SERRA ROSE

Eternity

Copyright © 2025 by Serra Rose

First published in 2025 by Serra Rose in Melbourne, Australia.

Editing: Ellen Klowden

Proofreader: Heat & Heart Editorial

Cover design by Miblart

For permissions, inquiries, or further information, please contact through:

www.serrarosewrites.com

First edition

ISBN (paperback): 978-1-7638448-7-2
ISBN (hardcover): 978-1-7638448-9-6

This book was professionally typeset on Reedsy.
Find out more at reedsy.com

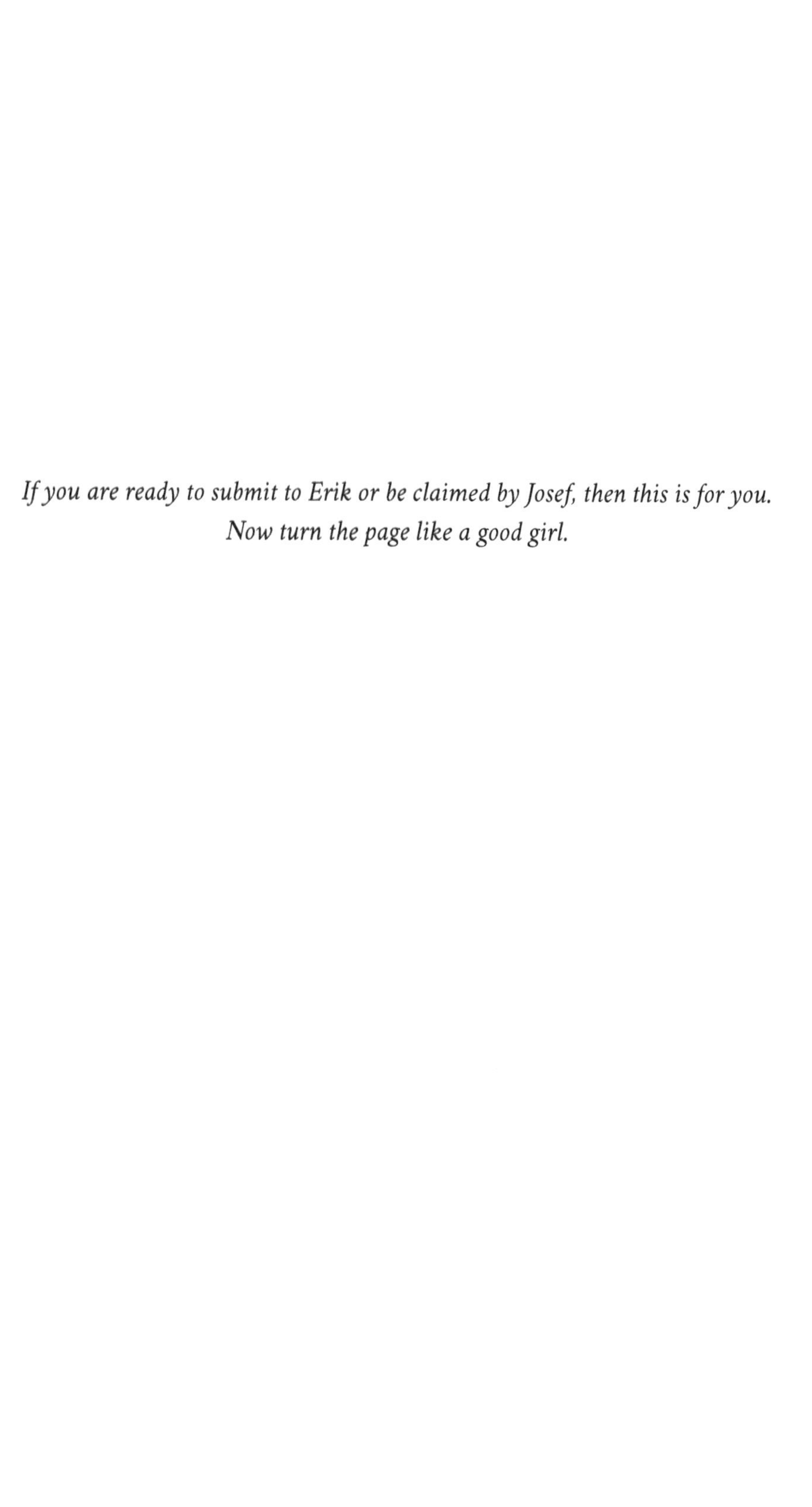

If you are ready to submit to Erik or be claimed by Josef, then this is for you.
Now turn the page like a good girl.

Translations

Old Norse

Draugr - vampire-like creature
Tyr - God of war
veiðimaðr minn - my hunter
Ek ann þér, ek elska þik - I cherish you, I love you.
gamall hermaðr - old warrior
Ástkærr minn (masc) / Ástkær mín (fem) - beloved
hermaðr minn - my warrior
Mjölnir - Thor's hammer

French

Prenez position - take your position
Ma chérie - My darling / my love.

Italian

Mi Amore - my love
Bastardo - Bastard

Vampire clans

Famiglia di Sammarinese - Name of vampire clan in San Marino
La Voz - Name of vampire clan in Venice

Content Warning

This book is intended for readers who are 18+. It contains detailed scenes of consensual sexual intimacy. It also includes themes and scenes that may be triggering for some readers.

Eternity is significantly more violent than a reader might expect based on prior books in this series. I'd like to remind you that in this world, there is nothing romantic about vampires, and if you remember from Consumed, war has been declared. You'll see vampires in their true nature, not shackled by The Accords. You'll see them as they are.

Please be warned, you'll also see:

Decapitation

Stabbing

Death

Violence

Slicing of throats

Tearing out of hearts

Rough sex

Hands around throats (some air restriction)

Predatory behaviour (non-sexual - vampires preying on humans)

People being burned alive (event discussed, not happened on page)

Graphic physical violence with head trauma (gore)

Arrow in eye

Remember to be kind to yourself. Your mental health matters.

A sensitivity reader from the LGBTQ+ community has read Eternity

Authors note

This far into the series, you know me, you know my writing is in British English. Words are spelt different to American English. You might think you see typos in this book, but rest assured, it's just written in British English, not American English. I am an NZ/Australian author and have made these choices to stick to the spelling we use on this side of the world.

Chapter 1

Spain - Ninth Century

Our enemy wasn't human. Deep, animalistic growls echoed in the night around us. No human made those sounds. Myself and my men had never come across such creatures. They moved with the swiftness of Tyr, their red eyes blazing as fangs tore into throats, taking the life of men who stood no chance against them. Steel struck flesh, blood spilling across the ground, only for their wounds to close moments later. They mocked our desperation with laughter, revealing their strength as they faced us barehanded. I longed for my home, to be making weapons, not holding them against beings who couldn't die.

We'd marched into a slaughter. Arriving in this village during the day, everything had appeared normal. The people hadn't fought us, simply let us take what we wanted. I'd thought it was too easy and should have voiced my concerns. We didn't know what protected them. The moment the sun set, a nightmare had descended upon us.

"Draugr!" someone screamed.

The word only added panic to the men around me. We were fighting for our lives, and we were losing.

"*Tyr*, give me strength. Grant me victory, let my enemies fall before me," I pleaded, forcing down my fear. Only the desire to survive remained. I would not die on foreign soil. Determined to see my family again, I gripped my axe tight, as one of the creatures ran at me. The sight of her filled me with a fear that clawed at me—nightmarish as blood dripped from her mouth. She struck me in the chest, pain stealing my breath. I swung my axe, hitting nothing but air as she disappeared. I'd never encountered such strength and speed. Only the gods should have such abilities.

Her blow from behind drove me forward, and I swung my axe blindly.

Let my blade hit home. I sent one last plea to *Tyr*, hoping he could hear me.

She appeared again and lunged. My axe connected below her chin, the impact jarring through my arm as I sliced her head clean off. Her body crumbled to the ground. Her eyes bored into mine, unseeing, but still they raised the hairs on the back of my neck.

"Erik killed one of them!" my brother, Magnus, shouted from next to me.

I'd been so focused on what was in front of me, I'd forgotten everyone was there. Now their roars of victory erupted from what remained of our forces. It felt like only seconds since these creatures had attacked. We outnumbered them, but we were outmatched.

I'd proven that they could be killed after all. Tyr had heard me! Filled with a renewed hope and triumph, I cheered with the rest of them, unable to hold back a grin. This would be a story told for generations. Erik Haraldson: the one who killed a creature with inhuman strength and speed.

"Their heads!" Magnus's voice boomed over the noise from behind me. "Remove their—"

His words died. Frowning as I turned, I found a woman with her mouth to his throat. His eyes rolled back, and he moaned in pleasure, wrapping his arms around her. Around us, many of the men I'd travelled with also moaned in pleasure as these creatures latched onto their throats, slowly losing colour in their faces. Others screamed in agony. Fury slammed into me, and I was moving without thinking. Axe high, I ran at the woman sucking on Magnus's throat, releasing a cry of rage. She let go of my brother and he dropped to the ground, his moan a soft exhalation of breath. Her red eyes focused on my face, lips curved into a slow smile, revealing sharp fangs. Blood—my brother's—smeared over her mouth, dripping from her chin. I had already sent one where it belonged; she would soon follow.

In the blink of an eye, she became a blur. Suddenly behind me, she wrapped one arm around my chest, and yanked my head to the side. My struggles to free myself had no impact against her strength. Her fangs pierced my exposed flesh, and I slipped into bliss, consumed by the surge of pleasure. I understood why Magnus had reacted the way he had. She was drinking from me, lips on my throat soft, bite filling me with wave after wave of warmth and need. For her.

My axe slipped from my fingers and hit the ground with a soft thud. I had to hold on to the need to fight, or I'd be next to fall. Again, I asked Tyr for strength to defeat my enemies. I grabbed the dagger in my belt. My mind was foggy, and I clung to the desperation that would help me survive. My brother lay on the ground at my feet with a smile on his face, still wrapped in the same sensations that now ensnared me. So many had already departed our world, not fighting, but embracing their deaths as these dark beings fed from them.

This will not be how I die! I lifted my arm across my own body, and I plunged my dagger deep into her neck.

She growled, and released me. I couldn't stand and fell next to my brother. She pinned me beneath her, smiling down at me, and pulled the dagger free. Her blood sprayed, splattering over my face. The taste of her blood sent fire through me, leaving me wanting more. I'd never tasted such delight. A need gripped me and I reached up, smearing my hand through the wound, and brought my fingers to my mouth.

She spoke in the language of the people there. Not only could I not understand her, but I couldn't focus on anything but how her blood tasted. Fear claimed me. My craving for her blood was unnatural. Would the gods turn their backs on me? Would Odin still allow me into the halls of Valhalla? I licked my fingers again, unable to stop, groaning as I did.

She spoke again. Still unable to understand her, I swallowed down the blood, wanting more. The sounds of battle around me became sharper, overwhelming. The shadows seemed to recede, and deep within, I knew it was because of her.

"What did you do to me?" I demanded.

"You are Bestowed," she said in my language, smiling at me. "It's powerful, isn't it?"

I groaned again at the taste, unable to resist licking more. The scent of blood and the echo of heartbeats overwhelmed me. I turned my head, gazing at my brother. At the blood on his throat. His heartbeat thundered. *How am I hearing his heartbeat?*

"Do you want more?" she asked, lowering herself and baring her throat.

More? Her offer horrified me, yet I couldn't tear my eyes away, even as the gaping wound closed. Hunger clawed at me, and her heartbeat was a slow drum, compared to mine—rapid and terrified.

I glared. "No! Get off me!"

Her laughter rang from her. "Aren't you hungry?" Her voice dropped to a whisper, but her words sunk into me, like a command. "Do you not feel that need creeping through every fibre of your soul?" She snapped her teeth at my jaw, lips brushing my neck again. I leaned my head back, baring my throat. "Oh, is it my blood or my bite you hunger for?" she asked.

Both. I wouldn't admit that to her, though. "What are you?" I asked, sliding my hand across the ground, trying to find my axe. Maybe it was within reach.

"Vampires," she said, then glanced across at the head of the creature I'd killed "You're the first human in this world to kill one of our kind. Brave. I want to *keep* you."

She bit me again. When her fangs sunk in, I didn't try to fight it. Unable to resist, I licked at her blood from my fingers again.

'Don't deny what your body craves.' Her voice was *inside* my head. *'It's alright, young warrior.'*

Her face filled my entire vision. There was an unnatural beauty to her that I couldn't ignore. I reached towards her face, fingers smearing her own blood over her cheek. I was about to die at the hands of a seductress, and wasn't sure whether to welcome my death, or reach out to the gods for help. *Would they help me?*

A male creature approached, and lifted her from me. His arms encircled her as they kissed. I turned my head, seeking my axe.

He spoke to her in another language, the one she had used earlier.

"No, I don't want to kill him," she said, still speaking in Northern tongue.

He stared down at me with a frown, and again I couldn't understand him as he pointed around us..

My fingers wrapped around the wooden handle.

She caressed his face. "Luis, this one is Bestowed. See his red eyes! He already feels hunger, and through our new blood bond, his strength and the warrior within him makes me want to keep him."

Red eyes? I didn't know what that meant, but it couldn't be good. *Gods, don't let me die, or become like them. Tyr, Thor, Odin.* I hoped someone would hear me. But even as I called for them, my hope died. I was not going to see the sun rise. If only I knew what the man was saying.

Luis frowned, turning his red eyes to me. "Why would you give him your blood?"

His words hadn't changed, yet I understood them. As I sought to understand, a raven sounded, flying overhead. *Odin!* First Tyr had helped me kill the other one, now this. Was he here to welcome me into Valhalla?

I rose to my feet, axe in my hand, the world around me unsteady. She laughed.

"He's relentless. He stabbed me, and got a taste of my blood. Now he wants more, but won't admit it." she said. "I want to keep him."

"You want a thrall?" Luis asked.

"No, I want to turn him," she replied gleefully.

Turn me? The words both confused and terrified me.

Luis approached me. I tried not to look at the blood on his face. His eyes flickered down to Magnus, and he advanced to where my brother lay.

"Leave him!" I demanded. "Face me, vampire."

His laughter was heavy with arrogance. "You think you can fight me?"

I pointed to the head at our feet. "I killed one of your kind; I'll kill you, too."

"Luis, I want this one," the woman said again. "I don't know what it is. He's good to look at; he'd be useful if more of his kind were to invade." She tilted her head at me. "Perhaps we can share him. He looks like he'd be able to handle the both of us." Her smile widened. "He looks like he'd be well endowed."

Luis picked up my brother like he was nothing, throwing him over his shoulder. "If that's what you want, my Beloved. The rest are dead. We'll save this one for him."

The woman pulled me to her. "Drink, human. Your body craves it."

She'd held on to my dagger, and sliced across her throat, blood welling up.

I lifted my axe and swung, only for Luis to stop it with one hand. "She's offering you a *gift,* friend, take it. Your other option is to join your people. Look around you: they're all dead."

I realised for the first time that all one hundred men I'd travelled with were dead. The silence that filled the place of their voices was deafening. Many of them hadn't even fought, so they wouldn't be dining with the gods. Panic set in. I was not going home. I'd never see my family again. *Odin, watch over them.*

She was so close, her scent overwhelming, pushing away thoughts of returning home. She smelled like rain on a warm morning at the start of summer. Sweet and earthy. And her blood called to me. A deep need rose, and no longer able to resist, I let her guide me to drink from her. I didn't try to fight it any more and licked her bloody throat with a groan before pressing my mouth against the deep cut she'd made.

I couldn't get enough. The taste of her blood was the only thing I could focus on. I moaned, suddenly wanting more than just her blood. I wrapped my arms around her back, grinding myself against her, wishing I could strip her down.

Strength coursed through me, the hunger deepening. I gulped down her blood like my life depended on it. The cut closed, and the growl that rose from me surprised me. I licked the remaining blood from her skin.

The woman pulled me off her, and gripped my chin. "I am Queen Amara. This is my beloved, King Luis. What's your name?" she asked.

"What's happening to me?" I asked. "Why did I drink your blood?" I still wanted more, but I couldn't move. My fear was closing in again, but something else was, too. A shadow wrapping itself around me, a spark inside of me waning. "What will it do to me?"

My knees buckled, and she caught me before I fell. "You're dying," she told me. "The blood you've taken will push you into slumber. When you sleep, your body, every part of you, will be remade. You'll awaken like me; immortal, strong, but hungry." She stroked my cheek. "Will you not tell me your name?"

"Erik."

"I'm going to keep you, Erik. You're mine now," she replied.

She lowered us to the ground, supporting my weight, lips brushing mine softly.

I hadn't wanted that. I looked up at her, fighting to stay awake. "Why? Why did you do that?"

She smiled. "Don't worry about that now. Sleep, my warrior. I'll wake you from your slumber."

I wasn't afraid to die, but I *was* afraid of what I was about to become. She slid her tongue over my cheek. Licking me. No, licking the blood on my face.

"Don't bury them," I pleaded. "Burn them on the water."

"We will honour their deaths," she agreed.

Good. That's good.

I closed my eyes.

Small ripples lapped at the boat as I gripped it, my brother's corpse inside. Deep tears marked his throat from my fangs, eyes forever closed. He'd fought me as I drank him dry. I'd growled like a berserker, hungry for his blood, with no memory of who he was. His last words had been whispered: "It's okay, brother."

I didn't know what I had done until I regained my memories a day later. Single mindedly ravenous for the blood that flowed through his veins I had fed from my brother; drained him dry to sustain this new, strange body with newfound strength, instincts and reflexes. Waist-deep in the cold river, I waited for the grief to come, but I found no such emotion. The memories were there, he had been important to me, but nothing sentimental flowed in me for the body on this boat—for the man who grew up beside me.

Light steps approached from behind me.

"Erik?" Amara asked.

"I need a moment," I told her.

She waded through the water. Her worry flooded through our blood bond. I returned my gaze to the boat. They'd saved him for me, realising at his final whispered words that he was my brother. With my senses now stronger, the sickly sweet stench of decay and rotting meat overwhelmed me. But I needed to prepare to send him on his way. I didn't grieve him as I thought I would and it confused me. There was no emotion in my body that felt even remotely like sadness or grief for his surviving family. Nothing but a cold detachment. I did however still hold to our traditions. Magnus deserved a proper funeral so he would be welcomed into the halls of Valhalla as a warrior, to feast eternally with Odin. It was the right thing to do for the brother I'd known most of my life.

"You can grieve for your brother," Amara said. "It's alright, Erik. We're not completely heartless."

I couldn't find the words to express my regret. That I'd killed my own brother. Or that the grief didn't touch my heart as I would have thought. "I don't feel the pain I should," I admitted. "I'm the reason he was here. It's my honour to give him a funeral, but his wife will never know what happened. I have to go home, tell her he died in battle." It was a lie, but she didn't have to know that.

She touched my arm. "If you go home, it's likely you'll tear through your entire village. They'll see what you are, and will run screaming. That is something irresistible to our kind."

Our kind. Her words sank in. I was a vampire, a creature who could never die. I would never go to Valhalla, dine with the gods, or see my brother again.

"No, but you'll dine with us," she said with a smile. "Let your family go. Let your gods go. *We're* your family now. You're a god amongst men."

I already missed my family, and my home, but I couldn't be their deaths.

"Light the fire, Erik," Amara said in her gentle voice. "Let this be how you let go of the part of you that died. You'll see your home again. Let those you love die first. Let me show you what it means to be an immortal."

Luis approached with a flaming torch, handing it to me. He and Amara returned to the bank at the river's edge.

"Goodbye, brother." I laid the torch in the boat, and pushed it out. Something in me snapped into place as my brother's body burned. My life, as I had known it, was over. It was time to embrace my new life. Accept the gift Amara had given me.

Her presence blazed through my bond with her. I turned from the burning boat, meeting her eyes. She smiled, Luis next to her. Her hand reached out for me, and after a moment, so did Luis's.

"Won't you join us?" Luis asked.

I accepted their outstretched hands, and was pulled towards them. Amara's hands slid over my chest, down, sliding under my tunic. Luis pressed in behind me.

"Bare your throat," he commanded.

I did as he asked, and Luis bit into me, feeding only for a moment.

"My beloved has claimed you. She wants to share you with me." Luis said. "We choose you to nest with. I am already your King, but understand. I am also the alpha. That is our way when we nest. You kneel to me. You obey me. Then, you can worship my beloved; your Queen."

Amara leaned forward, her lips pressed against mine. Hot with need, I kissed her back, but Luis pulled me off her. "Do you understand?" he asked. "I'm the alpha."

"Submit to him, Erik," Amara said.

I fell to my knees bowing my head. "You are my King, and my alpha," I agreed.

A hand grabbed my hair, pulling my head up. Amara smiled, her fangs glinting. "You're mine, my sweet young warrior," she purred and lowered herself to kiss me. I wrapped an arm around her waist, need overtaking me. We were blood bonded, and I wanted her more than any woman I'd ever wanted before. I was ready for an eternity with her. She gazed into my eyes. "Bare your throat. Let me have what is mine."

Chapter 2

S*witzerland - Twelfth Century*

Vampires had taken everything from me. Not vampires—plural. *One* vampire. He haunted my dreams every night. His smug smile drove anger and hatred through my heart. With a young family, I'd left my homeland many years before, to flee from the creatures that terrorised the night. But their plague had followed; there was no escape. I never thought I'd lose my family to them. I relived that night every time I closed my eyes.

I awoke in the middle of the night to the low moan of my wife. Confused, I opened my eyes to find another man in our bed. A shadowed figure pinned my wife beneath him. His mouth pressed against her throat as her hands moved over his body. She squirmed against him, moaning again. The only detail I could see in the dark was his shoulder- length blond hair.

"You want more, don't you?" he whispered.

She whimpered.

"Get away from her!" I threatened, reaching for my dagger.

He raised his head to look at me, his beard also blond. "Go back to sleep, human. I won't hurt her, or you. Let me feed, and I'll be on my way."

I should have been terrified. This man was a monster from the shadows we'd all been afraid of for years. Rage coiled deep inside me. I was tired of running from these nightmares.

"I said get away from her!" I said louder. "That's my wife!"

I tried to force him away, pull him off her. He growled, wrapping his hand around my throat. Even in the dark I could see his fangs. I'd never come face to face with a vampire before, and his grip tightened, showing me his strength.

"I'll give you one warning, human. Let me feed in peace. She'll know only pleasure from it, and I'll spare you both. Anger me, and you'll regret it. I'll make sure it hurts if I have to show you why angering me is a bad idea. I have a temper."

My wife ground herself against him, turning her head to gaze at me. "Josef, it's okay," she said. "He's not hurting me."

He gazed down at her. "You like my bite, don't you?"

She nodded. The vampire released his grip on my throat.

"Tell your husband that tonight, your blood, and your body are mine. He can have you back in the morning. I'll give you back to him in one piece, unharmed."

He stroked her cheek. The sight of his affection for her only enraged me more. I gripped my dagger tight and plunged it deep into his back. Grey light, the first hint of dawn, spilled into the room, and his red eyes bored into mine. The sun would be up soon; he'd have no choice but to retreat.

"I told you to get away from her!" I challenged. "Return to your shadows, or I'll find a way to kill you! Leave before the sun rises."

A menacing growl rumbled from him, dread and fear closing in. Before I could stop him, he lowered his head and tore out her throat.

"No!" A raw, agonised scream erupted from me. The vampire climbed off my bed as my wife's blood gushed from her wound. Her terrified eyes locked on mine, and her final breath came out a wet, choking gurgle. I pressed my hand against her throat, trying to stop the bleeding. But she had no throat left.

"I did warn you," he said. "You should have let me feed in peace."

Life left my wife's eyes. "I'll find you, and kill you," I promised.

My dagger was still in his back. "You'll have to do a lot more than a dagger to the back," he said, laughing. "I've granted you mercy this time, Josef."

"Mercy? You killed my wife!" Agony ripped a hole in my heart, leaving me broken and empty.

"Yet you still draw breath. Consider yourself lucky you're not bleeding out next to her after stabbing me. I can be a reasonable man. If you had been, your wife would have had a moment of pleasure, and I would have left the two of you alone."

He was gone, leaving me alone with the body of my dead wife. I pressed my forehead against hers. My hands trembled, sticky with her blood, and I wailed as I cradled her face. Anguish was a knife twisting inside me and tearing out my soul. This would be my moment of grief, as I decided I'd let her death harden my heart. I would find him and kill him. I had to find out how to kill vampires first. I would pull an army to my cause. Others who had faced the same loss.

I kissed my wife's lips. "I swear to you, that his blood will stain the ground beneath my feet, even if it costs me my own life. I will join you in peace, knowing I have avenged you. If I die before I end him, our son will take up my mantle."

I sighed at the memory, hating that I was cursed to relive her death, and breaking further when I'd discovered my son and his new wife had met the same cruel fate. So I'd met with people from surrounding villages, others who were tired of the monsters that came from the dark. I convinced them to fight back.

It took a while, but we captured vampires, torturing them until we discovered that wood and fire were lethal against them. More joined us. But in the war that broke out, I only cared about one vampire. Every time we faced the vampires, I searched for *him*. I gave in to a dark hatred, becoming empty, not caring who died in my war against them. Against him.

I left my tent ready to take my watch. The night around me filled with the chatter of men, sharing stories of battles from days before. Ice trickled down my spine, and I caught the shadows of five figures on the edge of our camp, watching. They retreated into the forest, but one lingered at the treeline, turning back. It was too dark to see clearly, but the chill down my spine suggested he was looking at me. The one I hunted. I reached into my tent for a bow, arrows, and a wooden stake.

"I need twenty men!" I commanded. "With me now! We're going hunting!"

Twenty men I'd personally recruited scrambled to grab weapons and belongings and follow me. I barely waited for them to follow as I marched into the forest, determined to find him. I had a wooden stake in my boot, but it was the bow strapped to my back that I valued. I'd put an arrow into his heart. This was it; there was no coming back from this hunt.

"What's your plan?" a young man, new to the fight, asked when we got deep into the forest.

"Set up camp," I said. "Draw them to us."

With the fire lit, I welcomed the warmth, listening to the hiss and crackle before me. I accepted a drink, keeping my focus on our surroundings. The vampires were probably watching us. I downed my drink, grateful for the numbness it brought. Drowning out the grief and guilt. Before long it became a struggle to keep my eyes open.

When I came to, the cold wrapped around me, the absence of the warmth of the fire unsettling. How long had I been asleep? Voices from above me made my blood run cold. They were not those of the men who'd followed me into the forest. I opened my eyes to find five people standing over me. Vampires. Three men and two women, who weren't even looking at me. I quickly closed my eyes again.

"I have an idea. We turn one of them." The one who spoke sounded young, barely older than my son had been. "Put him back among his people. When he wakes up, he'll likely kill them all." His laughter echoed in the silent night. "An insider, in our ranks. He'll tear them apart."

I listened to the camp around me. No one was raising an alarm at the vampire's presence. Three men had been beside me next to the fire when I'd closed my eyes. *Are they dead?* The unnatural silence pressed in.

"But we can't leave him here among his people as he slumbers," a woman said.

"Then take him from the camp. When he wakes up, send him back." The third voice was one I knew all too well. I fought against the violent impulse that screamed to attack him.

The vampires laughed. "So which one, then?" the first vampire asked.

"That one," my wife's killer said.

My eyes were closed, but I had a feeling he was pointing to me. The words chilled me to the bone.

"Why that one?"

"He has a personal hatred of me after I killed his wife," he admitted with a chuckle. "Carlos, remember the night you had to pull that dagger from my back? You'd just killed the young couple two houses over."

Two houses over. I had discovered who was responsible for my son's death. And his young wife. Pain exploded in my chest, as fresh as the day it had happened.

"I did wonder how you'd managed that," Carlos said. "Yes, that couple was delicious. Their fear sent me into a frenzy."

The vampires laughed. Anger and sorrow burned within, and I struggled to bury my fear. They were talking about turning me. This was it. This would be the fight of my life—I would not let them turn me. I didn't care if I died trying to take him down; he and Carlos had already taken everything from me.

"We've faced each other a few times," my enemy said. "He has a burning rage for us. He is a fighter. I'm not entirely sure there's much humanity left within him. He's a man with nothing left to lose. He was there the night war was declared."

"The night Amara died, you mean?" a woman's voice this time.

There was a pause.

"That's right. We talked. He made threats. He admitted they were declaring war with that fire they started. He didn't care that humans were dying—only that we were."

"One of them is awake. That scent," Carlos said. "Whoever it is, is listening to us."

"They'll all soon wake up," the one I hunted said.

"Their drink put them out for an hour," the woman said. "But it will wear off soon."

Did they poison us?

I was lifted, thrown over a shoulder. My cloak slipped, exposing me to the cold. I forced myself to remain still as they carried me from the safety of my camp. I opened one eye, trying to work out how I was going to get out of this. My bow had been on the ground next to me. The only thing I had on me was a wooden stake tucked into my boot.

"You want to turn him, don't you, Erik?" Carlos asked, with amusement in his voice.

Erik. I finally knew his name.

His laughter was cruel, dark. "There's something poetic about becoming the maker of the man who hunts me."

I would not let him near me. I only had a small window to drive my stake into his heart. If I was lucky, I would have time to kill Carlos before one of the others tore my throat out. But I'd die knowing I had avenged my wife and son.

I was dropped on the ground, the impact rocking through my bones, leaving me winded. I opened my eyes as someone kicked me. Cold smiles surrounded me.

"Will you make him a feral?" Carlos asked.

A long silence stretched out. "That idea does appeal," Erik admitted. "But you're the Father of Ferals, not me. Maybe you should turn him."

A feral! My heart quickened. That was even worse than being a vampire. Ferals were mindless, trapped in endless bloodlust. I would lose myself. That was worse than death.

"Furious little human!" Erik said with a smirk. "Get up, Hunter."

I sat up, glaring.

"I assume you heard our plan for you," Carlos said.

"I'll kill you before I let that happen," I promised.

Fear tore at my chest. They surrounded me, and I had no way out of this. One wooden stake, with no one to help me, against five vampires. Unless I could get one to kill me, I was going to become a vampire.

"Why me?" Carlos asked with a smile that made me want to punch him. "I'm not the one who killed your wife."

Their laughter only added to my rising fury. "I don't need a reminder of who took my wife from me." I snapped, burying it. I would not give them the satisfaction of my fear. "But you're the one who killed my son and his wife." I glared at each of them. "You're all monsters."

"From what I hear, so are you," Carlos said. "You're already suited to be one of us, already a killer. At least when you join us, you'll savour every drop of blood, the scent of fear, every life you take. Don't you hunger to feel alive again?"

"I'd rather you kill me," I said.

A woman vampire spoke up. "I want this one. Erik, I know you like the idea of turning him, but I want him. Not to make him a feral, either. I like his spirit. I'm yet to become a maker."

A gleeful smile spread across Carlos's face. Excitement danced in his eyes. "The vampire hunter turned vampire. Betrayed by their own."

"The first," Erik added. "I believe men look up to him, because he's the one who rallied the army that now hunts us."

"I'll never betray other Hunters!" I muttered.

Erik crouched beside me, eyes glinting in the moonlight. "You will. Because as a vampire, they won't be your people any more—just prey. You'll hunger for them, and no matter how much you take, you'll never get enough. Their lives will be meaningless to you; all that will matter is the bliss in their veins." He reached out to me, gripping my chin tightly. I couldn't move as he gazed into my eyes. "Oh, that defiance. I admire the fight in you, but it will fade. No one fights what we are. All that makes you human will die. You'll come to savour the pleasures of this life, and find dark joy in your new existence."

My flicker of fear turned into a flood of terror. I had no way out of this. I had to fight, in the hopes they'd kill me instead.

Erik's eyes turned red. "Oh, that scent of fear. You'll never get enough of that, either. Many will run from you, and you'll kill them all."

I reached for my stake and rammed it towards his chest, only for his hand to grip my wrist tightly.

"Let me go!" I demanded.

"I'm not going to hurt you, Josef. You and I can be friends. Once you're a vampire, I'm sure we will be. I can teach you to hunt. To seduce them so we can claim their bodies as we feed. To have them beg for your fangs and your cock."

My fear melted into desperation as they all stared down at me in silence. "Please don't turn me."

"Erik, will you turn him?" Carlos asked.

Erik took my stake from me and discarded it, before standing. "I'll let Ana turn him. She doesn't often ask for much. As long as I still get to hunt with him. I want to see what he's capable of."

"Of course," Ana said.

"We'll need to bury him, so the others don't find him," Carlos added.

Bury me?

Ana knelt down. "It's alright, you'll be in slumber. You won't know you're buried. I'll be buried with you. We all will be, while the sun's up."

I couldn't breathe. They were going to make me a vampire. The very thing I hunted. A fate worse than death. Instinct took over and I was on my feet, facing Erik.

"I'll still kill you," I promised. "Vampire or human, I'll stand over your corpse."

Erik flashed me a friendly smile. If he hadn't been my enemy, I would have been tempted to smile back. "If you're able to hold on to your hatred of me, then I welcome the challenge."

Then I was on the ground, pinned down. I struggled, trying to escape.

Ana's red eyes gazed into mine. "You do have spirit. I can't wait to see that when you turn."

I roared and shouted, desperate that someone—anyone—from the camp would hear me. Panic seized my chest as I thrashed against her grip, but her hold was unbreakable. I headbutted and kicked her, the sound of my useless struggle mocking me.

"So feral," Erik noted. "Relax, Josef, you'll enjoy this part. Just as your wife did."

"Don't you talk about my wife," I threatened.

Unable to do anything else, I spat at him. My spit hit him in the face, and he merely wiped it off, his smile not fading.

"He is a fighter," Carlos said. "I hope that part of him remains. That will be useful."

Ana lowered her head, fangs piercing my throat. I froze, the warm pleasure taking me by surprise. I moaned.

"Remember that first bite?" Erik marvelled, eyes on my face as I fought the sensations of vampire venom. "That moment when venom hit your system?"

"It was intoxicating," Carlos agreed.

They were all watching me.

Don't stop fighting! I strained against the dark pleasure the vampire's bite awoke within me. I punched her, both my arms immediately pinned by Erik and Carlos. Ana continued to drink from me, my struggles growing weaker. When she finished, she lifted her head, my blood on her mouth and chin.

"He's a lovely taste of fear and strength," she purred. "There is still plenty of fight in him."

Erik leaned forward, licking my blood from her.

"Oh yes, he does taste good," Erik agreed. "I imagine that's what righteous fury tastes like."

Carlos mirrored Erik, licking Ana's chin, slow and deliberate, a growl rumbling from him. But when Erik dropped to lick my throat, I froze—heart hammering. My mind screamed to flee or fight, but they still held me immobile. I was trapped, as Erik's tongue traced the mark Ana had made. I hated him. I bucked against their grip again, but she'd taken too much of my blood for me to have much fight left.

Erik gave her a dagger—mine that I'd stabbed him with the night he'd killed my wife. She sliced into her own neck. Determined to not let her put vampire blood in me, I sealed my lips closed tight. If I didn't drink her blood, I'd die. That was better than the alternative. I'd be reunited with my wife and son.

She lowered herself, throat close to my mouth. The scent of blood sickened me, as it ran over my lips.

"Drink," she whispered. "Embrace what you're about to become, Josef."

Fingers probed into my mouth, forcing my lips apart. Her blood flooded in and I choked, wanting to reject it. Oh, how I wanted to reject it. *No! Stop!* My hope died. A deep hunger had awakened, and a groan vibrated in my throat as I tried to ignore what my body was demanding. I shook with the effort, but my ability to resist the fire her blood ignited in me crumbled. I swallowed, and I closed my mouth over her throat.

I growled, holding Ana tight. She let me drink for a few moments, before pulling out of my embrace. I tried to lift myself up, desperate for more.

Erik laughed. "There you go, no more fighting. Let it happen. I look forward to meeting you when you awake, my friend."

I glared at him, fury simmering beneath my surface. *I'll kill you all.* My mind whispered, but every beat of my dying heart dragged me closer to my death. I felt myself fade, yet fought against the darkness that closed in, its weight pressing in from all sides. My body was shutting down, but my eyes remained on Erik, until I could no longer hold them open.

Chapter 3

My memories crashed over me as I watched Hunters from the shadows. Men I'd recruited, burning the bodies of the men I'd led into the forest. To their deaths. I hadn't just killed them, I'd torn into their throats, taking joy in their screams. I'd laughed as they tried to run. The Hunters expressed horror at the brutal massacre, worrying about where my body was.

I remained hidden, my body instinctively claiming the shadows. The army I had built was now my enemy. The moment I revealed myself to them, they would try to kill me. I'd given the order myself, that if any Hunter became a vampire, to take them down. There was no hiding what I was—my fangs were not retracting.

'Come, Josef, I'm here.'

I'd tried to ignore the voice of Ana, my maker. There was a connection between us, and I shut myself off from it. I couldn't go back to my life, but I wanted no part of her. I needed to bide my time, to work out how to kill them. Especially Erik. But her voice became more persistent, commanding. The image of a river pulsed through my bond with her.

'It's okay, Josef,' she said. *'You're one of us now. Come, join your new family. I know you haven't fed in a couple of days. Come hunting with us, you must be hungry.'*

She was right. The hunger gnawed at me, and I considered taking one of the men in front of me, watching for anyone I could separate from the rest.

'Leave them,' Ana commanded.

Her voice became hard to deny. I turned my back to the Hunters, following her summons. Once I saw Erik, I'd tear his throat out as he'd done to my wife.

I found her waiting for me at a river. The whisper of water over stones had become almost thunderous, each of the rocks clashing under the pressure of the current.

She smiled. "Josef, do you remember who you are?"

"I remember," I said. "You turned me into this, for what? To be your personal attack dog against the Hunters?"

I hated to admit it, but I was already seeing myself as different to the Hunters. I wasn't one of them anymore.

"Look around you," she said instead. "Appreciate your strength. Learn to love the night; that is your world now."

I took in my surroundings. My eyesight pierced the darkness that night brought, every detail clearer than if it were day. I raised my fist, fingers curled and relaxed again. My muscles thrummed with power, my body tightened; readiness rippled through every fibre of my being. No longer human, I was a different kind of hunter. A predator.

"Don't get lost in your new-found power. It can be intoxicating," Ana said, then her voice hardened. "Come here. Tell me, what do you feel? Tell me about the men you killed."

Much of who I was lingered, echoes of the broken man who had lost everything. That man had died in this war I'd started against vampires, in which I had given up my own humanity. But in his place a darker self had awakened. The sounds of screams whispered through my mind, the feel and taste of their hot blood; the scent and flavour were no longer disgusting to me, but were now mesmerising. It was intoxicating, and left me wanting more. The echo of their heartbeats and the scent of their fear; a bliss I had never known until that moment. I had spent my human life ignorant to the delights these new senses gave me, and the predatory desires singing beneath my skin.

I didn't want to like it. I didn't want to want more. The pain of losing my family had been replaced by the insatiable hunger, strength, and vampire instincts. But I wasn't ready to let go of my resistance.

"Will you embrace your true nature? If so, accept me as your maker, and join us. Or would you rather resist?" Ana asked.

"You got what you wanted. You made me a vampire, and I killed twenty Hunters. Let me go."

"He's trying to fight what he is," Ana said to the others who surrounded us silently. "That resistance is weak, though. It's the echoes of the last of his mortal self holding on. Let that part of yourself go, Josef."

The rest of the vampires closed in around me. I lifted my eyes to Erik. A rage that burned hotter than anything I could have felt as a human forced a growl from me. I sped towards him, wrapping my hand around his throat. But he only laughed, waving back the others. His hand rested on mine.

"Looks like he has a temper," Carlos noted. "Just like you, Erik."

"I know you're trying to hold on to who you are. Leave your humanity behind, Josef. You're not that man any more," Erik said. "Join us for a hunt.

Embrace what you are."

I tightened my grip. "I'd rather tear your throat out. The same as you did to my wife," I glared at Carlos, "and son. You took everything from me."

Erik pulled my hand from his throat, the look of amusement replaced by one of sympathy. His hand gripped my shoulder. "I'm sorry for what I did, Josef," he said. "I did not intend to kill your wife that night. I was hungry, and your interruption of my meal—and stabbing me—I lost my temper. You didn't deserve that."

I studied his face, finding his words genuine.

"I fell into a frenzy," Carlos added. "That spicy scent of fear is irresistible, as you've probably learned. They were dead before I realised it."

"That's about as close to an apology as you'll get from him," Erik laughed.

Carlos smirked.

I never could have dreamed that the men who'd killed my wife and son would have apologised.

"Let go of that pain," Erik said. "You're not human any more. We're not meant to resist our nature. Hunt with us, just once before you do whatever it is you want to do. We won't hold you to us."

"One hunt," Ana agreed. The others repeated the words.

Their words awoke the yearning in me, to *hunt*. New instincts that were already embedded deep within. At first, the man I was clung to his fight, his humanity. They had forced this existence on me. But darkness had seeped into every part of my soul. I wanted to give in to the bliss I'd experienced when drinking from the Hunters, to lose myself in the red haze that had taken me.

I shook my head, trying to hold on to who I was. For my wife. The memory of her rose up, but with it, the truth that I had tried to hide from in drink and killing vampires. I'd used my grief for my three loved ones to propel me forward in starting the war against vampires. I'd become something I myself hadn't recognised. Even in the times I'd faced Erik, he'd recognised I'd let darkness in, telling me there was no coming back from that. I could almost laugh at my own stupidity. At such a hopeless cause. The useless pursuit of a grieving human.

"I'm the reason she's dead," I murmured. "I got her killed."

"I killed my brother," Erik said. "I was the reason he was in the village protected by vampires instead of back in Norway. He was the first I fed on when I awakened, and I killed him. As a young vampire I felt that guilt, just as you do. But what we are, what you are now, we're not meant to hold on to that remorse."

"To let go of the man you were, you need to let go of your guilt and grief," Ana agreed.

I let my resistance crumble.

"How?" I'd held on to anguish for so long. "I'm tired of the pain."

"Grieve what you lost," Erik suggested. "Then embrace what you are."

"Let the man you were go," Ana said. "He's dead. Maybe that human part of your soul is reunited with your wife and son somewhere. Let yourself be a new man. Discover who you are without the burden of humanity."

Carlos shrugged. "I heard having a drink can help. Let the frenzy take you. Take joy from the scent of fear, and their screams."

My eyes swept over all five of them, seeing no hostility, only warmth. They had already accepted me as one of them.

"I will join you for a hunt," I decisively declared.

"Great, I'm hungry!" Carlos said, a wide smile crossing his face.

Erik chuckled. "There's a village nearby. How about we go there."

I followed them in silence, lost in my thoughts. It took me a while to realise Carlos was walking next to me. "Their screams echoed through the forest," he said. "It was difficult to resist following that scent of fear. I fought off a frenzy listening to such music. But I also heard your laughter. You may not have had your memories, but you were still you. That enjoyment you felt, that is you, Josef. So when we feed, let yourself enjoy it, as you did then. Revel in your new nature."

"Carlos is all about their fear and screams," Erik said. "While I do appreciate the spice of fear, I much prefer seducing them. The sweet flavour for their desire, the sound of their moans, the warmth of their bodies as they beg for more, squirming beneath me."

"You'll learn what your hunting preference is," Ana said. "But whether fear or desire, blood is still blood. Falling into that intoxication, drunk on their blood, that's euphoria."

"Let's run!" Erik said and smiled back at me. "Think you can keep up?"

They were gone, but I could still hear them, and followed. The speed with which I easily caught up left me stunned. Laughter burst out of me.

"There it is!" Erik rejoiced. "Hold on to that joy. Welcome it. We'll show you what other pleasures there are. And I don't just mean in hunting or feeding."

I said nothing, and we stopped on the outskirts of a village. I knew the village all too well.

"We…uhh, the Hunters watch this village," I blurted. "All the villages around here. They ask us…them for protection."

"Oh, we know," Carlos smirked. "Thank you for telling us, though."

We walked forward, and I grabbed Erik's arm. "Why can't my fangs retract?"

"You learn to mask your vampirism," he said. "Freshly turned fledglings have no control. It's normal. Your eyes are red, too."

"It's beyond the fangs and red eyes. though," the other woman added. "Even with your fangs and eyes hidden, humans can see there's something unnatural about us. Our human face is like a mask, concealing our dark soul and inhuman quality from their eyes. Our unnatural beauty."

"Even with the mask, they're drawn to us," the third man said. "The pull of the vampire. Humans cannot resist us."

"Yet many can sense the danger in our presence." Carlos noted. "I rather enjoy the look of fear and confusion when humans try to understand the trickle of ice down their spines."

"I did," I admitted. "I felt you all before I saw you. From the other side of the camp." I met Erik's eyes. "I thought it was my chance to finally kill you."

Carlos grinned in response. "We wanted someone to follow," he said. "We wanted to draw a Hunter in. We were going to send you all back in pieces. We watched you all from the shadows as you fell asleep, thanks to Ingrid putting sedatives into your ale. It wasn't until we were standing over sleeping Hunters that I got the idea to turn one. I didn't realise you and Erik were already well acquainted. Nor that we'd lured the one who recruited the army."

"Less talking, more hunting," the other man said.

"Giuseppe, calm yourself," Carlos laughed. "We *are* hunting. I want to learn more about our newest addition. He's one of us now, and—"

"I'm not," I argued. "I agreed to hunt with you, not join you."

"He's got you there, Carlos," Erik quipped. "But I'm with Giuseppe. Let's hunt."

"I can wake them," Ingrid offered, running her hand over Erik's arm. "Run to a house screaming for help. Bring them out. Their curiosity never ceases to be their demise."

"Bring the whole village out, give us something to choose from," Carlos said.

Erik pulled me back. "You might want to cover your ears," he advised me. "She's about to scream, and if you're not used to your new senses, it's going to hurt."

I put my hands over my ears, still wincing at the onslaught of Ingrid's high-pitched scream. Before my eyes, she transformed. Losing the graceful movements of a vampire, stumbling forward, almost clumsily. She'd become more human-like.

"Help me!" she called, reaching a door and banging on it before moving on to the next house. "Please, someone help me!" The panic in her voice sounded real.

"She sounds so human," Carlos remarked. "It's eerie."

"It's a game we like to play," Erik replied.

It wasn't long before humans started coming from their houses. Only a week before, I would have been marching through with weapons, surrounding them with other Hunters to protect them. Now, overwhelming hunger pulled me forward. Ana pulled me back.

"Let your hunger choose," she said. "Find one you want. Do you want to give chase, like Carlos, or to seduce them, like Erik?"

Her words made no sense. Deep within, my hunger mixed with the darkness now a part of me. I growled, and pulled out of her grip, stalking forward. I was surrounded by heartbeats and the scent of fear, and a state of mind rose up. I was no longer a man, but a creature that hungered to sink my fangs into flesh, to bite. Another growl rose from me.

Laughter behind me echoed.

"I think he's already in frenzy," Giuseppe observed. "Do we try to control him?"

"No, let him go," Carlos instructed.

I let their voices fade. Gripped by instinct and hunger, I ran directly at a human, my momentum taking us to the ground. Eyes met mine, widening in terror. "Vampire!" he screamed. I pushed his chin up and to the side, biting into his throat.

'Josef, let me share this one with you,' my maker's voice in my head gave me pause. I lifted my head. Her eyes were red, and she leaned forward, licking the blood that dripped down my chin. The sensation was strange, enjoyable. *'I'm your maker, let me enjoy your kill with you.'*

I exposed the other side of the human's throat for her. She lowered her head, biting him. I returned to my feeding, letting the familiar haze that I'd enjoyed only days before take me. When the human's heart stopped, I moved until I found another, not yet satisfied.

The haze lifted as a tongue slid over my chin, another across my cheek. Ana and Ingrid knelt over me.

"Why does that feel so good?" I asked, sitting up.

"It's natural," Ana reassured me.

"You look like you enjoyed the feed," Erik commented.

"You went straight into frenzy, the moment you caught a whiff of their fear," Carlos noticed. "Do you remember anything?"

I recalled the last few moments. Their fear, their screams, their blood. Warmth had spread through me, their heartbeats pounding through my head. The ground beneath me swayed, my movements slow. "I do. Why do I feel like I've had too much to drink?" I asked. "I feel like I'm drunk."

"Because you are," Ana said. "You're blood-drunk. A delicious effect of over-feeding. You only needed one, maybe two. Instead you tore into *three* throats before we could stop you."

"You're the one who thought to stop him," Carlos laughed. "I would have let him feed until he passed out."

She lifted my chin. "I suppose I should teach you to use your venom, so they enjoy your bite."

"Three?" I asked. "I killed three humans?"

Erik crouched down. "You did. And you loved every moment of it."

I couldn't argue. The rush, the thrill of it shivered through every part of me. The taste of blood lingered, rich and intoxicating. I licked my lips.

"Notice you called them humans?" Erik pointed out, and helped me to my feet. "Your view of them has already changed. You cast yourself as different to them."

"That's because they're food, and your mind has already made the distinction," Carlos said.

"You are an animal," Ana said with a smile. "I enjoyed watching you in motion."

"You've embraced what you are," Ingrid congratulated me.

"Do you feel guilt? Or do you want more?" Erik asked.

I met each of their gazes, all waiting for my answer. I had wanted to hold on to who I was, but that man had died for a cause I no longer held. I gave in. I surrendered to the darkness within, and smiled.

"I want more," I affirmed.

Glee filled their eyes.

"Will you lead us to slaughter our enemies?" Carlos asked. "Lead us to the army you built, and become their downfall?"

Once more, I smiled. "I will."

Chapter 4

V*enice - Fourteenth Century*

The sun bore down in our courtyard, and I'd taken shelter under the tree my father had planted the day I was born. My father sat in the heat of the sun, straight-backed, his black linen shirt one I'd sewn. I smiled up at him. He wiped his forehead with the back of his hand.

"You're not supposed to move!" I complained.

My father's laughter rumbled from him. "Then perhaps you'll bring me some water. You have me sitting in the scorching sun without cover, while you sit in the shade." His smile widened, eyes crinkling. "Will you allow me to see your masterpiece?"

I turned my focus to what I'd drawn. He was a painter, and I'd wanted to follow in his footsteps. To be an artist as talented as him. But as I studied what I'd drawn, I hesitated to show him. "It's not finished."

He walked towards me. "My treasure, I'm sure it's perfect. You're more talented than I was when I was your age."

A soft, glowing warmth stirred in my chest. I turned the sketch around to show him, nervous as his silence stretched out.

"I'm so proud of you," he said, emotion in his voice. "My daughter—the artist. You'll have your work in a gallery before me."

I hoped he wasn't saying it to make me feel better. He lifted his eyes to meet mine. "Aria. You must stop doubting yourself."

I hugged him. His arms wrapped around me, comforting. "Thank you for letting me draw you," I said.

"I am proud of you," he repeated. "I always will be. Don't ever give up, Aria. You have something special."

"There are my artists," my mother said, walking into the courtyard.

Light filled my father's eyes as he turned. "Marisa, my love," he said, drawing her close.

He lifted his hand to cup her cheek, her eyes full of warmth as she beamed up at him. I knew my parents loved each other very much and were openly affectionate.

"My beautiful wife, you and Aria are my greatest treasures, and I appreciate every moment with you both," he murmured in a low voice, words he repeated often.

He kissed her and I turned away, allowing them privacy. They spoke in low voices as I examined my artwork. Still seeing fault, I lifted my eyes to the portrait my father had painted of me earlier that morning. I wanted to be proud of what I'd done, but next to his art my sketch looked like the scribbles of a child. I let out a sigh.

My father turned towards me. "That is too loud of a sigh to be happy. What's wrong?"

"She is her worst critic," my mother said. "She doesn't see what we see." She smiled up at my father. "Giovanni is here to see you. Let me comfort our daughter, while you attend your meeting."

My father laughed, his deep chuckle that always lightened my heart. "The duty of being a Barone never ceases. Bring him in. I'm sure Aria would like to see her uncle before the meeting."

My uncle walked into the courtyard, grinning at me. His smile and eyes were similar to my father's.

"Aria! My favourite niece!" he called out.

"I'm your *only* niece," I returned.

"That reminds me, when do I get other nieces, or even nephews?" my uncle asked. "I want a nephew named after me!"

"Your current niece isn't enough?" my father joked.

I laughed. "Why would he name a nephew after you when you didn't name any of your sons after him?"

My uncle opened his mouth and closed it, while my father laughed. "She makes a good point. Why do I not have a nephew named Matteo?"

"Because one Matteo Barone is enough for this world," my uncle finally found his words. Then he caught sight of my sketch. "Aria, you're improving," Uncle said in the tender voice he always used when he spoke to me. "Be careful, Matteo, you'll soon have some competition. Perhaps you'll be sharing studio space."

"Aria is most welcome to share space in my studio," my father said. "Excuse us, I'm sure this won't take long."

I overflowed with pride as my uncle led my father from the courtyard. My mother joined me at the easel.

"You've done well to catch his likeness," she told me.

Warmth filled my heart, and I savoured it. "Can I draw you?" I asked. "I want to practise."

He didn't come home that night. Or the next. Or the one after that. Days stretched into a week—one of confusion and heartbreak. When we went to his studio, it was empty. Every brush, every canvas, every unfinished painting—another question we couldn't answer. Uncle Giovanni stood there, too, as lost with his brother's absence as I.

"Why would he leave?" I asked my mother, voice trembling, tears running freely down my cheeks. A week had passed, and no one had seen him.

She shook her head, eyes red and swollen. She couldn't hide the uncertainty. The same fear that had been pressing against my chest since that first day.

"I don't know," she whispered, voice breaking. "I don't know…" her words trailed off.

Hope was slipping away for both of us. His disappearance had made our world unsteady. Our villa had never felt so cold, so dark. My portrait remained next to his, and I promised I wouldn't draw again until he returned. The house still smelled faintly of him. Every night I went to bed, I hoped to hear his footsteps, his booming laughter as he joked with my uncle, and the comfort of his voice as he whispered, "I love you, my treasure."

Every day we hoped for his return, refusing to believe he would abandon us. Every time the sun set, we were met by the cruel silence of his absence. Uncle Giovanni would stay with us well into the night, holding on to what little hope remained.

I sat outside watching the gondolas glide past, lanterns flickering, moonlight reflecting on the canal. A shadow fell over me, and fear curled around my throat. I lifted my eyes and gasped.

"Papa!?" I cried out.

He stumbled forward and stopped. "Aria," he breathed.

"Papa, it's you! You came back to us! I knew you would. Mamma will be so happy!"

His eyes were in shadow, and he wore the same clothes he had been wearing that day. I wanted to run to him, to feel the safety of his arms around me. He moved slightly and the light of the lamp behind me cast across his face. Instead of the familiar brown eyes so like my own, his were crimson—blazing with something I didn't recognise. His lips were parted enough to reveal long…fangs? I took a step back, a chill slithering down my spine. Not understanding what I was seeing, I grabbed the lamp, holding it up.

He tilted his head, gazing back at me. "I can smell your fear, and hear your heart beat."

I took a trembling step towards him. "Papa? What…happened to you?"

"I'm sorry, I couldn't stay away. Please don't be scared of me, Aria. I would never hurt you. Or your mother. Where is she?"

"She's inside with uncle Giovanni," I said. "They'll both be happy to see you. We weren't sure if you were dead or if something happened." I couldn't look away from those fangs, from the red eyes. "Something happened. Where were you?"

"She can't see me like this," he said. "Neither of them can."

He took a step back, and I did run to him then. I wrapped my arms around him. "Please don't go," I pleaded. "We need you."

He flinched at my touch, arms not enfolding me in his warmth as I had hoped. His body was cooler than I expected for such a warm night. I lifted my head, once again taking in the red eyes and fangs. He wasn't human.

"What are you?" I asked.

"I'm still me," he said, voice almost a growl. "I'm just…" He stepped back. "How can you bear to look at me?" he demanded. "Are you not afraid?"

"Because you're my father," I said. "You've never given me any reason to fear you. Come inside. Please, Mamma and Uncle will want to know that you're alright."

He hesitated. "I can't show her this." He pointed to his mouth. "They will run from me."

"Wait here!" I ran inside, grabbed a cloak and returned to my father. Relieved that he hadn't left, I gave him the cloak. "Pull the hood over your head."

He did as I suggested, pulling the hood down low, concealing his eyes.

"You'll have to show her eventually," I said. "You can't hide your eyes forever."

"Aria, please come inside." My mother walked outside then and froze, eyes on my father. "Matteo?" Her voice trembled.

"It's him," I said.

"Why are you wearing a cloak?" my uncle asked, following my mother outside.

My mother wrapped her arms around my father. "Matteo, you've returned to us. We were worried sick about you! Where did you go?"

My father didn't move for the longest time, then slowly he wrapped his arms around her.

"It's not important," he said. "I'm here now. I'm not leaving you again, Marisa." He kissed her on the top of her head and lifted his eyes to me. "My love, my treasure. I'm sorry."

I stepped into their embrace, filled with joy, while also wondering how he was going to hide his face from my mother in the morning.

"Where were you?" Uncle Giovanni asked. "You were gone for *a week*, Matteo. You have no explanation?"

He pulled away from us. "I'm tired," he said. "Can we talk in the morning?"

My uncle relented and the four of us went inside. My perfect life really was perfect, and nothing would take him from us again.

The following night, screams pulled me from my sleep, and I sat up gasping. Another scream, my mother's. I climbed out of bed slowly, heart pounding.

"Mamma?" I called out. "Papa?"

Only silence answered me, and I lit my lamp, leaving my room. My feet padded softly on the floor as I followed where I thought the sound had come from. I ran, bursting into the courtyard as a loud, anguished roar made my blood run cold. My father sat on the ground under my tree, my mother in his lap. My lamp lit up the horror before me in a ghastly yellow glow. Her eyes were open, but she wasn't moving. Her throat had been torn open; both she and my father were covered in blood. He stroked her cheek with such tenderness, as he always did. "I'm sorry, Marisa," he whispered.

"Papa?" I stared down at him in shock. "Papa, what did you do?"

His head snapped up, and a wild glint shone from his eyes. A guttural growl tore from his throat. I flinched, forcing myself not to move, as every instinct screamed at me to run.

"She's dead," he whispered, voice broken. "I didn't mean to, Aria. She saw me and ran from me. I lost myself."

Pain punched through my chest so hard I could barely breathe. I let out a soft, broken sob. Unable to speak, I reached a trembling hand towards my mother. "No." My voice was barely audible. "Papa, no. You said… you said you wouldn't hurt us. We have to get a healer. She can't be…" Tears blurred my vision. "No."

"It's too late." His voice was hollow. "Run, Aria. Go to your uncle, and never come back. You'll be safe with Giovanni. He will protect you from the monster I've become."

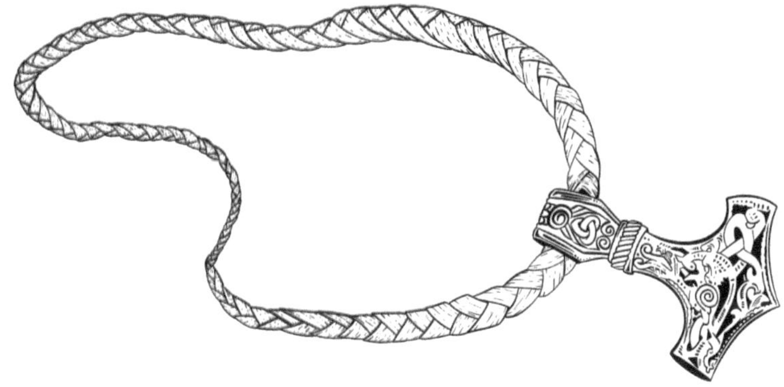

Twenty years later.

I left the house, defeated. The woman had been another dead end, unable to help me. But I knew she knew something. She hadn't denied the existence of vampires. Instead, she'd told me to go home. To return to my family. I smiled, thinking of my sons, and my husband. Maybe she was right.

Overhead, dark clouds hid the setting sun as I made my way to where I was staying. The wind pulled at my cloak, and I hoped it wouldn't rain, and that I would get back before it got too dark. I turned down a street, my thoughts on my father. I had only been a child and lost both parents in one night. He'd told me to run to my uncle, and we both refused to believe he was dead. The twenty-year search had led us nowhere. Family had always been so important to my father, and I didn't want to believe he'd abandon me. My uncle missed him as much as I. We both wanted him to come home.

I hurried down the unfamiliar street as the sky darkened, night fast approaching. Fear slivered down my spine, the feeling of threat driving my heart to my throat. I turned another corner, and gasped. Two people stood under a tree in front of me, caught in an embrace. The man lifted his head, turning towards me. Blood trickled from his mouth and down his chin. Fangs, red eyes—and blood.

"I'm sorry, I…" I stepped back. "Vampire," I whispered. Not one who looked like he welcomed my presence. Not like my father would.

He licked his lips, releasing the woman. Her body crumbled to the ground, and she breathed in with a deep sigh.

"Well, don't you smell delicious?" the man said. "A little bit of perfume, a touch of fear. Are you lost?"

He advanced, and instinct screamed at me to run. I couldn't tear my gaze from the thin line of blood that trickled down his chin.

"You know what I am," he said. "You're not a Hunter, are you?"

I could only shake my head.

"So how do you know about us?" he asked, gliding forward again.

Something about the glint in his eyes spoke to a deep instinct in me. Without another word, I turned and ran. Behind me, a low, menacing laugh chilled me to the core. My heart pounded as I ran. Tears streamed down my cheeks. I'd spent twenty years trying to find my father, only for another vampire to find me. I cried out for Venice, wishing I hadn't left in search of my father. Longing to see my husband and sons again. They would never know what happened.

There was only silence behind me, no thunderous footsteps. I risked a look over my shoulder, not seeing him. *Maybe he didn't give chase.* I stopped running, turning around to find the street empty. I breathed a sigh of relief, and turned around again, stopping in my tracks.

He blocked my path, eyes red. "I do like when you humans run," he declared. "You interrupted my meal. I'm hungry." He stalked towards me. "So you'll do."

I took a step back, but the vampire moved fast. Too fast. He towered over me. I couldn't breathe, choked by fear as I peered up at him. *I'm going to die. I'm sorry. Papa.* Tears welled up, stinging my eyes. and slid down my cheeks, and a whimper of regret rose up from me.

He only grinned. "A whimper already? I haven't bitten you yet."

I ran again, but before I could get far, he knocked me to the ground, pinning me down.

Fear tightened around my throat.

"Are you going to kill me?" I whispered.

He traced fingers down my throat. "I'm not supposed to, but your fear makes it hard to resist."

I was about to die far from home, and my family would believe I had abandoned them. Grief for my husband and sons suffocated me.

"I have a family," I whispered. "Two young boys."

He smiled, wiping away my tears with his thumbs. "Oh I do love to hear my meal beg." He dropped his head, licking my throat. "Relax, it won't hurt."

His fangs pierced my throat, and waves of heat and desire crashed over me. Pleasure replaced my fear, and I clung to him, strangely wanting more. I couldn't fight him, but I didn't want to. *How is he doing that?* Something else to add to what I knew about vampires. I was going to die, but instead of fighting my death, I'd embraced it. I embraced him.

"I know about vampires because my father…he's like you…a vampire," I gasped. "A vampire. I need to find him. His name is Matteo Barone. Please…"

Black spots were creeping in when he stopped, lifting his mouth from my throat. "The Feral is your father?"

I didn't know what he meant by 'The Feral.'

He studied my face, mouth and chin covered in my blood. "You want to find The Feral?"

My heart was erratic, too fast. "The Feral?" I asked. I was fading.

"Matteo Barone. He's known by many vampires as The Feral," he said. "If you're his daughter, then he's from Venice. That explains the Hunters' presence. They're watching you, aren't they?"

I clung to him, darkness creeping up. He'd taken too much of my blood. I could only nod. If only I'd been able to find my father before I died. I could have told him it was alright. That he had grandchildren. That his brother still hoped he'd come home.

"Damnit, I have a soft spot for damsels in distress," the vampire muttered. "I want to help you find your father. To see that family reunion."

Warm liquid poured into my mouth. I spluttered, panic squeezing my chest. *Am I drowning?*

"Drink. I'll make sure you see your father again. You have my word," he said. "If it takes ten years or a hundred, you'll see him. As a vampire, you'll be reunited with your father.

He was feeding me his blood. I latched on to his throat. I'd never set out to become a vampire, but somehow felt this was right. I would see my father again.

Chapter 5

<u>Bonus Chapter from Consumed</u>

San Marino - 2045

Of the vampires who had followed King Giuseppe into Venice,

two were missing. Including our King. The entire clan crowded around them.

"Where is King Giuseppe?" I asked. I wished he had taken me with him. I'd been trying to get into Venice for twenty years. Frustration surged through me that I had missed an opportunity.

"King Giuseppe is dead," Ricardo declared. "He challenged King Carlos and lost. The Feral killed him."

The Feral! I wanted to ask more questions.

"Are we at war with them?" another vampire, Carmen, asked.

War? I hoped not.

"King Luca swore we had no quarrel with them," Ricardo said.

Giuseppe had recently taken Luca to be his Second, after Marco's death. It had been unexpected; many vampires in the clan were older than Luca, more suited to the position. Many questioned the decision. I suspected Giuseppe's grief had affected his choice.

"Where is he?" I asked.

Pierre met my eyes. "He remained back to speak with Carlos. He will return soon." He addressed the clan. All fifty of us. "They have a siren. Her voice was incredibly powerful and had us all on our knees. Giuseppe did not care to warn us before he led us to what could have been our end. His death was deserved. As was Marco's. To not only challenge The Killer, but The Feral and a siren, too."

I fought down the urge to growl. Rage burst through me at his talk of my maker. Dead or not, I was still loyal to Marco. Pierre had been in our clan for at least a hundred years, but he was a vampire without loyalty.

A smirk crossed his face. "Luca has not yet taken a Second. Who will challenge me?"

I knew why he wanted the role.

"Is it the role you want, or the clan?" I challenged.

He flashed his fangs at me. I laughed. Stupid child. He was not that much older than Luca. As a six-hundred-year-old vampire, *I* was among the eldest in the clan. I wasn't certain Luca as a King would make us the strong clan we should be. But neither would Pierre.

I stepped forward. "*I* challenge you," I spoke out, showing him my fangs.

Pierre tilted his head as he eyed me. "You are more suited for a King's Queen."

A shudder tore through me as I absorbed his words.

"No," I argued. "I challenge you for becoming *Second.*"

"There will be no challenge," Luca said. "I pick Aria for my Second."

The clan knelt before Luca. I joined them. "Thank you, my King," I said, shooting a triumphant look at Pierre. He glared back. I would have to be careful with him.

Luca looked over the clan, and he let out a sigh. He hesitated, and uncertainty crossed his face. "King Carlos has taken control of our clan. He will allow me to be King, but I answer to him. To ensure loyalty, I am bonded to Josef Alfaro."

Everyone reacted in shock, their voices filling the den. This had been my clan since Marco turned me. It was not unheard of that Kings or Queens who were challenged would absorb the clan of the loser. But no one wanted to belong to a new King. I could see that in their faces.

"Why did he not send anyone here to oversee his new clan?" I asked. "Are we to expect Josef to join us?"

I knew exactly who Josef was. Every time I had tried to enter Venice, it was Josef Alfaro and Erik Haraldson who stopped me. They always called King Carlos, who had forced me out. The idea of Josef arriving in San Marino filled me with excitement, but I wasn't sure why.

"King Carlos will not absorb us," Luca said. "The rest of you can go. I will talk with my Second." He waited for everyone to leave, then turned to me. "I want you to go to Venice in a few days. I will let Josef know to expect you. I hope to please Carlos. Make sure to appeal to him and The Feral. There is no reason we cannot maintain a close friendship with his clan."

I forced down the grin that would have given me away. No one in the clan knew that I'd tried to get into Venice for the last twenty years. Nor could they know why. Only Marco knew. Venice had been my home, and over the centuries I had returned many times, to maintain a close connection with my descendants, and those of my uncle's. They knew what I was, and the day I received a message from Lenora of my father's return had been the best day of my existence.

"I will do what must be done," I agreed. "Will I be expected to take an offering with me?"

Luca considered this. "Perhaps. I'll think about that."

It occurred to me that Luca was in over his head. He was so young, and there could potentially be a challenge to his rule. Pierre or Ricardo were the most likely candidates. *Wouldn't it anger Pierre if I beat him to that, too?* I almost laughed at the idea.

Luca grabbed my arm. "Marco was your maker, wasn't he?" he asked, his voice gentle.

I nodded. "He was. I'm still feeling the effects of his death." It was as if it were *my* heart that had been ripped out, and now an emptiness filled me.

He gave me a sad smile. "I know what it feels like. I want to make sure you are not going to go to Venice for revenge. Carlos is very old and strong. His clan are loyal to him. They will tear you apart if you try anything." He closed his eyes and sighed. "Giuseppe didn't stand a chance. I don't want to see that happen to anyone else in my clan."

The idea of revenge hadn't occurred to me. "I will be there to represent our clan," I promised. "I will meet with King Carlos, and with his Second, in peace."

His eyes narrowed. "Be careful. Matteo Barone is as feral as they say he is. He tore out our former king's heart before any of us could move to protect him."

I smelled fear. "You have nothing to worry about, Luca. We will give them no reason to attempt to kill any more in our clan."

I had lived six hundred years, but the next few days were the longest in my life. I approached Venice in what had once been King Giuseppe's boat. As expected, Josef and Erik met me. Josef laughed.

"How many times will it take for you to learn?" he demanded.

"You're expecting me," I told him. "I am King Luca's Second. He sent me to meet with your King, and *his* Second."

The pair of them exchanged a look filled with amusement.

"An interesting turn of events that no one could have foreseen," Erik said. "He will not be happy to see you. Does Luca know he sent the *one* person whose presence would anger our King?"

I remained silent, my heart pounding. This was the moment of truth. Whether they would send me back, or take me to their den.

"Surely Luca wouldn't be stupid enough to do anything to deliberately anger King Carlos," Erik said to Josef.

I watched them both. Erik was clearly from the days of the Vikings. His long, blond hair was tied back, and he still maintained a long but neat beard. His grey eyes focused on me with interest. Josef's blue eyes held the same interest, his dark hair shorter. They towered over me, and I decided that they were likely an intimidating duo. But instead of the expected fear, I found myself overcome by pure lust. I'd always been drawn to men like this.

They both breathed in deep, their eyes turning red as they closed in. They could smell my lust. I held still, waiting.

Erik leaned in, taking in my scent. Their own arousal spiked. "Well, don't you smell delicious," he said with a fanged smile.

There was silence for a moment, and I suspected they were talking through a blood bond. Both of them ran their eyes down my body. Josef moved around behind me, and he breathed in again.

Erik placing his hands on my hip was unexpected, and he pulled me towards him. Josef wrapped his arm around my stomach, and moved forward. I was locked in tight between them.

"You'll have to excuse us," Josef said, his breath tickling my ear. "It's been awhile since we've had a woman that our King didn't claim as his. We only have two females in our clan. Now he has the young Huntress, too."

I had a good idea what they were talking about, but I held my breath. The thought of fighting them occurred to me. To make them work for it.

"Ours," Josef declared, his hand grasping my chin to lift it, to expose my throat.

Exhilaration surged through me, and I decided against the traditional fight. I was from another clan, and not a new vampire. It was likely they expected me to make them work for it. Instead, I lifted my head high, inviting them to bite.

The two of them struck fast, sinking their fangs into my throat. Their venom flooded me and I let out a moan, my knees suddenly weak. Erik pressed himself against me. I could feel his erection through his trousers and ground myself against him. Josef's hand slid down into my jeans, pushing aside my panties. His fingers slid through my wetness, and a growl rose from him. I let out my own growl.

They removed their fangs, but their lips remained on my throat, their soft kisses sending a deep shiver through me. Their tongues slid over my skin, cleaning away blood. They had marked and claimed me, and I wanted it. I wanted them. I yearned to claim them, but this wasn't my territory. I would have to wait.

"Ours," Erik agreed when they released me. He gazed deep into my eyes. "That is just a taste of the pleasure we will give you. Voice your thoughts."

I grabbed a fistful of hair on the back of Erik's head and pulled him into a deep kiss. Then I turned, and with the same fervour, I kissed Josef. I pulled away from Josef, Erik's hands still on me, Josef's fingers still inside me. Their lips trailed hungrily across my mouth, meeting each other's before their teeth scraped over my jaw.

Josef lifted the fingers he had slid into me, towards his mouth. I grabbed his hand, pulling his fingers into *my* mouth.

His breathing changed as I sucked on his fingers, and he groaned.

"You cannot taste me yet," I declared, releasing his hand. "This is a business trip. Perhaps later we'll have time for pleasure."

I wanted these men to take me, and I struggled in turning down their advances. I would have let them both fuck me in the very place we stood. But I had something else I needed to do first. Someone else I wanted to see. A reunion that was long overdue.

I gave them each a soft kiss again. They were so close to me, wanting more. And I stepped out from between them.

They both growled, and moved forward. I held my hands up to stop them. Raw desire glinted in their eyes.

"Business," I said again, my hands pressed against their chests.

I saw their internal struggle as they forced back their nature, their eyes returning to the normal colour.

"Oh, I love a determined woman," Erik's voice grumbled from him. He groaned. "You're *ours*, but we'll wait. You'll be worth the wait."

The smile he gave me sent a flutter through my stomach. Damn, I hungered for him. For both of them.

I snapped at his jaw playfully. "Perhaps when your King isn't waiting on me," I reminded them.

I had a villa, the very one that I had lived in with my parents. I could take them to that, let them claim me all they wanted. I hoped they played rough.

Josef lifted my hand, pressing his lips to my fingers.

"Come on then, I suppose we should present you to our King," Josef finally said. "At least now, you'll have protection."

To be claimed was an honour. I'd been claimed by two incredibly hot men, to whom I'd been attracted the first time I lay eyes on them. It meant that if Pierre tried anything, he had no right to me. It also meant I was tied to these men, and they would likely expect me to join *their* clan. With Marco dead, and Pierre closing in, I wondered if I should.

We approached the villa that I knew all too well. Lenora had told me they'd removed Pietro and his family and taken over what had once been my family home.

They stood in front of me as King Carlos entered the room with a human woman. The scent of her made my canines ache. Clearly, my arrival had interrupted his meal. I had fed before arriving in Venice, but to have a human right there, still warm from desire for the men before me, it was a struggle to keep my fangs from emerging.

"My King," Josef said. "Luca has sent a representative."

I realised they had not referred to Luca as 'King'.

"Then present her." Carlos demanded. I couldn't see him with the two men blocking me, but he sounded irritated. "Standing in front of her does not hide her scent. You know the warnings I have given her."

"We ask that you not harm her," Erik added. "She is Luca's Second."

"Why does it matter?" A new voice had entered the conversation. One I knew. *He's here!* "Carlos clearly doesn't like her presence. Why would you bring her here and make such a plea?"

"Because they claimed her," Carlos said with laughter. "Alright, step aside, let me officially receive her, then."

They moved to the side, and I dropped to my knee immediately. I bowed my head. He wore only jeans, and I'd caught sight of a wolf tattoo on his bare chest. The Immortal Wolf was only one of many names he was known by.

King Carlos spoke to the human woman in another language. Likely Spanish. She replied. He pulled her to him for a kiss before releasing her, and then he spoke again. The distinct scent of lust rose from her.

I lifted my eyes up slightly, glancing at the human woman. There was no glazed-over expression of a trance, and she'd been marked. King Carlos had claimed a human.

"Lower your gaze," the King's Second commanded.

I dropped my eyes immediately. It stung to have him speak to me in such a formal way. That he hadn't recognised me. I reminded myself I'd been twelve, and human. Centuries ago. He would not be expecting me.

The King chuckled. "Matteo, I think you enjoy this too much."

The laughter that boomed from him set off memories of a human girl. She had died centuries ago, but she was still here.

"King Carlos," I said. "My King's Second." I could have sworn my voice cracked.

I wanted to turn my head. To meet the eyes of the man to his right. But suddenly I was nervous. I'd dreamed about this reunion for centuries. Only Marco had known, and he had helped me try to find him.

"On your feet," King Carlos commanded.

I rose, careful to keep my eyes down.

"You've finally found your way into Venice, then." King Carlos chuckled.

"I was named as King Luca's Second, and he wanted to send me here to meet with you." I informed him.

King Carlos moved away from me and sat in a large chair. The human woman took one beside him. I stared at the woman.

"Are we to discuss matters in front of her?" I asked as I took a seat.

A growl broke from King Carlos. "You will show my Queen the same respect you show me." He leaned forward. "Now tell me your name. And why you have been so determined to enter my domain."

Queen? A human? This did not match anything I had heard of King Carlos.

Finally, I lifted my eyes to the man who stood next to King Carlos.

He looked exactly as he had the last time I'd seen him. Over six hundred years ago, crouched on the ground, anguish in his face as he held her body in his arms. He'd told me to run to my uncle, and never return. Now, he met my gaze without recognition, curiosity glinting in his eyes.

"My name is Aria *Barone*," I emphasised, not looking away. Vampires around us gasped. Erik and Josef swore. I'd used the name he'd recognise instead of the name of the human I'd married before my mortal death. His eyes widened with shock, and he shook his head in disbelief. King Carlos turned his head, eyes darting between the two of us.

"I have been trying to find you for a very long time, *Father*."

Chapter 6

My father stared at me in shock. "Aria?"

Choking on emotion, I could only nod. His face reflected the same storm that surged inside me. He didn't move. The red-haired vampire touched his arm, the contact pulling him out of his trance. He cleared his throat and turned his eyes to King Carlos.

"Everyone out," King Carlos commanded his clan to regain himself after his own shock. "This is a family reunion that deserves privacy. Leave the den." He rose from his chair, his human moving with him. "Aren't you supposed to hug or something?" Carlos asked. His hand tightened over my father's shoulder in a comforting gesture, before he turned towards the red-haired vampire. "Sorry, sweet siren, that includes you. Perhaps you'd like to join Camila and I for a human meal. She hasn't eaten yet."

She followed him and his human from the room, pausing at the door to gaze back at him. The look in her eyes gave away that she was still a young vampire. She had to be less than fifty.

Josef and Erik stopped in front of my father. "We didn't know," Josef said. "If we'd known who she was before we claimed her…" He looked at me, words cutting off. "Matteo, I'm sorry."

"I wanted it too," I said softly.

My father didn't react, his eyes still on my face. A tense look passed between them before they quickly followed King Carlos through the door. A dark-haired woman and a man with shoulder-length, brown hair remained. The woman left quickly, but the man gazed at me. As if he knew me. Then he, too, was gone.

My father's eyes moved quickly across my face. "There's no question who you are; you are my daughter." Then he was in front of me, wrapping his arms around me. Strong arms that I remembered, offering protection, safety to a child of twelve. "Oh, Aria. My treasure. I've thought a thousand times about you. About the life you had. About all I took from you." He let out a sigh. "Never in a hundred lifetimes did I imagine you'd…" His voice broke. "How?"

I leaned into his embrace, tears streaming down my face. Hearing him call me his treasure, made me feel like that child again. Good memories of my human father flooded me. "I went looking for you," I admitted. "I never gave up on finding you. I found my way to San Marino and interrupted a hungry vampire instead."

"Who?" he growled. "Who ended your life? I'll kill them."

The pain in my chest flared. "Your king already killed him." I said, trying to push down the anguish. "Unfortunately, it drove my King to mad grief, so he returned with revenge in his heart."

He pulled back, looking down at me. "Marco?"

I gave a small, trembling nod, letting another tear spill over. "I felt his death. It was as if my own heart were being torn from my chest."

His thumb wiped away my tears, and it was almost as if the last six hundred years hadn't happened. I was twelve years old again. He was my father, comforting me.

I hugged him tight. "I found you." I said. "I tried so many times to see you."

"That's right, you've been trying to enter Venice," he recalled. "Why didn't you tell Carlos who you were? He would have let you in."

I sighed. "Because I wanted to stand before you and present myself. I didn't want you to hear from someone else that your daughter still lived." I couldn't hold back the small smile. "But that doesn't matter any more!"

I could feel him shake his head. "I can't believe it. I should have been there, to protect you. See you grow, marry. I never met my grandchildren."

I smiled and we both stepped back. "They knew all about you," I told him. My oldest, I named after you. My youngest I called Gianni."

"I finally had a boy named after me." He chuckled. "Gianni. Your uncle Giovanni would have loved that." He sat down, indicating for me to sit next to him. "What was your husband like?"

"We don't have to talk about that right now. I have plenty of time to tell you. Our descendants protected me. They let me have the villa that used to be our home. I know you were still here for a few years. Everyone was terrified of you. But when I went looking for you, I never found you. I refused to believe you were dead."

"Gabriela pulled me out before the Hunters found me. I was not allowed to return to Venice for many centuries," he explained. He leaned forward. "Aria, what I did to your mother. What you saw that night..."

I touched his arm. "Papa, it's okay. I know the hunger. I know what you went through, and I don't blame you for anything."

"You can't know the pain of destroying your own family." he murmured.

"I am my father's daughter." I replied. "I did the same thing. Despite Marco's warnings, I tried to return to my life, only to lose control. I came to, my husband's blood dripping from my chin, his eyes forever closed. Marco found me crying over his body, and helped me understand we're not supposed to live in their world. I'm glad the boys weren't home then. That they didn't have to see that." Instead, they'd believed their mother had abandoned them, their father had been killed. "I saw them after that night, from the shadows. It was so hard to stay away from them."

Sympathy crossed his face. "Oh, my little treasure, you should have grown old, with your husband. I wish I had known. I would have found a way to come home."

I shook my head. "We don't need to regret anything, Papa. I've found you. That's all that matters." I laughed. "I see you found happiness in someone else."

He said nothing.

"I saw the way you looked at each other. She's important to you," I added.

He nodded. "There is a long story with her, but yes. She is my beloved. I still hold your mother in my heart. I never stopped loving her. But Quinn is my whole world."

I thought of my mother. "She'd want you to be happy. I'm glad you found Quinn. She's young, though; did you never find someone in all this time?"

He stood. "Perhaps we should go for a walk."

We left the villa that had become my home the night he had told me to run. My mother, dead. I'd banged on the door in the middle of the night until my uncle answered. He'd listened to me, and hugged me tight. Thoughts of my uncle brought a lump to my throat.

Outside, few humans were around, but I didn't pay them any attention. Only to my father. He was here, beside me. My chest burst with joy as I gazed up at him.

"Do you want to see our villa?" I asked. "It's still mine."

"I'd like that," he agreed.

We walked side by side. We were father and daughter, but almost the same age in human years. I was a couple of years older than he was.

"Did you continue with your art?" he asked, hope in his voice.

I nodded "The Hunters took the first picture I drew of you, but I did another sketch. Of you and Mamma, and it's still hanging in the villa today," I said proudly.

We arrived at the villa, and he hesitated, eyes wide. The familiar building did not look uncared for, nor abandoned. My descendants had cared for and upgraded it over the centuries. Even twenty years away and it still looked lived-in. Still with the classic architecture and overlooking the grand canal, three gondolas were secured to my private dock. The villa was true display of wealth. I smiled at it fondly, pleased to be back.

The shock hadn't left my father's face.

"Are you okay?" I asked.

His eyes were wide. "I was in madness the last time I lived here. I never thought I'd return."

"You've been here twenty years. You didn't come back?" I asked.

He gave a small shake of his head. "This is where I killed my wife, and tore my daughter's childhood from her." He winced. "It's also where I killed my father. Your uncle was here once when I returned from a hunt. I think it broke his heart to see me the way I was." His eyes grew intense. "How was my brother? I wish I could have thanked him for raising you."

I stared at the ground. "I turned him," I admitted. "But he died. Those damn Hunters. They never left us alone. Obsessed that you would come back for your family. They hunted us for years until their descendants took over. He was only a century old." The pain of watching my uncle hadn't faded over the centuries. As his maker, I'd felt his death. "His last words were that when I found you, to tell you he loved his brother; his only regret was that he didn't have the opportunity to tell you himself."

My father's face reflected his loss, eyes darkening with the storm of grief.

"I wasn't myself when he saw me," he said. "I was in feral madness. But I remember through the red haze that he said he missed me. And that I'd be proud of the young woman my daughter was growing into. I must have maintained enough of myself to not try to kill him as I did our father."

I took a step towards the villa and paused. "He knew I'd become a vampire, and he returned to this villa every night for a month while I watched in the shadows. He spoke aloud, hoping I'd hear him. I revealed myself, and he only showed joy at seeing me." I smiled, wanting him to come into what had once been our home. "Would you like to see your family? I drew pictures of every one of our descendants."

He followed me towards the villa. I opened the door and tapped the pin into the keypad to deactivate the alarm. Lenora would know immediately that I had returned. She'd set the pin to be my birthday at least thirty years ago. Inside—grand rooms with Renaissance Frescoes, the furniture still vintage, although our original furniture had since been replaced.

I led him to the main gallery, showing him the portraits of my husband, and my children. "Meet your grandsons," I said.

He stood speechless, captivated by the portraits.

"That's Matteo, and Gianni." I laughed at the memory of my sons. "Matteo looked so much like you." I pointed to the portraits of them as children, before showing him the sketches of them both as young men. My eldest son Matteo really did grow into looking like my father, while his brother had resembled my husband more.

He swayed, then stepped back, dropping into a nearby chair. A tear slid down his cheek.

"Papa!" I stepped towards him. "I'm sorry, I shouldn't have brought you here!"

He smiled at me. "My treasure, no! You have given me a gift!" His eyes shifted, returning to the pictures. "What were they like?"

I smiled. "As children, they were trouble. But they grew into well-mannered young men who drew a lot of attention from the women. Matteo was the one everyone drifted towards. He named his first daughter Marisa, and was overjoyed to see me when I could no longer hide in the shadows. Gianni was quiet, and found peace in painting and reading."

I pointed to the next portraits. "That's their children. My eldest grandson also looked like you."

"You leaned into your talents," he said with pride. "I'm so proud of you, Aria. Your mamma would be, too."

Warmth enveloped me. "My father was an artist. I wanted to follow in his footsteps. I sometimes painted, like you. But sketching was my chosen medium."

We walked into the courtyard, where I was hit by the memories of our last day in which we were both human.

"I hope your King will let me return now that he knows who I am. This is my home," I affirmed.

"I'm sure he will not deny my daughter her home," he agreed. "I suppose you'll need somewhere outside of our den to nest. I've known Erik and Josef for a long time. I know their sexual appetite. Especially Erik's. Josef is more of a partner I would have thought ideal for you than Erik. I certainly don't want to have to listen to what they're doing with my daughter."

I glanced at him. "I was wondering when this would come up. Please don't be angry at them."

"Is that what you want?" he asked. "To be claimed by *two* vampires? There's quite an age gap between you."

"I'm not…" I hesitated. This conversation was *a little* uncomfortable. "I'm not that little girl any more, Papa. I'm a six-hundred-year-old vampire with a taste for blood and sex. I *like* the fact that they claimed me. If I weren't in such a hurry to see you, I would have let them…um…"

An awkward silence stretched out between us.

Horror flitted across his face. "This is not a conversation either of us is comfortable with. If it's what you want, then I'll let them off the hook." A joyful glint reflected in his eyes. "I suppose I *could* make them squirm a little first."

We walked down the hall, and I pointed out who each of our descendants were.

I laughed. "Will I be expected to stay in Venice? To join your clan? I'll claim this villa for my nest, but I'm still technically of another clan."

We walked around the villa. "You're of a clan that Carlos took control of. I think he'll be open to letting you stay here, if that's what you want to do…with your new *friends*." He turned his smile up. "As his Second, it's within my power to invite you to join our clan, if you want. It's likely Erik and Josef will want you to join, too."

I smiled. "Thank you Papa. I'm grateful for your blessing."

He wrapped his arms around me again. "*You* are the blessing. I hope we can spend more time together. Tell me all that I missed. Of my brother, and of your life."

Chapter 7

As I walked beside Josef, the streets of Venice shifted from the noisy bustle of tourists to only the occasional echo of footsteps or a hushed whisper in the dark. Silver moonlight and shadows draped over the city reflecting from the canals. But I tried to ignore the humans with their loud heartbeats and the scent of blood. I was too focused on Aria's revelation.

"Matteo's daughter," Josef grumbled for the third time. "We claimed *Matteo's* daughter."

"Relax," I told him, pushing down my own worry. "Let's wait and see what happens."

"Relax?" he scoffed. "You've seen how protective he gets over Quinn. This is his daughter. His flesh and blood. One that he thought was dead."

He had a point. "Let's not panic yet." I grabbed his wrist, and pulled him towards me. He put up no resistance, his hand resting on my waist. "She wanted it as much as we did. At no point did we force anything on her. She would have fought us if she didn't want us. She bared her throat."

My hands rested on his hips. He pressed his forehead against mine.

"I've seen him go feral," he said. "I always hoped we'd never be the ones to push him to that point."

"She's a grown woman," I reminded him. "With a mind of her own. Matteo knows that. She's not the child she was when he last saw her." I hoped my calm would seep through to Josef. "Besides, do you think Carlos would let Matteo do anything?" I reached up, caressing his cheek. "Let's not worry about something that hasn't happened yet."

Humans walked around us, seemingly comfortable with our open affection in public. Possibly locals who recognised us. I didn't look up to confirm; I only saw Josef. I needed to calm the panic inside him. To take care of him, as was my responsibility in our connection.

"It doesn't change anything," I said. "We claimed her. She allowed it. She's ours."

The woman was a true beauty, but that wasn't what drew me to her. In a way, she reminded me of Amara, the smile she'd given me as I claimed her. The spark of defiance, as if she were considering fighting me before giving in.

He let out a breath. "I want her, Erik. I want the two of us to claim her, for her to claim us. I touched her, and she was already wet. I want to bring humans in to feed from while we fuck. I want it to last for days."

The scent of his lust set off my own. He was talking about *nesting*.

I grinned. The memory of my time with Amara and Luis flooded back. I'd been so young then, so willing to join their nest. Amara and Luis had awakened a part of me that might have remained dormant if I'd remained human. It had taken a week to create the bond of the nest, someone always hunting and bringing back humans to feed the nest. We only stopped to sleep and feed. The nest had lasted for centuries, until Amara's death had put an end to it. Fuck, I still missed my maker.

Our eyes locked and he cupped my cheek, breath cool against my mouth. I grasped the back of his neck, rough as I pulled him towards me. His lips were soft, and I brushed them tenderly with my own at first before parting his with my tongue. Fierce heat awakened in my chest, wild and lustful, and I pushed him back until he hit a wall. He groaned into my mouth, body tight against mine.

Nothing existed but the two of us, our kiss becoming ravenous. Our hearts pounded against one another, and growls rose from both of us. Overcome by my need for him, I forced myself to stop.

"Ek elska þik," I whispered as we pulled apart.

"I love you," he repeated back, eyes on mine.

A gondola glided past, the strings of a violin breaking our silence. But I didn't look away.

Josef bared his throat, something he did when he wanted us to feel close, especially after such a heated kiss. My lips brushed his throat before I bit him. I was first generation, and I found satisfaction in drinking from other vampires. Amara had been that source until her death, after which Ingrid had become the one to satisfy me. When we left Melbourne, leaving Ingrid behind, Josef had fulfilled that role.

Very few knew that Amara was my maker, not even Carlos. Vampires didn't put importance into who one another's makers were. Some, like Gabriela, flaunted that they were first generation, while I'd preferred not to. Only those I'd fed from over the years had known - my venom was somewhat more potent than that of other vampires.

As I fed from Josef, our bodies pressed against one another. My cock strained against my trousers. Josef's hand slid down, groping me. My tongue and lips were still wet with his blood as I trailed kisses up to his mouth again. This time, our kiss was long, our tenderness lingering as the world around us faded.

'Submit to me, Josef,' I whispered through our bond.

What we'd started with Aria left me unsatisfied, needing completion.

He dropped to his knees, gazing up at me with that spark of love mixed with hunger. The look alone had the power to send my heart soaring.

"I submit," he confirmed.

Then he unbuckled my trousers, pulling my cock free. His mouth wrapped around it, tongue swirling over my head. Pleasure pulsed at the sensation. His eyes never left mine as he bobbed his head, his mouth pushing me towards the release I desired. Our earlier worry was swept away by blazing lust. I groaned and panted, grabbing the back of his head. His eyes glinted as he returned my stare.

"I'm your alpha," I said.

His words were muffled as he continued his movement. I grunted again as warmth spread out, my orgasm barrelling towards me. His fangs scraped over flesh as he moved, my cock hitting the back of his throat.

I pictured him and Aria together as I watched. The idea of stroking myself as the two of them fucked, filled me with joy, and I came, my eyes rolling back in my head with almost *unbearable* pleasure.

My body twitched, and Josef rose to his feet, finding my mouth. I tasted my own seed, and his kiss was ferocious, full of want.

"You're my alpha," he affirmed, panting. "Will she submit to you? To us?"

I smirked. "She will. I will teach her to recognise me as the alpha of our nest."

Hunger sparked from Josef's eyes. I knew what he wanted.

"I'm not giving you the satisfaction you want," I told Josef, delighting in the control. "You'll have to wait. You'll have to *earn* it from Aria." I tucked my cock back into my trousers, and buckled up. "Let's hunt. Hopefully when we're done, Matteo will be in a mindset in which he's ready to speak with us."

I started to walk away, waiting for Josef's reaction. He growled, and I grinned over my shoulder at him. "It'll be worth it," I promised. "You and she will start it for us."

"You torment me," he grumbled, hurrying to catch up. The tone in his voice was not of anger, but desire.

"You must wait for your reward," I said. "What do you feel like for dinner?"

"I wouldn't mind visiting the gallery," he said. "You know how much I love the taste of willing volunteers, yearning for our bite. But those willing to *pay* for the thrill of our vampire's kiss tempt me so much more."

The gallery was in Carlos's territory. But our King had agreed, that if we only fed within the gallery, and didn't hunt, he wouldn't see it as trespassing.

It was the time of night in which humans were sitting down to eat, the rich and inviting aroma of their food wafting from their houses—herbs, tomato, and garlic. Their dull chatter carried through the walls; about mortal lives I had long ceased to understand or care about.

"Everything's changed," I murmured as my thoughts turned to what had occurred the last few days. "We lost two vampires but gained a human. This will be interesting."

"I'm happy that Carlos found his Queen," he admitted. "We'll all feel their absence for a long time, though."

Lorenzo and Annika's deaths had shaken the entire clan. No one blamed Carlos for killing Annika; we understood his reason. He'd been in a difficult position, and he had decided to protect Camila. Yet knowing that did little to soften the pain of our grief. We'd lost two members of our clan, and it hurt.

"Camila's going to feel that, too," I said. "Humans feel guilt heavily. She will likely blame herself. Being the only human in a vampire clan, and exiled from her own community, she has a lot to struggle through."

Josef nodded. "Perhaps former-Hunter-to-former-Hunter, I can help ease her through that. I think we may have a lot in common."

I laughed, Josef's turning a fond memory. As a human, he'd hated me with an intensity that had piqued my interest. He'd even tried to hold on to who he was, but he'd surrendered to his vampiric nature so quickly, and we'd become fast friends. "Remember how much you worried that vampires would hate you?" I reminded him. "They welcomed you, as quickly as we welcomed Camila. Despite the fact that you'd killed people we knew."

He grinned. "I remember you promised to protect me from anyone who took issue with my presence. I never imagined we'd have another Hunter join us."

"We have the most unique clan," I commented. "A feral, a siren, an assassin. Two Hunters, one of whom is still human."

Josef chuckled. "Don't forget the Viking."

I growled. I hated that title for my people.

"I love how offended you get by that." Josef grinned at me.

"I will push you in the canal," I threatened.

Josef's laughter rang out. "You wouldn't."

We found our way to the gallery. The stone building before us echoed those around it. Tall pillars framed the entrance, and windows with rounded arches reflected the moonlight. It was late, but it would be a few hours before the gallery closed. It did, after all, belong to a vampire. I led Josef through the doors.

Chapter 8

Inside the gallery, a mixture of light and shadow danced across the marble floors, Matteo's art on display alongside human artists'. Moonlight poured through tall arched windows framed in limestone. The air had the faint scent of polish and turpentine, a blend of old and modern varnishes to preserve the artwork. Frescoes ghosted the ceiling, their colour softened by centuries. Vaulted arches stood proudly between the galleries rooms.

"I always did admire his talent," Erik said as we stopped before one piece, a sunset of Venice. It had 'Not for sale' over it. Matteo had once gifted this very painting to Quinn, luckily, as it was the one piece that meant the most to him, and it had escaped the fire.

"I didn't realise he was putting this one on display," Erik observed.

"I think Quinn insisted he display it," I said. "I heard them discussing it one night. She said it was a work that needed to be displayed because of the emotion captured in it."

"Emotion?" Erik asked. "All I see is a sunset."

"Artists, and those who know art, have a keener eye for what's in a painting," I said. "I read that once." I pointed around the gallery. "How many of these humans do you think are here for the art, and how many are here for us?"

Only a few people were there; low voices and footsteps echoed in the empty space.

"It's him," a whispered voice brought a smile to my face as I examined each of the humans. Some did show a genuine interest in the art.

A woman in a black dress wandered around the gallery, not even looking at the art. A couple; the woman wearing a red dress, showing tattoos, a small leather collar around her neck. Her dark hair hung down around her shoulders. The man had his hand around her waist possessively. Unshaven with a few days' growth, and black hair, he had the same build as me. The two of them watched us with interest. It was clear that the pair knew exactly who and what we were.

"The couple," I said with a grin.

"The lady in the black dress," Erik returned. "I've seen her here before."

The woman in the black dress caught us looking back at her. She gave a tentative smile.

I chuckled. "You're right. She isn't even bothering to pretend to look at art. However, that couple looks like they'd be right at home in a BDSM club." I grinned. "We should start one of them next. King Carlos could run it." I gave Erik a side eye. "Although, you'd spend as much time there as him, watching all the action."

Erik smirked. "You could come too, we could take the collar." His hand closed around my throat. "I'd punish you publicly," he whispered. "You'd be on your knees, submitting to me and begging me for release."

The thought of it set me ablaze. My cock was still hard from having sucked him off but receiving no release in turn. "Promise?" I asked, voice raspy.

Everyone in the gallery had noticed us. We moved towards the room filled with nude pictures of my clan; minus Matteo, the artist. I held the curtain open for Erik, then followed him through. The assistant smiled up at us—someone Quinn and Lenora had personally selected to run this part of the gallery. I placed my hand on her shoulder.

"Hello, sweet thing," I whispered in her ear. "Perhaps today is the day you'll let me bite you."

Her heart fluttered, cheeks turning pink in the dark.

"Josef, I am glad you're here," she said in an attempt to maintain professionalism. "There are three people in the gallery, hopeful that someone would show tonight."

I raised an eyebrow at Erik, meeting his amusement.

"The lady in the red dress had time with Andreas a couple of days ago, but today requested Erik," the assistant said. "The man with the suit is her husband, interested in joining in. The woman in the black dress was taken by Carlos, but indicated she'd be willing to have…and I quote, 'anyone's lips on my throat, as long as he makes my panties wet.'"

"Her," I said quickly. "I have a sweet tooth tonight." While the taste of fear in blood was intoxicating to us, Erik had taught me the art of seduction while feeding, and even after all these centuries, desire-laced blood remained a treat I couldn't resist. We had a human already wet for us.

I turned around to find Erik in front of Lorenzo's painting. I glanced at his and Annika's faces, pain squeezing my chest.

"Erik?" I prompted.

"Hmm," he didn't turn around. We'd only burned their remains days ago, and had forgotten about the paintings.

"Was this a mistake, coming here?" I asked.

Finally, he turned away from the portrait and gave me a wide smile that didn't meet his eyes. "Not at all. You had a craving, so let's eat." He lowered his head to speak to the assistant. "Perhaps in the morning you can have someone take down the portraits of Lorenzo and Annika," he said. "They won't be returning."

"Oh, did something happen?" she asked.

"They died." Erik replied, his voice breaking.

"Oh." The awkward silence that followed was deafening. "I'm sorry." There was real sympathy in her voice. "I'll have them taken down immediately. In the meantime…"

She was waiting for our pick.

"*All* of them," Erik said. "I'm feeling a little hungry tonight. Bring them to my room. We're sharing."

Erik pulled back the curtain to the room next to his painting, and pressed his thumb to a panel that Andreas had installed. The computer recognised his thumbprint and the door opened. He propped it open, and I followed him into the soundproof room. Inside were candles, which Erik took time to light. Two lounge chairs sat opposite each other, a request Erik had put in so we could share whenever the moment arose. There was a small fridge in the corner, in which he kept bottled water, and on top was a box of what humans called 'snacks'. Foods loaded with sugar to help them after the light-headedness that came with blood-loss. Along the back of the room was a bed made with black silk sheets.

I pulled my shirt off, and took a seat in one of the chairs. Erik removed his, and waited by the door. It wasn't long before the humans stepped through the curtain, pausing as they took in the room. Erik leaned forward, breathing them in, eyes turning red.

"Mmmm, they smell delicious!" he said, voice low. "I'm Erik. This is my beloved, Josef."

I smirked at their surprise to find two of us.

"I'm Adriana," the woman in the black dress said, as Erik closed the door behind them.

"I'm Matthew and this is Caterina," the man said.

"Who wants to go first?" Erik prompted, closing the doors.

Adriana stepped forward. "Me," she said. "I didn't realise there would be two of you." Desire flickered across her face as she took us in.

"Come here," I instructed her. "I want to breathe you in, see if you smell as delicious as Erik says."

A shiver passed through Adriana, my words having their desired effect. She moved across the floor, eyes on me. She stopped before me. I patted my leg. "Sit, make yourself comfortable."

She sat on one leg, leaning back against me. I pressed my face to her throat, taking in a deep breath. Underneath her jasmine perfume I noted a hint of strawberry. Her heart rate picked up.

I grinned at Erik. "You were right."

He laughed. "You doubted me?"

Adriana turned her body to meet my eyes. She touched the pendant that hung around my neck. "What's this?"

"It's called *Mjolnir,*" I said. "Erik gave it to me as a gift, a few years ago."

I moved her hair from her neck and slid my tongue over where I would bite. I lifted my eyes to Erik, and he was leaning against the wall, eyes focused on her face as his smile widened. The woman also looked at Erik.

"Are you just going to watch from over there?" she asked.

"I'll feed when I'm ready," Erik replied. "Josef, bite her. Give her what she's paying for."

I sunk my fangs in, releasing venom into my bite. The woman gave a soft whimper and she squirmed against me. Erik chose that moment to approach us, only to kneel before her. "I'm going to bite you on your thigh," he said. "Are you okay with that?"

She could only nod, and raised her dress, allowing Erik access. He pulled her panties down, and bit between her thighs. Her whole body jerked in response. His venom was stronger than mine. She let out a moan, and I wrapped an arm around her body before she could slide from my lap. I closed my eyes, surrendering to the pull of the feed. Her pulse beat against my lips, thundering in my ears. Her blood was rich and sweet with desire on my tongue, and my body responded to the bliss as ripples of pleasure surged across my skin, warming my own blood. A calm quietened the inner beast, as I sunk into the red haze. Movement pulled me out, and I opened my eyes.

Erik's mouth was above her pussy, eyes on her face. Again, she nodded and he started to lick. I released her throat, licking away the blood that trickled from my punctures. With my free hand, I turned her head slightly, and lowered my lips to hers. She reached up, grabbing the back of my head as if to hold me there. Her soft lips parted, a whisper of a moan escaped as she allowed me in.

The couple remained at the door, their own arousal rising from them as they watched. I pulled back from the kiss, meeting Caterina's eyes.

"Help yourself to the bed. Enjoy each other while you wait," I told the couple, and returned to the kiss.

I met Erik's red eyes, his hunger powerful through our bond. He'd only taken a taste before starting to eat her out, and the desire in the room was affecting him. The woman was squirming against my erection, her kiss becoming hungry. Erik growled, the woman's heart skipping. Tremors started jolting through her, Erik pushing her towards an orgasm.

On the bed, the couple started stroking each other, their breathing quickening. Adriana moaned again in response to Erik's tongue. She reluctantly pulled from the kiss, eyes meeting mine.

"Am I allowed to ask for more?" she pleaded. Her hand rubbed against my crotch.

The effects of our venom had taken hold of her, and I panted with need myself. I reached down, undoing the zip and button on my jeans, relieved for the release of my cock from the denim. Erik pulled my jeans to my knees, and started to kiss my thighs, lips blazing across my skin. His movements were tender, yet hungry simultaneously.

"Is that what you need?" I asked Adriana, almost forgetting myself.

She nodded and lowered herself onto my cock. Her body pulsed around me, and Erik's beard brushed against my thigh as he remained where he was, watchful. I placed my hands on her hips, and lifted her up a little, sliding her down my shaft again. She leaned her head against my shoulder, breathing hard. I continued the motion, lifting her and lowering her onto me again. With each movement, an ache unfurled inside me. Part hunger, part desire. Erik's eyes burned into me, watching my face intently. Our gazes locked, and only the two of us existed. Time slowed down.

"Oh god," Adriana gasped, pulling me back to the present. "Please bite me again."

I bit her, and her whole body tensed, squeezing tight, gripping my cock. A drawn-out moan rose from her, and I squeezed her breasts, running my hands over her body. I hadn't been going nearly long enough for my own orgasm. Erik's fangs sunk into one thigh and his hand brushed over the other. He released more venom than usual into his bite. It flooded through my blood, pushing me to come as the human did. I groaned against the woman's throat, determined not to show the humans that I was almost seeing stars.

The woman caught her breath, and Erik helped her to her feet. He carried her to the bed, and the couple moved out of the way. I re-buckled my jeans and grabbed a bottle of water and a chocolate bar, taking them to Adriana. Her breathing hadn't yet calmed down, eyes wide, a dreamy smile on her face. The couple watched us, waiting. But instead of inviting them over, Erik closed the space between us with a growl, grabbed me by the throat and pushed me up against the wall. His hand lifted my jaw roughly, forcing my eyes to his before lowering his mouth to mine.

'Submit to me,' he demanded through our mental bond. *'Every ounce of you. Now.'*

I submitted to his demanding kiss, melting against his body. The kiss was filled with primal need, dark and consuming; both of us clawing at one another.

'You get me heated watching you,' he whispered, voice pouring over me.

'Then shall we continue with our meal?' I offered. *'We still have two more yearning for our bite. Satisfy them, then you have me all to yourself.'*

Then as one, Erik and I turned to the couple. They hadn't moved, watching us, their breathing accelerated.

"Ready?" I asked, reaching out my hand.

Chapter 9

I walked through quiet Venice streets with my father. It was a bittersweet moment, and I burst with joy. We crossed familiar stone bridges, our footsteps silent. The lamps cast a yellow glow over their surroundings. Then we hunted in San Marco; his territory. To hunt with my father was a moment I'd never considered. My sole focus had been on our reunion. I took my fill and pulled him from his human.

"They call you 'The Feral,' I commented as the humans fell to the ground behind us. "I always wondered why."

He nodded. "The night you ran to your uncle, my maker called me back. I was so overcome by grief and guilt, I killed her."

"You were in feral madness," I acknowledged, finally understanding. "Oh, Papa, I'm so sorry."

"It's not as much of a struggle as it used to be," he admitted. "Quinn's presence calms 'The Feral."

"Then I'm glad you found her," I said with a smile. "Perhaps when we return to your den, you can introduce me to her."

Delight filled his eyes. "I'd like that."

We walked in silence for a while, side-by-side through the Venetian streets.

"You just missed Carnivale," he said, breaking the quiet that had settled between us. "We make something special of it as vampires. Feeding in the open, the intoxication."

I laughed. "I've spent many Carnivales here, blood drunk." I grinned up at him. "Oh, do you remember that mask you painted for me? The red and gold one."

Delight lit up his eyes. "You remember that? You were so young."

"Of course I do. I wore it everywhere three weeks after. Until it mysteriously disappeared, only to reappear the day before the following Carnivale," I recalled.

"You were so proud of that mask." Warmth filled his voice. "Your mother didn't want you to break or damage it. She wanted to see you wear it the following year."

We stopped at a gallery. I smiled up at the stone building, one I was familiar with, but it now had the Barone sigil above the words, 'Art Gallery.' "Is this it?".

"It is." The pride in his voice was unmistakable. "Would you like to see my art?"

Excitement bubbled up "Papa! Your dream!"

Wistfulness passed over his face. "I never thought I'd have the chance to hear you call me that again. It warms my heart."

"We have a chance not afforded to many of our kind," I agreed.

He led me into the gallery. "Do you want to display your art in here?"

Elation unfurled within me. "Really?"

"This was part of the dream. To have our art side by side," he recalled. "My little artist."

I admired the art around us. "I almost gave up," I admitted. "You went missing the same day I drew your portrait. We never thought we'd see you again. Mamma hugged me as we cried with your portrait in front of us. We didn't know what had happened. I thought you'd left us."

My father's arms wrapped around me. "My little treasure, I would never have left you and Marisa willingly."

The child I had been, it was *her* tears that escaped my eyes. "You were gone for a whole week," I said. "So in my sorrow, I swore I'd never draw again. You inspired me to draw, and you were gone."

My chest ached at the memories. His arms tightened around me.

"I'm sorry," he whispered. "I fought to get back to you both. She didn't turn me straight away. She fed from me for a couple of days before she forced her blood into me."

"She forced you?" I asked.

He pulled back, looking down at me, a storm in his eyes. "I would never have picked this," he admitted. "My life was perfect. I loved my family and had everything I could have wanted. I did not choose this over you. Either of you."

"Do you hate what you are?" I asked in fear. I'd never met a vampire who didn't take to this life, but knew it occasionally happened. But would King Carlos have taken someone with such a dislike of our nature?

He sat on a bench in front of a painting. I sat next to him.

"I hated what I did to my family," he said quietly. "I hated that my life was torn from me. That I never got to see you grow up, get married, and have children. But I never hated being a vampire. I think I did feel a little guilty, that I enjoyed what I'd become, when I'd caused such devastation for my own family, whom I believed I could never see again. Fifty years passed and I realised I never would have the opportunity to hug my little treasure. To tell her what had happened."

Understanding came over me, as I'd done the same to my own husband and sons. "We have a second chance," I emphasised. "Let's not waste it on regret."

"You becoming a vampire isn't what a normal father would want," he admitted. "But you're right. I am grateful that Marco turned you instead of leaving you to die. I wish I could thank him."

I turned away, stifling the rising emotion. The loss of my maker had left an ache that would take time to heal from.

A separate room with a black curtain over the door drew my attention. "What's in there?"

Amusement crossed his features. "That's an experiment."

Curiosity bloomed. "What kind of experiment?" I prompted.

"There are nude paintings of the others. Humans pay for private time with the model or models of their choosing."

"You have a feeding gallery?" I asked, laughing. "Can I see?"

Before he could respond, I made my way towards the private gallery and lifted up the black curtain. The scent of Erik and Josef mingled with blood and the scent of pleasure. They'd been here recently. Fed, and more. I took in the sight of the paintings, immediately picking out Erik and Josef. The tattoos on Erik caught my eye before it was drawn to his cock. He'd posed in a way that showed no shame, flaunting his body, daring people to look. I smiled at Josef's bold hands on his hips, desire flooding my body.

"Are you after anyone in particular?" A woman asked. "Fifty thousand for half an hour."

"She's one of us," my father said. "My daughter."

The woman nodded with understanding, as if she knew 'one of us' meant vampire.

"The two who were here; how long ago did they leave?" I asked.

"They left about ten minutes ago, and were well satisfied. They are popular," she replied with a smile. "The clients were also very happy."

I couldn't wait to see their appetites, both in feeding and in bed. The thought of it made heat pool low in my stomach, and my fangs ached. I could almost feel their lips on my throat, their fangs biting into me. I yearned for both of them.

"That is something no father should be subjected to," my father said from behind me.

I glanced over my shoulder, confused.

My father grimaced. "Humans have such weak senses, I would never have thought I'd wish for it now."

Realisation sunk in, followed by horror. He could smell my lust. "Okay, maybe we should go," I said and hurried away from the room with naked pictures of Erik and Josef and the scent of their satisfaction.

"Quinn is nearby, and would like to meet you," my father said once we left the gallery. "Officially."

I smiled. "Of course." I was excited to see the woman who had won my father's heart. "So, do I call her Stepmother?" I joked.

He scoffed. "I don't think she'd appreciate that."

"I imagine it was difficult to leave her children," I said. "Do they know she's still alive? How long has she been a vampire?" My curiosity about Quinn burst forth in questions.

"She's been a vampire for twenty years," he informed me. "She had no children."

I stared in shock. "You made her a vampire with no children?"

He smiled. "She didn't want any. Times have changed: a lot of women like to focus on careers these days, rather than having children. She had a career in singing. It's actually how we met. She's a siren, and Called me, tying the two of us together. Since that day, she was fated to become a vampire. It's her Siren Song that helps calm the feral within."

So, *she* was the siren Pierre had been talking about. My father's voice softened when he spoke of her, and his eyes lit up as they always had when he looked upon my mother.

"Did she have to give up singing?" I asked.

"I could never give up singing," a female voice with an Australian accent said behind me. I spun around. Her smile was one of warmth.

She embraced Matteo, and he kissed her on the forehead. There was a deep love in the gesture, and I couldn't help but smile as I watched them.

"*Mi amore,* it delights me to introduce you to my daughter," he said.

It felt strange hearing him call her by the same name he used to whisper to my mother. His voice spoke the words with such familiarity—Mi amore—his tone filled with the same love he always spoke to my mother. I should have been happy for him, but the sound of it dragged up the pain of a child. I swallowed it down. Seeing him happy again, how could I resent that?

"Hi, Aria. I've heard so much about you. I'm happy you were able to reunite with Matteo," she said.

Her red hair had been the first thing I'd noticed earlier, and there had been something familiar about her. I met green eyes that shone with genuine joy, and a wide smile. Her cheeks were peppered with light freckles, her pale skin a contrast against the Mediterranean colouring of my father.

"Didn't you see any sun when you were human?" I asked with laughter. "I thought Australia was a sunny country."

Her laughter was like music, with a lightness to it. "I like her already," she said to my father, then shifted her eyes back to me. "You clearly don't know Melbourne," she joked. "But I worked a lot with my music at night. You should have seen my sister, though; she was darker than me. She and my dad got their colouring from the Māori side of my family, while I got the pale Irish."

"I actually recognise you," I said, recalling why she looked familiar. "Your pictures were everywhere when I went to Australia twenty years ago. Humans were sad over your supposed death."

"When were you in Australia?" my father asked me.

"Hours after you left," I said. "Your former Queen was not happy to have us there asking about you. I assumed something had happened, so left quickly before she had a chance to challenge our presence there. But I remember that photo of the two of you in masks. It didn't occur to me at the time that you'd be with my father. I assumed you'd been his meal, not his beloved."

Quinn beamed at Matteo. "They loved to use that photo of us. We were only together in the public eye for a short time before your gallery burned down, but it's as if we were the hot new celebrity couple."

My father kissed her, the two of them smiling. "They knew little about us and what we were to each other. My beautiful siren, you had me under your spell from the moment I heard your voice. That photo only showed the love we already had for one another."

Quinn's eyes shifted towards me. "Sorry if this makes you uncomfortable."

I shook my head. "My father was equally affectionate with my mother. I'm happy he found you. I think my mother would have liked you."

Her smile widened, and my father's embrace around her tightened.

"Matteo says you hunted together," Quinn said. "I bet that would have been surreal."

Warmth spread across my chest, unexpected but welcome. This young vampire—who had my father's heart—radiated sincerity, and I couldn't help but respond with a smile.

"Oh, it was!" I agreed. "Maybe the two of us can spend some time getting to know each other?"

Her eyes sparkled with joy. "I'd love that! Maybe you can join us at the bar this weekend. I'm singing. I'm sure Matteo and Carlos can let us hunt without them."

"Maybe not this weekend," I said. "I don't know how long I'm going to be with Erik and Josef."

My father frowned, and Quinn laughed. "I'm sure we'll have a chance afterwards," she said.

My father cleared his throat. "Carlos is calling us back," he said. "He would like to speak with you."

Chapter 10

Quinn and my father led me back to their den.

The male vampire with shoulder-length brown hair who'd looked at me earlier, stood in front of the door, and eyed me up and down. He smirked, but stepped aside. "Carlos is waiting," he said. I was surprised to find he spoke with an Austrian accent.

"Thanks, Andreas," Quinn said. "Have you hunted yet?"

I let the conversation fall behind me as I walked through the door. Moonlight filtered in through the windows across the marble floor, tapestries and paintings lined the walls, and I breathed in the scent of home. A chandelier hung from the ceiling, but most of the lights remained off. Not that any of us needed them to see.

Once again King Carlos sat in the chair, his human next to him. I dropped to my knees before him. Quinn and my father entered behind me, silent.

His human woman laughed. "I don't think I'll get used to people kneeling to you," she said in her Spanish accent.

"They bow to you too, my Queen," he affirmed. "As do I." He then addressed me. "On your feet, Aria. There is no need for formality, given who you are."

I stood. I had met King Carlos a few times while trying to enter Venice, his reputation matching his actions with the ferocity with which he removed me. Standing in front of him intimidated me more than any of those previous meetings.

"This is an unusual situation," he said. "I do wish you'd told me who you were, but I understand your need for your father to be the one you spoke to. I apologise for my approach to you."

I nodded. "You were only protecting your territory."

"Indeed." King Carlos looked at me with a small smile, expression transforming before me. No longer the hardened glare, but somewhat friendly. "Matteo tells me you have a villa elsewhere."

"I do," I agreed. "Up until you arrived, it was my home whenever I returned to visit my descendants."

He met my eyes. "How did you know Matteo was here?"

"Lenora sent me a text message when Pietro suspected his sudden move from this villa had been due to vampire compulsion. They assumed it was my father, as no other vampire would go straight for the family home."

I recalled the message. *'I believe your father has returned to Venice.'*

"They were certainly quick to approach the villa and make themselves known," King Carlos recounted.

"I kind of see the family resemblance," the human added, looking from me to my father. "The same dark wavy hair, and shape of their face and skin tone."

King Carlos leaned back in his chair. "Yes, I suppose you're right," he agreed. "Matteo, you may want to leave for this conversation."

My father smiled down at me and squeezed my shoulder. "Come and see me afterwards," he said, and led Quinn from the room.

"My Norseman and former Hunter were here earlier, asking for some alone time with you," King Carlos informed me. "They seem to believe you're the one they've been waiting for. They've wanted a nest for some time, and thought you would be ideal. I want to hear what you have to say on this."

"They did claim me," I said. "I certainly would have let them know if it wasn't something I wanted."

King Carlos rubbed at his chin thoughtfully. I glanced at the human, curious. She gave me a smile. There was no fear in her eyes, only my own curiosity reflected back. Once again I found myself wondering how King Carlos, with all I had heard about him, could take a human and name her Queen.

"You're wondering about my Queen." King Carlos wasn't asking, as he watched me.

I shifted my eyes back to him. "I'm sorry, I wasn't trying to be disrespectful," I said.

He leaned forward. "Voice your thoughts."

"You have a certain reputation. This is a little unexpected," I admitted.

He reached for the human's hand, face softening as he gazed at her. "It was for me, too. When we stopped trying to kill each other, Camila became more than just a Hunter. I saw who she was underneath."

I took a step back, fear choking me. "Hunter?"

Camila rose from her chair. "Please don't be afraid of me, Aria. I'm no longer a Hunter. I would never harm you." She stepped towards me, her scent of apples and vanilla curling around us.

"But you've killed vampires?" I asked. "King Carlos, a Hunter in a vampire's den..."

I had never feared Hunters, but then they had never been inside a den before that I knew of. Sitting there next to the King as if she belonged.

King Carlos stood. "Aria, do you trust that I would never put you at risk? Or your father."

I met his eyes. "From what I know about you, yes."

"Then trust that this former Hunter is no threat to you. She has been exiled from her community, and is under my protection."

"You fought in the war against the first Hunters." I looked between the two. "Yet you love a Hunter?"

His eyes crinkled as he brushed his hand up her arm. "I do."

"And you, um, Camila. You love King Carlos?"

They smiled at each other, and I relaxed. There was only adoration in their gazes. No Hunter would look at a vampire that way. He lifted his hand, brushing fingers over the twin scars on her throat. He'd marked her.

"Will you turn her?" I asked.

Camila lowered her eyes, and returned to her chair.

"If and only when she asks," he said, grabbing Camila's hand.

"She let you claim and mark her, but doesn't want to—"

Carlos held his hand up to silence me. "You didn't mean any disrespect, but this line of questioning is becoming just that," he said. "My Queen will tell me if she wants me to turn her, and any vampire who doesn't like that can keep their thoughts to themselves."

I bowed my head. "I'm sorry, King Carlos. I've never heard of a human being claimed in this manner. Do you not worry about her ageing? If she's your beloved, do you not want her with you for all eternity?"

A twitch of panic crossed his face but quickly smoothed over. Camila's heartbeat sped up, and I caught something else in her eyes. *Interesting*. Did she already know that she would have to make that decision? Had she already made it?

"I will not discuss such matters with you," King Carlos said. "How about we get to what you want to address. The reason you're here."

I had completely forgotten about the reason I'd been allowed into Venice. "Luca wanted someone here to ensure the ties between our clans are of unity," I said.

King Carlos laughed, and returned to his chair. "Your new King wanted to make sure to not displease me. Wise. I must admit, I am surprised that Giuseppe chose Luca for his Second to replace Marco."

I diverted my gaze.

"Oh, I didn't expect that," he commented.

"Expect what?" Camila asked.

"You were surprised, too, weren't you, Aria?"

I didn't move, staring at the floor.

King Carlos moved towards me with swift speed, lifting my chin until our eyes met. "You don't want to betray your King," he said softly. "This isn't betraying him. In a way, I am your King, allowing him to rule in my place."

There was no malice in his eyes. "It was a surprise," I admitted. "I think Giuseppe's decision was grief-fuelled. There may be a challenge."

"I need you to be honest with me, Aria. Should I be putting someone else in that position?" he prompted.

My heart sped up a little. I was betraying my King.

"I have fed from the Bloodking, and have the power to *compel* the truth out of you," he added. "I don't want to do that, though. Especially given you're the daughter of my Second."

"I think he was foolish to not know what kneeling to you would mean," I said slowly. "He handed our entire clan over because of his lack of understanding. That alone is an indication that he is not King material."

Guilt pierced my heart. I'd always struggled not to speak my mind, but to speak of my King in such a way was dishonourable. King Carlos narrowed his eyes at me.

"I appreciate your honesty," he said. "I may have to make the effort to travel to San Marino in the next few weeks. Meet the clan that I have taken control of. I didn't have a chance to meet those who came here. At the time,

Lorenzo did notice one looking towards Celeste, though, as he hid behind others. I'll be interested to know if he knew her, or if I'll have someone trying to claim that which is already mine. If you point out any of these would-be challengers to me, I will make sure they are not a problem." His smile was menacing. "No one will *dare* challenge me."

I struggled to find words.

"Erik, Josef!" he called out, stepping away from me.

They were in the room in an instant. Erik met my eyes, his glinting red, fangs showing between his lips.

"I think it's best you two leave the den with your new friend," King Carlos said. "I know what you're hoping for, and I don't think doing that within Matteo's hearing is a good idea."

Erik's eyes darted to mine. My heart skipped as sheer hunger crossed over his face. "Yes, my King," Erik glanced away from me towards Josef. "We need to pack."

"Why? We're only going to end up naked, anyway," Josef said with a grin.

King Carlos laughed. "Erik isn't talking about clothes."

Josef's smile widened. "What do you have in mind?" he asked Erik.

"Leave that to me," Erik replied. "Grab a few clothes anyway; we still need to hunt."

It didn't take them long to pack. Then we were leaving the villa.

My father approached us, with Quinn.

"Matteo—" Josef began.

"I'll say the same thing I would have if we'd been human," my father said, cutting Josef off. "Be good to my treasure. Treat her well. I only want to see her happy." He winked at me. "If not, I'll rip out your throats."

Erik smirked at me before meeting my father's eyes. "So, do we call you 'Papa'?"

The silence stretched out, my father glaring from Josef to Erik. Next to him, Quinn met my gaze, laughter dancing in her eyes. She had the kind of smile that was contagious.

"You're twice my age, you will never call me that," my father declared, and marched away.

Chapter 11

The walk to my villa should have been quick. Erik and Josef couldn't keep their hands off me. We stopped many times, as they caged me between them, touching and kissing me.

This time Erik pinned me against Josef, and grabbed my jaw. His kiss was fire, and when he pulled away, he held my lower lip with his teeth. I wanted to get to my villa, but I couldn't deny either of these men. Already wet, I wanted one of them inside me right then. I brushed my hand against his crotch. He let out a small breath, his cock straining against his trousers. I slid my ass back slightly, pulling a hiss from Josef.

Their bite was unexpected and I closed my eyes, letting their venom propel me higher. Once again the strength of Erik's caught me by surprise.

We finally got to my villa. I led them inside and deactivated the alarm.

"Looks like you need an updated security system," Erik noted. "I'm sure Andreas could set something up for you. Scan your eye or your fingerprint. He set up security for our den, and nothing goes undetected."

I led them through the villa to the bedroom that had been mine for over six hundred years. Chandeliers hung from the ceiling, unused due to vampire sight. Red velvet curtains were tied, large windows revealing the canal that the villa overlooked. Modern furniture that Lenora had helped me pick out over twenty years before filled my bedroom. Black wooden bookshelves and dresser, a black framed bed, large enough for five people. Venetian masks and art lined the wall, some painted by my father, some I'd done myself. Being back here made me feel like I'd returned home and contentment filled my heart.

The moment we entered my bedroom, Josef immediately grabbed me, eyes red, gripping my jaw. Erik moved towards the bed, laying back.

"I'd like that taste now," Josef growled. "Stand with your back to the wall."

His commanding tone took me by surprise. "This is *my* home," I said. "You don't—"

My words cut off as he pushed me against the wall, dropping his hand to press against me through my jeans. I sucked in a breath, pushing against his fingers.

"What were you saying?" he asked with a smirk.

"My nest," I gasped as he pressed harder.

"This will go a lot easier if you don't resist what Josef wants," Erik suggested. "He wants his taste. You're in our territory now, little trespasser."

Erik lay on my bed, hands behind his head. My red silk sheets beneath him almost matched his eyes.

"No more teasing," Josef said. "Remove your jeans now. I'm *hungry*."

My pelvic muscles tightened at his words. Josef grinned, breathing in deep.

"Good, I know you're ready. Give me what *I* want, and I'll give you what *you* want."

I removed my jeans, and Josef tore my tee-shirt over my head. He reached out, hands skimming over my body. His touch sent a tremor through me. On his knees, he forced my legs apart. His finger slid through my wet centre, and a growl rumbled from him.

"She's already so wet," he said to Erik, desire lacing his voice. "She's ready for us."

"Of course she is," Erik said from my bed. "Move, let me see her. I want to see every inch of what is ours."

Josef's finger curled through me, and he shuffled to the side. Erik had removed his clothes, his erection hard to miss. The painting had been accurate in that department. His entire body was covered in tattoos. Norse designs that hinted at stories. I wanted to trace my tongue over each and every tattoo, to hear him moan as I licked him over his entire body.

I grinned over at Erik, "Are you going to stay over there?" I asked, eyes on his cock.

Josef laughed. "Oh, he'll join in when he's ready," he said. "He likes to watch. It'll give you some time to prepare yourself." He took his hand from me, putting his fingers in his mouth. "Mmmm, Erik, she's delicious."

Erik gave me the once over. "Touch yourself," he said. "I want to see you come apart at your own doing."

I whimpered, his words sending small shivers through me.

Unable to resist, I slid my own hand towards my wanting pussy.

Growls rose from Erik and Josef. I shifted my eyes from Erik's erection, watching Josef undress. I yearned to touch him as I touched myself. Josef had a tattoo that matched Erik's. *La Voz.*

"Let me touch her, Erik," Josef pleaded. "Let me taste her."

"Wait," Erik replied. "You'll taste her when she comes. The rest of her body is yours to enjoy."

Josef smiled at me as I slid my finger through my own wetness. He leaned forward, and lifted the hair from my neck. His hand grasped my chin, pushing up, exposing my throat. His tongue slid over it.

"No biting," Erik growled. "Not yet."

Josef's teeth grazed over my jaw, and he lifted his head. The heat of his gaze was scorching before he leaned in, breath caressing my mouth. I parted my lips, welcoming him in. Our kiss burned slowly, heating up like the embers of a fire reigniting. The hardness of his cock against me, my own fingers, and his demanding tongue all had me whimpering into his mouth.

I reached for him with my free hand, which he grabbed, slamming it against the wall over my head. He trailed kisses over my collarbone, then his tongue darted out. More kisses, followed by licks as he moved towards my breasts. His warm mouth closed over my left nipple, the movement of his swirling tongue setting off a gasp. I momentarily forgot to continue pleasuring myself.

"Don't stop," Erik growled next to my ear. I had been so distracted with Josef I hadn't seen him move. "I'm going to kneel in front of you and make sure you continue. I'm going to touch myself, watching you touch yourself."

Oh fuck, these two knew how to push all the right buttons. As Josef's thumb stroked my wrist, his mouth over my nipple and his other hand brushing the underside of my breast had me panting. My nipples had hardened, my clit throbbed, and my skin flushed. But gazing down at Erik on his knees, stroking himself sent a shiver up my spine. Every nerve in my body felt exposed, each sensation of Josef's touch, my own, and Erik's breath had my whole body flashing hot, and tensing.

The fingers that circled my clit became a point of pleasure, pulling me towards my orgasm. Chasing the release, I moved them faster.

"Good girl," Erik said, reaching for my hand. He pulled my fingers into his mouth for the briefest of moments before guiding my hand back. "Mmmm, you're so wet," he said, and started to pump himself faster. "Get ready to bite her," he instructed Josef, and moved himself closer to me.

Josef grunted into my breast, watching my face. His lips stretched into a smile against my skin. Erik's free hand reached up, wrapping around Josef's cock. I moaned, and my back arched. Heat unfurled and I raced towards that moment of pure euphoria. I was on the edge and needed—

"Now," Erik instructed.

Fangs sunk into my inner thigh, and my throat, and I cried out as a wave of pleasure hit me, hard. The sheer ecstasy, vampire venom and the intensity of the moment pushed me into black.

Chapter 12

The noise Aria made would never be described as human. An animalistic wail that ended as her body slumped, and Erik moved fast. He caught her in his arms.

"What happened?" I asked, eyeing the room for a threat.

Erik chuckled. "She came so hard she blacked out."

"You gave her your full venom, didn't you?" I shook my head in disbelief. "I told you, you need to let someone *adjust* to your concentrated venom before giving them so much."

"I got caught up in the moment," he admitted with a smirk. "But I'll be more careful."

He carried her to the bed, laying her over the red silk sheets. He kissed her forehead before turning towards me. "You're right, she tastes divine," he said. "Let me taste her from you."

Before I could move, he pulled me towards him, our bodies up against one another, his hard cock crossing mine. His tongue forced my lips apart. I could taste her blood from him.

Aria's arousal remained in his mouth also. He'd tasted her briefly.

"Let's tie her up," Erik suggested, and reached for his bag. He pulled out restraints and a blindfold.

"What else do you have in your bag of tricks?" I asked, reaching for it.

He pulled it out of my reach. "It's a surprise."

I growled in frustration.

Erik turned his crimson eyes to me. "Are you growling at me?"

Oh fuck.

I dropped to my knees. "I'm sorry," I said. "It was a growl of frustration, not *at* you."

He grabbed my jaw, tilting my head up. I caught his hungry smile. His thumb ran over my lips.

"If you wanted me on my knees, you could have said so," I commented, reaching for his cock, ready to bring it to my mouth.

He laughed. "It's not time for that right now. But I would like to feed from you, while you drink from me."

I was on my feet in an instant, and exposed my throat to him. I took in a sharp intake of breath when he bit me. He was injecting his full venom, almost enough to make me come; if I hadn't had twenty years to get used to it. I clamped down on his shoulder, our blood bond pushing through me. It wasn't just the presence of his mind, it was as if our hearts beat as one. When we fed from each other, our bond strengthened. I could sense satisfaction emanating from him.

We pulled apart with reluctance.

"She'll wake up soon," Erik said. "Help me restrain her."

"What if it's not her thing?" I asked, grabbing the leather cuffs from him.

He grinned. "Oh, I have the feeling she'll like it. If not, we'll simply untie her."

We worked quickly, and Erik placed the silk blindfold over her eyes.

"The first time I saw her, I wanted her to join us," he admitted. "Our beautiful trespasser. That spark of defiance as she glared at us."

We'd both confessed our love for one another, Erik and I, not long before that day. We'd just arrived in Venice. But the first time I'd laid eyes on her, I'd been captivated by her bravery as she attempted to enter another vampire's territory, despite our king forcing her out. "I do wish she'd told us who she was," I said, drinking in the sight of her. The scent of her release pulled at me, her thighs wet. "We delayed that reunion with her father. And we could have spent the last twenty years with our new nest mate."

"What's done is done," Erik replied. He pulled me close, licking his blood off my chin. I'd deliberately been messy when I fed from him. "I love when you leave a mess."

A low rumble vibrated from my chest. When he finished, he lifted his head, allowing me to clean my own blood. Then he wrapped his arms around me. I returned the embrace, filled with warmth.

"Whatever happens with Aria, I'll not neglect you," he promised. "You were mine before she was. Carlos can share his many lovers; we can do the same. You are mine, and I am yours, for eternity. She will be *ours,* too."

There was no need for words as we remained in one another's arms. My love for Erik was everlasting. I had no fear of him forsaking me for another. We both shared a long history together, even before we gave in to our desire.

What had started as hate, had changed when I became a vampire. Despite me hunting him for years, he'd been eager to stand with me as I adjusted to my new existence. He and Ana had taught me to hunt, each having their unique preference. He'd been the one to teach me about putting venom in my bite, and I'd convinced him not to use it on Hunters. He'd been there with me when I'd led the vampires into camps, resulting in a great loss for the Hunters. I'd become a high priority then, Hunters demanding my death. I'd earned the names, 'traitor', 'a curse', and 'an abomination'. Both of us had lived a life of what humans called 'enemies-to-lovers' in romance books; over hundreds of years. I'd lost my family to vampires, only to embrace my new immortal family willingly.

"You know, I recognised the darkness in you," Erik murmured, in response to my thoughts, as my mind was wide open to him. "You'd given up your humanity long before you became a vampire. With a push from yours truly, of course." He chuckled. "Maybe that's why I chose you that night when Carlos suggested turning a Hunter."

"Admit that you enjoyed those last few moments of tormenting me," I said with a smile. "Every time we faced each other, you were so smug and annoying."

His body shook. "It *was* entertaining watching you think you could take on five vampires with a stake from your boot. But I couldn't help but admire you when you stood to face me. You had nothing to lose, and you faced someone who could have easily killed you. In my centuries as a vampire, I don't think I'd come across that many humans with such courage."

I pulled out of the embrace. "There aren't many humans left with courage like that. Most of them would piss themselves if they knew we existed. With the Bloodking declaring war, I'm hoping that means The Accords no longer apply."

"Oh, I would say they'll be quickly declared invalid," Erik agreed with hunger in his eyes. "Although, we will have to hunt outside of Venice if we're in a killing mood. Our agreement and peace with the Barones still stands."

I turned towards Aria. "Maybe when we've nested, the three of us can hunt."

"The thrill of the hunt, when we're not restrained by irritating Accords," Erik said. "I think you're right. That would be a delight." He took in a deep breath, letting it out slowly. "It has been too long since we've been allowed to revel in our nature. To give chase, to torment them." He growled. "To seduce them, so they're begging for our embrace and bite, even with their final breaths."

As if the idea turned him on more, he yanked me to him again, rougher than before. "We can fuck as we feed."

His lips and tongue were demanding.

Before I could yield to the kiss, Aria stretched out. She moved her head towards the right, then the left. Her hands flexed against her restraints. Instead of fighting against it, she simply smiled. "Well, that was unexpected."

Chapter 13

The softness of silk sheets brushed against my skin, and darkness covered my eyes. I could smell Erik and Josef, and their hearts beat in rhythm. Their murmuring voices had lulled me back to consciousness. I'd interrupted something: their fast responses to me waking up didn't hide that they'd been kissing.

My arms were secured over my head to the headboard, bound at the wrists with something unyielding. And by the smell of it, it was leather.

"Well, that was unexpected," I managed.

I'd come so hard I'd blacked out. That had *never* happened before. I'd been fingering myself, but it was their bites that pushed me over. The effects of their venom and my orgasm lingered, ripples of pleasure still lapping at me. Small tremors still shook my body.

Erik laughed somewhere to my right. "You do make wondrous sounds when you come. Absolutely delicious."

I smiled in his direction. "I wish I could take credit, but your venom probably had a lot to do with that. Do you often inject your full venom?"

"I told you," Josef said from my left.

"Are you complaining?" Erik asked, closer.

The mattress sank as he pinned me beneath his body. I couldn't see him, but could feel him. Every sound felt amplified. Our heartbeats, the soft draw of his breath which brushed over my lips. His chest barely touched mine, but my skin blazed from the contact. I wrapped my legs around him, his cock against my thigh. His rough beard against my chin hinted at what he was about to do, and I held my breath. Then he kissed me. His kiss was different to Josef's—rougher, with a hunger to it. Insistent. Demanding. Consumed by desire, I returned his intensity. I pulled at my restraints, the need to touch him overcoming me. Hands pinned my arms down.

"Mmm, you taste as sweet as I knew you would the moment I saw you. Are you ready to continue?"

"Let me touch you," I panted.

With gentle hands, Josef pulled my legs from Erik, binding my feet with leather straps to the corner posts.

Erik pressed his cheek against mine, his facial hair once again tickling my cheek. "You're ours," he reminded me. "You touch us when we say you can." His weight pressed down next to mine. "Let us take our fill."

"Are you ready?" Josef asked.

Before I could answer, hands slid over my body—Erik's touch rough and possessive, igniting sparks beneath my skin, Josef's gentler, almost reverent.

Lips brushed against skin. Fangs pierced my throat, then breasts, and thighs. Bites that didn't last long, but enough to awaken a deep need that spread like fire. Tongues moved over sensitive places. Warm breath caressed me. In the dark, everything felt accentuated. The aroma of my own arousal mixed with theirs. My pulse and ragged breaths echoed in rhythm with theirs. The low rumbles from them sent small quivers through my body.

Their intoxicating scents overwhelmed me. Erik smelled sharp, like hot metal. Josef had a softer scent, more earthy.

"You let us claim you, but you need to make it official," Josef said. "Do you accept that you are ours?" Once again his lips made contact; tracing the edge of my jaw. I parted my lips in invitation, aching for his kiss to claim my mouth, as he had already claimed my body.

"I am yours," I confirmed. "And you will be mine when I claim you."

"We have a King, but in this nest, with the three of us, you will recognise me as the alpha." Erik whispered before nibbling on my ear. "Submit to me, Aria. To us."

More kisses moved across my body, their hands caressing me as they moved, leaving heat in their wake.

"My villa," I said, stubborn. "My nest. You submit *to me*."

Josef chuckled. "You're the one tied to the bed, sweet thing."

"I don't care," Erik scolded, pressing his lips to my throat. "You will recognise me as your alpha." His fangs pierced my throat. He bit deep, marking me, his venom sending my mind spinning again. "I will give you what you want, I will worship your body. But you will know who has total control over your pleasure. You will know that I am the eldest of the three of us, and that gives me the power of our trio."

"Alpha," Josef murmured in agreement as his fingers brushed my lips. "I would tell him what he wants to hear, if I were you." His lips caressed my collarbone. "Or we'll punish you. We could always make you listen as we fuck each other."

I said nothing, and they retreated in the dark. My skin blazed, wanting their touch.

"Please, don't stop," I pleaded.

Sounds filled my ears of skin brushing over skin. They were touching each other, kissing each other. A low groan, a growl.

"Please," I said again, trying to shake my head free of the blindfold so I could at least see them.

"Who's your alpha?" Erik repeated.

Defiance rose up. This was my nest. Yet even as I clung to my stubborn pride, I couldn't deny the way his words whispered to a raw, primal part of me. His commanding tone made my pulse quicken. I squirmed, needing someone to touch me. I surrendered.

"You are," I said finally with a whimper.

"What do you say?" Erik prompted Josef. "Should I give her what she's so clearly desiring?"

"Make her work for it," Josef said with a smile in his voice. "Make her use her words."

Their breaths whispered against my skin, and I tried to lift myself up, desiring their touch.

"What am I?" Erik asked.

"Alpha," I panted in desperation. "You are my alpha, Erik."

Chapter 14

"What am I?" I asked.

"Alpha," Aria panted. "You are my alpha, Erik."

Her submission both empowered and exhilarated me, and a dark satisfaction coursed through my veins.

I had once knelt before King Luis and spoken those same words. To hear someone say them to me filled me with warmth. *I have my own nest now.* My thoughts directed to the maker who would never hear them. If Amara had been still alive, I knew she'd have been proud of me.

"That's a good girl," I said, and Aria shivered. *'Oh, I think she likes being called a good girl.'* I said to Josef.

She needed to be teased, so I ran my hands across Josef's chest, down to his abs. He leaned forward, his soft lips brushing mine. A whimper escaped Aria's lips and I smirked. Josef rested his hands on my waist, my skin blazing at his touch. My heart burst with affection, and I suppressed the urge to pin him beneath me, to dominate him until he made the sounds that I loved so much. We were here for Aria, to complete our nest, and had plenty of time for each other. Instead, I let my breath caress his ear.

"Good girls get rewarded, don't they Josef?" I whispered.

"They do," he agreed, his own need igniting through the tether connecting us.

"Would you like to reward our good girl, while I watch?" I prompted.

Josef's eyes smouldered with his lust. Not just for Aria, but for the inferno our kiss had sparked in him. I gave him a reassuring smile. *'Soon,'* I promised. *'When the three of us have claimed each other.'*

'I want to claim her first,' he responded.

'Then claim her," I said back. *'And I will claim both of you.'*

He started kissing her ankles, moving up slowly. Aria squirmed under his lips. Before long, he was holding himself over her, his cock between her legs. "Are you ready for me?" he asked her.

"I'm ready for my reward," she whispered.

Josef pushed himself in slowly with a grunt, dropping kisses on her jaw, cheeks, and throat. I moved from the bed to a chair to get a better view. The muscles on Josef's back rippled; his movements were deliberate, slow and gentle. Each thrust of his hips elicited a combination of low moans and whimpers from her.

I couldn't look away, as desire crept through me. An ache coiled in my gut, twisting around my spine as I witnessed their horizontal dance. I gripped my own cock, and moved my hand with slow strokes, in time to match their rhythm. My nerves screamed with need, sensitive to my own touch. Heat pulsed across my skin, this sight of them, smell of their lust, sound of their pleasure drove me higher. I let out a jagged breath.

Aria's head turned towards me, a small smile on her lips.

"No, focus on me, sweet thing," Josef growled, and grabbed her jaw, bringing it back. "Focus on my cock, inside you. My body against yours." He lowered his head. "The brush of my lips." He kissed her.

Oh fuck. His words didn't just have an impact on her. Watching the two of them kiss would have had me on my knees if I wasn't already seated.

Aria's hands flexed again as she pulled against the restraints. Despite Josef's words, his eyes hungrily followed the movement of my hand, the glimmer of burning desire unmistakable, before returning his attention to Aria. Out of sheer desire, he drove his hips faster, deeper.

"I want to claim you," Aria panted.

"I won't stop you," Josef returned. He lowered himself, his throat within easy reach for her. "We can both claim each other if you'd like."

"Yes," she panted. "I claim you, Josef Alfaro,"

"I claim you in return, Aria Barone."

Her name jolted a reminder of who her father was, but I pushed it aside, not willing to think of Matteo while watching Josef fuck his daughter.

She lifted her head and bit into his throat. Josef sank his fangs into the curve of her shoulder, and I yearned to touch them both. To watch vampires blood sharing in such intimacy was a pleasure that I didn't want to miss. I rose from my chair, running my hands over Josef's back. A small shiver passed through him that I felt through our blood bond.

I leaned over and kissed his back, lips trailing upwards, as my hand rested on Aria's side. With their fangs still locked on one another, they stilled. The high of their blood sharing flickered through the bond I shared with Josef.

"Let me join the fun," I instructed.

The other side of her throat was exposed. As I bit, her entire body jolted. Her blood was sweet, heavy with desire and pleasure. She groaned against Josef's throat. She had formed a bond with Josef, and his mind was wide open. Her own mind fluttered through his. In her presence, there was strength, with a gentleness inside her. That alone made me desire this woman more, her energy once more reminding me of Amara. As I drank from her, a whimper escaped. I hoped she wasn't going to black out again.

I released her as she and Josef finished feeding from each other.

"Fuck," Josef panted. "That's intense."

His eyes were red and dazed from their blood sharing. I leaned towards him, licking Aria's blood from his lips and chin. He pressed his mouth to mine in a hungry kiss as his momentum with Aria began again. I grabbed the back of his head, heat pulsating through my body. Josef groaned against my mouth.

"I can hear you kissing," Aria said.

"Feeling left out?" I asked her. I lowered myself to whisper in her ear, "When Josef's finished, it's my turn. Do you think you can handle me?" I traced my thumb over her bottom lip, still wet with Josef's blood. "I want your mouth wrapped around my cock first." I licked blood from my thumb, before dropping my lips to Aria's.

As the two of them moved in rhythm with one another, the need to touch them overcame me. To touch her. To claim them both.

"Change position," I told Josef. "Sit up, pull her into your lap."

Josef followed my instruction, untying the bindings, but leaving her blindfold in place. He leaned against the headboard, she turned around and he pulled her into his lap. One arm slid around her, holding her in place. She settled back onto his cock, leaned her head back against him. I crawled forward. My breath brushed over her skin and she shivered.

"I want to worship you," I whispered. "While Josef claims your pussy, I claim your mouth."

She lifted herself, driving back down onto Josef's cock. Bliss flowed through my connection with him, and he ran his hands over her body. I kissed her inner thighs, moving up to her navel. Aria panted as she moved, her hands reaching for me.

"Josef, hold her arms," I commanded.

She didn't fight him as he pinned her arms to her side, lowering his lips to kiss her throat. She squirmed against Josef, lifting her head. I couldn't look away from the exposed curve of her neck. I moved up, claiming her mouth. Massaging her tongue with mine. The kiss grew in intensity, pulling a growl from me.

"The first time I saw you, trying to enter our territory, I knew you'd return," I whispered. "I saw that defiance in your eyes, and hoped you would. Today is twenty years in the making. You were always going to be ours."

"I could taste your arousal," Josef added. "You wanted us as much as we wanted you. Even as Carlos injured you, I knew we'd taste your blood." He lowered his hand down, rubbing her clit as she slid down on his cock again. "We knew we'd taste you."

"Your very presence demanded respect," I said. "I actually thought you were a Queen."

Aria moaned and lifted herself up again.

I moved my own fingers over her clit, replacing Josef's. With my other hand, I cupped his ass. "You're both mine," I declared.

They panted faster, their orgasms close. I traced my thumb over her again. I now lay against her, my own cock hard between her legs.

"Say it," I growled. "Obey your alpha."

Josef grunted, his body tense, and Aria's moan indicated her own release nearing.

"We're yours," Josef said, breathing hard as he spasmed. "Aria is ours, and we're yours."

"For eternity," Aria gasped, trembling. "We're yours until the end of our days."

Chapter 15

I came down hard from my orgasm, the taste of Aria's blood still on my lips. Erik's hand still squeezed my ass as he declared we were both his. His weight bore down on Aria, and I hooked my leg around his. He kissed Aria, and she pulled her arms from my grip to wrap them around him. The warmth of her around my cock left me as she rose up, slipping off me, and Erik entered her. They were about to fuck right on top of me.

A presence pressed against my mind, one that I'd forced into the background.

'Not now, Luca,' I grumbled. *'We're in the middle of fucking your Second.'* I sent a wave of smugness through our blood bond, followed by annoyance at him interrupting me.

'Josef, please, I need Aria to come home. It's important,' he returned with a hint of urgency to his voice.

I sighed. "Aria, your king requests that you return to San Marino," I said.

Erik stopped moving, a growl rumbling in his chest. "Tell Luca to learn his place. Carlos is his king, he does not make demands of us," he told me. "I will not be interrupted."

More than anything, I wanted to ignore Luca. For Erik and Aria to fuck on top of me, to watch them both share blood. For the three of us to be bonded, to spend days nesting. I wanted to be selfish and ignore the requests of a new king who had knelt to King Carlos. But Carlos had chosen me to bond to Luca, and to ignore his request would be going against my King's interests.

This was going to piss Erik off, and I didn't blame him.

"It's urgent," I said.

Erik bared his teeth, his nostrils flaring. "What does he want?" he demanded. "What can be so important that he disturbs us at this moment?"

'What is your reason for calling Aria home?' I asked Luca. *'This better be good.'*

'It's Pierre,' he replied. *'He's challenged me, and I need my Second at my side. Perhaps you can stand with her, as the voice of King Carlos.'*

I sighed. "We're about to lose Carlos the clan he only just acquired," I said. "Pierre has challenged Luca."

Aria groaned. Erik didn't move.

"It's okay Erik," Aria whispered, kissing him softly. "We can nest when I get back. I will return. We have plenty of time. This will not take long. Pierre is ambitious, but not as strong as he likes to think he is. He's young, and probably won't have the loyalty of the older vampires."

Finally, Erik lifted himself up, echoes of his annoyance and disappointment weighing heavy on me. I moved towards him.

"We will finish it," I promised. "The moment we return."

"We?" Aria asked.

"Luca suggested my presence as the voice of Carlos might show strength," I said.

"I'm not letting either of you out of my sight," Erik said. "Whoever has challenged Luca, has challenged King Carlos. Which means he challenged all of us. We will speak with our king. I'm sure he'll agree."

Erik's protective nature shone through as he glared at us, daring us to oppose him.

"We'll speak with Carlos," I agreed.

We quickly dressed and returned to the den.

"My King, we have a problem," I said the moment we entered the villa.

His voice came from his bedroom as he whispered to Camila, apologising for the interruption. The clink of chains thudding against wood indicated they'd been playing.

"Damn, I missed out on our King on the St. Andrews cross?" Erik muttered. "What I wouldn't give to see Camila exercise her control over him. It would be quite a sight to see."

I chuckled as we waited for Carlos. Apart from our King and his human lover, the den was empty. Everyone was likely out hunting. Carlos entered the room, naked. Surprisingly, his eyes were blue, fangs retracted. He'd always encouraged us to be ourselves in the den, so to see his human mask was unusual—but logical for one with a human romantic partner. "You interrupted me," Carlos grumbled. "We'd just started, so this better be important."

I took a knee before Carlos, Erik beside me. A moment later Aria did, too.

"I'm sorry, my King," Erik said. "We were interrupted, too. I feel your annoyance."

Carlos folded his arms over his chest. "Speak," he grunted.

"Luca reached out," I said. "He says he's been challenged. He asked for

Aria to return home, and for me to stand with them, as your voice."

Carlos's eyes narrowed. "Challenged?"

"Pierre is ambitious," Aria repeated her earlier words. "It's likely he can get some support behind him. But there will be those older than him who won't support him. He's of similar age to Luca."

"Do you want to stand behind Luca, or is there someone who would suit the role better?" Carlos asked.

I studied his face as he watched Aria.

"You want someone else?" she asked.

"I thought about what you said. Your king is young, and has already been challenged. Maybe he needs to be replaced." He turned his attention to me. "Josef, you go with her. You speak for me. Anyone who doesn't yield to my orders, kill them." His focus returned to Aria. "I trust you to name the next king…or queen. Whoever this Pierre is, *not him*. I don't like that he's challenged me."

We rose to our feet and I turned to go, Aria and Erik with me.

"Erik, you stay here," Carlos commanded.

Erik spun around. "What?"

"You're bonded with Josef. I need you to be my link to what happens in San Marino. If we're needed, Josef will tell you. This doesn't need to be hostile, unless Pierre makes it so."

Erik met my eyes before addressing Carlos. "We don't know what they're walking into. Two vampires, against a clan?"

Carlos approached Erik, his face softening as he reached for his face. Erik caught his hand, the two of them staring the other down. "Please Erik, don't fight me on this. I need you here so we have an open line of communication. I'll send Andreas with them. If we're needed, it won't take us long to get there. I'll have our cars ready. If it comes to it, we'll take the whole clan."

Erik was first generation, but so was Carlos now, in a way. He'd become stronger since exchanging blood with the Bloodking, but if Erik wanted to, he could easily defeat Carlos in a fight. Yet he'd never challenged Carlos. He'd never boasted being first generation, only telling me when we bonded.

Neither moved, the two of them glaring at each other.

'Erik?' I spoke in private, needing him to not challenge Carlos. Our king was yet to speak to me about my challenge a few days before. *'Andreas is a fighter and a true creature of the shadows. No one knows what he's capable of, so they're likely to underestimate him. He doesn't have a reputation like the rest of us. For a reason. Carlos is right: you're needed here. If we need the clan, I can reach out.'* I glanced at Aria. *'No one knows she's Matteo's daughter. We can use it as a threat. She's The Feral's daughter. No vampire in their right mind wants The Feral coming for them.'* I grinned. *'I'm not exactly helpless, myself. I don't need protecting, Hermaðr minn. I know what you're worried about. This won't be like that.'*

I hoped using Erik's native tongue was enough to pull him out of his aggression.

Finally, Erik released his breath, and stepped back, his eyes on my face. Carlos visibly relaxed, too. I wondered if he feared a day Erik would oppose him. First generation or not, Erik was known for his strength and temper.

"We should go," I said out loud.

Andreas walked in. Erik moved towards me while Carlos filled Andreas in with the plan.

"Do what you need to, and come home," Erik commanded, and grasped the back of my neck, pressing his forehead against mine. "*Veiðimaðr minn.* I let you go to Spain alone and could do nothing while those damned Hunters tortured you. Anyone attacks you, tear out their hearts, and save them for me."

I cupped the back of his neck. "That won't happen again, *gamall hermaðr.*"

We pulled apart and he turned to Aria. "Who am I?" he asked her.

"You're my alpha," she whispered.

He smiled. "Good girl. We'll finish what we started. When you two get back, nothing will interrupt our nesting. It'll be the three of us *for days.*"

I stepped in behind her, scraping my fangs over her neck. "If the chance takes us, me and you may have to use your bedroom in your den," I offered.

"Alright, you three," Carlos said. "Josef, you're my voice. Andreas and Aria, do what Josef says. Once you're in the den, you're in Aria's territory, and she is still Luca's Second."

"Yes, my King," Andreas, Aria and I said in unison, before turning around and leaving. I had no idea what to expect in San Marino.

"Josef," Carlos called me back.

"Yes?"

"I hope you all enjoy your freedom to be vampires," he said. "To revel in your nature. It's been a long time. I want to hear all about it."

I frowned, not understanding what he meant. "I already revel in my nature, my King."

"I know you do. But we've lived by The Accords for too long," he said. "We've forgotten who we were before they existed."

Andreas laughed. "Are you giving us permission?" he asked.

A dark chuckle came from Carlos. "I am. The Bloodking has declared war. Any day, humanity will learn of us. The Accords no longer exist."

I studied his face, finding him genuine. And elated, I cheered. Aria's hand grasped my arm in shock.

"Now I wish I was going," Erik grumbled. "Don't enjoy yourself too much."

"Thank you, King Carlos," I said. "We will celebrate. Hunters today will not be prepared for a world in which we are not muzzled by their irksome Accords. They will learn why their ancestors feared us so much."

Chapter 16

I watched the three of them leave.

Carlos touched my arm. "They'll be okay, Erik. If anything happens, you'll know."

"I think we should *all* be going," I warned him. "Luca is a young king; he was bound to be challenged. This *Pierre* has not bent the knee to you. We storm their den, you install a king or queen of your choosing. Someone who will not challenge you, but recognise your power."

He smirked. "If it comes to that, that's exactly what I will do. Trust me, Erik."

I forced myself to relax. I'd come too close to challenging him, and it unsettled me. "I do, my King."

"I know, old friend. We'll worry when there's something to be concerned about. Have confidence in Josef and Andreas. Until then, perhaps I can get your mind off it. I have an offer that you might enjoy. A distraction, if you will," he said.

"I'm listening."

"Camila has been exploring her desires in the world of kink. She isn't resistant to the idea of being watched. In fact, she was quite enthusiastic at the idea of it when we fucked in the gondola. She's accepted my… polyamorous nature. I would quite enjoy having you watch us."

"It does not surprise me at all that you fucked her in a gondola." I considered his offer. "I have to admit the thought of watching you with someone as dominant as you does have appeal. And did I hear chains? It's been awhile since you've used the cross."

"You did, indeed," he said with a wide grin as we walked towards his bedroom. "She was feeling brave. I hope she'll let me put her on it next." Once again, I was his confidant, his words that of the vampire trusting me with his innermost thoughts. "Erik, I know it's unexpected, but all those years I took control, I never knew the thrill of having another dominate me."

"I'm pleased you've found another way to ignite that spark," I said. "I'd welcome a chance to watch. Will I be allowed to touch you?"

"She's the one to ask about that," he said. "I'm letting her dominance shine." He paused. "Maybe let me check with Camila that she's comfortable first. I don't want to put pressure on her by bringing you in unannounced."

I let him go into his room first and speak with Camila. She hesitated, and her heart skipped. She must have nodded, because then Carlos called out to me.

"Come in, Erik," he welcomed me, voice on the verge of elation. He wanted me to see him in this new role, an honour he would not grant many.

Carlos had concealed his vampirism when he came from his room, so I did the same before opening the door. Inside, I found Camila shackling him to the cross. She wore thigh-high black boots, and a leather corset. A candle, ice, various floggers, and a riding crop had been placed on a table next to the cross.

I'd seen Carlos experiment with his dominant nature over the years, giving him guidance. To see him in the sub position was not something I could have expected. Over the centuries, I'd been his confidant as he learned about that side of him. Now he was guiding someone else. And a human. I couldn't hold back my grin. He met my eyes, and smiled back with sheer joy. My heart swelled with pride for my king.

Camila looked up at me with a shy smile. Carlos reached down with an unrestrained hand. He tilted her chin towards him. "If there's anything you don't like, he'll leave. As always, speak up if you're uncomfortable. What's the safe word?"

Though I barely knew Camila, I recognised the glint of fierce determination within her eyes as she glanced my way again.

"Red," she said, and took a deep breath, letting it out. "No, I'm okay."

"I usually stroke myself when I watch," I said to her in a calming voice. "Are you okay with me doing that?"

She nodded. I stepped towards her, gently touching her shoulder to reassure her. "Don't be scared of me, Camila. I won't hurt you. I understand you're learning about what you like; it's okay if exhibitionism isn't part of that. Thank you for inviting me in to watch, but this is your space, and I'll respect that. Yes, I like to watch. I also like to touch. Only if you want me to, though." I met Carlos's eyes again. "I will keep my hands to myself, and my king."

I knelt on the floor and bowed my head. Camila returned to shackling Carlos to the cross.

She stepped up to him, to whisper in his ear. "Are you comfortable?" she asked.

He smiled down at her, pride shining from his eyes. "I am, *mi Reina*."

"I'm going to blindfold you," she said, reaching for a black silk scarf.

I recalled a blindfolded Aria, the memory overtook me with warmth. I refocused my attention on Camila. She pulled the scarf over his eyes, securing it. As she moved towards the table, he tilted his head, tracking her movements. She returned with ice, rubbing it over his chest, around his nipples, and down to his torso. A small breath broke from him, arms flexing against the cuffs. His nipples hardened.

The sight of Carlos in such a position, bound to the St. Andrews cross, drew me forward. Every inch of him exposed and vulnerable, the strain of his muscles, his erection. I wanted to touch him, to run my hands over his hard body. My King.

Camila turned to me, a playful gleam in her eyes. "You said you like to touch. Do you want to touch him?"

Heat coiled in my chest. My fingers itched to trace over his body, my body anticipated pressing against him.

"I do," I breathed.

"Erik wants to touch you," she whispered in his ear.

A slow smile spread across Carlos's lips and he turned his head towards me for a second before returning to the bowed position. "I would also like that," he panted. "Erik leaves no part of me untouched."

Camila stepped back. "Touch him."

I was not one to let a human command me, but Carlos had named her his Queen. So I obeyed. I rose to my feet, and pressed my hands against his body, feeling him shiver beneath my touch. "This is a new look for you, my King," I murmured to him as my fingers traced the ridges of his abs. I leaned closer, kissing his chest, leaving a trail of heat over his skin. He squirmed under my lips, his whimper turning into a growl.

A small breath escaped Camila, and I smiled to find her eyelids lowered as she watched us, lips parted.

"Oh, your girl and I have a lot in common," I said to Carlos. "Voyeurist tendencies. I like her already."

"My *Queen,*" he reminded me.

"Perhaps I can take my clothes off?" I asked Camila. "I do like to feel my King's warm body against mine."

It was likely I was asking too much for the first time she'd allowed someone into her space. She met my eyes, a heavy silence between us.

"*Mi Reina*, he's in our space, so it's okay to give him commands. He will comply. You're in charge, remember. If you want him to take his clothes off, voice your thoughts."

Over my shoulder, Camila's uncertainty melted away from her eyes. "Erik, take your clothes off."

Her voice was unwavering, commanding.

"As my King's Queen commands," I said, and quickly removed my clothes.

I faced her, already hard. I tried not to smirk as she gaped at my cock, then contained herself.

"Continue touching him," she suggested.

I turned back to Carlos. Her movement drew my attention, as she picked something up from the table. Carlos turned his face towards the sound.

"Erik likes pain, too," Carlos said to Camila. "He taught me much of what I know. Punish him if you need to. He won't mind."

I smiled at the way he was topping from the bottom. Guiding his Queen.

"Are you in agreement, Erik?" she asked.

"I am," I agreed.

"You will not join our bed," Camila said. "But I would like to see you touch Carlos. Lick him. Kiss him."

Once again, the resistance in me rose up. For a human to use such a tone with me, this would be an adjustment. I pressed myself against Carlos, my cock wedged against his, between our bodies. I licked his throat, digging my fingers into his hips. Carlos lowered his head, breath cool against my ear.

"Thank you, Erik," he murmured. "For letting my Queen play. I know it'll be unusual, having a human tell you what to do."

I scoffed as I licked him from navel to throat. A low rumble emerged from each of us.

"You're okay with it?" I asked.

He smiled. "Know that I am happy with whatever she commands," he whispered back. "I awoke this beast in her, so I will help her flourish."

I studied his face. "Okay, I'll play along. This is unlike you, though. To submit to a human…"

His jaw tensed. "It changes nothing. I am still your King," he declared, voice firm.

Kings and Queens knelt only to the Bloodking. His submitting to a human was technically grounds to lose his status, so I couldn't blame him for worrying. I had no desire for the role, nor did anyone in the clan. The dying young man I had met hundreds of years ago deserved his power, and I couldn't be prouder of what he'd built here, who he'd become. The loyalty of our clan he'd earned.

"Yes, King Carlos," I agreed.

"I hear talking, but see no licking or touching," Camila said.

A sharp sting across my ass cheek brought me heat. I groaned, nuzzling my face against his neck as thoughts of Amara's punishments overwhelmed me. I wrapped one hand around his cock, kissing his jaw.

Another strike followed. "I'd love another, if it would please you," the plea slipped from my lips, as warmth and pleasure embraced me.

She complied, this strike harder, the sting sharp like lightning across my back. A low rumble vibrated from my chest, need and want reminding me that I had not had the satisfaction yet with Josef and Aria. My lips pressed against Carlos's throat, fangs out before I pulled back my desire to bite. A groan broke from Carlos as another strike stung my flesh, my body shaking against his. I howled, falling into ecstasy from the pain, surrendering to my baser instincts. Needing to bite, to share the pleasure, I turned, grabbed the human and pushed her against the wall. She cried out, fear rising from her. I was in mid-strike when Carlos's voice pulled me back.

"Erik, *stop*!"

As the King I'd knelt to, his voice had power over me. I stared down at Camila, her chin trembling slightly, her eyes wide, glinting with fear. I released her arm and stepped back.

"I'm sorry," I said, dropping to my knees before Carlos. "You know I wasn't trying to hurt her, my King. I simply got carried away, drawn into my own pleasure, and she is a human with that scent of arousal."

Carlos's eyes were still covered, but he tilted his face in my direction. I waited, unsure if I would face his anger. I'd come close to breaking one of our most important rules. To not hurt one claimed by another.

"Camila, are you okay?" he asked. "Did he hurt you?"

"I'm okay," she confirmed. "I'm not hurt. He only startled me."

"Erik, maybe you should leave," he said. "Being rough and getting lost in the moment is one thing, but she is human. You could have hurt her."

I rose to my feet. "Yes, my King, I'm sorry." I took a step towards the door.

"Wait," Camila spoke up. "Carlos, if he didn't mean to hurt me, and was enjoying himself, does he have to leave? He was lost in the moment. He said himself he wasn't trying to hurt me."

"Erik."

I spun around. "Yes?"

"Do you think you can maintain control if I allow you to stay?" he asked.

Camila smiled at me.

"I promise," I agreed.

Carlos smiled. "Care to start from where we left off?" he said. "Before you mistook my Queen for a snack, I believe your body was pressed against mine. Camila, maybe don't strike him again."

I returned to my position, once more our bodies warm and hard against one another. In an attempt to smooth over his mood, I leaned forward, my lips hovering over his. Warm breath brushed against my lips. He closed the gap, and when his mouth crashed into mine he wasn't gentle but claiming—like the King he was. I groaned into his mouth, pushing harder against his body. His heart beat against my chest, mine matching its rhythm. With one hand on his waist, I pulled from the kiss to find Camila had moved closer, her breathing picking up.

"Did you like that?" I asked her.

She nodded. "It looked like you were enjoying that."

"Oh, I did, very much," I agreed. "I think you've discovered another kink, young Huntress. Watching others in intimacy is a delicious thrill. Would you like me to continue, or do you want him to yourself? I did come in to watch the two of you, after all."

"Kiss him again?" she asked. "One more time."

I nuzzled my cheek against my King's, and reached down, running my fingers over his cock. I kissed his throat.

"Bite him," Camilia said, voice dropping to a whisper.

I froze.

"My Queen, that is one command he cannot comply with," Carlos said. "He cannot bite me. In my world, not all vampires can feed from one another." He moved his head, burrowing into my neck. "But I can bite him," he grunted against my flesh, his fangs ready. "And I have to admit I am a little hungry after the heat of that kiss."

"Sorry," she whispered.

"Don't be sorry," I added. "You'll learn our ways."

"Carlos, bite him," she breathed.

Carlos bit deep. A low, contented groan vibrated from his chest as he fed. His venom spread warmth and pleasure singing through me, and my hands traced over his body. I tilted my head to watch Camila. Her eyes met mine—wide, captivated.

"It seems your Huntress enjoys watching vampires feed from one another," I whispered. "Almost as much as I enjoy your bite."

Carlos lifted his mouth from me, licking blood from my throat. "She's wishing it was her under my fangs right now."

I licked my blood from his chin.

"If it pleases my Queen, perhaps that water bottle?" Carlos asked.

I stepped back as she uncapped the bottle, pouring water into his mouth. He drank heavily from it, and she washed around his lips, removing all traces of my blood.

Carlos gave me a small smile. "I can't have her being Bestowed off your blood when she kisses me," he said.

I examined his mouth, sniffing. "No scent or sign of blood," I confirmed. "Rinse out once more just to be certain."

Camila did as I suggested.

"If my Queen will allow it, perhaps Erik can kneel," Carlos encouraged. "I do enjoy having him suck me off."

Her tongue darted out, licking her lips. "Yes, kneel to your King," she instructed me.

I fell to my knees before Carlos. Rising slightly, I kissed across his torso, and my hand dropped low to cup his balls. Carlos's breathing accelerated, and then I lowered my lips to the tip of his shaft, running my tongue over the sensitive skin under the head. I tasted his pre-cum. Camila's breathing accelerated.

The groan that rose from Carlos encouraged me to close my mouth over his cock, taking in his length. His hands pulled on his restraints again. Camila stepped forward, ice in her hand once more, and moved it from his shoulder, down to his chest. Water trickled down to where I lapped it up before returning to licking his erection. I moved slowly, watching his face.

"Faster," Carlos pleaded.

Camila brought the riding crop down to his chest with a sharp crack. Carlos shuddered, a guttural whimper slipping from his lips.

"Do not speak," she commanded in a hard voice.

"Oh—fuck," the words tore from Carlos, raw with desire.

She pressed the tip under his chin, lifting his head. "I told you not to speak. Do I need to remind you again?"

He visibly swallowed. "No, I'm sorry, *mi Reina.*"

"Good." She dragged the crop down his chest, eyeing me. "What are you waiting for?"

I let his cock slide through my mouth again, and as I pulled back, I stroked him. Only two pumps, but it was enough to elicit another sound from him. He seemed incapable of words, only long moans and a full body shiver as she struck him again.

The intensity of her stare travelled between Carlos, and myself. She had worn a hardened expression when I first saw her, when she'd tried to kill

Carlos. Now, her features almost made her look like a different person. Her eyelids were partially closed, her pupils dilated. Her faster breaths affected her whole body as she watched us. She looked softer, more vulnerable.

"Do you like seeing his cock in my mouth?" I asked her.

She nodded, her gaze sweeping over my body before lifting to Carlos's.

I grabbed his base, holding it as I licked over the head. Then, to frustrate Carlos, I pulled him deeper slowly. His cock throbbed, and small quivers started in him. I took him deep, and a twitch shook the cross and chains. He panted, leaning his head back. Camila stepped up to him, pouring hot wax down over his shoulder. He whimpered, and she leaned forward, planting kisses over his chest.

"Are you a good boy for your Queen?" she whispered. "Should I tell Erik to speed up for you?"

He whimpered again.

"Use your words," she commanded.

"Please, *mi Reina,*" he panted, finding his words.

Each time I pushed down, Carlos drove his hips forward, pushing his cock deeper.

"Do you want to come?" she teased.

"I do," he gasped out.

Camila's touch on my shoulder surprised me.

"Should I let him come?" she asked.

I took my time in answering her. Carlos grunted again, trying to jut forward.

"Answer her!" Carlos roared in desperation.

"Maybe I need some convincing to finish him off," I teased before she could punish him again for speaking.

Her eyes shone with understanding and she gave me a subtle nod, raising her hand.

"Don't hold back," I told her.

She struck me hard across my back with her riding crop. "Finish him off. Swallow it all when he comes."

I took in the sight of her smile, her glinting eyes, and the scent of her.

Tense and hoping for my own orgasm, I wrapped my hand around Carlos's cock.

"I do hope you'll let me watch when you're ready to reward him," I said. "I need release, too."

Without another word, I returned to sucking Carlos. I moved at the pace I knew he liked. One that would have him convulsing.

Chapter 17

Carlos's body trembled, glistening with sweat. Whimpers and moans tore from him, his hips maintaining a rhythm to match mine. He came with a guttural groan, his body rigid and trembling. I swallowed down all that he released. Breathing hard, he smiled down at me, his fangs on display. Camila swept forward, touching him. I stepped back, watching the rise and fall of his chest under her hands and his shiver when her lips grazed his jaw. She planted a kiss over his mouth.

Their bodies moulded together.

"I want to get you down from this," she said. "Watching that..." she stopped, breathing hard, eyes darting towards me.

Still on my knees, I grinned. "It's okay, you can speak freely. Did you enjoy seeing him come into my mouth?"

"I did," she confirmed without hesitance. "I want you inside me," she breathed, sliding her hands over his chest. "Your fangs and your cock."

"Perhaps Erik can help take me down and we can move our activities to my...*our* bed," Carlos replied.

"Erik?" she turned to me.

I stood. "I can do that."

The restraints were made with leather, lined with padding. I undid the buckle, first releasing his leg, before freeing his wrist. Camila did the same. Together, we eased him from the cross, supporting him and guiding him to the bed. I lay him down.

I stood back as Camila climbed on to the bed. She peppered kisses over his body, rubbing her hands over him as she did. Then she reached his shoulders, massaging his muscles, taking her time. He lifted his head, and she kissed him, before removing his blindfold.

His declaration of love for her a few days before had surprised everyone. But it wasn't hard to miss as I watched them. The way he looked at her with tenderness as she moved her hands over his shoulders and arms. The affection was returned, as she murmured to him, kissing him as she eased out any pain.

"You really do love each other," I muttered in amazement, finding myself to be the centre of their attention.

Camila removed her corset and climbed off the bed, facing me. "I gave up my world for his," she reminded me. "Can I touch you? Just once?"

"Only if I can touch you," I said with a wicked grin.

"Hands above the waists," Carlos declared.

I kept my body motionless, letting her explore at her own pace. Carlos watched intently as I lifted my hand to cup her breast, rubbing the underside with my thumb. Her gaze lingered on my body, fingers tracing over the ink etched into my skin. Then with a slight intake of breath she leaned forward, her lips brushing over my chest. I held still as she trailed kisses from one side to the other.

"Sorry," she whispered. "I wanted to try."

I tilted her chin up to look at me. "Never apologise for exploring yourself," I said. "Do you mind if I return the gesture?"

Uncertainty flickered in her eyes. But she nodded. With a deliberate slowness, I lifted a hand to her shoulder, brushing over her soft skin before lowering my head. I kissed the curve of her shoulder with tenderness. I shifted from her shoulder to her throat and back again. Her hand pressed against my chest slipped down to my abs, her heart racing, her breathing accelerated. I let fangs slide over her—without biting—as I kissed up her throat again, to her jaw and pressed my mouth to hers. She stiffened, pushing at me.

"No," she said firmly. *"Red."*

I stepped back. "My apologies," I said. I'd gotten caught in the moment again, gone further than she had asked for.

She smiled. "It's okay. I don't think I'm like Carlos. Your lips on my *body* felt nice, but on my *mouth,* it felt a little too intimate."

I nodded in understanding. "You're a one-man woman. I apologise for crossing that line. Why don't you rejoin your beloved, and I will simply watch."

She returned to the bed and climbed on top of Carlos, before casting a look back at me. "I didn't mind the touching," she said. "The kissing, either. Up until..."

"I understand," I spoke in a gentle tone.

Carlos brushed her cheek. "What would you like to do now?" he asked.

She turned her attention back to him.

"You know what I want," she told him. "Take back control, King Carlos. Let the vampire out."

He flipped them both over, his hands gripping her tight around her arms. A deep rumble issued from him as he lowered his face to her throat, breathing her in. I took a step forward, concerned that he was using too much strength in his grip. He turned his head, hissing at me, his red eyes wild. Her breaths were of desire, though. She wasn't struggling against his grip, so I backed off. That explained the bruises she had. She liked pain. She was well suited for Carlos.

"Bare your throat, *Cazadora,*" he commanded.

The scent of human blood filled the air as Carlos fed from Camila. She writhed underneath him.

He lowered himself, not yet entering her. Camila's answering whimper was the invitation he needed, and he eased into her. She made a small trembling sound, digging her fingers into his back and lifting her hips. My cock pulsed, and I wrapped my fingers around the base, sliding my hand over the shaft. Pre-cum leaked from the tip, spreading over my cock as I moved my hand.

"How's my good girl?" he murmured. "My beautiful Queen." He placed kisses over her face. "It's been such a big night for you." He started to thrust, taking his time. "First time using the cross, you looked so good in that corset. You struck me, you struck Erik. It's so brave of you, letting Erik in to watch. It makes me so happy that you're getting along with my clan. They're *your* clan too, now."

Camila turned her head towards me. Her pupils were dilated, lips parted as Carlos slid into her again. Her eyes dropped down to my cock, as I pumped in time with Carlos's movements. I rose to my feet, giving her a better view, as I continued slow, even strokes. Carlos glanced over at me, lips stretching into a smile.

"Do you like that, my dirty Huntress?" Carlos panted. "Do you want to watch Erik get himself off, as he watches us?"

She forced her focus back to Carlos, their eyes locking as he drove himself in slowly at first, then picking up the pace. He pushed himself in deeper, rougher, her gasps with every thrust piercing me. Heat pooled, my breathing accelerated as their pace quickened. My hand slid over my cock, gaining momentum. The room was heavy with the sounds of skin against skin, quiet gasps, the scent of lust driving me crazy.

"Listen to him. He's panting. Listen to that sound of him stroking himself. Watching us has him hot. He's pleasuring himself, Camila. Watching us."

She whimpered again.

"Use your words," he instructed her.

"I want to see," she gasped.

He met my eyes. "Move closer, Erik. I want her looking at me as I fuck her, but I want her to see you, too."

I did as he asked, positioning myself so I could see him enter her. Each thrust went deep, the two of them panting. He kissed her throat, but didn't bite. He brushed his hand down the side of her body, before gripping her thigh. Her lips parted and he kissed her. My body pulsed, sparks of heat tingling under my skin. Carlos's muscles flexed with tension as he held back his full strength.

The energy between them enveloped me. She dug her fingers into his shoulders, he tightened his grip on her thigh, and I let my hand glide over my cock. Their momentum picked up, becoming raw, unrestrained and carnal. Camila met his every thrust with her own, breath ragged, hand grasping the sheet beneath her.

Her body started to tense, breathing changing, and she moaned again.

"Are you close?" Carlos asked.

"I am," she breathed. "Carlos…"

His movements were unrelenting. My strokes over my own cock pushed sparks through me, pleasure and shivers snaking around my spine.

Camila moaned Carlos's name. He grunted in response, the two of them coming together. I found my own release, my satisfied grunts drawing both their attention. I came into my hands, climaxing hard. Carlos peppered kisses over her again before claiming her mouth. When they pulled apart, he pushed her hair back.

"Would you like to have a shower, or lay here for awhile?" he asked.

"I want your arms around me," she replied. "Then we can shower."

He smiled. "Good, because I'm not sure I can move yet."

"Thank you," I said, meeting Camila's eyes. "I hope you'll let me watch again." I took a knee. "Queen Camila."

I grabbed my clothes and left the room. Carlos was particular about aftercare, and usually preferred that to be only between him and his lover. I wiped my hands on my tee-shirt before pulling my trousers on.

As I made my way to my bedroom, Celeste approached. "She let you watch?"

I smiled. "I think she will fit in with the clan easily. Are you alright? Sharing him with a human?" I wondered how Quinn felt, too. Although, she'd been the voice of reason when we'd all demanded Camila's death. She'd recognised that our King was in love. "Or that she's a Hunter," I added. "Especially your painful history with Hunters."

"I do not blame her for what happened three hundred years ago." She glanced back towards the door. "I think she is a good lover for him. I've never been jealous of his other lovers, I don't intend to be so over her. I want to get to know her, but I think she's a little scared of us."

We walked down the hall together.

"Well, we did demand her death," I said. "Plus, she's been raised to hate vampires. It's going to be an adjustment for all of us."

Celeste shook her head. "I still can't believe he fell in love with a human."

"Not just a human, a *Hunter*," I agreed.

"Where is everyone?" Celeste asked. "Oh, and weren't you nesting with Josef and Matteo's daughter? Have you finished already?"

I laughed at her smirk. "No, she got called back home. Josef and Andreas are with her," I explained. "Trust me, when they return, we will be nesting for days." I pushed down my worry. *'Hurry up and come home, Josef. I already miss your presence.'*

Chapter 18

We stopped at the San Marino border.

"Your territory might be smaller than Venice," I noted.

"It's not just San Marino that belongs to us," Aria said. "Giuseppe claimed the surrounding cities, too."

"I think we should enter on foot," I suggested.

"Agreed," Andreas said from the back seat. "We're entering their territory."

The small fortress country still reflected the charm of Italy, and we were surrounded by rolling hills. Its mountain loomed high above us, bathed in moonlight and shadows.

I wanted to suggest we hunt, but this was not our territory. The absence of vampires started to unsettle me.

"I don't like this," I stated. "It's too quiet."

"Is that your Hunter instincts?" Aria joked.

"Maybe," I said, keeping a sharp eye on our surroundings. The scent of pine trees mixed with smoke, pale cobbled paths winding ahead of us. The mountain towered high, a castle on its peak. "Pierre would know Luca is linked to me. He would therefore know Luca would call for help. He wouldn't know how many vampires I'd bring with me." I scanned the streets. "Was he one of the vampires there when Carlos killed Giuseppe?"

"He was," she confirmed.

"So he knows the power within our clan. The Feral. The Siren. And that King Carlos would be too strong for him to face alone," I pointed out. "He *doesn't* know about our ace up the sleeve. Andreas, I think you should do what you do best," I said. "Stay close, though."

Without a word, Andreas let himself become one with the shadows. I couldn't even hear his heart beat. An interesting ability that was easy to forget about until it was needed. None of us had known him as a human, so we didn't know how he possessed such an ability, or even if he had been human in the first place.

"What the..." Aria frowned.

"A gift of his," I explained. "He manipulates shadows. An excellent camouflage."

"I can still see you, I'm still here," Andreas said from beyond the shadows.

His voice was like a whisper in the wind. If we'd been human, we wouldn't have heard it. Aria stared at where he'd been.

"A true creature of shadows," she said. "Josef, perhaps you should reach out to Luca. Find out where he is."

'Luca, we're here,' I spoke through my blood bond with the young King.

'Where are you?'

'Josef?' Luca's voice was shaky. *'You're here?'*

Dread flowed through from our bond.

"He seems afraid," I said to Aria.

Aria led the way, and I signalled to Andreas to follow. The road beneath us started to incline. My kind did not feel the fatigue humans would from walking uphill, so we were able to appreciate the beauty of the city around us.

'We're coming for you,' I told Luca. *'Are you at the den?'*

'I don't know. He caged me. I'm not sure the clan is aware of what he's done,' came Luca's answer. *'Please keep Aria safe. Pierre will challenge her next.'*

It made sense, to take out the King in secret, take control in his "absence."

"Why cage him? Why not kill him?" I questioned aloud.

"He's caged?" she asked and stopped in mid step. "We *can't* go to the den. Pierre will be waiting for me. If he's taken control, or if he's about to, I don't know whose loyalty he has. That's unlikely to include the older vampires, but if I show up, we're walking in blind."

"Do you have somewhere else we can go to regroup?" I asked.

She changed direction. "I'm not supposed to know about this, and I don't know if Luca knows about it. Marco told me if there was ever a time the den got attacked, to get the clan there."

When she spoke about Marco, her voice carried a wistfulness.

"You cared about him," I stated.

She took a while to respond. "He was my maker, and my lover. But he was not my beloved," she said. "He's supposed to be the one stepping into Giuseppe's role. Our King made a poor decision in choosing Luca for his Second to replace Marco. Pierre's heart would have been torn from his chest the moment he thought to challenge Marco."

Compelled by sympathy, I pulled Aria into an embrace. "I'm sorry you lost him," I said. "Giuseppe fed from Matteo. Carlos was justified in what he did. Giuseppe deserved the punishment Carlos handed him. But I don't think any of us considered that Marco's death would be felt by another."

She leaned into my body. "Giuseppe got Marco killed, and chose a child to replace him. We're in this mess *because* of him." The fury in her voice made it obvious that if Giuseppe were still alive, she'd try to kill him herself.

"We'll take Pierre down," I promised. "And anyone who stands with him. Luca knelt to King Carlos. My King will not surrender this clan or territory without a fight." I tilted her chin up. "Perhaps, if you're lucky, you'll see first-hand why they call your father The Feral."

We continued walking, but this time I kept my arm wrapped around her.

"I heard stories," she admitted. "My uncle tried to shield me from them, as I was just a child. But people talk. I heard about the screaming, and how torn up the bodies were. Their throats were ripped to shreds."

I grinned. "They screamed because he didn't know how to inject venom into his bite. Carlos had to teach him. He'd killed his maker before he learned how to be a vampire, to enjoy the hunt, the feed. But it became a need for him. He *needed* them to scream. Took pleasure in it the same way Carlos revelled in fear. He was smug over the fact that Quinn became a screamer because of him." I laughed. "You probably didn't want to hear that."

She shook her head in amusement. "He was a terror. Everyone feared 'the monster of Venice' coming for them. Then after a few months, rumour spread that he was one of the Barone brothers. And they worked out it was my father, since he hadn't been seen in a while. When I became a vampire, Marco promised to help me find him. Every time we heard about The Feral, we followed the lead, only to be too late. I went to Australia mere hours after you all left."

"You went to Australia?" Andreas asked from behind us.

"Well, when an art gallery with Matteo Barone's name on it burns down, and there are vampire-like murders, it's a little hard to ignore," she confirmed. "I'm lucky Marco was with me, though. Gabriela wasn't too happy that I was there asking about my father."

I stiffened at the reminder of Gabriela. I hadn't thought of her for a long time.

Aria studied my face. "Are you alright?"

I forced a smile. "Yeah. Our former Queen had a fall from grace. Power changed her. Over time, she wasn't the friend to us she'd once been, but brutal, unforgiving. Carlos did what he could to shield many of us from her punishments. He was a king to us for what he endured, long before he was even a King. I wished he'd formed his own clan after the war when the Bloodking suggested it. I would have joined him, and I know Erik would have too. I was with Erik when she paid him a visit before we left Melbourne. She'd already challenged Carlos, almost killing him. She demanded Erik kneel to her if he wanted to protect Carlos. He told her the best way to protect him was to be a part of his clan. That he'd rip her apart if she went after Carlos again. Your presence, asking about Matteo, she probably would have killed you if she could."

"Yeah, I got that sense," Aria agreed. "As soon as we returned, I received a text message from Lenora, that my father had returned to Venice. I knew that if he'd removed Pietro from his old family home, he was there to stay."

I gave her a squeeze. "And so it began. Twenty years of trying to get into Venice unsuccessfully. You could have made it easier on yourself though by saying something."

She leaned her head on my shoulder. "And miss out on having you and Erik meet me every time?"

We both laughed, and our freshly forged blood bond pulsed between us. Her very presence sang through my blood, our dark souls fused.

"Well, if your King dying is what it took to finally bring you to us, then I wouldn't change this," I said.

She stopped and turned, eyes darting over my face. A slow smile spread over her face.

"I like your company, too," she declared. "Come on, we should get to the safehouse."

The climb beneath us became steeper, and we approached a marble bust with a face I knew too well. We made no sound, but humans who passed by did, their footsteps echoing in the silence.

"Why does your former king have a statue of him?" I asked.

Aria laughed. "He compelled someone to carve him instead of an Italian general. Occasionally humans recognised him, but no one remembered him."

"Naturally," I quipped.

We neared the top. "This is it," she said finally, pointing to a large house made of stone. "It's a safehouse, made to be a replacement den in the event our current one falls."

"Stop," Andreas instructed us. "Keep walking. Don't go inside."

"Andreas? What is it?" I asked.

"You have humans following you. Hunters," he said. "Walk to the end of the street, turn left."

"If we turn left, we'll be cornered down a dead end," Aria argued.

"Trust me," came Andreas's response.

I scanned the streets, finding the humans he was talking about. I'd been so focused on Aria, I'd ignored my surroundings.

"So much for all the Hunters going to Rome," I muttered. "Are they locals?"

Aria laughed. "We had a local family, until about twenty years ago. I took most of them out. The only surviving one ran after he failed to kill me by blowing up his entire facility. Although, they did have distant cousins here at the time, too. A Hunter you might be familiar with. Australian, white hair."

I couldn't remember the Hunter's name. Quinn's friend. "She was in Venice, a few days ago," I said. "Instead of killing her, Quinn let her go. She told her to retire from hunting," I said. "So, if they're not local Hunters, why are they here? Do any from your clan kill? Are you on Hunters' radar?"

Aria's eyes darted towards the Hunters. There were five of them. "We don't kill, we stick to The Accords. I don't know why they're here, but let's take them on a hunt." She pointed down the street. "Want to have some fun?"

"It's been a long time since I've had Hunter." I grinned. "What do you have in mind?"

"Let them corner us," she said. "It'll be like having dinner delivered."

Chapter 19

Andreas had saved our fangs. Neither I nor Josef had been paying attention. I wanted to kill the Hunters, but I wanted to have fun with them first, for daring to hunt us.

"Andreas, let them corner us. They will fan out, to close in. Take out whoever's in the middle," I instructed. "In their panic, Josef and I will take down one each. Leaving two to question their life choices. When they run, we give chase."

"You've done this before. I like it," Josef said, voice heavy with approval.

"I've had the same family of Hunters tracking me since I was a child. So Marco and I came up with creative ways to deal with them," I admitted. I missed Marco. He would have been gleeful at our hunt. He also would have picked up on their presence earlier. "How did we not notice them?" I wondered aloud.

"I almost missed them, too. Because they're not talking, and keeping their distance," Andreas said from his place in the shadows. "This is why King Carlos chose me to accompany you."

"It also explains why no vampires greeted us," Josef added, as we turned down the dead-end street. "No vampire will be out while Hunters are in town." A low growl rose from him. "The last Hunters who ambushed me tortured me for days, so I'd like to stretch it out with the two we give chase to. I want them to beg for their lives."

I checked over my shoulder to make sure the Hunters were following. "They will," I promised Josef.

"Hunters recognise him straight away," Andreas said. "Hunter turned vampire. They have been trying to kill him for centuries. He's probably at the top of their list."

"I'm not just *a* first Hunter like everyone calls me," Josef said. "I was *the* First Hunter. It's why Hunters were so offended by my becoming a vampire back then. While their descendants might not know, they still hate me just as much."

The heartbeats of the Hunters were calm, steady. I'd soon change that.

"I'd be right up there with you in being a prime target," I said to Josef. "The daughter of The Feral. I don't think I'm in the global Hunter records, but the local ones definitely know who I am. I think they hope I'll lead them to my father. They have hunted me, generation after generation."

We reached the end of the street and turned around as five Hunters advanced.

"*Prenez position*," the Hunter in the middle said.

The others started to spread out.

"They're French," Josef muttered. "Interesting."

Before I had time to consider what he meant, the Hunters raised their crossbows.

"Good evening," Josef said in English, taking a step forward to stand under the street light.

"Josef Alfaro," the leader said, and smiled.

There was no surprise in his voice.

'Why do I feel like he expected you?' I asked Josef through our blood bond.

Josef didn't reply, only taking a step forward again. "You know my name, do I get the pleasure of knowing yours?" he asked. "I can't say I've had such a large welcome group before. Did you forget to follow the Bloodking to Rome?"

"Shut up, leech," one of the Hunters said, earning a glare from their leader.

I edged towards Josef. "I'm a little insulted that there's only five of you," I said, laughing.

One of the Hunters released an arrow. Josef staggered as it struck his shoulder, the dull thud a reminder of pain I'd endured many times. It penetrated our blood bond and I fought back a gasp. Hunters and their cursed arrows. Josef hissed in pain, before growling. "When all your fellow Hunters are dead, you'll be the one who begs me to spare you," he declared.

"Shit," Andreas' voice came from the dark. "There's more. Josef, I count twelve other Hunters. It's an ambush. They came out of nowhere."

"Something's not right," I murmured. *How the fuck did this many Hunters elude three vampire's senses?* "Humans can't see in the dark, but they tracked us, without those night goggles, and remained silent."

Josef scanned the Hunters around us. "Fuck, why didn't I see that before?" he muttered. "Their eyes are *red*. They're *Bestowed.*" He turned slightly towards where Andreas was. "Andreas, stay hidden." He grabbed my hand. "We need to leave, before they completely surround us."

We ran, Josef taking another arrow, this time in the back. The Hunters' voices of frustration echoed behind us. I was grateful that while Bestowed did have our hunger, sight, and hearing, they didn't have our speed.

I ran towards the safehouse, but hesitated. "They would have heard us; this house will be compromised," I muttered.

Josef growled. "They've taken ground from us." He pulled the arrow from his shoulder as I pulled the other one from his back. The wound closed up, but he'd probably need to feed soon.

Andreas joined us, slipping into sight. I was still amazed by the revelation of his abilities. Surely he must have had ties to a demon bloodline—maybe a shadow demon—before he turned.

"They weren't trying to kill you. Hunters don't miss. Not that poorly. They had a perfect shot," he said.

We moved away from the safehouse, watchful and wary.

"Why are there Bestowed Hunters here?" Josef asked. "Especially now? The timing is suspicious."

"Let me go and watch them," Andreas offered. "They won't know I'm there."

Josef frowned. "I don't like that at all. There are too many Hunters for one person.

I touched Josef's arm. "They never saw him. We need to know more."

Once again, Andreas's eyes remained on me for a moment. I smiled, curious. His lips lifted into a small smile.

Josef's suspicions were starting to take shape in my own mind. Bestowed Hunters were unheard of. To be here, now, when Luca was caged couldn't just be bad timing.

"Be careful," Josef instructed Andreas. "Maybe we should meet in the nature park before sunrise?" he asked me.

I pointed in the direction of Montecchio Nature Park. "Meet us there. I'll take Josef hunting."

Andreas turned, and was gone in the blink of an eye.

"You need to feed," I told Josef. "Lucky for you, my favourite hunting ground is close."

I led him to where I'd hunted with Marco over the centuries.

"You need to consider the fact that these Hunters might be connected to Pierre," Josef stated. "The timing is too much of a coincidence."

"Why would a vampire align with a Hunter?" I wondered. "For *any* reason?"

"I don't know," he admitted. "When I was human, nothing would have convinced me to do so. I hated vampires with every fibre of my soul. That hatred is still alive in Hunters today."

Curiosity got the best of me. "What was it like? Being a Hunter one day, a vampire the next?" I asked.

He smiled. "The man who I had spent so long hunting after killing my wife offered me an outstretched hand, offering friendship. I don't think I ever imagined what that friendship would become. Enemy to lover and nest mate."

"Erik?" I asked, raising my eyebrows.

He chuckled at my expression. "Erik was the reason I became a Hunter, and the reason I became a vampire. It was Carlos's idea to turn a Hunter, but Erik's the one who picked me. He found humour in the man who hunted him becoming one of them. I didn't fight what I was, but I didn't immediately want to join them. All it took was one hunt, though, and there was no denying what I was. He became a good friend. Taught me much of what I know about being a vampire."

"You didn't hate him?" I asked.

His deep laughter rumbled through him. "Of course not! I woke up a vampire. How often are vampires able to hold on to that part of their humanity? I led him and the others to massacre the Hunters with a smile. I was incapable of holding on to the hatred. I released my pain, and haven't looked back since."

"Do you miss her?" I asked

His silence stretched out as we walked. "I loved my wife, but I lost the ability to hold on to the sorrow and anger over her death when I turned. That inability to grieve humans is something we've all experienced. We can feel it at first, but it quickly fades. Anything we do hold on to is because we think we should. I remember what she was to me. She was everything," he admitted. "We'd fled what is now Spain to escape vampires when my son was born. We thought Switzerland would be safer." He scoffed, then his silence filled the space between us. "I wouldn't be the man I am today if not for her. Or her death. I failed to protect her, and only quickened her death, but I'd be nothing but dust, with her and my son." He kissed the side of my face. "I wouldn't have met you."

A warmth settled in my chest, spreading out in the form of a smile. "You're a charmer, aren't you?"

He lowered his head to whisper in my ear. "Is it working?"

I pressed my hand against his chest. "Hunt first. Seduce later."

He chuckled, but his arm was around me tighter as we continued walking. I leaned into him, finding comfort in his presence.

No one was around. We'd have to enter a house to feed. "Did you know that's what they had planned for you?" I asked, leading him towards a house I'd fed in before. A husband and wife without children.

"Yeah, they openly discussed it in front of me. I tried to fight it, but as you know, that first taste of vampire blood, and you want more." His lips curved into a smile, and my stomach flipped. Damn, I could gaze at that smile all day. "I actually felt sorry for the human I'd been. Poor fool. Hunting vampires got him killed. He would have preferred to die trying to take vampires down, fighting to the last breath. Instead, I was blessed with a new life. One of blood and pleasure. I killed and betrayed humans who once followed me, wanting their blood and screams. Their fear was intoxicating. That's the same fate these Hunters will face, Bestowed or not."

"Will we be punished for breaking the Law of the Bestowed?" I asked.

Josef laughed. "Not when they've been unleashed to take us down. This is war, Aria. It's us or them. Besides, my King gave us permission to kill, remember."

War. I'd been turned long after the war ended, yet it had never truly left our world. But he was right. The laws no longer applied.

"Let's eat," I commented, and opened the door, letting Josef in first.

In the kitchen, he stopped me. He faced me, stroking my cheek. "You were created in a world where The Accords have always hung over your head. I only experienced a small time during which they didn't exist, but it was enough. Alongside Erik, I followed Carlos into his rebellion against

The Accords. Soon, the Bloodking will announce our presence to the world. We will live as vampires are supposed to. Without fear. Hunters will be the ones looking over their shoulders. The three of us will hunt, and bathe in the blood of Hunters. I will smear blood over every inch of your body so the two of us can lick you clean."

A small shiver rippled through me at his words. "Why don't we start now?" I said. In normal circumstances, I would act with caution to avoid drawing Hunters. But they were already here.

I led him to the bedroom where the couple lay sleeping. Their hearts beat in rhythm, their breaths deep.

"I've heard a lot about you and Erik," I said. "How...seductive you both are."

Josef smiled down at me. "Is that so?" He grabbed me by the waist, pressing himself against me. "Do we live up to our reputation?" He pressed his nose against my throat.

My pulse quickened, waves of heat coiling within me at the husky edge of his voice. *How is he doing this?* It had been a long time a man had set me on fire like this.

"Seduce her," I whispered, pointing to the woman. "Make her beg you to fuck her as we take pleasure in her blood. Then for desert, the spice of fear as we terrify him. Then we kill them."

A small smile played on his lips and he turned towards the woman. "I like the sound of this."

Chapter 20

I approached the sleeping humans, hunger burning through me. The rich scent created by venom in their bloodstream lingered. They'd been fed from before. I crawled over the bed until I had the woman pinned beneath me, my fangs lengthening. She let out a deep breath in her sleep, but moved enough to expose her throat. I brushed the soft skin below her ear. Her eyes opened.

"Jason?" she asked. "What are you doing?"

"No," I whispered. "I'm not Jason."

"Who are you?" Panic filled her eyes.

"Don't worry who I am, simply take pleasure in my bite, and I may give you more," I promised.

"B-bite?" Her fear threatened to pull me into a frenzy.

Aria crawled over, eyes red. The woman trembled beneath me in silent fear. I rubbed my cheek against hers. "It won't hurt," I said. "Bare your throat, and enjoy the effects of our venom." I caressed her throat again.

The lamp turned on from the other side of the bed, flooding the room with light. "Who are you?" The human male had woken up. "How did you get in my house?" He caught sight of my red eyes and fangs, and scrambled backwards out of bed, tripping over his feet as he bolted for the door.

Aria cut off his escape before he reached it. "Don't move," she said.

He froze, her compulsion taking hold, yet his fear remained strong, heart thundering. Aria turned him around so he could see the bed.

"Please don't hurt me," the man pleaded.

Me. Not *us*. He'd said nothing about the woman. Disgusted, I scowled at him. "No thoughts of your wife? No pleading for her?" I put anger into my voice. "You tried to run, leaving your wife alone with two vampires. Coward!"

Fear flickered in his eyes, the scent almost enough to drive me deeper into a frenzy.

I lowered my mouth to the woman's throat again, licking it. As I sunk my fangs in, she whimpered, squirming beneath me.

"Share?" Aria asked, back on the bed.

I held my hand out to Aria, pulling her in. Aria bit a moment later, and the two of us fed in silence. There was nothing like the bond of sharing a drink. The woman didn't fight us, affected by our venom quickly. I growled in contentment. Aria's hand slipped under my tee-shirt, running it over my back.

I released the woman at the same time Aria did. I leaned forward, licking the blood from her lips. I played with her hair, running a hand over her arm.

"I want to strip you naked, pin you to the bed, and claim you right in front of these humans," I declared. "I want to get blood drunk from them."

An insistent yearning overcame me, and I couldn't resist. The scent of her, the warmth of her body both drew me in. My lips crushed against hers. With a soft exhalation, her lips parted, yielding to me. She tasted like the woman's blood, lips soft, and tongue urgent, desperate against mine. I growled as I deepened our kiss, not wanting it to end, to wrap myself in the warmth that came with kissing this goddess. I pushed her to her back, beside the woman. Aria lifted her hips, hooking one leg over my ankle.

"You bit me," the human woman said. It wasn't an accusation, more of wonder. Our venom had her in a state of want.

I pulled from my kiss with Aria, both of us breathless. "I did," I agreed. "You're delicious. You enjoyed it, too. Even now, my venom is pumping through your blood. You want more, don't you?"

Her eyes shifted to my mouth. "You're vampires. Oh my god, vampires are real." The last word dropped to a whisper.

I smiled at her lack of fear. Partly our venom removing her fight, partly because of a fascination as she gazed at the two of us. Unlike the man who was one scare away from wetting himself.

"We are," I confirmed to the human. "Don't be afraid."

I wanted to enjoy Aria's presence, our bodies hard against one another. She rotated her hips, and the contact of her against my cock ignited me. I ran my teeth over her earlobe, giving her a gentle nip, savouring the shiver that passed through her body.

"I'm not afraid," the human breathed, pulling me out of the moment. I'd briefly forgotten she was there.

I let my smile linger on Aria before tearing my gaze from her. "Do you want me to bite you again?" I asked the human woman.

"I do," she whispered.

I shifted closer to the woman and traced my tongue over her soft throat. The small puncture marks from my earlier bite were already sealing closed with the assistance of my venom. She gasped softly, baring her throat.

"Please," the husband begged. "Let me go."

"If you want more, you can have me," I told the woman, ignoring her husband. "Take your pleasure as I feed. Tell him it's okay. That you want this. Tell him to surrender to us, and he too, can enjoy our bite."

She was clawing at my tee-shirt, the soft curve of her neck inviting, a temptation I couldn't resist. My lips brushed her skin.

"Jason, it's okay," she said. "I want this. You will too."

A memory rose up. My wife, human, telling me it was okay as I fought to protect her, but losing her anyway. My smile widened. This scene mirrored that night, and I was the monster that would kill them both. But instead of trying to protect his wife, the man had tried to run.

"My lovely friend wants me to seduce you," I murmured to the woman.

Her heart quickened.

I growled softly and breathed her in. Her scent was like warmth in the sun, with the sweet addition of desire. "Oh, sweet thing, do you want me to seduce you? In front of your husband?"

The woman's eyes darted towards the male, and back to me. "Yes," she pleaded. "Bite me. Seduce me."

"I'm going to have some fun with your husband first," I whispered into her ear. "He abandoned you instead of protecting you. Men should protect their wives, not leave them to die at the fangs of vampires alone."

"Please," she whispered. "My husband can watch."

"She likes you," Aria noted, reaching for my cheek. "A true master of seduction."

I winked at her. "I'm not even trying." I kissed the human woman. She didn't hold back, lips parting, hands sliding over my chest. "Are you saying you'd rather I drink from you, claim your body, as your cowardly husband watches?" I asked the woman.

"Yes," the woman said.

"You've fed from her before, haven't you?" I asked Aria. "I recognise that need to be bitten. This is not a new sensation for her."

"Marco and I may have been here a few times," she admitted.

I shook my head. "I think she's addicted to venom." I kissed the human woman softly. "I have to admit, I love when they beg."

"She smells delicious," Aria said, and turned towards the man, breathing in his fear. "But then, so does he."

I lowered to speak in the woman's ear. "We can smell your lust. That's the effect of my bite. I will give you what you want." I caressed her throat, running my fingers over where my fangs had marked her. Biting again, I allowed the red haze to pull me under. Vaguely aware of Aria joining in, I couldn't stop; I didn't want to. The woman's hands slid over me, but she soon became too weak, her heartbeat rapid. We stopped feeding, and watched as her eyes closed, her breathing stopped. Her heart stilled.

"Time for some fun," I declared, and the two of us turned our attention to the man.

He stared at his wife in horror, saying nothing, frozen in place by Aria's compulsion.

"Do you want to run?" I asked him.

He nodded.

"What do you think?" I asked Aria. "Feel like a chase?"

"I do like to work for my meal. But wouldn't it be more fun for him to die next to his wife? To lay his eyes upon her corpse as we kill him too?"

"No," his voice trembled.

"He smells…" Aria didn't finish her sentence, a low growl rising from her.

"I know," I said, putting a hand on her arm to calm her. "Why don't you bring him over."

"Come here," Aria instructed. "Lay down next to your dead wife."

He returned to the bed, unable to fight Aria's command. Soon, he was on his back next to the woman. "You killed her," he said, meeting my eyes.

"And you did nothing to protect her," I said. "You ran. At least *I* had the courage to try to kill the vampire who took my wife from me."

Erik's mind pressed against mine. *'Reminiscing times past?'* he asked.

I laughed in response. *'Humans aren't what they used to be,'* I replied. *'I'm feeding with Aria, and this trembling, poor example of a man tried to run from us as we killed his wife. He didn't fight for her at all.'*

Aria started to lick my chin.

Erik's amusement faded. *'You killed?'*

'I did," I confirmed. *'You were there when Carlos gave us permission.'*

'Josef, I don't care that you killed. I care that I wasn't there to enjoy it with you. Let me watch through your eyes while you kill the man. Then I want you to fuck Aria up against the wall. I want you to open yourself to me, so I can feel everything.'

I kissed Aria, letting Erik in. "Erik's with us," I said. "He's watching. He wants to enjoy the kill."

Aria grasped my jaw, gazing deep into my eyes. "Would our alpha like to choose how we kill?"

The man whimpered.

Erik's answer reverberated through me, his need to watch so strong I felt it as my own. I kissed Aria, hard. "He wants to watch while you feed first," I explained. "To see the human succumb to your venom. Then scream in pain as he feels only your fangs. The death he deserves."

"No venom?" she asked.

"No venom."

She smiled and moved towards the man.

"Please don't kill me." His voice was barely audible, but the tremble was noticeable. "I don't want to die."

Aria crawled towards him. "You're human," she stated. "Your mortality means that you will die. There's no escape for you."

I pushed the woman's body from the bed and sat back against the headboard. I was a man who liked to go for the kill, not watch it in action. But Erik wanted to see. *'Do I at least get to enjoy the kill. too?'* I asked him. *'I'm almost intoxicated.'*

'Wait,' he instructed me.

Aria struck fast. His eyes rolled back, and he moaned. Aria fed in silence, then lifted her head, turning to look at me. "Won't you join me?" she asked. "It's no fun with you over there. Especially when he starts to scream." She bared her fangs. "Please, Erik, let Josef play."

'It is hard to say no to that woman,' Erik grumbled. *'Do as she asks.'*

I didn't hesitate, and joined her in the feed. We let the man enjoy our bites for a moment longer, then released him, and struck again without venom. With our fangs buried in his throat, and without venom, he felt the pain, and struggled against us.

"Please stop," he begged. "You're hurting me."

I lifted myself from his throat to whisper in his ear. "If there is one thing in this world I despise, it's cowards," I growled. "You deserve this."

Then I tore into his throat, letting the blood gush. He grunted in pain.

Erik's disappointment flooded through me. *'Josef, your patience has not improved. I had hoped you'd drag it out more.'* He chuckled. *'Enjoy the kill, though.'*

'I am!' I replied, giving myself to the red haze and laughing. *'I am enjoying the kill, Erik. Very much!'*

The tearing of flesh and Aria's growl were as intoxicating as my own feeding. I let his blood gush down my throat, the red haze pulling me under. Then the blood flow stopped, and Aria moved closer to me.

I licked at her chin. "Erik wants you against the wall," I commanded. "Take your clothes off!"

She slipped out of her clothes, movements slow, teasing as she took her place—back against the wall. I wanted her blood, to claim her. The human blood still fresh in my veins, I was blood drunk. *'Oh Erik, I have missed the kill,'* I said in silence.

His laughter rumbled through my mind. *"I miss seeing that glint in your eye as you kill. I miss killing with you. Tell Aria I'm alone in her room, and I'm naked.'*

"Erik's naked," I said, stripping off, stalking towards her. "He's alone in your room. Our nest."

Aria smiled. "Does he want to watch me touch myself?"

Her hand slid down, eyes on my face as her fingers rotated around her clit.

'Fuck,' Erik's voice was laced with raw lust, and his desire jolted through me like lightning.

I watched her, breathing in the irresistible scent of her arousal. I used my link with Erik to make sure he could get it through his own senses. He growled in my mind.

"Josef, you're not the voyeur," Aria said, and held her hand up to me.

I didn't resist as her fingers pushed into my mouth. I groaned, and pressed against her, sucking her fingers. Her other hand dropped to stroke my cock. Her touch pulled a low rumble from me.

"Kneel," Aria whispered. "I want your mouth there."

A shiver tore through me, and I immediately dropped to my knees.

'Worship her,' Erik said through my mind. I could almost hear him panting and knew he'd be stroking himself soon enough. *'I want to hear her moan, see her eyes roll back.'* His growl rumbled through me. *'Bring her to her knees.'*

I let my burning need show through my eyes. Her own blazed as she stared down at me. I pulled her thighs apart, grasping her hips and kissed her gently.

"I need you to be rougher than that," she breathed. "Come on, Josef, I want to feel your tongue, your lips. Touch me. Make me feel it."

Carnal desire took hold, and I stood, turned her around. and pushed her against the wall. I pulled her arms up over her head, pinning them to the wall with one hand. With my free hand, I slid my fingers into her pussy, my cock pressed against her ass, our warm bodies pressed together. I lowered my head, nipping at her throat. She whimpered.

"How's this for rough?" I asked, pushing her harder into the wall.

Chapter 21

Josef had me pinned against the wall, his fingers rotating around my clit. I ground my ass into his cock. Frustrated by the lack of fangs as he nipped at my throat, I tried to pull my arms out of his grip. His fingers tightened.

"Now, now," he growled. "You wanted rough. This is what you get." He snapped at my jaw, before biting my shoulders and neck.

His fingers continued their rhythm, dominant, demanding. The muscles in my pussy clenched. I turned my head and his mouth found mine, hungry and all-consuming. He tasted of the humans we'd just fed on. I slid my tongue over his canine, but found no fang. I groaned in frustration.

He smiled against my mouth and stepped back a little. His fingers left my clit, moving to my stomach. He pulled me from the wall, then pressed down on my back, guiding me to an angle he was satisfied with. His hand released my wrists, and I felt the head of his erection at the opening of my pussy.

"Hands against the wall," he commanded, as he grabbed my hips.

Somewhat intoxicated from feeding, I held the wall, shooting a look back at him. His eyes were slightly unfocused.

"You're blood drunk," I laughed.

The corners of his mouth lifted, amusement dancing across his face.

"Perhaps," he said lazily. "So are you."

His hips rolled forward, and his cock drove into me. He pulled back and thrust again, eyes holding mine. I clenched around him as he slid into me. I exhaled as he drove forward, his cock striking deep.

He maintained a fast, rough rhythm: each time he pushed forward, his grip on my hips tightened. Heat radiated from my centre to my stomach and up my back. He dropped one hand, playing with my clit. The pressure of his fingers - deliberate, teasing - sent an ache through me. My breath came in ragged gasps. A spark of pleasure ignited deep in my belly and I released a moan, raw, full of want. His breaths came in short, each movement sending waves of warmth through every fibre.

I met each forward motion of his hips with my own rhythm, chasing the ecstasy. His movements no longer gentle, the intensity between us spiralled.

"I knew you had it in you," I breathed as he thrust again. "Not always a gentle lover, are you?"

He growled. "You asked for it," he panted.

I still wanted more.

"Rougher," I gasped.

His answer was a fast thrust hitting deep, eliciting a moan from me. He continued his momentum with his fingers, ripples of pleasure growing, spreading out. His grunts and ragged breaths fuelled me to slam back into him, my walls gripping him.

"Oh, fuck!" I cursed, toes curling as pure pleasure crashed over me.

As I came, Josef leaned forward, sinking his fangs into my shoulder, his body behind me tensing. A grunt vibrated against my skin, and my fangs dropped down. I reached for his hand, biting into his wrist. Blood sharing during sex after a fresh kill jolted me with energy.

We caught our breath, and he pulled out of me, leaving me empty. He turned me around and pulled me to him, wrapping his arms around me.

"Erik got himself off," Josef informed me. "He stroked himself by watching through my eyes. He says we need to hurry up and get back, because he wants his good girl's lips wrapped around his cock while I fuck you."

"Then we should probably meet Andreas in Montecchio Nature Park," I said. "The sooner we finish here, the sooner we can return to our nest."

We quickly dressed, and paused, taking in the sight of the bodies. The man's throat had been torn into, a pained expression on his face. On the floor, the woman looked like she had enjoyed her death.

"When we find Andreas, I wouldn't mind more of that," Josef said pointing to the humans. "The thrill of the kill is exhilarating, and I know he would take joy from it. Like you, he was born into a world of The Accords, but his first few years consisted of killing on battle fields."

I smiled up at him. "You're more bloodthirsty than I realised. I must admit I do like how rough you get when you're blood drunk."

He grabbed my arm, yanking me towards him. "It's the kill," he admitted. "It does bring out my rougher side. The first humans I killed in my beginning as a vampire were Hunters. Without fear of punishment."

I kissed him. "Well, we do find ourselves with an excess of Hunters here. And a vampire who seeks control of my den."

"I'd like to know who Bestowed the Hunters." His eyes darkened. "Let's hunt some Hunters. Get some answers before we kill them."

We left the house, Josef's arm wrapped around my waist. I leaned into his warmth. He'd become less of a stranger, and I found enjoyment in being alone with him. What had been raw desire had softened, his presence filling me with thrilling anticipation.

"How long before you climbed into the bed of your wife's killer?" I asked, amusement in my voice.

Laughter burst from him. "I was wondering when you'd ask me that." He took a while to continue. "We grew close fairly quickly. But not as lovers. Not then. It was a friendship that I never could have foreseen. A few close calls in the war, in which we both saved each other's asses. Especially when the Hunters realised I was a vampire."

We turned off the street we were on as I directed us towards the nature park. Both of us kept watch for the Hunters.

"We blood bonded in Melbourne when Quinn freed us from Gabriela's command," he said.

"Siren?" I asked with laughter.

"Siren," he confirmed. "When we arrived in Venice, with Matteo's knowledge of the city, Carlos split it into hunting territories. Erik told him he'd share a territory with me." He got a faraway look in his eyes. "He invited me to hunt with him on the first night. We came across a party, and got a little blood drunk. We were walking past the same place he and I claimed you. He turned to me and said: 'I love you, Josef. Not as a brother, but as I loved Amara. I have loved you for a long time but—' I didn't let him finish and kissed him before asking him what the hell took him so long." Josef's face had lit up.

"You loved him too?" I asked.

The scent of blood drew both our attention. Josef pulled me behind him, moving with grace until we found its source. A vampire was feeding nearby, the human pushed up against a stone wall of a house, his throat bared. She was known to do more than feed with her meals though, so I led Josef away.

'She's from my clan,' I informed him through our bond. *'Her name is Carmen.'*

'Is she safe? Can she be trusted?' he returned.

'I don't think anyone can, until we know what's going on,' I said.

'Agreed.'

We were silent until we made it to the nature park.

"To answer your question, yes, I loved Erik," he admitted. "I didn't know it until that moment. As soon as he declared his love, I had to show him my own. He then told me he'd once been part of a nest, and commanded me to kneel for his alpha. I didn't even hesitate and dropped to my knees so fast. He promised we'd find another; even if it took a hundred years, we'd complete our nest."

I laughed. "So, what took him so long?"

"He loved Amara, and mourned her death so much that he wasn't looking to love another. Eventually, he realised he could no longer ignore what was stirring within."

"Wait, Amara?" I asked in disbelief. "As in, the fourth original? She's his maker?"

"The very same," he confirmed. "Amara wanted him, so she and King Luis formed a nest. Unfortunately, in Amara's death, Erik and Luis ended. Both of them grieved her too much."

I grabbed his arm. "Josef, are you telling me that Erik is first generation?" I now understood why his venom had been so potent. How had I not figured that out?

"He is," he said.

"The first generation are stronger than the rest of us, more bloodthirsty, their venom more concentrated," I recited. "They can be satisfied with vampire blood. How has this gone unnoticed? Does King Carlos know? I've heard so much about Erik, but not that."

Josef chuckled. "It's not something he advertises. Especially after he lost his maker so violently. He doesn't go around biting a lot of vampires, and those he does keep his secrets."

"Why isn't he King, then?" I pondered. "With his power, he's *stronger* than King Carlos. But he kneels like he's equal to the rest of you?"

"There's a lot you don't know about Erik," Josef said in a low voice. "While yes, he does have power to overthrow a king, that's not who he is. If the world knew he was first generation, many would offer to follow him. He doesn't want that. We discussed him becoming king when we were released from Gabriela's command, but he was reluctant to do so. We bonded in preparation to form a clan of our own, and then he got the idea to invite Quinn to be our Queen, as it was her voice that freed us. Others in the clan had the same idea. But when she and Matteo knelt to Carlos, Erik told me we should follow their lead. That Carlos would make a great king, and it was our fate to join his clan."

"He has no desire to be more?" I asked.

"None," Josef agreed. "He is a warrior, and will defend his clan, and his King, but he doesn't want more than that. All he wants is to take in the pleasures of being a vampire. Feeding, fucking, reading books." Josef grinned. "Watching TV shows that upset him."

"Why does he watch TV shows that upset him?" I asked.

His face lit up, amusement reflecting from his eyes. "There's an old TV show on a well-known figure from his people, but they got a few things wrong historically, so he gets annoyed by it."

The concept of this made no sense. "Then why does he watch it?"

Laughter burst from Josef. "A question we all ask him many times." The amusement died from his eyes. "He gets homesick. The TV gives him a small taste of what he misses. Even if the portrayal is inaccurate, it reminds him of what he can't have."

The shadow of sympathy wrapped around my heart; I understood his pain. Like Erik, I'd had to give up my life, just as my father had. The modern world had changed, while we remained - unchanging, eternal. Yet alongside that ache, awe stirred. I'd been claimed—no, chosen—by a first generation vampire. That alone was a privilege granted to a rare few. One I did not take lightly. Joy swelled in my chest. My body sang.

"Don't treat him differently," Josef advised. "It's part of why he hides that from people. He's seen how people treat the first generation, and he hates special treatment. When I found out, I made the mistake of being in awe, as I know you are. I can feel it through our bond. He told me to get it out of my system and never do it again. That he was still him."

I absorbed his words quietly. How could I not treat him differently? Everything was different now.

Josef looked around. "Damn, where is Andreas? He should be here by now."

I listened, hearing nothing out of place. No heartbeats, no footsteps, nothing. "Could he still be watching them?" I asked.

Josef turned towards where we'd come from. "Maybe. But he knows we'd meet him here. The sun's coming up in a couple of hours, so he'll want to be with us to find somewhere safe."

"Then we should find him," I said.

We left the park, returning to where we'd last seen Andreas.

"I have his scent," Josef murmured, and followed the trail.

We walked for five minutes before the scent of blood reached us. Vampire blood. Josef growled as he crouched over the dark splashes on the pale cobbles.

"There's human blood here, too," I said, pointing to the spray. "A lot of it."

He nodded. "That's too much blood for a human to lose. So he killed someone. Good. Why did he reveal himself?"

The streets were empty, silent, offering us no answers.

"It can't be good that he's injured, though," I pointed out.

"No. Either he's gone to ground, or someone took him," Josef frowned. "He wouldn't leave us waiting for him, though. So that leaves the latter."

"This is feeling more and more like an intentional trap," I said. "Do we call in your clan?"

"No, not yet," Josef insisted. "We can handle a few Bestowed Hunters."

Chapter 22

I returned from Aria's villa as Carlos was leaving. He eyed me up and down, nostrils flaring.

"Again?" Carlos asked, eyes gleaming. "Are you trying to see how many times you can jerk off in one night?"

I grinned. "Aria and Josef had fun without me. But at least I got to watch through Josef's eyes. You're going out so close to dawn."

"Going hunting," he said. "I didn't want to leave Camila, but I needed a decent meal without risking her too much."

"Happy hunting," I said.

"I need you to do me a favour," he added

"Anything," I agreed.

"Camila's trying to adjust to her life among vampires," he said. "After you all called for her death a few days ago, she's trying to start afresh and offer an olive branch. Between that and how she's been raised, there's a lot she wants to work through."

"I imagine that would be quite traumatic," I acknowledged.

He nodded. "She's having nightmares, so it's going to be a process. I've tried to calm her mind. It worked for Quinn once, but Camila's mind isn't ready to let go of everything she's endured. She's talking to Celeste right now, and she may approach you. Please let her feel welcome, and part of the clan."

"Okay," I agreed. "Although after earlier, she should feel more relaxed with me."

"You're the one she's most nervous about, *because* of that," he said. "Help her relax."

"I will," I promised.

Once he left, I entered the kitchen to find Matteo and Quinn cooking again. "What are you making this time?"

"'Death by Chocolate'," Quinn said with joy. She lifted up a bottle of chocolate sauce. "Then, Matteo's going to cover me in this and paint me while I eat some."

I dipped my finger in the dessert, savouring the taste of the warm, melted chocolate before smearing it across her cheek. She caught my wrist, and with a small smile, brought my finger between her lips. With slow licks of her tongue and fangs grazing the tip, I smirked when she let go.

"Careful, I bite back," I warned in a playful tone.

She bared her throat, running a finger over the smooth curve of her neck.

"Please do," she said with a laugh.

Matteo pulled her towards him, gazing down at her. "You missed a little," he said, and licked off the chocolate I'd smeared on her face.

Quinn gave a soft whimper, the two of them lost in one another's eyes.

Camila and Celeste's muted voices filled the silence.

"How's the new addition to our clan?" I asked.

Quinn turned her head in the direction of their voices. "She has many wounds, and I don't mean the marks and bruises Carlos left," she said. "I think there's a little trauma there. I mean, her father sent her here alone. That has to be a heavy burden. I heard her talking to her brother yesterday. He doesn't like that she chose a vampire, but at least he won't turn his back on her."

"Her sister will be here in a few weeks," Matteo added. "It'll do her good to have family around her. As long as no one tries to kill any of us."

I shrugged. "Have fun with your 'Death by Chocolate'," I said, and returned to my room.

In the mood for reading, I grabbed a book and sat in my chair, wishing Josef could be in his. Reading together in silence had become a favoured pastime, as had discussing our books. I'd collected many books of various genres over the years. I did enjoy what humans wrote about vampires. It intrigued me—occasionally they captured our true natures, but mostly they romanticised us. I also liked books on magic wielders—which humans called witches—ghosts, demons, shifters and other creatures of the paranormal world. My current read was a book that had a vampire with the name Eric, and the character fascinated me.

It wasn't long before footsteps moved towards my door. There was a long silence before she knocked lightly on my door. I smiled at the thudding of the human heartbeat on the other side.

"Come in, Camila," I called out, closing the book I was reading.

She pushed the door open and stepped into my room, eyes wide as she looked around. She displayed fresh bruises, and the stitches from her throat had been removed, but the scar was still an angry red. Carlos had bitten deep in an attempt to hide his mark from her father. She caught me looking at it.

"It's still his mark," she explained. "Even though that one hurt, I wear it proudly."

"I'm glad," I said, listening to her heartbeat. A slight scent of fear rose from her. I put away my vampirism, letting my human mask show. Her shoulders relaxed. "No one here will harm you," I said to her. "You have no reason to fear us. Human or not, you're part of our clan. We will protect you as if you were one of us. You *are* one of us."

She gave me a faint smile. "Am I that obvious?"

"Only to those who can smell fear." I put my book down and stood. "You forget, I've seen you in your most vulnerable moments. Naked and fucking my King. Did you trust me then?"

She nodded. "I did. Your efforts to comfort me were appreciated."

I smiled at her. "Then you have no reason not to trust me outside your bedroom."

She stared at my axe and shield that hung from the wall, then at the books that filled my bookshelves. Her gaze finished on a single painting on my desk, of my brother. One that Matteo had painted from my descriptions of him. He'd done a good job of capturing Magnus's likeness.

"My brother," I said to her. "Magnus." I hadn't spoken his name in a long time. "He was the first human I fed on when I awoke from the slumber of transformation. I killed him."

She gave me a sympathetic look. "I'm sorry."

I gave her a small smile and waved around my room. "Please, come in. Make yourself at home."

"Wow," she whispered, looking around again.

"Not what you pictured?" I asked with a grin.

She met my eyes. "Not exactly. Carlos's room has everything out in the open. You said you taught him all he knows, so I guess I expected yours to be the same."

I laughed. "Carlos's room reflects who he is. He does not hide who he is, and sees no reason to hide his…tastes. I like to be more…discrete. It adds mystery."

She glanced again at the books. "Your bedroom doesn't reflect what I thought about you."

"Vampires can't read, and enjoy literature?" I asked. "What do you like to read?"

Her shoulders sagged.

"I was never allowed to read anything that wasn't Hunter-related," she admitted. "The history of the war. The brutality of vampires. Early records. Individual profiles. That kind of thing. Every Hunter learns from a young age about some of the more brutal vampires. There are a lot with certain reputations. I remember learning about Josef. Oh, and The Original Three."

I searched my shelves. She'd never read fiction, so I wanted to find a book for her. "I've heard human women love to read romance. There's an obsession with morally grey men." I chuckled, giving her a wink. "I have to admit, I do see the appeal. I'd love to see their take on us." I grabbed a book that I knew to be heavy with vampires, BDSM, and kink. "Maybe you'd enjoy this book. I know I did. Josef did too. You've lived the enemies-to-lovers trope, so you might enjoy that type of book. I'm sure Carlos will enjoy the effects it has on you."

She took the book, reading the back. "Thank you," she said.

I pointed to the chair Josef had claimed for his own. "Please, sit. Be comfortable. Let us talk."

She sat, the book in her lap. I took my seat opposite her.

"As you said yourself, you've seen me naked," she said. "It's difficult to face you after that, and not feel a little awkward."

"That's true, but you've also seen me naked," I reminded her. "You struck me. I got myself off to the two of you fucking." I grinned again. "Your mind is not adjusted to the vampire world yet, young Huntress. What you humans would deem as awkward, does not have to be so for us. Don't let the human mindset be what determines how you see things. You're in *our* world now."

She gave a tentative smile. "Quinn said it took her a while to get past that." She dropped her voice. "She also said that she's had you and Josef in her bed at the same time as Carlos and Matteo."

I shook with laughter. "Quinn's been spilling all our secrets. Wouldn't it be a shame if I spilled some of my own!"

"None to spill!" Quinn called out from the kitchen.

I shook my head in amusement. "I could still find something on you!" I threatened, and returned to my conversation with Camila. "Understand, you've left behind your life, and everything you know. We've all done the same when we became vampires. Although I do think it was difficult for Quinn, since she was a public figure in Australia. When we first arrived, she was afraid of Australians showing up and recognising her. We weren't exiled like you, though. You'll likely experience grief for what you've lost. Let that be what guides you to become who *you* want to be. A human Queen in a vampire clan, discovering herself, and all her kinks."

"Your clan is accepting. I'm not so sure other vampires will feel the same. Even Aria was afraid when she realised I'd been a Hunter," Camila observed.

"You have to understand, Hunters have never infiltrated a vampire's den before," I explained. "Not to the extent in which they're sitting next to the king the way you do. If one isn't expecting it, that can be enough to awaken fear in visiting vampires."

She nodded slowly. "I hope I was able to ease her fears." She stifled a yawn.

"You're doing well to stay up so late. This is a time during which humans are usually waking up. You've already switched to vampire hours," I acknowledged.

"Trying to," she agreed. "Carlos is having a pre-dawn hunt before we can go to bed. It's taking an adjustment to sleep during the day. Carlos usually wakes up in the middle of the afternoon wanting attention."

"Attention I'd say you're more than willing to give him," I joked.

"Of course," she said, meeting my eyes without flinching.

He'd probably be awhile, likely checking the city for any unwelcome presence. It would mean at least an hour before he returned. Just in time for the sun to rise.

I picked up my book. "Then perhaps get some reading in. I do like to read while in the presence of others reading. I find it pleasant."

"Sure," she said, and opened her book.

I watched as she started to read. She pulled her legs towards her, folding them under. She glanced up at me once before returning to the book. I opened mine and started to read where I'd left off. I fought the desire to skip parts—the scenes that weren't about the vampire Eric.

We read in a comfortable silence for half an hour before a distinct scent of lust rose from her. I glanced up, already knowing how far into the book she was. She seemed oblivious to the world, lips parted slightly.

"Enjoying that, are you?" I asked in amusement.

She jerked in surprise. "Oh, I forgot. You can…oh, um."

I laughed. "You got into that book, so much that you forgot I was here."

"Yes," she admitted. "I also forgot I was sitting across from someone with your senses." Her eyes glimmered.

The front door to the villa opened. Carlos's telltale footsteps announced his return. "Why don't you take that book to your bedroom? Carlos is home. I'm sure he'd love to help you work through that."

She rushed to the door and turned back. "Thank you, Erik," she said. "This was very different to our first meeting."

As she hurried from my room with the book, I realised that she was talking about my attempts to lure her into a feeding room at the gallery. I couldn't hold back the chuckle.

"Did you take care of my Queen?" Carlos's voice was low, but I could still hear him from the other side of the den. "Ease her fears?""

"I did," I agreed. "I gave her a book that she seems to be enjoying. I think you'll like the effects it has on her."

His laugh was low. "Thank you Erik. Any word from Josef?"

"None yet," I said.

His footsteps indicated he was heading towards his bedroom. "Report anything out of place."

He growled low. Camila's heart skipped. They'd likely be busy for a while.

I reached through my bond with Josef. *'Josef? Is there anything to report to our King?'*

A splinter of fear was quickly doused. *'Nothing we can't handle,'* he replied.

I sighed, worry churning in my gut. *'Why do I feel like something's happened?'*

'We're okay,' he said. *'It's been an eventful night. We've found a safe place to shelter during the day. I'll report back tonight.'*

He was hiding something. *'What aren't you telling me?'* I demanded.

'Nothing to tell,' he said and ended the conversation by shutting himself off from me.

Dread flooded through me. Something wasn't right. I started towards the door. Carlos would want me to report anything to him, but he was already busy with Camila. Instead, I made my way towards the kitchen.

Chapter 23

"Josef." Aria interrupted my pacing. "You need rest. We both do. I wouldn't mind your company while I sleep."

I turned to find her sitting on the side of the bed in the black silk pyjamas she'd found. Her eyes dropped to my bare chest and torso.

The house we were in was occupied by a young couple who were currently under compulsion not to move. We weren't hungry, but we'd agreed it would be useful to have food nearby. We'd pulled the blankets off their bed for them to be warm in the corner we'd given them. The delicious aroma of fear wafted across the room.

Aria met my eyes and reached out. "There's no use worrying when we can't do anything. We'll find Andreas. Then we'll go after those Hunters and kill them."

"We'll need to make sure they don't turn," I said.

"Then remove their hearts," she suggested. "There's no coming back from that."

A choked sob from the corner of the room drew my attention. I walked towards the humans huddled together, and crouched down in front of them. I reached out to brush the woman's trembling cheek. She flinched at my touch, another sob catching in her throat.

"Awww, are you afraid?" I asked, voice gentle.

Her gaze flickered to Aria and back to me, and she gave a small nod.

I let my smile become cruel, baring my fangs. "Good." My fingers slid through her hair, tucking a stray strand behind her ear. "So tell me…" I leaned closer, my breath on her lips. "Is it me you fear?" I lowered my voice to a whisper. "Or is it Aria that sends your heart racing?"

"You," she said.

My smile widened. "Good," I said again and traced my thumb over her face, watching her pulse flutter in the hollow of her throat. That subtle twitch beneath her skin held me captive. I brushed my fingers down her neck. Her skin was soft beneath my fingertips. Their fear rose in waves, reaching into my inner beast.

"That scent of fear is making my mouth water," Aria murmured from behind me.

The human woman didn't move, eyes wide, unable to look away from me. The man held her hand. I hissed, darted forward, baring my fangs. She jumped, crying out.

"I don't know if I'm going to be able to sleep with such an appetiser so close," I said. "Maybe I should take you to bed. In case I wake up hungry, it'll be good to have a snack close by."

"Leave her for dessert," Aria said. "Maybe we can have a drink from him before we go to sleep."

I gazed into the woman's eyes, exerting my will over hers. "It's okay. You live a little bit longer than your lover. Go to sleep. I'll wake you tonight. We'll have some fun." Her eyes closed and she fell back. I turned my focus to the man. "Stand up," I commanded. He had no fight against compulsion; his body obeyed without hesitation. He rose to his feet. "Walk towards the bed," I instructed. "Offer your throat to that beauty over there."

He did as I commanded him, and I followed. He dropped to his knees in front of Aria and tilted his head back, glassy eyes staring into mine. There was terrified panic in there.

"Let's not kill him yet," I said. "We'll be hungry when we wake, and it's been a long time since I've given chase. A proper hunt."

She smiled. "That sounds like fun." She turned her attention to the human. "Offer him your wrist."

He held his arm up to me, not from compulsion, but out of fear.

I groaned. "I'm more of a throat man."

Aria tilted her head, running her fingers down her own throat. I couldn't look away, and I growled. She gave me a look of pure seduction. The human's heart raced again.

"Mmmm that scent, I can't resist," Aria said, and struck fast.

I grabbed the offered arm, and pulled it to my mouth. The moment my fangs sank into the flesh, and blood hit my tongue, I almost moaned in pleasure. Filled with the spice of fear, his blood was rich, and I struggled against the red haze. We didn't want to kill him, but with that much fear, it was a challenge to maintain control. I released him and eased Aria off him. She moved her hand over my abs, eyes gleaming.

Damnit, I was hard, but I needed to sleep. Yet I couldn't hold back. I pulled her to me, cleaning the blood from her chin. The action ended in a kiss again.

"We should sleep," she said.

"We should," I agreed.

"I would love to sleep with your arms around me," she suggested. "Maybe with him nearby, in case we wake up hungry."

I pulled the man to his feet. "Get on the bed," I told him. "The far side."

He did so without a word. I dropped my jeans, advancing on Aria as she lay with her back to me. I wrapped my arms around her. The human stared in fear.

"We should release him from his fear," Aria suggested.

I laughed. "Wouldn't want his heart to burst."

She reached for him. "Shhh, it's okay. Go to sleep."

He was asleep instantly.

I kissed the back of her neck. "Erik knew something was wrong," I said.

Her hand moved, shifting through my hair. "It's okay. We'll find Andreas. There was no need to worry any of them yet."

I knew she was right, but Andreas's disappearance had me worried. He liked to watch from the shadows, but would never leave us without an explanation.

"The sun is rising soon," I said. "We can't do anything until tonight anyway."

I closed my eyes, letting sleep claim me.

A hand covered my mouth, and I opened my eyes to find Aria had a finger pressed to her lips. I frowned.

'Someone's in the house,' she whispered through our bond.

'Vampire or human?'

Instead of waiting for an answer, I sat up, my senses sharp. There were multiple heartbeats downstairs. Too fast to be vampires', but they moved too quietly for humans.

'The Bestowed Hunters!' I realised. *'How did they find us?'*

She only shrugged and shook her head. Footsteps on the stairs indicated they were coming up to the first floor.

'They've spread through the house. Cut off all our exits,' Aria's darted towards the lightening window. *'That's our only way out.'*

I indicated the humans. *'Bite him. If he's bleeding, they will be overcome by the scent of blood and will be less likely to follow.'*

I rushed over to the human woman, tearing into her throat deep enough for the scent of blood to fill the room as Aria did the same. The humans would bleed out within seconds, but it would be the distraction we needed. I pulled my jeans on. Then I grabbed her hand and we ran straight for the window. At the last second, I threw up my arm to cover my face.

The breaking of glass shattered the silence. Shards of glass pierced my skin, and we landed on the lawn below. Above us growls echoed in the night as some of the Bestowed Hunters gave in to their hunger. Others fled from the room, their footsteps thundering as they ran down the stairs.

"I was hoping you'd do that," a voice said with a French accent.

Beside me, Aria tensed.

A tall vampire leaned against a tree, his arms crossed over his chest. His black hair was combed back, hazel eyes filled with amusement. Beside him, five Hunters had their crossbows pointed at us. More moved in from both sides, closing us in. I had seen him somewhere before, and it bothered me that I couldn't place him.

"Pierre," Aria grunted.

He smiled at her "I'm surprised you didn't bring the rest of the clan with you. I was hoping you would. Especially your feral father."

Aria growled, uneasiness pulsing through our blood bond.

'What is it?' I asked her.

'No vampire knows who I am. Marco and I made sure of it. Which begs the question, how long has he been working with the Hunters?'

Pierre smirked at her. I stepped forward.

"What vampire betrays his own kind to team up with Hunters?" I demanded. "And Bestowing them? They don't deserve the gift of vampire blood."

"Josef, it's good to see you again." Pierre took a step towards us.

"Again?" I asked.

He tilted his head. "You don't remember me? Remember when you lived in France? About three hundred years ago?"

I studied his face again, and a memory snapped into place. I *did* know him. He'd been human then. The fight, the blood. I'd wounded him, left him to die.

"Hunter," I growled.

Arrows fired at us. Without hesitating, I wrapped Aria in my arms, turning to shield her with my body.

Chapter 24

In the kitchen, Matteo and Quinn were locked in an embrace, drawn into a deep, lingering kiss.

"Erik," Matteo said when they drew apart, voice rough as he caressed Quinn's cheek tenderly. The two gazed at one another, their love just as clear in their eyes as it had been twenty years ago. "Whatever that book was you gave to Camila, it has her hot under the skin."

The sounds of Carlos and Camila fucking came through from their bedroom. Camila demanded that Carlos bite her, and her moan indicated he had.

I laughed. "Just something I thought she'd like. Looks like I was right."

"Twice in the same night," Quinn added. "The girl has a lot of stamina, to do that with a vampire."

Matteo kissed her forehead. "If she's anything like you, he'll wear her out just like I wore you out. Remember that night I painted you? You couldn't keep your eyes open. Passing out as I carried you to my bed."

"You can't wear me out now," she breathed, her suggestive smile a promise. "Although, I wouldn't mind if you wanted to try."

"I do admire that she's trying to get to know us," Matteo added, returning to our conversation. They'd likely hurry off to their bedroom before long. "I think many humans would take longer to adjust to her situation."

Quinn laughed. "She's with Carlos."

Only three words, but they explained everything.

I winked at Quinn. "I remember you trying to work through your fear," I reminded her. "When you were stealing Matteo's art from his studio, you were terrified. But you impressed me with your determination to control it."

She shrugged.

I lost my smile and addressed Matteo. "I hate to tear you away from your beautiful beloved, but I need to discuss something with you."

He untangled himself from Quinn. "Excuse me, *mi amore*, I'll be back soon." He tilted her chin up. "We can finish our discussion when I get back."

Her eyes glinted. "The sun will be up soon," she reminded us both as we made our way outside.

Outside, the sky had lightened, humans local to Venice already starting their day.

"I assume the reason you're talking with me and not Carlos is because he's currently busy?" Matteo asked.

"You assume right," I confirmed.

"You heard back from Josef. What did he say?"

I frowned. "He didn't say much, but my gut tells me something isn't right. He was holding something back."

Matteo and I walked in silence for a moment. Gondolas that had parked for the night drifted past, gliding towards the docks where they'd meet the day's tourists. "Maybe he just wanted alone time with Aria," he suggested.

"I admire the way you've accepted that we claimed your daughter," I said. "But no. Something wasn't right. Something's happened, and he was determined to handle it himself, I think."

"You're thinking he doesn't want to worry you. Or us," Matteo surmised.

"Yes," I confirmed.

"Then it's not serious yet. If Josef thought they needed help, he would call you. After what he went through in Spain, I don't think he would take that lightly."

Before I could respond, pain echoed through my bond with Josef. Shards of pain in my shoulders, chest, and arms. Having leapt through windows before, I knew exactly what that pain was. I brushed a hand down my chest, almost expecting to find glass there.

"Something is definitely happening," I said. "He just jumped through a window."

"This close to sunrise?" Matteo asked.

Instead of pushing into his mind, I waited. A splinter of fear, and then agony. I fell to my knees. gasping in pain.

"Erik?" Matteo prompted.

'Josef!' There was no answer. I reached into his mind, only to find darkness. *'Josef?'* I tried to see through his eyes, but there was nothing, his mind unresponsive to me or my presence. I'd promised never to force my way in, so if he were awake, I'd be forced out and met with his anger.

"Josef's been shot from behind," I gasped out. I counted the points of pain I'd felt. "They missed his heart. Shoulder, between shoulder blades, lower back and his thigh. I think he's unconscious."

Matteo must have called out through his bond, as Quinn was there a moment later, followed by a shirtless Carlos.

"Erik," Carlos said, hand on my shoulder. "What's happening?"

I rose to my feet again. "I don't know. I'm certain Josef jumped through a window, and was shot."

"You were right to follow your gut feeling," Matteo said.

The first rays of dawn breached the horizon, eliminating the last of night's shadows. We retreated back to the den.

"Celeste," Carlos beckoned.

She joined us in the kitchen.

Carlos addressed us all, expression solemn. "We're going to San Marino. You have ten minutes to get ready. Sunglasses, pack a bag with clothes. Matteo, have our cars readied."

I hurried to my room, using speed to grab my magically enhanced sunglasses and throwing a couple of tee-shirts and pairs of jeans into a backpack. *'Hold on, Josef, we're coming.'* I instructed him, even though it was unlikely he could hear me.

In the kitchen, I paused at the sound of Carlos and Camila arguing.

"No, absolutely not," Carlos said with a tone that left no room for argument.

"Carlos, please. You tell me I'm part of the clan, but want to leave me behind? Would you leave Quinn or Celeste behind?"

"You know it's not because you're a woman. I've never been about that," Carlos maintained. "It's because you're human. We don't know what we're walking into. I will not risk you."

"You know there are Hunters, if Josef has been shot. I was a Hunter. I can help," she insisted. "My weapons, and my father's weapons will still be at the house." Her tone was tight at the suggestion of going for her weapons.

Carlos let out a frustrated sigh. "Camila, we're entering territory that doesn't belong to us. I haven't cleared our entrance with the clan there; so, we might not be a welcome sight to those who don't recognise us. To also have Hunters in the mix—"

"Then let me call my brother in," she said. "Carlos, you cannot leave me behind. You told me I'm your equal. Let me be your equal."

My admiration for her increased. She was not about to back down, proving herself in my eyes to be every part his equal.

"She has a point," I said, loud enough so Carlos could hear. "Can I just add that she is quite impressive, facing off with a vampire king the way she is? I don't think she's going to back down. A true warrior."

"She came into Venice alone with no idea how many vampires were here," Quinn agreed from her and Matteo's room. "She survived you, Carlos. I don't think there are too many Hunters who can boast that."

"We know you worry about keeping her safe from other vampires, her being a former Hunter, but she's right. She's part of the clan," Celeste added. "She wants to be there for Josef and Andreas, and even Aria as much as the rest of us. They're her clan, too."

"She's your Queen," Matteo added. "She's doing the same as any other Queen would do. Why should her being human get in her way?"

"Alright, okay, just stop," he told us. He sighed again. "It seems the clan has spoken up for you. You're all right. Camila, you are part of the clan. It just worries me to put you in unknown danger. Call your brother in."

I could almost see her smile. "Thank you, everyone," she said to us, voice warm with gratitude. The gentle sound of a kiss broke the silence.

"Okay, time to go," Carlos said to all of us. "You're not going near that house, though," he added to Camila. "If you want weapons, your brother can bring them."

To my knowledge, the house Camila had lived in had been Hunter-owned, but the Barones had taken over ownership of it.

The six of us left the villa. Vampires donned magically enhanced sunglasses to shield our eyes from the sunlight. Camila wore a pair she'd picked up from a tourist stand. Quinn turned on the security system that Andreas had set up for the den, and Matteo sent a text message on his phone, calling ahead for our cars. I was not one to leave the safety of the den during the day, and it had been a long time since I'd felt the warmth of the sun on my face.

I led the clan to the boat. It was a short ride to the mainland. Carlos's red Corvette, and my black Jeep awaited us, humans handing over the keys.

"Quinn, Matteo, you ride with Erik," Carlos instructed.

On the road, I focused on driving, while also trying to connect with Josef. "Whoever's hurt him, I'll tear them apart," I grumbled, a storm surging inside me.

From the back seat, Quinn put her hand to my arm. I met her eyes in the rear-view mirror. She glanced towards Matteo. Every part the concerned father, it was clear he was worried about Aria.

"We'll get her, too," I reassured him. "She's mine, as much as Josef is. If anyone has hurt her, they'll meet both our wrath. You haven't been reunited with her just to lose her."

He turned towards me, eyes red. "If anyone has hurt her, I will show them why they call me The Feral," he threatened. "They'll regret the day they were born."

After centuries of hating his feral nature setting him apart from the rest of us, he'd finally found peace with who he was with Quinn. She'd accepted every part of him, and even had the ability to break him out when he fell into that feral nature. Matteo would never willingly let himself go feral.

"I'll be right beside you," I said. "I may not be feral, but I'll be just as vicious. I'll let my inner beast out."

"That would be a sight to see," Quinn added.

Chapter 25

Josef was still unconscious when we were pushed into the cage, his form limp in my arms as they'd forced me to carry him. He'd shielded me from the arrows with his own body and attacked Pierre, only for the French vampire to punch him hard enough to knock him out.

The cage was carved out of stone in an open, underground cavern, lights lighting up every inch of the room, leaving no shadows. Iron bars clanged as the door was slammed behind me. Andreas stood over a seated Luca, arms folded over his chest. His shirt was torn, bloody. He pulled an arrow from Josef, who groaned in pain.

"Aria, are you alright?" Luca asked.

Andreas pulled out another arrow. "They missed his heart," he reported.

"Why bring us here, though?" I asked. "And what happened to you?"

"I left the shadows to assist two vampires under attack," he explained. "One died, the other fled." He pulled the last arrow from Josef, and we lay him down. "Considering Hunters were heading to Rome, there are a lot here." He glared at Luca. "This one claims he didn't know."

"Who died?" I asked.

"Sorry, I don't know her name, nor that of the one who escaped," Andreas said, apologetic.

"Thank you for trying to help." I breathed through pain. Someone from my clan had died. "Luca, why are you still here? This isn't the cage under our den, you should have escaped."

"The bars are sealed magically," Luca said

Frustration rose up. "You should never have been picked as Second," I grumbled. "You're no King! Kings are warriors, ready to tear the heart from the chest of those who challenge them. You...you're a child!"

He said nothing. But I wasn't done with my anger. "How the fuck did you allow Pierre to cage you?"

Josef chose that moment to awaken. He sat up with a grunt. "That hurt," he winced, and caught sight of Andreas. "Good to see you're alive." He took in our surroundings. "Caged. Great."

I helped him up. "You took those arrows for me. You shielded me."

He gave me a smile. "Couldn't let them shoot you now, could I? Matteo would never forgive me for letting his daughter get hurt so soon after your reunion."

Overcome by gratitude, I kissed him. "Such honour," I murmured. "But you could have gotten yourself killed. My father would have been just as upset over you being hurt. Or killed."

"He didn't want to kill us," Andreas pointed out. "Otherwise, we'd be dead."

Josef glared at Luca. "You walked us into a trap." He met Andreas's eyes, then mine. "I know I'm the link to our clan through Erik. I *cannot* call them into this."

"Agreed," Andreas said. "Bestowed Hunters are dangerous. A vampire working with a Hunter and bestowing them? Worse."

Josef grimaced. "And some will be waking up soon, new vampires. We used fresh blood as a distraction. I heard them feeding right before I got shot."

Andreas nodded. "I killed one, so he'll be in slumber, too."

"The only good thing from that is for the first few days, they'll be more focused on humans," I added. "Not us."

"Aria—"

I cut Luca off, anger burning in my chest. "No. Sit there and shut up. Josef's right. You called us into a trap. I'm your Second, Luca, and you put me at risk, and the clan. Furthermore, you risked Carlos's clan. Your King's!" I moved to the other side of the cell, not wanting to be near him. "You're a weak King." I sat with my back to the wall.

Josef sat next to me. "He's still your King," he said in a gentle tone.

"He got himself caged, and dragged us into this mess," I said.

Josef faced me. *'Is this anger fear-driven? It won't help.'*

'I was worried about you,' I confessed.

Sheer panic had stormed inside me when I'd felt the impact of the arrows through his body as his arms wrapped around me.

He lifted his hand, caressing my cheek "I'm okay. I didn't die," he reassured me, and he pressed his forehead to mine. "We're okay, Aria. So is Andreas."

Andreas sat on the other side of me. "We may not be so grateful soon," he said. "We're caged. And either he's going to kill us, or they're going to starve us." He eyed the door. "Hunters are involved, though, and we know what they like to do to vampires."

I frowned, leaning back against the wall. "Can't you…you know, blend with the shadows?"

He indicated around the cell. "Not if there *aren't* any shadows." He laughed. "And I still wouldn't get through those bars. Or the magic.

"Why has Pierre gotten Hunters involved? How did he even manage to do that?" I wondered.

"He was a Hunter before he was turned," Josef said. "We met about three hundred years ago, when he was human. We were in Paris, and a vampire of Celeste's clan had gone missing. They suspected Hunters had her. Our attempts to rescue her were unsuccessful. We took injuries, and I mortally wounded Pierre. He knew who I was, so I figured he'd seen the portrait of me as a First Hunter. We retreated, unable to get past the Hunters' defense."

"I'm assuming their captive vampire is the reason he still lives," Andreas muttered. "I wonder if she's still alive?"

Luca's eyes turned red. Hunger glinted within their depths.

"When did you last feed?" I demanded.

He met my eyes. "Pierre challenged me last night before I had a chance to go hunting."

Josef and Andreas turned towards him.

"When?" I prompted.

"Two days ago," he confessed.

I huffed in annoyance. "You should know better than to wait between feeds," I grumbled.

"We should probably get some sleep," Andreas said. "One of us keeps watch."

"I'll take first watch," Josef offered.

"I'll watch too," I added.

Josef raised his eyebrows at me.

"You were shot with arrows, and punched. You're going to be hungry soon, too," I pointed out.

He gave me a mock-disappointed pout. "Damn. I thought you volunteered so you could kiss me. Lean your perfect body against mine."

I laughed. "That too. But I don't need Andreas and Luca to be asleep for that."

He smirked.

"I'm a little hungry, too," Andreas admitted. "Being stabbed hurt, and I didn't feed nearly as much as I would like to have. I was mid-feed when I heard the struggle and went to investigate."

It sunk over us like black fog. Andreas and Josef would be hungry soon.

"I've seen enough starving vampires to know what's next," Josef muttered. "I've seen your father starving, too. We'll sink into madness, and probably try to attack each other, desperate for blood. Until we get human blood, we'll be much like the ferals."

I'd been hungry before, but not to the point of starvation. Marco had made sure of that. Andreas lay on the ground, hands rested on his stomach. He smiled up at us and closed his eyes. I leaned against Josef.

'Erik would have felt you get shot,' I pointed out. *'What will he do?'*

He put his arm around me. *'I shut myself off from him, so I'm hoping he didn't feel it. If they come here, they'll end up caged, too. I won't risk my clan like that.'*

I nodded. *'I know. I'd do the same for mine. It means we're in for a rough couple of days.'*

He squeezed. 'We are. But we'll get through it. Somehow."

Chapter 26

We pulled up behind Josef's car. Sunlight spilled over San Marino, the towers high on the mountain standing watch over the city. Their silhouettes stood out against the pale blue sky. Houses were grouped together, stone buildings and terracotta roofs.

Another car pulled up behind us, and the door opened. A man climbed out, and I watched him in the rear-view mirror. Quinn and Matteo turned around. His skin was the same warm brown as Camila's. His facial features and eyes matched hers. Her brother.

"That's him," Quinn said. "How did he get here from Spain so fast?"

"He went to Rome to pull Hunters out," Matteo said. "He was on his way to retrieve Camila from what he believes to be captivity in Venice."

"He believes that?" Quinn asked.

"You'd be surprised what Hunters believe when it comes to us," I said. "It's likely he's having trouble accepting she's with our King by choice. I'm not sure having him here is a wise decision, so we should probably be careful."

I climbed out, followed by Matteo and Quinn. I moved toward the convertible. Celeste stepped out from the front seat. In the back, Camila had lain down, her eyes closed.

"Camila, we're here," Carlos said, twisting around, shaking her awake. "Your brother's here."

She sat up and climbed out. "Diego!" She ran towards her brother but stopped short. Three other Hunters exited the same car Diego had. They stood next to him, crossbows ready, watching us warily. Knives and stakes were strapped to them.

Typical Hunters.

"Diego, you brought *them* with you?" Camila's voice shook, and she stepped back, standing halfway between us and the Hunters.

"I'm a Hunter, Camila. You can't expect me to be stupid enough to come into vampire territory alone," he said with a frown as he eyed us. "Besides, I promised them I'd drive them back to Spain. They lost family in Rome and we couldn't retrieve the bodies."

Carlos climbed from his seat, sunglasses in place. Diego's eyes shifted to him, expression unchanged.

"Carlos," Diego said with a nod.

"That's *King* Carlos to you, Hunter," Matteo snapped, voice sharp.

Carlos raised a hand, silencing Matteo. The motion was calm, measured. The direction of his gaze never left Diego's.

Diego didn't flinch, staring back at Carlos. An uneasy silence settled around us.

"Wait, how do you know he's Carlos?" Camila asked in alarm, breaking the silence.

One of the other Hunters pointed to Matteo. "That's clearly The Feral." His attention turned to me. "He doesn't look Spanish. If anything, he's a Viking."

I growled.

Camila turned her eyes to me, then addressed the Hunter. "Rafael, maybe don't call him that."

"You're defending a v—"

Diego silenced the Hunter. "Our father uploaded the photo of you two into the Network," he said to Camila. "War may have already begun in Rome, but some Hunters are on their way to Venice, if they're not there already. They know what Carlos looks like now."

I tensed. We'd have to be careful when we returned to Venice.

"Why are you warning them?" the Hunter, Rafael, asked.

Diego sighed. Without answering, he hugged Camila tight. "Are you okay?" he asked her. "Is this the choice you've made? How do I know they haven't compelled you?"

"We can't *compel love*," Matteo explained.

"I'm okay, Diego," Camila reassured her brother. "They haven't compelled me, I promise."

He pulled away, and grabbed her jaw, examining King Carlos's mark. Next to me, Matteo watched the Hunters. Carlos circled to stand on the other side of me.

"Diego, stop. You're hurting me," Camila pulled out of his grip.

In a heartbeat, Carlos put himself between Camila and Diego. The rest of us closed in around her.

Diego stood his ground, him and Carlos face-to-face.

"I didn't come here to challenge you, Vampire," Diego said. "I don't agree with my sister's choice, or that you've marked her so roughly, but I'm not our father. I won't do anything to hurt her. If she says you haven't compelled her, I'll believe her, until I see evidence suggesting otherwise.

She mentioned you need our help?"

I laughed. "Need the help of a Hunter? Not likely."

"Let's cool our heads," Carlos suggested, not turning his attention from Diego. "For now, we have a common need, to protect Camila—"

"Not that she needs it," Camila added.

"As she insisted on coming with us," Carlos continued. "Despite our reason for coming here, mi cazadora is quite determined to prove herself, not that she needs to." he smiled down at Camila. "She wouldn't be left behind, so I'm hoping your presence will mean peace of mind for myself. She's quite stubborn."

"You don't need to tell me," Diego replied with pride. "I'm happy that you *couldn't* control her."

"So how about we put our animosity aside for her sake," Carlos continued. "Your help would be appreciated."

No one moved.

"You can't be considering that!" Rafael exclaimed.

"I'm going to do what I can to keep *my sister* safe," Diego affirmed. "If that means I have to make a temporary truce with a vampire, I will." He held his hand out.

Carlos turned his eyes to Matteo, then me. We moved to stand next to him before he grasped Diego's hand. The two shook hands, and I relaxed.

"I have to say, I appreciate you sending my father's remains back," Diego acknowledged. "I've heard about the condition he was in, and I'm not particularly happy with that, but thank you. He should be buried in Spain." He looked at Camila and back at Carlos. "What do you need help with?"

"We are not hired muscle for parasites!" one of the Hunters said. "You should be eliminating these vampires. They killed your father, and have abducted your sister."

"Shut up, Miguel," Camila demanded, rolling her eyes. "I haven't been abducted. Our father killed a vampire in *their* territory in cold blood, *without* confirmation that the vampire had killed. Our father didn't care for The Accords."

"She's right. Shut up!" Diego said in a clear voice to his fellow Hunter.

"And lower your weapons. I don't want any trigger-happy accidents to spark tension here."

The Hunters exchanged glances, but lowered their crossbows.

"Thank you, Diego," Camila said.

Diego one-arm-hugged his sister as we followed behind them. I kept an eye on the other Hunters, but they were keeping their distance, watchful of us.

"Someone called Pierre challenged the King here," Carlos revealed. "Three of my own clan came here to help. I believe they've since been captured, or wounded."

"Pierre?" Diego asked. "You don't mean Pierre Moreau?"

"I have no idea what his last name is," Carlos said. "Who the fuck is Pierre Moreau?"

"A Hunter from the seventeen hundreds," Camila answered. "He became a vampire. Only he didn't turn out like Josef. He took down three French clans before he disappeared. Other clans that fell in similar style were thought to be him."

Celeste turned her head towards Camila fast, but said nothing. I touched her arm. She only shook her head. Knowing her pain, I didn't push, but let her feel my presence.

"There's been chatter about him lately from French Hunters," Diego added, reading from his phone. "The same Hunters who are logging that they're in San Marino."

"That answers that question," Carlos muttered. "There *are* Hunters here."

"So this Pierre Moreau is a vampire, but still a Hunter?" I asked. "And he's part of the clan here?"

"Diego, this is Giuseppe's territory," Miguel added.

"I know whose territory this is," Diego grumbled. "I am not particularly interested in helping Giuseppe," he said to Carlos. "Who of your clan are we looking for?"

"Giuseppe is dead," Matteo revealed. "I killed him."

"I have even less interest in helping Marco," Diego said.

"I killed Marco," Carlos said. "The new King is a young vampire named

Luca. He knelt to me after Giuseppe died."

Diego's eyes swept over each of us. "So this is your clan now. Your territory."

"It is," Carlos agreed. "But I let the new King maintain his rule, bonding him with Josef so I could have direct communication."

"Josef Alfaro?" Rafael asked. "The Traitor is here?"

I grinned at Matteo. This Hunter knew his vampires. "He has almost as many nicknames as Carlos," I commented. "Spoken with the same level of distaste."

"We're here for the vampire who challenged Luca," King Carlos instructed, giving me a slight smile. "You can do what you want to Pierre. Kill Luca, too, if you want. I have no need for such a weak King. His clan will remain untouched, as will mine."

As we entered San Marino, I was surprised to find no one greeted or stopped us. "Stay alert," I said, loud enough for the humans to hear.

The city's overpowering scent of pine reminded me of my last visit here. I would probably have met Aria then if Giuseppe hadn't met me at the border with Marco to conduct our business.

"I don't need a vampire to tell me how to do my job," one of the Hunters declared, glaring.

Matteo chuckled. "Making friends, Erik?" he asked.

I grinned. "Always."

Once again, I reached out to Josef, but he was either ignoring my calls, or still unconscious.

"Three hundred years," Celeste commented. "You were in France. That's when I met you."

"I remember," Carlos dropped back to walk beside Celeste, speaking to her in French. He kissed her.

Diego watched with a frown. Camila smiled up at him. "It's okay, Diego; Carlos is polyamorous."

"We're all polyamorous in a way," I said, loving the word. "We're not limited by human ideas of what love should be, who to love, or how many we can love. But we love equally."

"And you're okay with that?" Diego asked in a low voice. "He fucks other people? What have you gotten into, Camila? And those bruises!"

"Please, Diego, let's focus on the task at hand," Camila insisted. "You don't have to like that I chose a vampire. I don't need your permission for who I love."

Once again, I admired Camila. She had a strong will, and I was certain she had become even more steadfast in the days she'd been with us. Breaking free of her father's influence and now standing up to her brother. She was finding herself.

"He claimed Quinn, Matteo and Celeste too, but named Camila his Queen and Beloved," I added. "That makes her his primary."

"He claimed you?" Diego's voice rose.

"We have an agreement," Camila snapped. "He's not going to turn me unless I ask for it."

Brother and sister glared at each other, but it was Diego that backed down first.

"Fine," he grunted, and eyed me. "If it's Pierre Moreau, you and Josef fought him in France. It's in the Hunter records. Josef left him badly wounded; next thing, he's a vampire. There is more to the record, but the French Hunters have it hidden even from the rest of us."

"Why would a Hunter hide anything from other Hunters?" Quinn mused.

Carlos grabbed my arm, and we dropped back, letting the rest of them pull ahead. Matteo glanced back and nodded. The other Hunters were still watchful, but let us have our distance.

"I don't like this," Carlos muttered. "There are Hunters here, and we don't know where Josef, Aria, or Andreas are. We know that Josef was shot, but we have no idea if the others are okay. If Pierre is the one he speaks of, we don't even know what he looks like, just that he's French. Have you heard anything from Josef yet?"

"I don't like it either," I agreed. "I remember France. We got word a vampire had been captured by the Hunters, but were unable to get to her. I believe she was of the same clan as Celeste; that's how you met. We fought a few Hunters. One of them recognised Josef. We were up against an army, though, so we retreated. Not before Josef killed one and inflicted damage on another, who I assume could be Pierre."

"Everyone, stay aware," Carlos said to the rest of the clan. "We don't know who the clan is loyal to right now, and if this Pierre is the Hunter Diego spoke of, consider us in enemy territory."

Chapter 27

I didn't know if it was day or night, only that I had been awake for far too long. I just wanted to close my eyes. Andreas and Luca took watch and I lay down on the ground, waving Aria over. She lay down, snuggled into me, still in the silky black pyjamas, using me as a pillow, and she fell asleep instantly.

I stared at the ceiling. The cell was made of concrete and rock, the lights irritating.

"Sleep, Josef," Andreas said. "If anyone comes down, we'll wake you."

I closed my eyes, but opened them again when footsteps approached. I tapped Aria, and she sat up, saying nothing. Pierre stood on the other side of the bars, flanked by two Bestowed Hunters.

"Thanks to you, I had to kill my own men," Pierre said. "There was no bond, and I couldn't have ferals wandering around my city."

I scoffed. "*Your* city."

"Good to see you again, Josef. This time, I have the upper hand."

"You have me caged," I said. "Why don't you step in here, and let's see who has the upper hand?"

Instead of answering, he turned his attention to Luca. "I have no use for you any more. You did what I needed." More Hunters entered, and Pierre opened the cage. "Kill him. We'll have some fun with the others as we wait for their clan. I need to return to the den, take my place as King."

Aria was on her feet in an instant. Andreas and I followed her, forming a line in front of Luca. Weak King or not, we weren't going to let him die.

"Get out of the way, Aria," Pierre snapped.

'He wants to keep us alive for some reason,' Aria said. *'Any one of us would kill someone in our way without a second thought.'*

I agreed with her, but didn't respond. "You're a traitor to your own kind," I growled at Pierre. "Working with Hunters?"

He laughed. "Funny. That's what Hunters say about you." Ten Hunters stormed into the cage. "Step aside, now."

I bared my fangs. They were Bestowed, but still human, and nowhere near as strong as a vampire. And I was hungry. Beside me, the others growled in warning. The Hunters approached anyway. I reached for one, ready to tear into her throat, but she shoved a dagger into my gut. Two other Hunters attacked in unison.

I hissed as white-hot pain tore through me, radiating from my stomach. I released the Hunter, staring down at a wooden stake and two daggers buried deep in my flesh. Fury ripped away my control, and I let the red haze rise up.

'Josef,' Erik's voice was far away, and I ignored it.

I sank my fangs into a throat and shook my head, leaving nothing but a gaping wound before facing another, whose red eyes were filled with fear. I snarled. Driven by hunger and fury, I took down three Hunters before agonising pain cut through my frenzy like a blade. A gasp. Aria's. I stopped, finding Pierre's hand inside her chest. She was trying to hold the pain and fear from me, but I felt it as my own. Terror thrummed through our bond.

Luca was on his knees, a sword to his throat, Andreas snarling as he struggled against the point of a sword to his chest.

"Stop, or I'll kill her," Pierre warned. "Let's see how The Feral reacts when he learns you got his daughter killed."

I froze. Blood of the three Hunters whose throats I'd torn out dripped from my mouth. A lot more Hunters had come in than I knew about. All of them had red eyes, Bestowed. We were outnumbered. Pain blazed in my chest, as if Pierre's hand were gripping my own heart.

"You choose, Josef. The Feral's daughter, or the weak King," Pierre demanded.

I was blood bonded to both Luca and Aria and would feel the death either way. I'd experienced my maker's death, a century after the war, and that of my own fledgling twenty years ago. Pain like no other. But the decision was simple. Luca's death would break Carlos's control of *Famiglia di Sammarinese*, but I couldn't hurt Matteo like that.

"Let her go," I said, resigned.

"Josef, please," Luca pleaded. "Carlos promised—"

"It's my clan over yours," I told him, meeting Aria's eyes. "She's not part of our clan yet, but she will be." I glared at Pierre. "I've made my choice," I softened my voice. "Do not hurt her."

"Do I observe some affection there?" Pierre scoffed. "I'd love to see that conversation with her father."

I didn't move, didn't blink, my eyes on his hand. Slowly, he removed it. I almost breathed a sigh of relief that her heart was not in his grip. Aria whimpered.

"Over there," he pointed to the other side of the cell. "All of you."

I pulled Aria to me, wrapping my arms around her protectively, and the three of us backed away. She gasped in pain, and I kissed the top of her head.

"You're okay," I whispered. *'You're alive, Aria.'*

She burrowed into my shoulder, trembling in my arms, both of us shaken. I tightened my embrace around her, resting my chin on her head. The world stood still for a moment, her pain through our connection subsiding as the wound from Pierre's hand closed. Echoes of the pain remained, and whispers of hunger began to shift through my veins. Mine? Or Aria's? I couldn't be sure. Maybe both.

I moved Aria behind me, and Andreas stood shoulder to shoulder with me. Both of us protecting her.

"Give me that. I want the honour of doing this," Pierre said, voice heavy with glee.

We blocked the view from Aria as Pierre took the sword from the Hunter and decapitated Luca. There was no way to protect Aria from the sickening sound of the blade cutting through flesh, or the loud thud of Luca's head, followed by his body hitting the ground. Pierre swung so hard, metal struck stone. I'd seen plenty of vampires killed in that manner during the war, some at my own hand when I'd been human.

I grunted in pain as my own throat felt like a blade was slicing through it. Luca's death was quick, but I still felt it, excruciating pain pushed through our collapsing blood bond. I fought to stay on my feet.

Grief flooded through from Aria. *"Bastardo,"* she hissed.

I watched Pierre give a satisfied smirk to the Hunters around him.

"King of the Bestowed," Andreas muttered. "Why topple a King for the role if you hate us that much?"

Pierre chuckled, a low sound. Light caught his fangs, glinting off the tips.

"How did you maintain the Hunter mindset?" I blurted. "Becoming a vampire should have killed that part of yourself."

Pierre's smile widened. "Why? Wish you'd been able to hold onto yourself when you turned?"

"I never looked back!" I said. "The slumber is supposed to remake everything about you. Give you that vampire nature to replace the humanity. That's what comes with experiencing a mortal death."

"Make me a killer?" he said with amusement. "Oh, I never denied my nature. Aria can attest to that. I gave in to my nature with joy. I also used my new-found strength to kill vampires in the most brutal way possible." He glanced down at Luca's head, and kicked it. "Sometimes nothing beats the blade of a sword."

Without another word he walked out. Leaving us alive and looking at each other in trepidation. The cage slammed shut, and Pierre paused, watching all of us.

"Why did you have to kill him?" Aria spat, pointing to where Luca's body still lay. "You challenged him and won."

"Because he had served his purpose." Pierre shrugged. "He got you all here. Now we wait for the rest of your clan. I assume you've called them for help."

"No," I countered. "I'll not call them into an ambush. You want La Voz, you'll have to challenge King Carlos on his territory."

Pierre left, taking the Hunters with him.

'Josef!' Erik's voice broke through again. I recalled hearing him when I'd been fighting. *'Josef, are you alright? Answer me, goddammit.'*

'I'm okay, Erik,' I replied.

His presence flooded in as I let him in - comforting.

'What happened, veiðimaðr minn?' Even his voice was soothing.

'Nothing,' I lied.

'Don't lie to me, Josef,' he growled. *'You know I felt your pain, and you fell into a frenzy.'* He paused. *'I know why you're doing this. It won't work. We're coming for you. All of you.'*

'Please, Erik, don't,' I pleaded, giving in. *'I won't endanger you. Or anyone else. Turn around and go home.'*

His silence disturbed me. I waited for him to reply. *'Erik?'*

'It's a little too late for that, my beloved. We're already here,' he said finally.

Chapter 28

I had cursed at the downfall of rain that began not long after we started to climb the slope of San Marino. We'd been trying to find them unsuccessfully all day, the rain washing away any scent of Josef,

Andreas, or Aria. Not having been to the den, we didn't know where it was. The sun was setting when we regrouped at the edge of a nature park, and I was finally able to connect with Josef. He didn't sound relieved. Instead, I was met by horror, our bond pulsing with fear and dread.

'Tell me what's happening,' I instructed Josef.

As he filled me in, I repeated it for those around me.

"Luca is dead," I said, meeting Carlos's eyes, then Matteo's. "Aria is okay. As much as she can be after having Pierre's fist in her chest. Pierre forced Josef to choose between Luca or Aria dying."

Matteo growled, but said nothing. Quinn touched his arm. The Hunters tensed, their eyes on Matteo.

"Andreas is with them, but unable to use the shadows. They're caged. And they're hungry."

Josef continued talking through our bond. I'd known he'd been blocking our bond, but something had happened to weaken his defence. Possibly hunger, but it was more likely Luca's death had sent his mental walls crumbling.

"There is an army of Hunters here," I relayed. "Fuck, they're Bestowed."

Diego and the other Hunter's brows furrowed. "Bestowed?" Diego asked.

"See, I told you, your Hunter records are lacking," Carlos reminded Camila. She smirked in response. Carlos pulled her into his arms, and murmured sweet words of affection to her in Spanish.

"'Bestowed' is our term for a human who has been gifted a taste of our blood," Celeste explained.

The Hunters recoiled and their gazes averted.

"That is no gift," Diego said, voice hard-edged. "Any Hunter who experiences that would chain themselves up."

"Well, these Hunters aren't chained up," I said. "On the streets walking around, they're as much a danger to your precious humans you like to protect as they are to us. Especially if they turn. Josef says they're not bonded. They'll turn feral."

'Pierre kept Luca alive long enough to bring us here,' Josef continued.

"Now he's using the three of them to bring the rest of us," I repeated to those around me. No wonder Josef wasn't happy to learn we were already here. "We've walked into an ambush and we face an army of Bestowed Hunters."

"It's okay, Erik. We've done this before," Carlos said, the affection in his face hardening to that of the General I'd known in the war. "This time we have Hunters on *our* side." He chuckled. "Somewhat similar to when Josef joined us."

"We're not on your side, Bloodsucker," Miguel said. "Don't compare us to that traitor."

I growled.

"Truce," Diego reminded them. "We need to be focused. If we have infected Hunters to face, they'll be stronger than us. Faster. Not as fast as a vampire, but still a challenge for us."

The battle was about to start, and lines had been drawn. I could never have imagined we'd have Hunters standing with us. I didn't entirely trust them, and it was clear they were as wary of us.

A glint of worry shone from Diego's eyes. I lifted my wrist, and tore into it with my fangs, holding it out towards the Hunters. "Care to even the playing field?" I asked with a smirk.

A shiver of revulsion shook Diego as he eyed my wrist.

Matteo chuckled. "Erik, your blood is far too old. What they need is something more…*feral*." He bit his own wrist, holding it out.

"Oh, no. I think they'd prefer royalty," Carlos chimed in. "The blood of a King, and a descendant of the Bloodking's line."

Celeste and Quinn laughed as Carlos bit his own wrist. Camila elbowed him, and he licked at his blood, pulling his arm away.

"Alright, stop!" Diego burst out, his eyes narrowed. "We will not allow ourselves to be poisoned with your blood. I don't know what Hunter in their right mind would have agreed to that, but if they did that willingly, then they are now our enemy."

My wrist sealed itself closed, and I shrugged, licking the blood from where the wound had been.

"But they're Hunters," the unnamed Hunter said.

"Not anymore, they're not. They stand with a vampire," Diego grumbled.

The Hunters looked around at us.

"What we have is a truce," Diego said. "There's a difference. Stop wasting time; we need a plan of attack." Then he turned his narrowed eyes towards Carlos. "King Carlos, I believe you're the most experienced among us in that department." He hesitated, and let out a slow breath. "I put my trust in you."

For a split second, Carlos seemed taken aback. I smirked at Matteo at Diego's slight of me.

"I guess I'm not as famous as our King," I said, chuckling. "My experience in the same war means nothing."

Diego met my gaze, unflinching. "Oh, I know *exactly* who you are," he said, eyeing me distastefully. "You have a reputation as brutal as that of your King. I'd rather deal with him. He's the one my sister is connected to."

Camila's light touch on my arm had me looking down at her. "He's trying," she vouched. "We've all been taught to hate vampires. It's all we've known."

I lowered my head to whisper in her ear. "I've known that animosity for centuries. I live to antagonise Hunters; let me have my fun, young Queen."

She smiled, eyes darting back to Diego. He had been watching us, and returned his focus to Carlos.

"Alright," Carlos interjected. "Before anything, we need to feed. Now, before you Hunters get worked up over that, we're also going to use it to draw the Bestowed Hunters to us. I want to see how many there actually are. Take them out."

"How do you plan to do that?" Diego asked, voice losing its hard edge.

"Once we've fed, I will leave my…human in here. Give us half an hour. Then we wait. The blood should draw them in. They'll be expecting us, but you'll be an unexpected surprise."

"That surprise might be enough of an advantage," Diego agreed, nodding. "We'll get more weapons while you're…hunting." He then addressed the other Hunters. "All Bestowed Hunters and any vampires with them are our targets tonight."

"Make sure you burn them, remove their heads or hearts," I added.

"Otherwise, in a day, you'll have ferals. You may think you know all there is with your histories, but unless you've faced a feral, you have no idea of their blood thirst and strength. Vampires in a permanent frenzy cannot be stopped easily. We at least have the ability to resist the call of human blood when we're not hungry. They do not. All they want is to kill. Many of your ancestors died trying to eliminate them after the war."

Carlos lowered his eyes to Camila, squeezing her hand. "*Mi Reina,* you go with your brother." He smiled at Diego. "I know you'll return my Queen to me unharmed."

"I'd never allow her to be hurt," Diego confirmed. "But you know she can handle her own."

Carlos laughed. "Oh, I know. She's not ready to watch me feed on another human, though, so she's safer with you right now."

Camila didn't argue, but her eyes showed doubt. Carlos kissed the top of her head. She followed her brother but glanced back at us once before walking away.

"Here, I know you gave up the life, but at least take this," Diego suggested, handing her a dagger. "I have a crossbow in the car you can use, too." He scowled down at her. "Don't look so miserable, Camila. I'll get you back to your vampire King when this is over." He elbowed her. "I missed you. I'm glad he didn't kill you." He looked back at us and smiled. "He seems genuine in his affection for you, at least. I don't understand it, but I won't hurt you. They're under my protection, for now."

"High praise from a Hunter," I said to Carlos.

"Come, we have half an hour to feed, and set our trap," Carlos declared.

Chapter 29

The three of us lay in a huddle on the concrete floor, in the corner furthest from the cell door. Josef held me in his arms, and Andreas pressed against my back. I had long healed from having my chest punched open, but the memory of the pain remained. Hunger had set in, and the heartbeats of the Hunters nearby only made my canines ache.

"By the time they find us, if they do, madness will have already taken us," I worried.

"Erik's begged me to let him track us," he said. "To use the bond to find us."

"Right," Andreas said. "I'm assuming you won't."

"You assume correctly," Josef agreed. "Lead them to an army of Bestowed Hunters? We've already lost one member at the hands of a Hunter."

"You did?" I asked.

"Lorenzo was killed by Camila's father," he explained. "We killed him for it, though."

"You all accept Camila?" I sat up, leaning my back against the stone wall. "You're okay that your King fell in love with a Hunter?"

"We've never denied who someone loves," Josef said. "It's a lot, with who she was, but she's not a Hunter anymore." He smiled. "I used to be a Hunter; no one held that against me."

"Erik even calls him Hunter in affection," Andreas said. "In his Norse language."

"I didn't know you spoke Norse." Josef laughed. "You have no reason to fear the young Huntress," he said to me. "She's as much in love with Carlos as he is with her. She may be human, but she let her heart make her choice. She's one of us."

"Now, what are we going to do about our situation?" Andreas pushed. "And the insane vampire who thinks he's still a Hunter."

"I don't understand Pierre," I muttered. "He's been with us for a century. He had every chance to kill us."

"Maybe Marco and Giuseppe's deaths were a convenience for him," Josef suggested. "It could be they were too strong for him? Without them, he could bring the Hunters in, challenge your new King, and put his plan into action."

As if he heard his name, Pierre entered the cell again, watching us from the other side of the bars. "You look hungry," he commented.

"Fuck off," I growled.

"You would have made a good King's Queen," he sneered at me.

"You're a Hunter, why do you care about being King?" I asked.

"He's tasted our power, and is addicted to it," Josef mused.

"You call Josef a traitor, yet *you're* the traitor," Andreas countered, standing. "You betray vampires and humans alike. You Bestow Hunters and bring them into the city. Risky, considering they're not bonded. What's to stop them from giving in to that hunger? You'd have an army of ferals tearing this city apart. If you're convinced you're still a Hunter, isn't it your job to protect the humans?"

"They've trained their whole lives to resist that hunger," Pierre said. "They know the risk."

"Where is the clan?" I asked. Despite my hunger, worry for my clan became a weight against my chest. I hoped he hadn't killed them.

"They're alive, if that's what you're worried about," he confirmed. "Although, Angelina is dead. Veronica got away to warn the clan that there are Hunters here. They're hiding in the den."

So *that's* who Andreas had helped, giving up his cover of the shadows. A surge of grief hit me all at once. For Angelina, and for the danger my clan were in. I wouldn't let him see that, though.

"Are you done taunting us?" Andreas asked. "I find your presence irritating, and I'm hungry, so forgive my short patience."

Pierre laughed, a low, chilling sound. "Bring them in," he said.

Human heartbeats echoed through my head, and I clung to Josef tighter. His grip on me was just as desperate, eyes turning red. Andreas straightened, but remained where he was. Two humans were led in by Bestowed Hunters.

None of us moved; the sight of humans held us mesmerised. Their heartbeats thundered within the cell, each beat calling to the predator within. My fangs lengthened; hunger taking over all thought.

"You look hungry," Pierre said again. "I'll leave these right here." He turned to the Hunters behind him. One was large, with brown hair; the other had darker hair, more slight of build. "Stay here," he instructed. "I have a Kingless clan to take control of."

"You'll kill them?" the larger Hunter asked.

Pierre's eyes were trained on my face. "First a little fun. Then I'll get to that. I need them to kneel to me before I do. As the other clans did. Destroyed from the inside by their own king."

He left. I watched the Hunters. They were fighting their own hunger. One licked his lips, the other's eyes kept darting towards the humans.

"Do you hear their heartbeats?" I asked the Hunters. "Don't you want a taste?"

Their jaws clenched, but they said nothing, only glared at me.

"What are you doing?" Josef asked.

"Pierre said they've trained to resist the hunger. But the ones at the house gave in and fed after we left behind those humans bleeding out, for a distraction," I reminded him. "It was too great a temptation, as it would be for any vampire."

"Quinn and Camila have been Bestowed; they'd know what the hunger felt like as a human," Andreas said.

"So has Erik," Josef said.

Andreas and I both turned our attention to Josef. "He has?" we asked in unison.

"He described the hunger. He'd never experienced such need. The vampire blood, even a small taste, pushes the body to want more. He said even the scent of his brother's blood was overpowering. But Amara offered him hers, distracting him from falling on his brother and feeding."

"The human mind isn't made to cope with that hunger," Andreas added. "The first Hunter I ever met I Bestowed for the fun of it. He had no resistance, and other Hunters killed him before he finished feeding."

Josef eyed the Hunters. "How do Hunters train for that?" He slipped out from my embrace, guiding me to lean on Andreas. His movements were slow, his hunger showing. The Hunters watched him warily. One raised his crossbow and fired it at Josef. Catching the bolt with one hand, he stood at the door.

"Who's hungry?" Josef asked. He gripped the bars. "Come here, sweet thing," he cooed.

One of the humans meant to tempt us walked forward. Before the Hunters could fire on Josef again, he used the tip of the bolt to slice open the human's throat. Blood sprayed, and the human crumpled to the ground. The remaining human stared in shock at his companion. His lack of screaming or running hinted at him being compelled. Compulsion or not, he was still terrified, and the scent of his fear emanating from him threatened to drive me into a frenzy.

I licked my lips at the scent of blood in the air, my hunger flaring again. But I held back, curious. Andreas's body shook next to mine. Both Hunters stared at the fallen human. The blood. The familiar glint of hunger showed in their red eyes.

"Go on, I know you want it," Josef said. "It's okay. You'll enjoy the taste. You cannot deny what your body wants. Consider it a gift."

One of the Hunters licked his lips again.

'Got him,' Josef said through our bond with satisfaction.

I moved to stand beside Josef, Andreas next to me. I caught the bigger Hunter's eye, leaning on his mind.

"A taste," I whispered. "Breathe that scent in. Doesn't he smell delicious?"

"Such a waste of all that blood," Josef muttered under his breath.

"So close, if not for these bars," Andreas agreed.

"You're the one who slashed his throat instead of feeding," I pointed out.

"Stop trying to compel me, bitch," the Hunter said. "Pierre already compelled me to resist your compulsion."

I growled in frustration.

"But did he compel you to resist *that*?" Josef asked, pointing. "Look at it. Imagine how it tastes. All that blood. Just for you."

The Hunters couldn't look away. Neither could I. Andreas had said it himself. If it weren't for the bars, we'd be feasting. Instead, we were caged and hungry as a human bled out right in front of us.

Andreas bit into his own wrist.

"What are you doing?" I asked, alarmed. *Is he already in a frenzy?*

"Maybe it's not human blood that you crave," Andreas said. "Perhaps it's vampire blood that you desire." He held his hand through the bar. "Feed. Give your body what it *really* wants."

The smaller of the Hunters moved across the cell as if in a trance. He stopped before Andreas, looking up at him before returning his gaze to the blood.

"Henri, stop!" the other Hunter shouted, raising his crossbow.

I moved closer to Andreas, as did Josef. The Hunter lowered his mouth to Andreas's wrist. He groaned, and lifted his eyes to the three of us. Andreas stepped back from the bars, and the Hunter followed.

"Dinner is served," Andreas declared with a grin.

I grabbed the poor fool at the same time Josef did. We pulled him hard against the bars, but he paid us no attention. I brought his wrist to my mouth.

"Need support!" The other Hunter cried out, and before we could feed, he fired every last bolt in his crossbow.

Five new Hunters ran down the stairs into the cell, firing their own. Bolts hit my body, and a Hunter pulled my meal away from me. A growl broke free as I tried to reach out for him, for anything close enough. Instead more bolts and arrows hit me. Andreas' and Josef's growls echoed with fury and pain.

I backed off, pulling the bolts from my body, their sting subsiding as I let them clatter to the ground. A thud followed by another pulled my eyes back to the Hunters. The head of the one who'd fed from Andreas had been separated from his body.

"He knew the risk," the larger Hunter declared to those around him.

Andreas smirked as the Hunters dragged the body up the stairs. The larger one remained, glaring at us.

"That was my cousin you made me kill," he said.

Andreas shrugged. "He knew the risk," he repeated.

"If you pull that stunt again, *you'll* be the one to lose your head," the Hunter threatened us.

He followed the others out, looking back once.

"Well, that was a complete failure," Josef said to Andreas. "We didn't get to feed, and now we're worse off than before. Now, I'm not even healing properly." He pressed fingers against an angry red scar over his ribcage.

I examined where I'd been struck. While my body was still healing, scars were remaining. I needed to feed.

“Actually, it wasn’t,” Andreas argued. “We learned quite a great deal from that.”

Chapter 30

I'd come so close to feeding, I could almost taste the blood. My jaw tightened, mood darkening, the taste of defeat bitter.

"Did I miss something?" Aria asked, tone indicating she was as displeased as I was.

"You asked how they trained," Andreas said. "It occurred to me that they may have been Bestowed multiple times. Humans have been known to become addicted to our venom. What if the same thing is possible with our blood? When you described what Erik said, I figured I'd put my theory to the test." He turned, eyeing where the dead human still lay, in a puddle of blood after I'd slit her throat. "Their training would have included someone bleeding in front of them. You saw how they struggled when you did that. I couldn't help but wonder if they'd be more tempted by the scent of our blood."

I paced the cell, bare feet pattering on the cold concrete. "But we're still hungry," I complained.

I glanced down at my bare chest again; angry scars remained where the bolts had hit me.

"Who did that?" Pierre had returned. He glared at Aria. "You're trying to get my descendants to feed?"

A Hunter stood at his side with a bow. Taking it, Pierre loaded the bow, pulling back the string. He aimed the arrow at Aria.

"Actually, it was me," I said. Aria had taken more of an injury than Andreas and I had. I wouldn't let her be hurt again.

"Shut up," Pierre said, and fired.

I moved fast to stop the arrow—the same instinct that had worked with the bolt minutes before—but my body wasn't responding. I was too hungry. As I tried to catch the arrow, I missed, and it pierced my neck. Agony ripped through me, and I grunted in pain, snapping the shaft and pulling it out. The wound closed slower than usual, but a mark remained. I needed blood. It wouldn't be long before I stopped healing completely. By that point I'd possibly fall into a frenzy. I could already feel it, deep within my chest, hunger clawing at me.

'Josef!' Aria's voice was pained. Her expression tightened, as if she'd felt the echo of pain through our bond.

Shit. That meant Erik would be feeling everything, too. I tried to close myself off, but I no longer had the strength.

'Josef.' Erik's voice broke through my pain. *'Josef, please let me find you.'* His voice was tight with desperation. *'We will bathe in their blood!'*

All it would take was to use our bond to reach out to him. To call for help. Erik would feel the pull, as would our King. They'd come. I wanted to see Erik, for him to open the cage, for the two of us to tear into the throats of the Bestowed Hunters. But I couldn't risk him, or the clan. Pierre *wanted* them to come, which meant he would have his army waiting for their arrival.

"That's the second time you've taken arrows for her," Pierre said. "I'm starting to think there's something between the two of you." He loaded the bow again.

I stood in front of Aria, glaring at Pierre. Andreas stood beside me, giving me a grim nod.

"Which one should I shoot?" Pierre laughed.

The large Hunter from before entered the cell and pointed at me. "Josef's the one who killed her," he said, nodding to the body on the ground. "He's the one who fed my cousin his blood." He raised a shaking arm to Andreas.

I'd wasted blood in killing the human to tempt Hunters, instead of feeding from her myself, or offering her to Aria and Andreas. My impending frenzy—and Aria's and Andreas'—were my own fault.

I stepped forward, growling. "Leave them alone."

"You know, you were an inspiration," Pierre said with a smug smile that made me want to punch him. "You became the enemy, destroying Hunters who trusted you. After our fight, I came too close to dying for comfort. Luckily, we had a vampire whose blood we could use to help me." He smirked. "But when I was struggling with hunger, from my, what you call 'Bestowed' state, I took inspiration from what you'd done centuries before. I could be the vampire that destroyed clans from within."

"You shouldn't have been able to hold on to the Hunter part of yourself," I pushed.

"You know as much as I do that some still have it in them to do so," Pierre countered. "I guess I'm one of the lucky few."

"That was a risk," Andreas said. "You risked a lot—for the sake of what?"

Pierre ignored him, and he spoke to the Hunters in French. Then he loaded the bow again. This time I had no energy to move, and the arrow hit me in the chest. The momentum landed me on my back. Aria and Andreas knelt over me. Erik raged in my head, but it was all swallowed up by pain and hunger.

Andreas gripped the arrow's shaft, eyes glinting. "My apologies," he said.

I braced myself. When he pulled, fire and white-hot pain spread from my chest; burning hunger seared my veins. A feral scream tore from me.

"Why are you doing this?" Aria demanded. "Torturing us? Why don't you just kill us?"

"Because it's not your deaths that will bring the others, it's your pain," Pierre said. "I have a chance to take down two clans. Until you bring them here, you'll only get pain."

Andreas helped me up, and I leaned on him for support, breathing hard. Each time an arrow struck, I descended more into darkness, pushed further towards frenzy.

"Josef, you're not healing," Andreas warned me. "Stop getting yourself shot."

The intoxicating scent of blood flooded my senses. I lunged across the room, curling my fingers around the metal bars, the jolt of magic stopping me from breaking free. Hunger and rage merged, pulling me under the frenzy. I snarled as I shook the bars. Mocking laughter echoed from the man on the other side of the door, red eyes filled with delight.

"Call them here, and I'll end your suffering," he offered.

I growled again in response, snapping my teeth.

'Josef, stop,' a woman's voice said in my head.

The vampire on the other side of the door pulled a human towards me. Trickles of blood on her throat held me immobile. I yearned to bite and let the blood flow. The vampire watched me as he pulled the woman to him, and lowered his mouth to her throat.

Once again I was hit by the scent of blood. The human's wrist was lifted towards me, and I lunged for it.

'Josef,' two voices called out to me, silently. I ignored them, ready to feed.

The moment my fangs pierced her flesh and I got a taste, the human was gone. Yanked from my grasp. I lunged for her again, unable to reach what I needed. Hands pulled at me, moving me away from the bars. I snarled.

'Josef, it's okay.' The woman's voice again. *'Josef, look at me.'*

Her hand cupped my cheek, pulling my gaze to her. But all I saw was the curve of her throat. I struck, delighted to be feeding, but annoyed that there was no sustenance in her blood. I was torn from her, thrown against the bars. On my feet in an instant, I advanced on her again.

"Josef, stop!" This time a male voice, echoing around me as a brown-haired man stood between me and the woman.

"He's already gone. Damn, I would have liked to have tormented him some more," the man on the other side of the bars said.

'Josef, come back. I know you're hungry, you need to bring yourself out of the frenzy.' Again, a faraway voice in my head. *'Grab the necklace. Focus on that. Focus on where you got it. On the person who gave it to you.'*

I clutched the pendant and a face flickered in my mind, emerging through the fog. Long blond hair, a beard, and grey eyes that met mine with a smile.

The two of us were naked in a hotel room, a human slept next to us, our fang marks in his neck and arms. Erik kissed me with a rough need that sent shivers down my spine, pinning me to the bed. His tongue teased mine, savouring me. My desire for him stole my breath, raw, unrestrained. A scorching hunger pulsed between us through the dark tether of our blood bond. He growled low in his chest—the sound primal, vibrating through my chest. Heat coiled deep within me, unleashing waves of hunger.

I was entirely his, our mouths and bodies pressed together, and he pulled out of the kiss, only to sink his fangs into my throat. I moaned as he released the full effects of his venom. My fingers traced over the tattoos on his chest. Erik pulled away, reaching for the Mjölnir pendant that had hung around his neck ever since I'd known him.

"This belonged to my brother," he said, removing it from around his neck. "I pulled it from his body before his funeral. I may not have grieved him the way I wish I could have, but he was still my brother, and I loved him. A piece of my heart, next to yours wherever you go. A token to bind you to me, to remind you who you belong to."

He held it out for me to take.

"I can't take this," I said. "Erik, you've always worn this. It connects you to your brother...to your gods."

"I think my gods have long since turned their back on me." A ghost of a smile appeared. "Now it connects us. My love is eternal, Josef. We're one."

Without waiting, he leaned forward, pulling the pendant over my head. His own, blood-infused body had warmed the metal that now rested against my chest. I held it in my fingers, speechless. This pendant meant everything to Erik. He kissed me again. "I love you, Veiðimaðr minn."

"Josef," Aria's voice tore me from the memory

Her brown eyes were full of concern. I reached for the mark I'd left in her throat.

"You're not healing," I said, voice rough.

She kissed me, relief flooding through our bond. "Neither are you."

'Josef?' Erik's voice was shaky.

'I'm okay,' I said, gripping his necklace again, anchoring myself in Erik's presence. "I'm okay," I said out loud to Aria and Andreas. *'Erik, I don't know how long this will work. I'm wounded and hungry. We all are.'*

'Then let me find you,' he pleaded. *'Let us end this.'*

I turned my head, where Pierre had been. He'd killed the human, leaving the body to taunt me, us. I glanced at the Bestowed Hunters. They were waiting to kill Erik. And Carlos. Camila. Matteo, Quinn, and Celeste. Cold twisted around my spine, seeping into my bones. I would die in here.

'I can't, Erik. I'm sorry.'

Chapter 31

Josef's desperation to protect me, and the clan, would have been noble, if I hadn't experienced his pain, and felt him slip into a frenzied state of mind. I struggled to retain a sense of calm. Someone was hurting him, and I wanted to tear them apart. I stood next to Carlos as we watched the human from the shadows. The human sat on a park bench not moving, blood trickling from Carlos's bite mark. The scent was tantalising, enough to draw out anyone with vampire blood in them.

"We need to be finding them," I muttered, clenching my fists. "Not hiding in the dark for inferior humans who think they can take us down because they have a little vampire blood."

"Come on, Erik, get your mind focused," Carlos instructed.

"It *is* focused," I growled. "On the pain Josef feels every time they shoot him. I had to pull him out of a frenzy. But he's still on the edge. He's wounded and starving, Carlos. And he won't let me track him."

He put a hand on my shoulder. "We will find them. This is how we do it. I need you here."

He was right, but it didn't change that I wanted to go on a killing spree until I found them.

"I'm here," I confirmed and pointed to the Hunters. "Why don't you get one of them to walk the human through the streets as if they're helping her? It might be faster. Higher chance of finding the Bestowed Hunters."

"I did think of that," Carlos agreed. "I'm not sure the Hunters want anything to do with something I've fed on."

I chuckled. "I love how disgusted they were. I think Diego can be reasoned with, though."

We turned our heads to where Camila waited with her brother. The crossbow in her hand was a reminder of who she'd been. But she didn't hold it like the other Hunters did, at the ready. She pointed it down, shoulders hunched like it was a burden. Her mouth was downturned, eyes doubtful.

"She's going to get herself killed," I worried aloud. "Whether she wants to or not, she needs to be as vigilant as she would have been before she met you."

Without a word, Carlos walked over to Diego and Camila. He closed his hands over hers, guiding her to raise the crossbow, the arrow aiming at his chest.

"I know you don't want this, Camila, and you'll never have to hold one again when we go home," he promised. He kissed the top of her head, then turned towards Diego. "We're moving our trap," he said. "You'll become part of it."

From where I stood, it appeared Diego was battling himself, before he nodded. "What do you need me to do?"

"Walk the hu-woman. Maybe walk her home as if you're helping her. They may have their guard down with another Hunter."

"It's better than waiting," Diego agreed.

Carlos returned to the woman on the bench, and Diego followed him.

"I never imagined I'd see the day we worked with Hunters," Matteo said. "Especially with the descendants of the First Hunters."

I forced myself to remain where I was. Camila and Diego were the descendants of Amara's murderer. The night of her death rose up from the depths of my mind, one I had relived many times, wishing I could have saved her.

I lifted my mouth from the throat of the human. Amara did the same. Her red eyes met mine before she pulled me to her for a kiss. I melted against her naked body, her warmth seeping into me. Luis dropped the other human he'd been feeding on, one hand on my hip, the other on Amara's as he bit into her throat. She, in turn, bit into mine. I let the pleasure fog wrap around me and bit deep into the human's wrist. Amara's fingers pressed against my chest, sliding down to wrap around my cock. I moaned as her hand slid over the shaft. Intoxicated and bursting with desire, I let the human drop to the ground, her heart taking its last beats.

Screams pierced my pleasure fog. Luis growled.

"Not now!" he muttered.

I chuckled, giving in to my need to touch Amara.

"Luis, our Erik is blood drunk," Amara whispered.

"Good," he murmured back. "Both of you, kneel to your alpha and your King.

We dropped to our knees.

"My King!" a voice called from outside. "The Hunters have found us! The village is on fire!"

Luis sighed. "Can we not have a night to ourselves? Must these Hunters ruin everything?"

Amara kissed him. "Go take care of it. We're not going anywhere."

Luis pulled on trousers and his black tunic and marched through the door.

"I should go with him," I said, standing.

Amara laughed. "You're not going anywhere, young warrior. I need you to keep me company while he performs his Kingly duties."

She pushed me towards the bed. I wanted to fall back, for her to kiss my chest, to wrap my arms around her. Instead, I kissed her forehead. "You know I have to," I argued.

"Why?" she asked. "Pathetic humans and their hatred of us, they're no match for vampires. Those with Luis are enough to handle whichever small group found us."

I did wrap my arms around her then. "Amara. I love you, but I'm the King's guard; I have to go. Nico will have my head if I don't."

She returned my embrace. "I'm so sick of these Hunters," she said. "Their obsession feels like it's only growing."

"They'll never be enough," I reassured her. "We'll outlive them, and everything will return to as it was." I lifted her chin and kissed her softly. "A taste of what to expect when I return with our alpha," I promised, quickly dressing.

I stole one last look, before I ran into the night.

I stepped straight into chaos. Smoke filled the air; flames licked at a building on the other side of the village. Hunters surrounded another building, and set fire to that in the centre of the village. There were more Hunters than before.

"There are humans and vampires in there!" someone said, running past me, covered in burns.

I growled, and I ran towards where the Hunters waited. Like Amara, I had grown tired of being hunted. We were the predators; it was unnatural for us to be pursued in this manner. A familiar scent pulled at me. I ran towards it and stopped when I saw him. I almost felt sorry for the pitiful human. Grief for his wife had pushed him into a dark place, and the hostility that shone from his eyes as he glared at me showed how much he loathed me. He lifted his bow.

Dark shadows appeared under his eyes, and deep under all the hatred, there was an emptiness. He was lost. I had done this to him. I had created this Hunter who wanted me dead. How far could I push him before he broke? I gave him my widest smile and his scowl deepened.

Responsible for recruiting others to join his hopeless efforts to eliminate us, Josef had attempted to kill me more than once. I should probably kill him before he recruited more. We'd have an army facing us if we weren't careful.

"Still following me, I see," I said with laughter.

"I told you I'd kill you," he reminded me. "I'm a man of my word."

"You did," I agreed. "But what's this obsession of yours costing you? Look at yourself, when was the last time you actually slept, or enjoyed life's pleasures? You barely look human any more." I pointed to the burning building where I could feel the heat even at that distance. "And that?"

"That is a declaration of war," he said. "On you and all those like you."

"You're killing humans, too," I pointed out. "There are wives in there. Husbands. Sons. Daughters."

"I don't care. There are vampires in there, too. That's enough."

"I thought you declared that you were protecting humanity from us. You've embraced darkness, Josef, and there's no coming back from that," I said. "You're as monstrous as you claim we are."

He glared and advanced on me, the strong scent of ale on his breath. "Don't talk to me about darkness after what you took from me."

Pain reflected in his eyes. But before I could say more, fury broke through my bond with Amara, quickly turning to fear.

'Erik!'

I turned, leaving behind the man I'd turned into a killer. Josef screamed my name, followed by a long cry of rage, but I ran.

'Amara?!'

'Erik,' her voice shook. 'I love you, Erik. Get to the river. Luis will need you.'

Her fear and those words filled me with panic. I broke through the door, barging into the house, and I found three hunters with arrows trained on Amara. A fourth stood over her, sword in mid-swing. She bared her fangs.

"Amara!" I roared.

Her eyes lifted to mine. 'Protect Carlos! He's the one who—'

Her words cut off and her head hit the ground, followed by the thud of her body. Her blood stained the sword, and I faced the Hunters. I bellowed in pain and grief, darkness threatening to swallow me. I let it consume me, falling into a frenzy.

When the red haze receded, I was covered in the blood of those I'd killed. I'd ripped open their throats and pulled their hearts from their chests. Only her killer lived.

"This is our declaration of war," he said, mirroring Josef's words.

"Then you better kill me now, because I will hunt you, and your descendants down," I promised.

Something hit the house from the outside, and flames engulfed the wall. Heat seared my face. When I turned back, he was gone, the sound of his retreating footsteps an echo. I stumbled towards where she lay, and lifted Amara's head. Her eyes—lifeless, glassy—bored into mine. Her skin was still warm, but the absence of her breath was a stake to the heart. It hurt to breathe, and my heart shattered into a million pieces. My maker, gone.

"I love you," I whispered, voice breaking. "If it's war they want, we'll give them war."

The memory brought pain as fresh as it had been then.

"Especially *his* descendants," I muttered in response to Matteo.

For the millionth time, I gazed at Carlos, wondering what Amara had been about to tell me before she died. He'd fallen for a descendant of the man who killed my maker, and I couldn't even fault him for that. Amara would have found it amusing. She'd treated Carlos like a son, telling me he looked like a son she and Luis had once lost.

I watched Diego and Camila again. We'd killed their father, and I'd enjoyed the sounds of his screams as I tore into his flesh alongside my clan. I didn't hate her, nor her brother. As Carlos and Diego talked, I couldn't hold back my smile. I could never have foreseen Carlos allying with Hunters. Or that I'd be beside him when he did.

Celeste touched my arm. "Are you okay?"

"I'm worried about them," I said, turning away from the Hunters. "If they fall into a frenzy, they'll attack each other."

"I'm not talking about them," Celeste said. "Carlos told me a long time ago that you were close to Queen Amara, part of a nest with her and King Luis. That while everyone was watching Luis grieve, you went quiet. He only discovered recently who had killed Amara. That Camila and Diego are descended from him. Did you know he killed her?"

Carlos's head turned slightly, listening, but remaining focused on what was ahead of him.

"I knew," I confirmed. "I saw her die. I carried her to the river, to King Luis." My voice dropped to a croak.

Silence descended like a heavy fog. The entire clan turned their heads to look at me in silent shock. I could feel their eyes on me, the pity.

"But I killed her murderer," I confessed, joyful at the memory. "Twenty years after the war. I stalked him for years, too. He knew I was hunting him. The last few weeks of his life was a torment as I played with him. But the night I killed him, Josef, Ingrid, and Ana were with me. I promised him I'd spend a thousand lifetimes avenging her death, that his descendants would suffer. I found some of his descendants, but lost track of them, until the night we killed Antonio. What a pleasure that was!"

When Camila's eyes met mine, I realised I'd spoken too loudly, sharing my revenge. No one said a word at my confession, but Diego pulled Camila closer to him.

"*This* is what you've accepted into your life," he said to her. "Is that what you want to be a part of? They're not like us, Camila, *this* is what they are. They take joy in killing, and the only thing that has stopped them has been The Accords. You can love Carlos, but he's no different to that one. The moment they declare The Accords are over, that's what the world will face once more. But you take *that* into your bed."

Camila cast me a look over her shoulder, hurt reflecting in her eyes.

Chapter 32

I sat on the ground in between Josef and Andreas, cold seeping into me. Another wave of hunger surged, my veins burning, and I buried my face in Josef's shoulder, whimpering.

Josef tightened his arms around me. "I know." He kissed the top of my head.

His chest bore jagged scars from the arrows he'd taken. I ran my fingers over them, tracing their ridges. The mark on my throat was unnatural. We needed blood, and I didn't want to imagine, if Pierre would continue with his torment, how long it would take for us to fall into a frenzy we couldn't be pulled from.

"This is only the first day," Andreas said. "It's going to get a lot worse."

Has it been only a day? It felt longer.

"Thank you, Andreas," Josef snapped.

I turned my smile to Andreas. Both of them had stood in front of me earlier. "You seem to be handling this better than me or Josef," I said.

Andreas shrugged. "I spent ten years being tortured," he revealed. "They killed my maker, captured me, and tried to find what they could about my ability. They starved me, force-fed me animal blood, cut me, the works."

"Animal blood?" The thought of being forced to drink something so vile churned my stomach. "Why?"

He shrugged. "Why do Hunters do anything they do?" he asked. "They recorded everything in their journals."

"How did you get out?" I pressed.

His gaze drifted to Josef.

"We were in the area," Josef added. "Erik, Ingrid, and I came across Hunters, and we were watching them when they led us back to where he was being held. I'd never seen a vampire so starved. We burned down that prison, left his tormentors inside so they burned to death. No record of Andreas remained to reveal his secret. It took at least fifty years before he started to talk to anyone. To trust us."

I pulled them both closer to me. "We'll get out of here, somehow."

I wanted to believe it, I wanted them to believe it. But hope was fading. Hunters didn't usually let vampires slip through their grasp.

"You need to stop taking arrows for me," I told them both, changing the subject.

"Not going to happen," Josef countered.

"I'm with him," Andreas confirmed.

"Why?" I asked.

"I'm old-fashioned," Josef said. "The need to protect my woman is a deep instinct," he added. "A long time ago, my attempt to protect my wife failed, leading to events that made me the man I am today. And I am going to do what I can to protect that which is mine."

"I'm not your human wife though," I pointed out. "I'm six hundred years old and can protect myself."

He gave me a squeeze. "I know. This isn't about you not being able to protect yourself. Even if it's useless, this is about my urge to protect those from my nest. That's why I'm not letting Erik track us through our bond. I'm shielding him as much as I am you. And the clan."

I met Andreas's eyes. "So, what's your excuse?"

Andreas smiled. "That's who I am, sweet angel. I protect my clan. You're Matteo's family, hence part of our clan."

Josef growled.

"Sorry," he muttered when he caught Andreas and I looking at him. "It's getting harder to not fall into that hunger frenzy."

He was right. I could feel the primal need rising up to sink my fangs into a throat. A mere taste of blood wouldn't be enough; I'd needed to tear into the flesh for the blood to flow. An ache snaked through my veins, gnawing at the control I'd learned centuries ago. All I could think about was the bliss fresh blood would bring me. That I'd drink until blood drunk. I struggled against the urge to growl and lunge at Josef's throat.

Josef ran his fingers over my neck. "Sorry I did that."

I winced at the twinge of pain. "It's okay."

To distract myself, I lifted my head, pressing my lips to Josef's. He kissed with the gentleness he had shown in our nest. His tongue caressed mine and I moaned, my bloodlust becoming desire for him. Wanting more, I pressed in harder, needing him to be rough, carnal. I ran my tongue over his fang. His arms tightened around me, caging me to him. Finally, his kiss became hungry, full of want as he tore at my pyjama top. Buttons popped out, and as his hand slipped up to cup my right breast, another growl rose from him. I growled, myself, nipping at his jaw, dropping kisses to his throat.

Hands pulled me off Josef, and I turned, snarling. Andreas pointed, and I realised Pierre was watching us. I hadn't heard him enter.

"What do you want this time?" I grumbled.

Josef panted, eyes on my body. But it was the way Pierre looked at me that had me pulling my top closed.

"Don't stop now," Pierre taunted, voice smug.

Andreas stood up, approaching the barred door. "Did you enjoy that? Watching them kiss? Watching them fight their desire to kill each other?"

Pierre smirked.

"Or is it her, that you like to watch?" Andreas challenged. "I saw your eyes when you caught a glimpse of her body. You may hate us, but you can't deny your attraction to her, can you? Vampire or not, she is a beauty." He leaned towards the bar. "You want to know something? Shhh, it's a secret."

Pierre leaned in, eyes gleaming, drawn forward by Andreas's offer of a secret. The moment he was close enough to the bars, Andreas's arm moved, striking quick as a snake; grabbing Pierre by the collar, and yanking him forward with brutal force.

Pierre's head clanged against the bars, and his teeth rattled. Before he could recover, Andreas pulled him forward again, and again. Blood trickled from the gash that emerged upon Pierre's forehead on the third strike, and he went limp, collapsing against the bars before Andreas let him slide to the floor in a heap.

Andreas exhaled slowly and stepped away from the bars. Fury turned his eyes red. "Never look at another man's woman. Have some respect."

The silence that followed had me curious about this mild-mannered vampire I knew almost nothing about. I pulled in a deep breath, searching for words to fill the silence. The scent of blood overwhelmed me. My control snapped. I was on my feet, and I lunged at the bars. I pulled at them, snarling. Hands grabbed at me, trying to pull me back. I turned, baring my fangs. Two men faced me. One, bare chested, scars lining his flesh. The other with brown hair, blood on his torn clothes.

"Aria, stop." Their voices meant nothing.

I darted forward, hitting the bare-chested one with my full weight, our momentum carrying us forward until we hit the wall. He pushed at me as I tried to bite into his throat. The other one wrapped his arms around me, holding me still. Growls and snarls rose from me as I struggled against the grip.

The man on the other side of the bars stood, his laughter echoing around the cell. "Looks like we've lost Aria. How long do you think you can hold her?" He put his hand on the door. "Perhaps I should let her out."

I stilled, the words offering a way out so I could feed.

"Oh, you'd like that, wouldn't you?" he asked. He slipped a key into the lock.

"Be sure what you're doing," The bare-chested one said. "She's likely to attack you."

I didn't take my eyes from the lock. But he stepped back.

"*Earn* your freedom, Aria," he offered, and pointed at the men in the cage with me.

I broke free, this time pushing the brown-haired one to the ground. I snapped my teeth, growling, trying to sink my fangs in.

"Aria, it's me, Josef." The bare-chested one pulled me off the other one. "Try to find yourself."

"It's no good, Josef," the brown-haired one said. "She's lost. She needs human blood, and until she gets some, she's not going to pull herself out of the frenzy."

'Aria,' the voice was inside my head. *'Aria, I know you're in there. Look at me.'*

I turned to look at him. I let him pull me to my feet. Then I sunk my fangs deep into his throat, and his blood spurted into my mouth.

Chapter 33

Pain radiated from where her fangs pierced my throat, and we hit the floor. She growled, biting deeper. Andreas lifted her off me, wrapping his arms around her. I rose to my feet, blood running down from where she'd bitten me. She snarled, struggling against his grip, glaring at me. I gazed into her red eyes, seeing nothing but the bloodlust. I held a hand out to her, and she snapped at my fingers.

Pierre laughed. "She's as feral as I've heard her father is."

I glared. "You wouldn't be so smug without that door. Maybe I should push her in *your* direction."

"Josef, I can't hold her much longer." Andreas grunted with effort. "You need to do something. Pull her out of it, or put her down."

I can't do that to her. "You're asking me to use the bond *against* her," I stated.

Andreas struggled to contain her. "Unless you want to hold her?"

I allowed my mind to connect to hers. She shook her head as if she felt my presence.

'Aria, stop,' I commanded. *'I know you're hungry. So am I. Come back to us.'*

Her eyes were empty as she tried to attack me again. Unable to find her under the bloodlust, I considered Andreas's words. To put her to sleep. Struck by an idea, I grabbed her jaw and leaned in, kissing her hard.

She froze, growl cutting off. I pushed my tongue into her mouth, and dropped one hand to her hip. Her body responded to mine. I'd never kissed someone deep in a frenzy like this before, and I could only hope she wouldn't try to kill me. Or bite my tongue off.

'Deep down, we're still creatures of desire,' I whispered to her. *'I'm here, Aria.'*

Her pyjama top was open, and she pressed her body against mine. Both our bodies lacked warmth, but I didn't care. Our kiss sent heat through me. I broke our kiss, checking her face. She didn't move, eyes on me. Still in her frenzy, there was no sign of the Aria I'd come to know the last couple of days. But for her to be still, she must be in there. I lowered my head to her breast, pulling a nipple into my mouth. Contentment rumbled from her.

Andreas moved away. "At least give them privacy," he said to Pierre. "Or do I need to smash your head against the bars again?"

I didn't hear what Pierre said, nor did I care. I watched Aria as I sucked on her nipple. Her eyes closed then opened again. A spark of desire lit up behind her eyes.

'Aria, are you okay?' I asked.

Still she said nothing, merely watching me.

"Well, that's not quite what I meant, but it's working," Andreas acknowledged.

Aria's head snapped around in his direction. I moved up, my tongue sliding over her throat as I kissed over the skin. My fingers ran over her body, and I dropped one hand, slipping it inside her pyjama pants to press against her clit.

She moaned and lifted her head, exposing her throat.

'I can't,' I told her. *'You need blood, Aria. You won't heal.'*

She reached for me, pulling me forward, her kiss desperate. Her fingers dug into my back. When she pulled back, she smiled.

"*There* she is," I said, kissing her forehead.

"That was pleasant; don't stop now," she whispered. She touched my neck where blood still trickled from her bite mark. "Sorry."

Ripping the bottom part of the pyjama top, she tied the strip around my throat.

"You look like the women who used to cover their throats with scarves," Andreas said. "As if it would stop us from feeding."

I chuckled. "You ripped your top," I said. "If I had my tee-shirt, I'd give it to you."

"You want to protect my modesty?" she asked.

"I do against him," I said, pointing to Pierre.

"Here," Andreas said.

We turned, finding him holding out his own tee-shirt. Aria accepted it and removed the pyjama top, pulling on the tee-shirt. "Thank you, Andreas," she said. "Now I don't have to tolerate Pierre's perverted stare."

The three of us glared at Pierre.

"Did you enjoy the show?" Aria demanded. Her voice was calm, but anger vibrated through our blood bond.

Pierre laughed. "You'll all be in a frenzy before long. Maybe I'll release you so *Famiglia di Sammarinese* can kill you."

"They wouldn't kill *me*," Aria said.

He raised an eyebrow. "I'm their King. They knelt to me. I told them you had killed Luca. Poor Luca, the young King, killed by his Second. You're a traitor to them."

"*You're* the traitor," she hissed.

A Hunter walked into the cell, speaking to Pierre in French.

"Anyone speak French?" I muttered, curious as to what they were talking about.

"No, but if Celeste were here, she'd know what they were saying," Andreas said.

Pierre turned his head at the name 'Celeste', eyes meeting mine. A chill slid down my spine. Then he smiled. "Your clan has their own trouble right now. Antonio Martinez uploaded a photo of his daughter with Carlos. Hunters have descended on Venice in the hopes to take him out. I almost wish I could go with my descendants. We'd take great pleasure in killing the Immortal Wolf. The atrocities he's committed over the centuries. Worse than yours."

I remained silent.

"He has your loyalty," Pierre noted.

"That's more than what you have," Aria said. "The clan may have knelt to you, but you haven't earned their loyalty."

"I'll have it when I drop your body, and theirs, in the den," Pierre said. "Not only did you kill Luca, you allowed these vampires into our territory."

Andreas growled. "If you intend to kill us, then what are you waiting for?"

"So much for waiting for the rest of our clan," I said.

"I don't need to. The Hunters in Venice will do it for me," Pierre replied. "You'll help this clan trust me, before I kill them."

Chapter 34

We followed Diego and the human at a distance. Camila walked with him, the two of them talking in low voices. Leaves danced in a cool breeze at my feet. I watched them twirl, struggling to hold in my impatience.

'Josef, we will find you,' I promised, annoyed that he was being stubborn.

"Incoming," Quinn whispered.

I followed where she was pointing. Two humans caught sight of Diego and Camila with the woman Carlos had fed from. From where we hid, we could see their eyes were red. Carlos signalled for us to remain where we were. They approached Diego.

"Who are you?" one demanded.

"Relax, we're Hunters," Diego said, pulling his tee-shirt up to show a crossbow tattoo over his ribs. "We were passing through on our way to Rome. I found this woman. She's been fed on. There must be vampires here." He eyed them. "I didn't realise other Hunters were here. I saw no record of Hunter presence here."

The man was a good liar.

The other held his phone up to Diego, before aiming it at Camila.

Shit. I grabbed Carlos's arm. "Josef said that's how Camila identified him," I whispered, hoping my voice was too low for them to pick up.

"Diego Martinez, did you realise your sister consorts with vampires?" the Hunter with the phone asked.

One of the Bestowed Hunters grabbed Camila. "Vampire sympathiser."

Camila struggled against the grip, anger and pain flashing across her face. "Let me go!" she demanded, voice sharp. She tried to pull her arm free, shoes scraping on the cobblestones.

"I wouldn't do that if I were you," Diego said calmly, glancing in our direction. His own voice was just as sharp.

Beside me, Carlos shook with fury, a growl rising from deep in his chest—menacing and promising violence. The Hunters looked towards it. Carlos moved first, the air rippling behind him. The rest of us followed, surrounding the Bestowed Hunters.

"You betrayed us to vampires?" one of the Hunters asked Diego.

"You betrayed *yourselves* by accepting vampire blood," he returned. "Let go of my sister, or you'll find yourselves without throats. I won't stop him, either."

I growled, baring my fangs. "Our King has claimed her, but she's of our clan, and we protect our own."

Matteo, Quinn, and Celeste nodded in agreement. Shock reflected in Camila's eyes, tears welling up.

"Release her now, or you'll find every one of your fingers broken for daring to touch her," Carlos threatened. "Then as Diego said, I'll tear out your throats and watch as you gurgle in your own blood."

"Come to think of it, Camila's never been one to threaten," Diego added. "I'd be more afraid of her wrath than that of the vampires."

Camila met his eyes and he gave a small nod. I wasn't sure what he'd said, but she seemed to take it as a sign of something. Diego stepped back, joining the Hunters he'd arrived with. Camila raised her knee which made a sharp thud when it connected and I flinched, almost feeling the Hunter's pain as he grunted, struggling to keep his grip on her. Then she shifted her weight, driving her foot forward in a kick releasing a shout. Her foot met her captors midsection with a satisfying thump. He released her this time as he stumbled back. Camila ran into Carlos's embrace.

"Are you okay?" he whispered. "Did he hurt you?"

She nodded. Carlos lifted her wrist, already red. "I'm not sure you want to watch this, *mi Reina*. But this is what happens when someone hurts you."

"You should know, we're not alone," one of them claimed.

Carlos smiled, guiding Camila towards her brother. "You mean your army? Do you know who I have with me?" He pointed to Matteo. "The Feral. Your friend has *his* daughter." He pointed to me. "That's Erik Haraldson. You have something of his. You also have members of my clan." He stepped towards one of the Hunters. "Perhaps I should leave a message for Pierre."

Before the Hunters could move, Carlos punched through the chest of one, ripping out his heart and dropping it to the ground. Camila gasped. He faced the other one. "Tell him we're coming for him." He towered over the Hunter. "I understand I have one of the worst reputations known to Hunters. If you haven't worked out who I am, I am King Carlos. I believe you know some of the names recorded in history for me. If you're not afraid, then you're an idiot." His grin widened, delight reflecting from his eyes.

I advanced on the Hunter a split second before Matteo did. He eyed both of us before glaring at Carlos. "I'll give him your message," the Hunter said. "I hope he kills all of you. You and those others."

Unable to hold back, I grabbed him. "Where are they?"

He remained silent, a fearless glint in his eye as his lips turned upward with a smug smile.

Carlos touched my back. "Let him go, Erik."

I growled but let him go.

"Run," Carlos said. "Before I change my mind and let him kill you."

The Bestowed Hunter hurried off.

Carlos eyed Camila. "Sorry, you know I had to."

She nodded. "I know."

"Miguel, follow him," Diego said. "Keep your location tracker on, so we can see where he goes."

One of Diego's men nodded his head, gaze sweeping over all of us, before he ran to follow the Bestowed Hunter. His boots hit the ground in quick steps fading into the distance. I clenched my fists.

Diego addressed Carlos. "I'm going to take this woman home. I'll leave my sister in your hands. Meet me in the park."

Carlos gave a curt nod. Without another word, Diego led the woman away, their footsteps gradually fading until only silence remained.

"Why aren't we following the Hunter?" I demanded. "He'll lead us right back to wherever Pierre is holding them."

"Erik, we need patience and calm," Carlos said.

Matteo growled. "Erik's right. Carlos, he has my daughter. I've only found her again. Josef and Andreas would march in there for any of us."

Carlos sighed. "I know. But I want to know how many Bestowed Hunters there are. I want them all in one place so we can kill them all. Quinn will have them on their knees. Not one of those Hunters will survive."

Carlos lifted Camila's wrist, stroking it gently with his thumb.

"I'm okay," Camila said again.

"I'm the only one allowed to bruise you, so I'll make sure that hunter that I allowed to live, will die painfully," he promised.

"You're openly killing now?" One of the remaining Hunters who had come with Diego asked. "You don't care about The Accords?"

Every one of us vampires laughed. Carlos approached the man.

"These are Bestowed Hunters," Carlos explained. "One step away from becoming ferals. Do you want to allow that?"

"No," he admitted.

"Good, then we're agreed." Carlos said.

"I wouldn't say I agree with vampires," the Hunter said. "But I don't want to see ferals return."

Carlos shrugged. "Let's wait in the nature park," he said.

"No," I said. "You go. I'm going hunting."

"Would your prey be food, or something else?" Carlos asked.

I crossed my arms over my chest glaring at him. "I will not wait on a human to find Josef, Andreas, or Aria!" I declared. "I don't stand with you on this, Carlos."

Shock darkened his face. "You've *never* opposed me," he muttered. "Erik, please, we need to be smart here. And united."

"I'll follow the Hunters, find out where they report to." I said.

"What if one of them sees you?" he challenged. "They were able to capture Andreas, Josef, and Aria. If we're not careful, anything we can do may get them killed."

"*You're* too busy trying to protect your Queen," I said. "*We're* here for people we've known for centuries. Matteo's just been reunited with his daughter."

"I need you to listen to me," Carlos said. His voice carried weight, the King's command wrapping around my will. "You knelt to me, Erik. You accepted me as your King. Listen to me now."

Reminiscent of Gabriela using her voice for centuries, I struggled against it. He'd said it himself, I'd knelt to him, accepting him as my King. His ability to command was stronger now, strengthened by his blood sharing with Luis. I dug into the power that Amara had given me.

I growled. "You would use your voice in that matter? With me? After what Gabriela did to us?"

Gabriela had once been a close friend. Carlos repeating her actions hurt.

I could have used my own power as a first generation vampire to fight against Gabriela's voice. But Amara's final words had always stopped me. To protect Carlos. So I had. Gabriela had come close to killing him a few times when he disobeyed or angered her.

Guilt flickered across Carlos's face. "You've never challenged me before, Erik. Why now?"

"Because I felt everything when Josef was tortured in Spain," I said. "I could do nothing. I won't stand by and do nothing this time."

"Stop. I'm with Erik," Matteo said. "I will go with him. We'll watch from the shadows, and I'll report back on everything."

Grateful to have Matteo agree with me, I smiled.

"I'll go, too," Quinn said.

I waited, watching Carlos. He looked at the three of us.

"Then we all go," he proposed.

I shook my head. "No, I think you should stay with Celeste and Camila. If anything does happen, Matteo and Quinn can call for help."

Carlos nodded. "Alright. I want a full report on any movement. Don't do anything without my say-so. Call for help if you need it, and wait for me."

I led Matteo and Quinn in the direction the Bestowed Hunter had gone.

Chapter 35

I couldn't remember anything about the frenzy, I'd been too deep into bloodlust. Stories of ferals were well known to vampires. We knew if we were hungry enough, we could sink into that same madness. My father had faced that, embedded within because he'd killed his maker, leaving him with no one to stabilise his new instincts and nature. No one to ground him.

Josef had brought me out by awakening my desire for him, and I was still heated, wanting his hands on me, and his lips. But the strength of his arms helped keep my hunger at bay. Memories rose up behind my closed lids. My mother and father dancing in the courtyard. The night my father disappeared. My mother's death. Seeing Vampire Hunters watching me, no matter where I went. Meeting my human husband. My sons. Marco pulling me from slumber. The first time I'd seen Erik and Josef.

Grief pushed against my chest. I hadn't feared dying like this since Marco chased me through streets and fed on me.

"I'm glad I met you," I said.

Josef kissed the top of my head. "As am I," he agreed. "I don't think I'm ready for goodbyes, though."

"Maybe we should be," I argued. "Perhaps say goodbye to Erik. Tell him to tell my father I love him."

"I suppose if I'm going to die, it's with a friend and his woman," Andreas added. "A beautiful one, at that."

Warmth swelled in my chest and spilled over into a smile. "Andreas, you're not flirting now, are you?"

He merely lifted one shoulder, lips curving upward.

Footsteps approached, but stopped outside the door at the top of the stairs.

"Martinez Hunters," someone murmured.

Great, more Hunters.

Josef straightened.

"Their King tore his heart out. They're working with the Martinez Hunters," the same voice said. "Including the bitch he marked."

I sat up, meeting Josef's eyes.

"They're talking about Camila and her brother," Josef whispered. "I'd say they know my clan is here."

"Carlos tore someone's heart out," Andreas repeated. "Sounds like he's in a good mood."

"One followed me, what should I do?" the Hunter asked.

"He'll lead them to us. Kill him," came the response.

"I hope it's not Camila's brother they're talking about," Josef said. "That would deeply wound Camila."

"Once Pierre finds out they're here, he'll want these three dead," the second Hunter said.

The tapping on a phone indicated someone was sending a message. The phone vibrated almost instantly.

Soft thuds across the floor announced the arrival of others.

"He said to kill them. He needs to stay with his clan right now."

"Are you sure he's not enjoying the King status a little too much?" someone asked.

"He said it's necessary. He needs their complete trust before he'll be in a position to kill them all. Then he'll call us in. The death of The Killer will help him gain that trust. The King of a clan who took over this one."

"Are you sure you're not making excuses for him?" another voice spoke up. "How do we know he hasn't lost sight of his mission? What if he enjoys being a vampire? You saw him feed last night. He was *laughing* when the person begged him for mercy."

"Don't question him," the response was urgent. "Do as he asks. Once we're done here, we'll go to Rome. He can get close to the Bloodking."

Josef scoffed. "They've obviously never met the Bloodking." He shook his head. "Luis is not an idiot, and is brutal when he kills. He makes examples of people."

Andreas sat down next to me, and I wrapped one arm around him. His arm slid around my shoulders.

"I've never feared death," Andreas said.

"When I was a Hunter, I knew I would die to bring down the vampire who'd killed my wife," Josef added. "I made peace with that, as long as he died too."

Andreas chuckled. "I don't think things went according to your plan," he pointed out.

Josef shrugged. "In a way, I did exactly what I thought I would. I fought, trying to resist what they were doing to me."

"I ran straight towards the vampires," Andreas said. "I saw a chance to become powerful. I was lucky they didn't kill me where I stood. Not that they would have been able to, with my ability. Luckily they saw that as useful, and gave me what I wanted."

Curiosity got the best of me. "Were you human? Or...?"

He laughed. "You're asking if I was a shadow demon?"

When I didn't respond, he shook his head. "I don't know. I asked myself many times. I inherited this ability from my mother. She said it ran in the family. But only one living member possessed it. I gained it when she died. We had every reason to believe we were human. We certainly weren't immortal."

"You didn't try to find out?" I asked.

He shook his head. "I saw no need. It's a useful ability that became more useful when I turned."

Five Hunters filed down the stairs, crossbows at the ready. We rose as one. Without a word, Josef and Andreas stepped forward, positioning themselves between the Hunters and me. Andreas' stance was rigid, the muscles in his back tense. Josef's body trembled slightly. I stared at the crossbow tattoo over his back.

"No," I said. "I will stand with you."

I stepped in between them, taking their hands in mine.

The Hunters didn't say a word. They raised their weapons.

'They're not Bestowed any more,' Josef said. He let go of my hand and stepped forward. "I see the vampire blood has left your system." He bit into his wrist. "Who wants some more?"

Andreas joined him, biting his own wrist. Once again, the scent of their blood overwhelmed me. I held on as I waited.

"Didn't you already try that?" a Hunter asked.

"Only one person can have this," Andreas said. "You can almost taste it, can't you?"

"You want the strength our blood gives you," Josef added. "Your body craves our blood."

I bit into my own wrist, knowing it wouldn't heal.

The three of us stood together, wrists held out.

Arrows were released. One pierced my shoulder, and another between my ribs. Pain pierced my chest and I gasped to breathe. Andreas hit the floor, an arrow sticking out of his throat. I pulled my arrows free and knelt down to help him. I eased the arrow out of his throat, and he sat up, eyes red.

I turned, finding Josef on his back. An arrow stuck out from his chest. Ice flowed through my veins.

"Josef?" I asked, approaching him. For a heartbeat, everything stopped. I put a trembling hand to his chest, around the arrow.

He opened his eyes. "There's no way Erik didn't feel that," he declared.

"Are you okay? Did it get your heart?"

He gazed up at me with a flicker of fear. "I don't know. There's nothing but pain."

Andreas joined me. "Sit up, let us help you."

Josef started to sit up but grunted in pain. Another arrow hit him. He gazed at me, and reached for my face.

"Let us pull it out," I whispered.

"He's coming," he said.

"Who?" I asked.

"Erik," Josef said. "I can sense him, he's close." He winced. "But so is the loss of control."

A roar filled with fury ripped through the air. Erik's. A second followed, and I knew my father was close, too.

Chapter 36

We found Diego's Hunter dead outside of a house. He'd been ambushed. A knife was embedded into his chest, his throat slit.

"A fresh kill," Matteo observed. "If we'd got here earlier, we could have helped him. I'd say we're two minutes too late."

I could sense Josef nearby. The echo of searing pain wasn't mine but his. He'd been shot again. It was as if the arrow had pierced my own chest. I rubbed at the spot where the sharp pain radiated through me.

"They're in there," I said to Matteo and Quinn. "Josef's in a lot of pain. And *hungry*." I pointed to the dead Hunter. "You better tell Carlos, so he can tell Diego."

"I hear fifteen human heartbeats in the house," Quinn added.

"Some are fainter, as if they're underground," Matteo noted.

I focused on the sounds within the house. "There are only three vampire heartbeats," I observed. "They're weak."

Pierre could be anywhere. The better action would be to wait, to find out where he was first, to take him out, too.

"I'm tired of waiting," I grumbled out loud.

"Agreed," Matteo said.

His eyes were already red, fangs at the ready. As were Quinn's. I let my own vampirism show.

"Any words of inspo before we march into the enemy's domain?" Quinn asked.

"Make them all suffer," Matteo said simply. "I want screams."

"Of course you do." Quinn laughed. "Erik? You got any?"

"We've lived a long time with The Accords," I said. "We've adhered to their laws. We've controlled our nature and suppressed our bloodlust." I pointed to the house. "There are Hunters in there who have never faced us unhindered by the laws their ancestors forced upon us. Any day, it will be declared that we are no longer bound by those cursed Accords. Let's show these Hunters exactly why their ancestors feared us." I put a hand on Matteo's shoulder, meeting his eyes. "Let go, Matteo. Let the feral out." I dug deep into the nature I had been forced to deny for centuries. "Show them what we are!"

The last words came out a growl. I embraced the beast within, and I let him loose.

"Well said," Quinn said and put her hand to Matteo's chest. "They're waiting for you, my sweet feral."

Matteo turned towards the house. He'd shed any sign of humanity; what was left was The Feral. A brutal killer who would tear apart his enemies. Good. So would I. For daring to touch what was mine. For taking clan members who meant the world to me. We marched across the road.

I was about to bust down the door when pain flooded through from Josef. They'd shot him again. He'd sustained many injuries and was too weak. I let the pain guide my anger and let out a roar to let Josef know I was coming. I would spill enough blood to soak the floor. I would spill it for Josef, Aria, and Andreas.

'*Erik,*' Josef finally reached out to me. My chest ached at how weak he sounded.

Matteo let out his own roar—raw, guttural and more animal than man. He slammed his full weight against the door, and it splintered from the force. Three Hunters stepped forward. Before any of them could raise weapons, we were on them. The world ceased to exist but for fury, hunger, and bloodlust. I lunged at a throat, my fangs sinking deep. His struggles were useless against me and only fuelled my beast within.

Reason dissolved under the red haze. The only thing I could focus on was his thunderous heartbeat as he fought for his life, the pulse spurting his intoxicating, fear-spiced blood into my mouth. I was unleashed.

Our attack drew the attention of more Hunters. We were outnumbered. An arrow hissed passed me. Another grazed my shoulder. I answered with another roar, tearing the offending weapon from the nearest hunter before plunging my hand into his chest. I gripped his heart and threw it at the next. I slashed the throat of another with my sharp nails and stood over him as he pressed his hand to the wound, gurgling on his own blood. Next to me, The Feral and the Siren faced other Hunters.

The room was filled with growls and screams. Matteo had sunk his fangs into a throat, his prey screaming and fighting against him. Without the euphoria that our venom brought, these humans would feel immense pain. Matteo had bitten deep, tearing, leaving deep wounds that resembled gashes left behind by a wolf. The screams cut off, as the Hunter no longer had a throat. With a fast punch, Matteo removed the Hunter's heart to make sure he didn't return in a day. Sheer joy filled his eyes. He always did appreciate the screams.

Drawn forward by the scent of fear, I removed the throats and hearts of more Hunters, and another scream broke—this time from a Hunter who met Quinn. She'd struck his jugular, blood spraying, and a dark glee filled her eyes as she gazed at me. She dropped the body, licking her lips, crimson streaking down her chin. I joined Matteo in licking the blood from her.

Raw hunger filtered across her face. It was the first time I'd seen her in such a frenzy. "I want more," she declared.

I laughed. The three of us moved as one, living death to those who dared face us. A sword pierced my side and I pulled on the blade, bringing the Hunter towards my fangs. No longer bound by the chains of Accords that had caged us for too long, we welcomed the screams, the splatter of blood, and the dark joy that came with it.

Finally, only one remained, and he ran at me. I pushed him against the wall, my hand crushing his chest. Wood splintered behind him from the force.

"Beg for your life," I commanded. "Scream, kneel, pray to your God." I breathed in deep. The scent of his fear reached into me. Tantalising and hard to resist. "Oh, you smell delicious. You could do with a little more fear, though."

"I will not beg," he choked.

"Look around you, your fellow Hunters are dead," I commanded. "You face three vampires; your courage will not help you now."

His eyes darted to the chaos around us, chest heaving. "You broke The Accords."

Behind me, Quinn spoke softly to Matteo, pulling him from his feral state.

"I spit on The Accords," I said. "They control us no more!"

"Stop playing with your food," Matteo said, and reached around me, tearing out the Hunter's throat.

I threw the body to the floor. "You could have let me have my fun. You enjoy their screams, I enjoy their begging." I licked at the blood on his chin.

"That was the first frenzy during which I have remained that aware." He tilted his head, as if even he could not believe it.

I smiled at that, something akin to pride in my chest. "You became one with your feral."

"I *am* The Feral," he affirmed.

I took in the sight of the bodies, and the blood we'd spilled.

"There are five more," Quinn said. "Their hearts are racing, and the fear…" she finished with a growl.

"Perhaps the screaming has them afraid," I said, pleased. Footsteps approached and I turned around. Carlos and Celeste stood in the doorway.

"You started without us," he said. "I'm disappointed."

Celeste gazed at the humans, kicking at one. "Did you leave none for us?"

I pointed to a door. "I think that leads through to a cell. You're welcome to them."

Carlos reached for my chin, his eyes boring into mine. "I haven't seen that glint for a long time," he said. "Welcome back."

"Where is your Queen?" I asked.

He pointed outside. "She and her brother are seeing to their friend they lost. I warned them they might not like what they saw if they came in here."

I didn't move as Carlos licked the blood from me. Contentment rumbled from his chest. "I love the havoc you've wreaked here," he said. "Let's finish them off and help our family. Where's Pierre?"

"Not here," I said. "We'll find him, though."

I stepped towards the door, and kicked it in.

Chapter 37

I lay down over Josef. His heartbeat thundered under my head, ragged breaths gnawing at me. I pressed closer to him; his skin as cold as my own. The thud of his pulse grew louder, darkening the edges of my vision, pounding waves against the aching hunger inside me. The scent of his blood sang to the predator within. It would do me no good but its sweet tang pulled me to the edge of another frenzy.

Carnage upstairs echoed through the cell. They were coming for us, but I couldn't hold back my bloodlust any more. Weak, hungry, and wounded, I was about to lose all control. Andreas lay on the ground next to us, and I reached for him.

The door banged open, smashing against the wall. Those remaining in the cell ran up the stairs. Growls filled the air, then the scent of sweet, stomach growling blood. I whimpered, and Josef's arm wrapped around my body. Andreas scooted in closer to us, and we huddled together in an attempt to resist the rising bloodlust. Every cell in my body roared for the warmth and life only human blood could give. Five people approached the door, watching us. They were covered in blood. It smelled human. They weren't.

"The cage is magically sealed," one of them said. "He's working with a Magic Wielder."

"Luna's magic was stronger," came another voice.

I lifted my head, watching them; a warning rumbling from me.

"Aria, my treasure, it's alright, we're here." The man looked familiar, brown eyes, voice pulling up something unsettling. Emotions. I shook them off and ran at the bars.

"Shhh, it's okay, we're here to help." he said.

I growled in response, shaking the bars. A blond man stepped forward, reaching through the bars. "Aria, stop. Who's your alpha? Me, remember. Submit to me."

"Really, Erik?" the other man grumbled. "Do I have to hear that?"

The words meant nothing to me. I snarled again, snapping at his hand. He didn't flinch when I drew blood.

"Celeste, Quinn, find them food," the one with curly hair said, and the two women left.

I didn't look away from the men who stood on the other side of the bars.

"Find a key," the curly-haired one responded. "One of those corpses should have one. That will allow us entry through the magic barrier."

The large one with familiar eyes reached for my chin. "We'll get you out," he promised, and started to search the pockets of the two bodies on the floor.

"Josef," the blond one reached for the man at my side, lifting a pendant. "Hold on."

We responded with growls, rattling the bars.

Thunderous heartbeats drew my attention to the top of the stairs. Humans! I waited, hoping they were for me. My fangs ached, and I yearned for the taste of their blood. Two women guided them down the stairs. Six living blood bags.

The door opened, and three terrified humans were pushed into the cell. With the fire of my hunger propelling me, I lunged, seized hold, and yanked one towards me, fangs tearing into the soft flesh of the woman's throat. I silently howled in triumph, and as her hot blood surged over my tongue, pouring warmth back into my starved and damaged body, I groaned.

Around me, the others fed with the same frenzy, their prey and mine crying out in pain. Their struggles were weak, our hold on them unyielding, as we took our fill. Warmth filled me, replacing the cold within my body. I drank until her heart fell silent. I let her lifeless body fall to the ground, licking my lips and lifting my eyes to those watching me. The remaining humans were pushed into the cage, wide-eyed and pleading. I approached a man.

"Please don't kill—"

I put my hand over his mouth to silence him, once again my fangs tearing a soft throat. The gush of his blood brought me satisfaction, the red haze lessening. My wounds healed, and strength was returning. When I'd drained him, I released the body, my mind slowly returning. I faced La Voz. My father pulled back the door and rushed forward, pulling me into his arms.

"My treasure, I'm happy to see you," he rejoiced in my ear.

"You, too, Papa," I returned, letting his embrace encircle me. I was safe, and welcomed the feeling.

Quinn and Celeste hugged Andreas next to us. Erik and Josef clung to one another. Erik lifted his gaze, meeting mine, and raised his arm. I reluctantly pulled myself from my father's embrace, and let Erik pull me into his arms alongside Josef. Relief that Josef was okay flooded me. I kissed Josef's throat, then leaned my head against his shoulder. His lips brushed the top of my head—a quiet reassurance—as he pulled me into his arms. Erik watched us both.

"You're my alpha," I whispered to answer Erik's earlier question.

His grin widened. "Good girl."

He lowered his head, and I lifted my own to meet his kiss. His tongue was persistent against mine, commanding. The taste of blood lingered on his lips and in his mouth. We met with rough want, his arms around both myself and Josef. Warmth unfurled across my chest. Josef kissed the corner of my mouth, and I yielded to his lips. Then Josef and Erik claimed one another's lips.

"I was as worried for you as I was for Josef," Erik murmured to me.

I lay my hand on Josef's chest, as he leaned forward, forehead pressing against Erik's. They stayed there for a moment before Erik crossed the room to Andreas. Not a word passed between them, but the two hugged tightly. One by one, Carlos joined them, my father, Celeste, Quinn, and Josef. The bond of the clan revealed itself in the way they stood together.

I couldn't help myself; I leaned into their warmth.

"Okay," Carlos said, grabbing our attention. "We should get out of here, maybe burn the house down to draw Pierre out of the shadows."

I leaned against my father again, heart swelling at the strength and comfort at his presence.

Celeste laughed bitterly. "After Hunters took out my clan, I've been waiting a long time to have a chance to kill some."

Carlos kissed her forehead. "Then I declare it's open season on Hunters. Except for those we came with." He eyed me. "Is there somewhere we can go that Pierre doesn't know about?"

"We have a safehouse that Marco told me about, but I'm certain the Hunters know about it," I said.

"Then we find a house and claim it. Let's go. Camila and Diego are outside."

We started up the stairs. Halfway, I paused, turning around to gaze at Luca's corpse. "We should take his body," I said.

Carlos returned to the cage, retrieving Luca and his head. We let him walk past before following him up.

"You had to be shirtless through this whole ordeal?" Erik asked Josef.

The two broke into low chuckles. "What can I say? Aria needed something worth looking at," Josef said.

Carlos turned around, raising his eyebrows at Andreas. "And you?"

Andreas shrugged. "She only had a pyjama top, and Josef broke the buttons. I figured the least I could do was give her my tee-shirt. Especially with Pierre taking an unwelcome opportunity to stare at her body."

I intertwined my fingers with his. "Such a gentleman," I acknowledged.

He smiled down at me. For a heart beat, I felt a pull to kiss him, a fleeting desire that faded. His smile filled me with warmth. I wrapped an arm around him.

Walking through the door, we found bodies of Hunters strewn around the house. It looked as if they'd been torn apart by wild animals, a gruesome sight.

"Well, that explains why you're all covered in blood," Josef said.

"A true work of art," Andreas added. "Our tormentors got the fate they deserved."

"Indeed," my father agreed, voice low. "They dared take my daughter, and members of my clan. It was only going to end one way for them."

"You should have seen him," Erik said to me. "The Feral at work. This is his masterpiece."

Quinn smiled up at Erik. "You were also an impressive sight," she said. "This is as much your masterpiece as it is his."

"Quinn killed her first Hunters," Matteo added with pride. "All without her siren powers."

"Oh yeah, she was all vampire. Almost as feral as Matteo," Erik remarked.

"Wait here," Carlos instructed. "Let me speak to Diego and Camila before you all walk outside looking like that." He passed Luca's body to my father, and Erik took the head.

We waited inside as he went outside.

"You should know, they're all covered in blood," Carlos said in a low voice.

"So are you," a male voice said.

Carlos laughed. "We killed Hunters. They had to die for what they did."

"They killed a good man," Diego said, voice tense with emotion. "They chose to be Bestowed. They got what they deserved. What's your plan?"

"We regroup," Carlos said. "We need to find somewhere. Our next target is Pierre."

"Who's he talking to?" I asked.

"Camila's brother," my father said. "They're working with us."

"I do believe he's softening to Carlos," Celeste added.

"'The enemy of my enemy is my friend,'" Andreas said. "It works."

Carlos returned. "Diego has a place. His father was here about twenty years ago after a Hunters' facility exploded. He organised this house for the only Hunter who survived. So we go, shower, sleep, and prepare to fight a vampire who likes to kill other vampires."

"*Finally*," Erik said. "He's going to regret the day he awoke from slumber."

Chapter 38

The house Diego led us to was a large one, with twelve bedrooms and five bathrooms. The kitchen was modern which opened into the living space. Matteo, Celeste, Quinn, and Erik had sped down to our parked cars, retrieving our bags.

"All this for one Hunter?" I asked.

Camila met my eyes. I hadn't had a chance to speak with her since I'd called for her death and challenged Carlos for not killing her. Her eyes held no fear or hostility, only warmth.

"It was built to house Hunters, to replace the facility that was blown up," she explained. Her smile faded. "There are cells underneath, too. For obvious reasons."

Aria smirked. "That was my doing," she told the Hunters. "Emiliano blew it up trying to kill Marco and me."

Their lack of response intrigued me. It seemed they weren't surprised.

"Take a room, have a shower, do what you need." Diego said, grabbing his bag from Celeste. "The sun will be up soon, and we're all tired. Maybe when the sun sets again we can regroup, and make a plan."

Carlos nodded to us, his order clear: listen to the Hunter.

"I'm not letting either of you out of my sight," Erik said to Aria and me. "You're coming with me."

In the room, he pulled our clothes off and pushed us into the bathroom. Under the hot water, Erik washed us both, gentle in his movements. He scrubbed at the blood on my face, and dropped a light kiss to my lips.

"*Veiðimaðr minn,*" he said.

My lips found his again, letting him feel my need for him, my relief to have him with me. I'd thought I was going to die without seeing him again, and while I had wanted to protect him and the clan, I was glad he'd not listened.

"Never do that again," he said. "I tell you to let me find you, you let me find you. Am I understood?"

I rested my hand on the back of his neck as our foreheads touched. Hot water cascaded over my shoulders and down my chest, the warmth soaking into me. "Yes, my alpha," I whispered.

"Dammit, you always know the words that will soften me when I'm trying to be serious," he grumbled.

"I'm sorry, Erik. I only wanted to protect you, and the clan," I explained.

His eyes softened. "I know. But you know I want to protect you, too. Our King wants us all safe. We've already lost enough. We're a clan. That bond is strong. I love you, Josef, and I will storm through Hel to get you back."

I choked on emotion. "*Gamall hermaðr,* your words fill my heart. I love you, I promise, I won't do it again."

Satisfied, he turned his attention to Aria, washing her as tenderly as he had me. His lips pressed against hers, and she melted against him. He wrapped his arms around her in a tight embrace.

"Josef's affection for you has grown," Erik said. "I feel it in our bond, and it has taken seed in my own heart. I want you to join our clan, to stay with us."

I wanted that too, more than anything. I put one hand on Erik's shoulder, the other on her hip. "We cannot expect Aria to leave a clan she's been with for centuries," I said.

Erik sighed. "After what you've both endured, I don't want to let either of you out of my sight ever again. I've claimed you both, you are mine."

She pressed her head against his chest, and her eyes met mine. "I want to join your clan, but I don't know if I can abandon my own. They've lost two Kings in a matter of days. Once we eliminate Pierre, Hunter or not, he makes a third. His Hunters have killed a member of our clan." She looked up at Erik. "My own affection for Josef has grown, and I, too, feel his love for you in my heart. I feel it as if it were my own."

I gave her a heated kiss, and the two of us took our time to wash Erik. I smiled at him as I washed blood from his beard.

"You let your beast out?" I asked.

He grinned, dark joy filling his eyes. "It reminded me of when you and I first hunted together with Ana. Nothing held us back. Having Hunters come at us like that was similar to the battles I fought when I was human. Even then I found it thrilling. The heat of battle, added with a vampire's nature, makes for a delicious combination."

When he'd walked into the cell, splashes of blood over his tee-shirt and dripping from his jaw, I'd been overjoyed. Aria had fallen in a frenzy again, and I'd felt my own pull me under. But I'd pushed it back long enough to catch a glimpse of our rescuers barging into the cell. Drenched in blood and the feral-like glint in their eyes, they'd appear a nightmare to anyone else. But to me, it had been a welcome sight.

"The Bloodking is bringing that back," I reminded him.

He grabbed my jaw, his kiss more forceful this time. He growled before showing Aria the same intensity.

"My maker once said I was a god among men. Humans will kneel before us," he said. "They will run from us."

I laughed. "Remember when I first turned, our first attack on the Hunters? They ran then, when they worked out they'd let in the enemy that had the face of a friend. They thought they could warn everyone I was no longer one of them."

Erik gazed at me with pride. "You were a sight to behold. You accepted what you were with such…" he paused.

"Grace?" Aria asked.

We both laughed. "Far from it," I said.

Erik turned the water off and stepped out, holding towels for us. I took mine, wrapping it around my waist. Aria pulled hers around her body.

"Savagery," Erik found his word. "He tried to hold on to his humanity at first. He tried to hate me. But he found he couldn't resist the call of the hunt. He was remarkable to watch. Once he gave in to his nature, we asked him to lead us to the Hunters."

"I walked into those camps unopposed and let the vampires in. When they realised what I was, they tried to run. Their fear drew me into a frenzy. It was intoxicating," I added. I grabbed a second towel to dry my hair. "Not an ounce of remorse," I said. "Yet somehow Pierre holds on to his humanity."

"The only time I felt guilty for killing a human was when I stared into my husband's eyes as the light died," Aria said. "I'd done the same thing to my sons that I experienced as a child. That guilt faded quickly though. I loved my husband, but he was simply food. It was a strange realisation."

"How many humans did you kill?" I asked with a smirk.

"Like any young vampire, I struggled to control my nature," she said. "I killed five in as many days. Marco wasn't a hands-on maker. He believed it was important for a vampire to learn their own control." She met my eyes. "In response to your earlier comment, I'm not entirely sure Pierre has held onto his humanity," Aria said. "I've known him for the last century. He enjoys what he is. Plus he's been after me for decades. The night we discussed who Luca's Second would be, he told me I was more of a King's Queen. As if I would join him." She curled her lip. "I had a feeling he was planning to overthrow Luca, but I never could have foreseen any of this."

I brushed her throat with my fingers. "When we've rested and fed some more, we'll kill him," I promised. "He'll be begging us to end it by the time we're done."

We collapsed on the bed, huddled together. It was a change from the hard floor of the cell. We were in enemy territory, just as we had been the night Carlos had accepted his role as King in Melbourne. "Shouldn't we all be in the same room?" I asked. "It's better in enemy territory like this."

Erik smiled at me. "I think we're alright. We have Hunters guarding us, a protective king, a feral and a siren." His eyes darted towards the door. "Plus our protective shadow. Why don't you come in, Andreas? No point standing out there alone, in the dark."

Andreas stepped forward, the shadows parting for him, pulling back over his skin. "You always know that I'm there before anyone else does," he said with laughter.

Erik smirked. "Once we discovered your useful trick, I learned how to sense you, even through the shadows. I always have to know where my clan are." He glanced down at Aria and me. "They're okay, Andreas. You're all safe, and Pierre will taste our anger soon enough. Perhaps you'd like to join us. Sleep here with us, if it will help you feel better?"

Aria reached her hand out to Andreas. "I agree," she said. "Stay with us, Andreas."

He hesitated only for a moment before taking it. The four of us curled up on the bed. I pulled both Aria and Andreas into my arms, appreciating what they had both endured with me. Erik pulled my back to him, embracing us all.

Chapter 39

Aria was gone when I awoke; Andreas and Erik were still sleeping. I needed to be moving. In the living room, I found Diego and Camila with the other Hunters, eating pizza.

Camila noticed me first. "Josef, you look better than you did this morning. How did you sleep?"

"Where is everyone?" I asked instead, to avoid her question.

"Aria is showing Carlos and Matteo where her den is," she replied. "They'll be back soon."

I took the chair next to hers and breathed in the aroma of the pizza. Tomatoes, cheese and olive oil, and the herbs delighted me. I saw no need to eat human food often, but loved to breathe in the aroma of it. Diego glanced at his companions and the three of them stood.

"I showered," I said as they walked towards the door. "So I know I don't smell."

"Diego," Camila warned.

Her brother stopped. "Sorry, I'm not ready to break bread with you," he told me.

I shrugged with a grin. "More food for us, then!"

They left, and Camila cast me an apologetic smile. "Are you feeling better?"

I gave her the once-over. "Are you asking if I'm still hungry? Does it worry you, sitting alone at a table with me?" I smirked, then realised my words came out harsher than I intended. I wasn't used to speaking with humans in this manner.

Her eyes widened. "No!" she said quickly. "I wanted to make sure you were okay. Carlos said you were wounded multiple times."

I looked at her for the first time. She didn't look at me with fear, but concern and empathy.

"I'm okay," I said, softening my voice. "Did you really have King Carlos and Diego working together?"

Her eyes lit up. "I did! They were both trying so hard. It wasn't smooth, but I was so happy that they were trying in the first place."

I eyed the door her brother had walked through. "They'll sit at the same table one day."

Uncertainty flickered across her face. "I don't know. I think them working together and Diego not trying to kill Carlos, or anyone else, is as far as we could get. Hunting has been Diego's whole life. He won't turn his back on me, but I don't think he'll ever change his views."

I reached across, my hand covering hers. "He wasn't here for us. Your brother doesn't give a fuck about vampires in trouble. He would have quite happily let us die. Or even killed us himself."

"Then why did he come?" she asked. "Working with Carlos, talking to me about being happy?"

"Because he wants to be in *your* life," I said. "I lived that hatred, and I know it's impossible to let go of. I wasn't raised in it, though. I imagine living it from birth would be a little different to my own experiences. But if your brother is putting aside that hatred to work with the man you've given your heart to, it is because he isn't ready to let you go." I gave her a small smile. "I heard he even warned you about the Hunters advancing on Venice after your father released the photo of you and Carlos. That's progress."

She considered my words. "You're right. Thank you."

I lifted my hand and sat back. I wanted to put her at ease. For her to trust me. That was essential, now that she was part of *La Voz*. "I knew your ancestor."

Her eyes widened. "You did?"

"We both fled the same village, and he was a good friend. He stood with me when I married my wife, and as I buried my family. The day I faced him as a vampire, I believe he was genuinely saddened, as if I had actually died. But that quickly turned to hate as we fell into our roles of soldiers on opposing sides."

She was silent for a moment. "And then you and Erik tormented and killed him."

I winced. "We did. You know what we are. He killed someone important to Erik." I saw no point in lying to her, curious as to how she knew. Maybe Erik had said something. I hadn't known at the time the reason for Erik's obsession with tormenting the Hunter.

Her eyes remained on my face for a long time.

"Can I ask for advice?" she finally asked.

"I don't know if I'm any good at advice," I replied truthfully. "That's not my forte."

"How do we get past this?" she asked. "I tried to kill you all. I have killed others of your kind. You all accepted me that night, but it doesn't change what I've done. Or that you all have dark histories that you wouldn't hesitate to return to."

"You gave your heart to a vampire, and you're wondering if you made the right decision?" I asked.

"No! I love Carlos," she said and let out a breath. "I guess I'm wondering what that means for me? I'm part of a clan with vampires who have all been killers. Does that make me a bad person?"

I leaned forward again. "It's okay that you believe the worst of us, that's what we are and we all accept what we are. But you're not a bad person, Camila. You're merely guided by your heart. You cannot help who you fall for. No one will force you to leave behind your humanity or morals. But you have to know what being with Carlos means."

She nodded thoughtfully. "It means my own humanity is already questionable." Her shoulders slumped, eyes lowered.

I touched her arm. "I had a feeling this would happen and I suspect being around other Hunters helped trigger this. You should talk to Carlos. There is a way to help remove that uneasiness you're feeling, but you've already stated you don't want to be a vampire. You're no longer a Hunter, but living with us? That's going to be an adjustment for you. For all of us."

She reached for my hand this time. "Thank you. From one former Hunter to another, I hope to learn from you about moving forward from that past. I think I have a lot I need to figure out."

I grinned. "Oh, it was different for me, joining the other side. I became a vampire; you fell in love with one. But I'll teach you or guide you in any way that I can."

"I may take you up on that offer." She winced. "Hunters are going to come after me too. Probably to get to Carlos."

Struck by an idea, I took a knee in front of her. "Then I pledge to protect you when you need it."

Her mouth hung open as she stared at me. The rest of the clan entered the room, watching. Carlos moved across the room towards Camila and helped her to her feet.

"Josef has offered himself as your protector," he said in a quiet voice. "What do you say?"

She gazed down at me. "Given that we're both former Hunters, I think it's fitting," she acknowledged with a small smile.

She whispered to Carlos. "Matteo is your Second, and advises you when you need it. As Queen of *La Voz,* perhaps I too need a Second."

Matteo stepped forward. "So you accept you are Queen? Our King's Queen, a former Hunter, a human. To take a seat next to our King, as Queen of the vampire clan of Venice; La Voz?"

She nodded.

Matteo turned his attention to me. "Do you accept the role of her Second? To not only be with her in our King's absence, but to ensure her safety in the upcoming war, should it come to Venice?"

I smiled up at Camila, swelling with warmth. This was unexpected. "It would be my honour."

Pride shone from Carlos's face. I stood.

"I look forward to spending time with you, Camila," I said. "I hope we can become friends once you've completed your self-reflection."

Carlos frowned. "What self-reflection?"

"Nothing to worry about," I reassured him.

Camila smiled wider. "I hope so, too." She faced the whole clan. "With all of you. I know you all accepted me. But I don't want to just be a human that Carlos has claimed. I want to be part of your lives." She smiled at Quinn. "Whether it's listening to your music." Her face lifted in Erik's direction. "Or reading a book with you in silence, I appreciate having a chance to get to know you all the last few days. This is the first time I've related to vampires like this."

"Welcome to *La Voz,*" Erik said. "Probably the most unusual clan in history." He pointed around the room. "An assassin," he said of Andreas. "The Feral. A siren. A former Hunter. The Immortal Wolf. A human."

I caught movement in my peripheral vision. Diego was watching. He met my eyes with a grim acceptance. I faced him. "Your sister is under my protection," I said. "That protection extends to her family."

He looked around at each of us, finishing on me. "One of the first Hunters, kneeling to my sister. I can't say I would have thought that possible." He crossed his arms. "I came here for my sister, but I also came to find reasons to kill you all. All I see is people going out of their way to make her feel welcome. I see no fear in her, or signs of compulsion. I also understand in Venice you have an agreement with the Barones, that you don't kill. So I promise you this. You're all under *my* protection. I will do what I can to keep you informed of any threats to your clan. That will ensure my sister's safety."

"See, progress," I said to Camila. She grinned and ran towards her brother, the two of them hugging.

"We have killed here," I said, indicating myself and Aria. "I don't just mean the Bestowed Hunters. We killed a couple because The Accords no longer exist. We killed a second couple to use their fresh blood to distract the Bestowed Hunters."

Diego frowned at me. "With that knowledge alone, it would be my job to kill you both."

Erik and Matteo growled.

Diego's arms dropped to his sides. "Maybe refrain from telling me shit like that. I'll look the other way just this once for the sake of my sister. But I don't want to hear such confessions. Truce or not, I am still a Hunter."

"I agree with my brother," Camila said in a quiet voice. "I have turned my back on being a Hunter, but it doesn't mean I'd suddenly be okay if you killed people. Even without The Accords, can we agree to peace, and not to kill openly?"

The room went silent.

"We can," Carlos confirmed after a minute. "Despite The Accords no longer holding us back, I'm sure we can refrain from taking joy in our natures." He made no attempt to hide his disappointment. "If you do not force restrictions on us as your ancestors did, I will keep the peace. We will give you no reason to come after us."

'That doorway has already been opened,' Erik whispered to me. *'And our*

King knows it.'

Diego nodded his approval, then met Carlos's eyes. "So, what's your plan? How will we take down this piece of shit Hunter vampire who Bestows Hunters and tried to kill your clan?"

Chapter 40

I'd been in many war rooms before, but none quite like this. Hunter and vampire stood side by side. Diego had a map of the city on his tablet, and zoomed in on the den. He'd plugged it into a device that cast the image on the wall. It never ceased to amaze me how technology had advanced. He had the images of both houses side by side. In terms of location, they were not far from one another.

"Do you want to start with the den?" Diego asked.

His companions sat at the back of the room in silence, and had refused to talk to any of us.

Carlos stepped forward. "The entire clan is inside. Bestowed Hunters killed a vampire. Thanks to Andreas, the vampire with her escaped. She would have seen that those Hunters were not normal Hunters. That would have driven them into hiding. Any attempt to enter, and they'll be extremely territorial. A few of them will recognise us from when Giuseppe led them to Venice. They may see us as hostile. We do not hurt them, though."

"They'll also be mourning their loss," Aria added. "If Pierre's told them I killed Luca, they'll be struggling to understand or even believe that. I've never shown ambition for such a title, and grieved Marco when he died." She looked down for a moment. "I was worried about how many would be loyal to Pierre, but if any were, they would have been at that house. No vampire I know would befriend Hunters." She glanced at the Hunters in the room. "No offence."

Diego shrugged.

"Our first issue is with the Bestowed Hunters," Carlos said. "We cannot risk them advancing on the den and causing unnecessary deaths."

He stepped back, indicating for Diego to take over.

"We face vampire blood-powered Hunters. We should assume that, with Aria, Andreas, and Josef free, Pierre would've shared his blood with them again. He knows *La Voz* is here, so he'll want to be prepared. Going by the large numbers of people outside the house, he's called in an army. All of whom are likely his descendants." Diego tapped his tablet, and a photo showed on the screen. In images taken from drones, we could see at least thirty people outside the burning house. "I've called in some friends who can help. They'll be here in an hour." He nodded to Carlos. "That gives your people time to feed before we head out. Please try to refrain from killing?"

Carlos nodded his head—an agreement I had no intention of keeping while away from Venice. "Because you asked so nicely." He smirked.

Camila jerked her head towards Diego. "You called people in? Who?"

"The Garcia Perez brothers," he said.

Camila's eyes widened.

"Oh, I know those names," Josef said. "They were in the Hunter records."

"How did you get your hands on records?" Diego asked.

Josef smirked, but through our bond he seethed. Not that I could blame him. Having now been tortured twice by Hunters, he had every right to his fury. I couldn't tell if he was resistant to us working with Camila's brother, though.

"Who are the Garcia Perez brothers?" Carlos asked, changing the topic. "Do I need to worry about my clan?"

"They're five brothers who are known to have sympathy for vampires," Camila explained. "No one in the Spanish Hunter community wants to work with them." She smiled at her brother. "Probably the best people to call in, in this situation."

I looked around at my clan in shock. "There are Hunters who sympathise with us?" The revelation was a foreign concept. We were enemies, and that was it. "How?"

"They believe that the true meaning of The Accords is peace," Diego said. "They align themselves with some vampires in their city to maintain that peace."

"They believe there can be peace, that we don't have to force laws on vampires to live in harmony," Camila added.

"You're talking about The Accords," Josef said.

Camila nodded. "They view them as muzzles our ancestors forced onto vampires, and that there could have been a proper truce without doing that."

"I like the sound of these brothers already," I mused. "Are they the only ones who think like this?"

Diego met my eyes. "There are some. They are usually ostracised from the Hunter community; some are known to share a city with vampires, running volunteer programs in which people donate their blood willingly. By fang or by needle, depending on their preference."

"Clubs, and other places similar to Matteo's gallery," Camila added. "Donation Stations."

"That wasn't in any of the Hunter records," Andreas said in a quiet voice.

"It's not exactly something Hunters like talking about," Rafael said. "We were raised to hate you, that you were our enemies. The Hunter Network is for sharing information about vampires, histories, Hunters' records. That's something we preferred to keep in the dark."

"I believe that might be the most you've spoken," I commented, grinning at him.

Rafael shrugged, returning to his silence.

"Perhaps we can get back to the topic at hand," Carlos suggested.

"So, you're calling in your friends," Matteo said, bringing us back. "Do they know you're working with vampires?"

"They know," Diego said. "They'll be researching each and every one of you on the way. They'll know your entire histories."

"And what colourful histories they are!" I added.

Diego's gaze paused on me before continuing. "We should assume that Pierre wants to keep his army separate from the clan, for now. This has been a long play for him; he's not going to panic and bring them in against an entire clan of vampires yet. But he's also likely to be angry that you killed at least half that army. They may have had a do-not-kill order before, but they'll kill you on sight, now."

"That makes sense," Josef agreed. "He wanted my clan here, anyway. Now that we're all here, his plan was to kill us all."

"As if he could take us all on," Matteo muttered. "Most of those Hunters were *Bestowed*, and they failed to take on three of us."

"If it were me," the other Hunter Diego had brought finally spoke up. "I'd have a lot more Hunters on standby that you don't know about. A backup plan. It's possible he has more Hunters than you've seen. You killed fifteen, he probably has fifty more." He stopped when he realised we were all looking at him. He'd made it clear he didn't like this team up. He shrugged. "What's the word you used? Bestowed? Bestowed Hunters who may turn into ferals are not something I want on the streets. They're dangerous. So, right now, I'm focusing on *them* being my enemy. I trust Diego's judgement, but don't expect us to be friends."

"Understood," Carlos said. "Focus on whatever you need to to get this done."

"Alright, so expect more. Expect them to be Bestowed too. And expect them to be willing to kill you." Diego reiterated. "They're our first target. Take them off the board before approaching the den. What we know about them: they'll have the same light sensitivity as vampires, the hunger, sensitive hearing, and sense of smell. They'll also be a lot stronger than us." He glanced at Andreas. "So is it vampire blood, or human blood they crave?"

"Both." Andreas said. "They've trained their whole lives for this. That means they've spent years being fed vampire blood to learn to resist the hunger. Our venom can be addictive, and we all remember how intoxicating our first taste of vampire blood was. Something that gives them all that advantage, plus the superiority that comes with it? In the cell, I could see that tempted them. But they have our hunger, so the scent of human blood will call to them, too."

"We can't compel them," Josef added. "Pierre has compelled them to resist any compulsion that *isn't* his."

Diego's eyes passed over Camila, expression softening as unspoken pain passed between them. She must have told him about Carlos's discovery of Camila being compelled by the vampire who killed their mother. "Maybe I need that," he muttered. "Especially when we go after Pierre. He's going to use his clan against us. We have no defence against that." He took a deep breath and let it out slowly. "Okay, so Bestowed Hunters who can't be compelled."

"And they have no problem killing other Hunters," Camila reminded us.

Diego cleared his throat and pointed to another house in the image. The drones had tracked the Hunters there. The image changed to blueprints of the house. "They have two entrances. The front, and the back. Vampires have a better chance of positioning at the back without attracting attention than we do."

"Erik, Josef, and Matteo," Carlos said. He pointed to a house on the other side of the road. "Andreas, I want you here. You'll see if any get out. Either warn us, or take care of them."

"Perhaps we should have someone with Andreas?" Josef suggested.

"I'll go with him," Aria offered.

I caught Josef's gaze. In the time they'd been caged, Andreas had stood next to Josef to protect Aria. It was possible he'd won her admiration in his actions. Was there more to it than that, though? He'd entered our room, and she'd welcomed him in. I'd known Andreas a long time, and he'd always been silent, had never attempted to disrupt anything. Always the shadow.

"That leaves Hunters with you," Diego said to Carlos. "And Quinn and Celeste."

Impressed that he'd learned their names, I smiled at Quinn. "It's possible the Bestowed Hunters know about you if Pierre has seen your power."

She chuckled. "Knowing about me doesn't diminish what I can do. I'll still bring them to their knees."

"Is there something I don't know?" Diego asked.

"Quinn is a siren," Carlos revealed. "Only, with her being a vampire, her voice has more of a kick to it."

"A siren?" Diego asked. "I thought they all died out."

"Their bloodline lived on," I said. "Their voices are magnificent to behold. It's quite the draw in the bedroom."

"If they're not using it against you as a weapon," Josef added.

We all laughed.

Diego turned to Quinn. "If you're using your voice against our enemies, do we have any defence against it?"

"If I hum from within, I can aim it more directly. I can draw them forward, pull them under my will, or even have them on their knees. You may still feel its effects. If I sing with intention..."

"It's like a bomb," I said. "No control, only destruction."

"I see," Diego said. "Is it possible for that to be a last resort?"

"Of course," she agreed.

"The Garcia Perez brothers will be here in time for us to leave." Diego cast his eyes around us. "I never thought I'd hear myself say this, but we need you at your strongest."

"Oh, don't you worry about that," I said. "I ate well recently. I'm at my full strength."

Matteo and Quinn laughed.

Diego glared at me. "Three of you were recently tortured. I want to make sure everyone is well fed, and up to the task. Are those three strong enough for this?"

"We'll hunt," Aria said.

"We'll be back in an hour," Josef added.

"You're not going anywhere without me," I said. "I'm coming with you."

"Oh, I'm counting on you coming," Josef joked.

"In that case, it might be a little more than an hour," I said. When I caught Matteo's frown, I only laughed harder.

"One hour," Carlos said. "Anyone else who needs to hunt should do that now." He hugged Camila and kissed her. "I'll be back soon."

We all left quickly. I grabbed Josef around the throat. "I hope you're ready. The three of us are doing more than hunting." I grinned. "When we've fed, I'll be hunting *you*."

Josef's eyes turned red.

Chapter 41

"How long has it been since we killed together?" Erik asked Josef.

They'd already made up their mind they'd kill together. I didn't comment on their disobeying their King.

"When Carlos led the rebellion against The Accords." Josef chuckled.

I'd killed with Josef, and it had awakened a joy I'd never imagined. No fear of The Accords. No holding back my nature. I led them to my favourite hunting ground. A mist clung to the mountain, and the thrill of a hunt buzzed through my veins. The streets were surprisingly quiet.

"I don't just want to hunt, but to give chase," Erik said. "I want the human running, that scent of fear." He grinned.

The idea appealed to me. "Then we should find someone, and let them go in Montecchio Park," I said. "We can chase them through the trees, they can scream or beg, whatever you want."

Hollow footsteps echoed from behind us.

Josef pointed. "They'll do!"

I watched the human couple. Erik approached them, steps loud, and movements less graceful.

"It always looks strange to watch vampires try to look human," I said to Josef. "So unnatural."

"Sometimes it's necessary," he replied. "To ease their fears, to allow us to get close before the hunt." He moved forward, walking as human-like as Erik's.

The two of them approached the humans.

"Don't scream," Erik said. "Don't struggle."

They threw the humans over their shoulders, and we moved swiftly to Montecchio Park. In the park, nocturnal creatures avoided us, their sounds blending with the night and the rustle of leaves. Deep into the park, and away from prying ears and eyes, Erik and Josef released our prey. The humans looked around.

"Who the fuck are you?" The man spoke with an American accent.

"Tourists, my favourite!" Josef said with a twisted delight. He stepped forward with an almost playful manner and hissed. The sound was enough to frighten the humans. "Time to run!" he said joyfully.

The woman's fear rose in waves, pulling me forward. "Vampires, like in the news," she whispered to the man. "You said they wouldn't be here, that San Marino would be too small."

"The news?" Erik prompted.

They both stared at us in terror.

"I don't want to be your blood slave," the woman pleaded, backing away.

"Blood slave?" I asked. "Why would you think we'd make you our blood slaves?"

Erik and Josef laughed. "Thralls," Josef said. "Hunters called them blood slaves during the war. A term I coined, admittedly, when I was human. They were never enslaved though, merely addicted to our venom. They always lived a life of comfort, well fed, protected, sheltered."

"The Bloodking still keeps thralls," Erik added. "I haven't been in the presence of thralls for a long time though. I do miss how much they begged us to bite them. Always offering their throat, or even their wrist. But those who offered their bodies too, they were my favourite."

He reached out for the human woman. "It's okay, you won't be our thrall." His fangs glinted in the moonlight. "You won't live long enough for that."

"Which one do we want first?" Josef asked.

With one finger under the man's chin, I brought his eyes to meet mine. "Would you like to go first?" I asked. He said nothing. "Run," I instructed. "If you can make it out of the park, you live."

The man took in his surroundings, as if unsure where to run.

"That way," Josef pointed.

The human ran.

"How long do you think it will take before he realises you pointed him in the wrong direction?" Erik asked.

The woman whimpered. The scent of fear didn't just call to me, it pulled a frenzy forth. My beast within wanted to give chase. I'd held back my nature too long.

"What do you think?" Josef asked. "Compel her not to move, or for her to run, too?"

"Let her run," Erik said. "It'll give us another chase when we've finished with him."

"Run," I told her. "That way." I pointed down the path that would take her deeper into the park, into the woods.

Once we lost sight of her, we followed the direction the human man had gone.

"Draw it out," Erik instructed. "Close in, but give him a way to escape. Give him hope, only to tear it away from him."

Josef chuckled. "It has been too long since we hunted like this, Erik."

"I know."

It wasn't long before we found the human attempting to hide behind a tree.

"Pathetic," Erik said from behind him. "You were supposed to run. We wanted to give chase."

Josef laughed. "This is the humanity I once tried to protect. That modern-day Hunters try to protect. Even the human I was would be disappointed."

Erik studied the man. "Pathetic excuse for a human. Maybe you deserve this."

The two of them made what looked like an obvious mistake. As they stepped towards the human, his eyes darted to his escape. He took the chance they'd given him.

Josef grabbed my arm. "Give him some distance."

"They always run," Erik remarked. "I stood and stared my death down. Beheaded a vampire in my fight for survival. Swung my axe and she ran right into it."

"I ran," I said.

They both looked at me, waiting for me to continue.

"I left Venice to search for my father, or anyone who knew about vampires. I'd spent years obsessed with finding him. I came here to speak to someone who I heard knew about the supernatural world. She told me to go home and forget about my father, that asking questions was dangerous. She told me to return to my family. I didn't realise at the time she was the Magic Wielder connected to the local vampire clan. I left and came across Marco feeding. He chased me. Mostly drawn by my fear, but also that he needed to silence me," I recalled. "He intended to compel me, but when I ran, he lost control a little. My rambling about my father pulled him out of it. If not for that, he probably would have killed me. He was hungry, and I interrupted his meal." I shook my head. "A woman wandering alone in the middle of the night looking for vampires found more than she could have expected."

I caught the sympathy in their eyes.

Erik lifted my jaw to raise my eyes to his. "A woman alone being chased by a vampire is a little bit different."

"Not really," I argued.

"Any one of us would have given chase. Even who you are now would have," Josef pointed out.

He had a good point.

"Did you hate Marco for that?" Erik asked.

"No!" I exclaimed. "I was grateful for the life he gave me. It took awhile, but I finally got to see my father again. As Marco promised." I couldn't help myself, and leaned forward to kiss Erik, then Josef. "Plus, I wouldn't have met you both if not for him."

Josef groaned when I pulled away from him, and he yanked me back, hard against his body. He lowered his mouth to my throat, lips sending heat through my entire body. Erik stepped in behind me, kissing the back of my neck. I tilted my head back, and he shifted to my throat.

"I think we've given him enough time. Can we eat, or do you want to play a little more?" Erik asked. "I want to feed so we have time to ourselves before we have to return.

"Let's eat," I agreed.

Erik lifted his head. He turned towards where the human had run. "Breathe that scent in, my friends. Enjoy the scent a little, savour it. Anticipate how rich his blood will taste."

I breathed in, the way humans did with freshly poured wine. With slow steps, I resisted the urge to give chase. The spice of fear. His terrified gasps. The sound of his heart.

"He hasn't gone far," I noted.

"He's hiding again," Erik said. "Ready?"

"Can I approach him first?" I asked.

"A beautiful woman in the middle of the most terrifying night of his life?" Josef laughed. "I like it."

"Like Ingrid," Erik agreed.

I traced my fingers over his arm before following the human. Erik and

Josef were not far behind me.

"Hello," I said, finding the human easily.

The whites of his eyes showed as he stared at me, his heartbeat racing. The pulse in his throat captivated me.

"Shhh, it's okay," I cooed. "It's just me and you."

"Are you one of them?" he asked.

I grasped his hand and pulled him to his feet. "One of who?" I whispered.

His eyes darted around us. Erik and Josef waited in the shadows, but close enough for him to see their silhouettes. He took a step back.

"No, please," he pleaded. "They're there."

I turned, taking in their red eyes and fangs, and the hunger. "There's no one there," I said.

"What? No. They're right there!" He pointed.

"What is it you see?" I asked. "There is no one there."

"T-two men," he said. "Vampires. I think they killed my girlfriend."

"Vampires?" I scoffed. "Vampires aren't real. Have you been drinking?"

He glared at me. "Did you not see the news? Vampires revealed themselves an hour ago. In Rome first. Then there have been sightings all around the world. They said The Accords were no longer valid and declared war."

Thrilled by this news, I smiled at him. "Do you know what that means?"

"No?" His eyes didn't leave Erik and Josef, even though he couldn't see them clearly in the dark.

"It means vampires can legally kill." I pointed around us. "So why would you and your girlfriend be out in the dark? That was a bit foolish, don't you think?" I stepped forward. "There could be hungry vampires out here, breathing in the delicious scent of your fear. Wanting to sink their fangs into your throat. Hungry for your blood."

His shoulders dropped, he visibly gave up. "You're one of them, aren't you?"

Finally, I flashed my fangs and red eyes at him. "I am."

He looked around. "Where are they? Did you kill my girlfriend?"

"She's still alive. But we'll return to her when we're done with you," I said and took another step towards him.

A strong odour wafted from him. He'd pissed himself. I scrunched my nose at the offending smell.

"Are you going to kill me?" he asked.

I grasped his hair, pulling his head to the side, brushing my fingers over his exposed throat. "We are. We're going to feed until we're blood drunk."

Erik and Josef took that as their invitation to reveal themselves. The human fought against my grip.

Josef planted a kiss on my lips before turning his focus onto the human. "Do you want to die quickly and painlessly? Or should we chase you a bit more?" he asked.

"Please don't kill me," he pleaded again.

Josef leaned in, licking the man's neck. "But we are hungry."

"It's time to eat," Erik said. "Stop talking to your food. No venom. I'm in the mood for screams."

I sank my fangs into his throat, and Josef did as well, next to me. The human cried out in pain, struggling as we fed from him. Behind me, Erik's hands slid over my stomach, lips on my throat. Pleasure ripped through me when he sank his fangs in. I moaned. His hand slid down, pressing against me through my jeans. With his solid body pressed against my back, his cock hard, and fresh blood in my system, I released the human, leaning into him. He growled.

"You still need to feed," he whispered in my ear. "You can't let Josef take more than his fair share."

"Won't you feed with us?" I asked. "Are you not hungry?"

Once more his lips pressed on my throat. "The thing about a first generation is we can take satisfaction from vampire blood. Now feed, Aria, you need it."

So I returned to feeding, euphoria wrapping me in warmth as I fed, with Erik feeding from me, hands possessive, and tight against my body.

Chapter 42

The woman seemed to sense us as we stalked her from the dark. She had gone off the trail and stumbled through thick undergrowth, her panicked gasps and footfalls breaking the silence of the night. She'd at least chosen to run instead of hiding, making this hunt more of a chase than that of the man we'd left taking his last breaths.

I deliberately stepped on a twig, which snapped loudly right behind her. She spun around, but I had already moved back. I chuckled, the sound carrying.

"I know you're there!" she cried out.

"It's your turn," I whispered from behind her, and turned her to face me.

She gasped again, panic shining in her eyes. "Is he dead?" she asked, accent revealing a slight southern drawl.

"Shhh, you don't have to worry about him any more," Erik said beyond her sight. "Why don't you give in, enjoy your death."

I lifted her chin, kissing her lips softly. It didn't take long before she gave in to my kiss, a soft whimper rising from her as her lips parted. She shuddered, melting against me. Erik and Aria closed in. Erik lifted her arm, stroking her wrist. She stared at us, wide-eyed.

"Please don't kill me," she begged, voice barely audible. "I don't want to die."

I brushed a tear from her cheek. "Oh, sweet thing, we've been freed. This is what we are. But unlike your companion, you'll not feel pain. You're the dessert, and we want that sweet tang of desire." The kiss would have already added that flavour to her blood.

Erik lowered his head, brushing his lips over her wrist. He met her eyes, giving her a fanged smile. She trembled, trying to pull her wrist from his grasp. He tightened his grip as I slid my arm around her back, pulling her in. Holding her to me. I breathed in, joyous at the scent of fear that overcame me.

"Aria, this is your territory. Perhaps you'd like to go first," Erik offered.

Aria didn't hesitate, and the moment she bit down, I followed, claiming the untouched side of the woman's throat while Erik fed from her wrist.

Our venom overwhelmed her. The three of us held her up as she squirmed from the sudden onslaught of desire and pleasure pumping through her. Her arousal mingled with her fear, heart racing as we fed in silence.

I released her as her heart stopped. The human dropped to the ground with a soft thump, and Erik was on me in an instant; grabbing my jaw, locking eyes with me.

"There it is," he said with satisfaction. "That *freshly killed and enjoyed every moment of it* glint. The freedom that we experienced, it's ours again, Beloved."

I leaned forward to lick at the blood from his chin. His hand grabbed the back of my neck and drew me into a kiss. Rough and irresistible. Caught in a spiral, it hit me that I was blood drunk. I pulled Aria towards me as Erik kissed me. When we separated, he let out a sound halfway between a grunt and a growl. He was as intoxicated as me.

"War has been declared," Aria said. "Vampires are out of the shadows."

"It's about time," Erik said. "Oh, the fun we can have. I want to see this news. What has been reported?"

"I wouldn't mind more feeding," I said. "We can feed until we pass out. This time give them a taste of our venom first. I want them to beg us to bite them."

"Once we've dealt with Pierre," Erik reminded me. "We're short of time, remember, and I have much I want to do to the two of you."

I smiled. "I want my own thralls."

"I want to see what the news says about us," Aria emphasised.

I followed him, taking joy from our fresh kills, their blood singing through me.

We let ourselves into a house, finding it empty and cold. I opened the laptop on the kitchen table. Typing in the word 'vampires' resulted in thousands of news results. I clicked on one that had been written ten minutes prior.

Vampires Exist!

It has been revealed that vampires are real. Not only that, but a war has been raging between vampires and vampire hunters for centuries. Today, they stepped out from the shadows.

One who calls himself the King of all vampires brought this truth to us, declaring war on vampire hunters, and any people who thought they could fight them. In the hours since, he declared that The Accords no longer stand, and he ordered vampires to show themselves. Since they revealed themselves, they have been slaughtering people in the streets. The King of vampires has taken people to be blood slaves, which they call thralls, and left a slew of bodies around Rome, thought to be those of vampire hunters. Governments worldwide have not responded yet. Globally, other vampires have revealed themselves, some declaring themselves Kings or Queens of smaller clans. They look human, until they display their red eyes and fangs. So we have no way to tell who is and isn't a vampire until it's too late.

Already, it has been discovered that there are underground clubs in which people allow vampires to feed from them, have sex with them, or more. There are donation stations, and a variety of other ventures in which vampires make money from people more than willing to bare their throats to these creatures. Many have said their bite brings pleasure. This reporter has not been able to find any such clubs, or been face to face with a vampire yet. So I put the offer out there: If any vampire wishes for their story to be told, please contact me. I will be discreet. All I want is to tell your story—for a small fee, of course.

Her name and email was at the bottom of the article. Elise Harris.

Aria's fingers ran through my hair as she read over my shoulder. Erik's hand rested on my shoulder, thumb massaging the back of my neck.

"Sounds like she's looking for more than just an interview," Erik noted.

I turned around to face him. "We could have some fun with this. Give her what she wants."

His eyes flashed. "Indeed. A few vampires may contact her though with the same idea."

"We'll have to make sure we get her attention then." I checked the news page. "She's in England. An easy flight to Italy."

"We could use my hotel in Verona," Erik offered. "The humans there know me, and are paid more than any in the city."

"Let's get through today, and I will reach out to her. I'll make sure she can't resist me over all others."

"It's real," Aria said. "We no longer have to hide."

I stood, turning around to face her. "Free feeding. Out in the open." I reached for Erik's arm. "Just as we used to."

"No punishment for killing," Erik added with a wide smile, fingers grasping mine.

I practically vibrated, giddy with elation.

I laughed. "The number of people we've killed since we've been here, it might draw Hunters."

"Let them come." Erik let go of my hand and removed his shirt, and reached for Aria. "We have forty minutes. I would like longer, but this isn't our nest, so this will have to do." He wrapped his arms around her, pulling her close.

The two kissed, and I stalked towards them, circling them. Erik's arm shot out, pulling me in, turning to kiss me. Aria tugged at my tee-shirt. I pulled away from Erik long enough for her to remove it. I pressed my lips against hers, as Erik's hands slid down my back. He then trailed kisses, starting between my shoulder blades, moving down. He reached around, and his fingers were swift to unbutton my jeans. I lowered my mouth to suck on Aria's nipple as Erik removed my trousers and boxer briefs.

Erik stood, his naked body pressed against my back. His cock between us. He and Aria kissed over my head. I rose, the three of us taking turns to kiss one other. First my lips met Erik's, rough and wanting, igniting sparks that spread like wildfire. Then I turned to Aria, soft and gentle with her, holding back the need to push her against the wall and sink my fangs into her throat. Then she and Erik kissed, and I ran my hands over both of them.

"Bedroom," Erik commanded. "Now."

We moved fast, continuing in the bedroom.

"Get on the bed," he told Aria.

She did as he asked. I approached, but Erik stopped me.

"You stay there and don't move," he instructed Aria. "Watch."

He dropped to his knees before me. His warm mouth closed over my cock, his tongue swirling.

"Erik," I groaned. "I haven't—"

"I know," he said. "You deserve this, Josef. I'll get mine in good time." He turned his eyes to Aria, who watched us hungrily. Her hand slid towards her wetness. "No," he growled. "Only watching for now. I want my mouth there when you come."

She whimpered, but removed her hand. He licked the pre-cum from the head of my cock, hands tight on my hips.

"You know, I have to admit I do like having you kneel to me…my alpha," I said, drawing out the last word as my cock hit the back of his throat.

His eyes lifted to mine, red and gleaming with desire. *'I'll punish you for that!'*

"Oh, please do!' I returned with a smirk.

His tongue and mouth awoke my need, waves of pleasure rippling out. He dropped one hand, cupping my balls. I let out a low moan, moving my hips in rhythm with his momentum as his mouth slid down my cock. I breathed in the scent of Aria's lust, her yearning flooding our bond.

Bonded to both Erik and Aria, I felt everything they did. Aria's pleasure at watching Erik suck me off. Erik's joy to have me back after his deep worry had finally faded. His protectiveness and an ache that pushed its way through me, too. My own pleasure swelled at each bob of his head. I flexed fingers through his hair, thrilled to have him back.

As he continued, he pumped his own erection. Overwhelmed by all that flooded through, my orgasm crashed into me. Erik didn't stop until his own release. Then he stood; kissing me again, tasting of myself and the blood of our recent meal.

"Stand at the end of the bed," he commanded. "Hold on to the footboard."

I did as he ordered, and he moved around the room, ruffling through drawers.

"Yes!" he hissed, and approached me from behind. "Eyes on Josef's face, beautiful trespasser," he instructed Aria.

Erik pressed two fingers, cold with lube, massaging around my hole. The motion was enough for me to suck in a breath. First one finger probed inside, thrusting in and out for a few times. I let out a sigh of breath as I adjusted to his finger.

"Relax," he whispered in my ear. A second finger joined the first, pushing in and out. My asshole tightened, the movement sending ripples of warmth and pleasure through me. "That's it," he murmured. "Get ready, Josef." His fingers slowly pumped, in and out for a moment longer.

Then he smothered lube over his own cock and placed his hands on my hips. "Are you ready?" he asked, probing his fingers in again.

"I am," I said.

Aria's eyes widened, darting down to my cock.

"Can I suck him while you fuck him?" she asked.

Erik's body was hard against mine, warm from our meal, tense from his need to claim me. "Very well," he agreed.

She crawled to the end of the bed, wrapping her fingers around my erection.

Erik pushed forward, the head pushing into my ass. He stopped, letting me adjust.

"More," I breathed.

He pushed in more, the combination of pain and pleasure a sweet torment. I exhaled, tightening my fingers onto the wooden frame. Slowly, Erik stretched me as he pushed his cock in deeper, bit by bit. My body tingled, my anus tight around him. Finally, his thighs rested against the back of mine.

"Are you okay?" he asked, panting.

I nodded as Aria's lips closed over my shaft, crimson eyes gazing up at me.

"Good boy," he whispered, sending a full body shiver through me. "That's my good boy."

He moved his hands to wrap around my waist, holding me tight against him. His teeth grazed my earlobe.

"Aria, wait for me to start, then make sure you keep the same rhythm," he told her.

Every nerve ending in my body felt as if it were being touched as he started to move. A low groan rose from my lips as his cock pulled back, then slammed forward again. As he repeated the motion, each time he pushed in, sparks of pleasure surged from my ass, up my spine. His thighs slapped against the back of mine, arms around me tightening at each movement.

Aria started moving, my cock in her mouth, finding a rhythm with Erik's momentum. Forward when Erik pulled back, withdrawing when Erik thrust into me. I grunted and growled, their pace sending waves of heat through me. Erik panted in my ear as we moved, and he grabbed my chin, turning my head to push a kiss against my lips. Raw desire sparked between us, and jolts of electricity burst through a fog. With the two of them working on me, I was racing towards an orgasm.

"How are you doing?" Erik asked me. "Look at Aria, lips stretched around you."

As I gazed down at Aria, the sight of my cock sliding into her mouth brought another grunt from me.

"She has a beautiful mouth," I rasped out.

"I'm going to move faster," Erik warned. "Aria?"

She couldn't talk, but she hummed, the vibrations pulsing through my cock.

Fuck! Small tremors started in my legs as my beloveds worked in unison, each movement striking my pleasure points. Warmth unfurled in my stomach, and I reached the point of no return. My body tensed, tightening around Erik.

"Oh, you're close," he murmured, and pushed in with a rough thrust, eliciting a long moan from me. "Make sure you swallow all of him down," he instructed Aria.

I panted and the wood under my fingers splintered, crushed in my grip as I reached my release, coming into Aria's mouth and letting out a loud roar. The tightening of my muscles around his cock pushed Erik to his own orgasm, his body behind me tensing with small quivers running through him. His animalistic roar drowned out my own, then he bit into my throat.

We stilled, breathing hard. Erik's fangs were still embedded in my throat, the venom stretching out my release. After a moment, he removed his fangs, tongue sliding over my neck, a growl emanating from him. His embrace relaxed, his lips brushing against my jaw. I leaned my head back, placing my hands over his. The warmth of his embrace steadied me.

"Look at the two of you," he murmured, still catching his breath. "So very clearly *mine*."

I melted into his arms watching as Aria licked her lips, smiling up at me.

After a few minutes, Erik pulled out of me slowly with another kiss to the back of my neck. "I'll be back," he said, walking towards the bathroom. "Then it's Aria's turn."

Chapter 43

"I want you to watch as patiently as she has." Erik pointed next to the bed. "On your knees. There. No touching yourself." He wrapped his fingers around my cock. "This, and your pleasure, belong to me."

Without a word, I knelt on the carpet where he'd pointed. He crawled onto the bed, up Aria's body. Pinning her under his weight, the two kissed.

She groaned into his mouth, the scent of blood rising. Her fingers dug into his back, and she lifted her hips, grinding against him. He lifted himself up, wiping his thumb across her bottom lip. He sucked on his own thumb.

"I can taste Josef on you," he said.

His lips trailed over her jaw and throat. "Are you ready to claim me, my beautiful trespasser?"

"Yes," she breathed.

He smiled and kissed her again before moving himself all the way down, pressing his lips against her inner thigh. He met my eyes with a smirk. "Both of you are so obedient. Maybe I'll have to reward you."

Excitement bubbled up and I beamed at him. Aria showed the same elation. Then Erik buried his face between her thighs, eyes remaining on hers. She groaned, pushing herself against his face. Between the scent of her arousal, and sounds of his tongue inside her, my cock started to swell again.

Even from where I knelt, I could see Erik's tongue was unrelenting, as he pushed Aria towards pleasure. She threw her head back, grasping at the sheets and at his hair. Whimpers and moans rose from her, louder and louder as she neared coming. I panted, yearning to kiss her, to bite into her throat. I wanted to feel her as she came. The closer she got, the more I felt it. Tremors started in her body, and my own trembled in response. My panting became louder, heavier. I fought against my need to move.

Aria let out a loud, long wail as she came. Erik lifted his head, her juices in his beard. He met my eyes.

"Do you want dessert?" he asked.

"I want a taste," I pleaded, eyes on his face. "My alpha."

His smile widened. "Have one, then."

I moved towards him, hungry, pushing my tongue into his mouth. His tongue pushed back, caressing mine. Aria bit into my shoulder, hands sliding over my abs, down to my erection. Torn between wanting Aria and Erik, I gave in to her. I turned around to kiss her, my blood on her lips. Erik licked where she'd bitten.

"You two deserve to have each other first," he said in a soft voice. "I'll sit and watch."

"Turn around," I instructed Aria. "I want you on all fours."

She didn't hesitate, turning around, glancing over her shoulder at me once. I grabbed her ankle and pulled her towards me, to the edge of the bed. With the curve of her cheek on display, I caressed her. Then I raised my hand and slapped her ass. She yelped but didn't pull away. I slapped again. Waves of heat passed through our blood bond.

"Oh, you like that, sweet thing?" I asked.

She wiggled her ass at me, so I gave her a third slap. I lined my hips, and guided my cock into her pussy. I pushed all the way in, and started with slow thrusts, letting her adjust to me. Her muscles gripped me as I drove into her. She moved in tune, forward then lunging back when I thrust forward. The sound of skin slapping filled the room, and Erik's heavy breaths. He wasn't just watching, he was stroking himself as he watched over my shoulder.

I slapped Aria again, and her muscles constricted around me. I groaned. With my thighs, I squeezed her legs together, her body's grip tightened on my cock. I growled, my next thrust deep, sending a shiver through her.

"Josef," she whimpered.

I chased my pleasure, the two of us moving in tandem.

"I want to have your arms around me when I come," Aria gasped. "I want us to bloodshare, Josef."

I pulled out, crawling onto the bed. She moved towards me, each of us on our side facing each other. I wrapped my arms around her. Our eyes locked and I re-entered her. As I gazed into her eyes, a wave of warmth washed over me. I smiled at her. Something had changed within. Looking upon her filled me with joy, and I let that feeling spread across my chest. I reached for her face, caressing her cheek. Taken by need, I kissed her.

"You're mine," I whispered, feeling the weight of those words. Their meaning had changed.

She gazed back at me, tenderness in her smile. Our movements were slow, gentle. She kissed me again.

Smugness from Erik ended our kiss. I found him watching us with a small smile.

Aria bit me. Flooded with her venom, I sank my fangs into her shoulder. Her blood hit my tongue and I groaned against her. The bond that we shared enveloped us, binding us together. The taste of human blood in hers was subtle.

We released each other and returned to our pace. Once again the warmth started to pulse through my body. I pushed in, pulling out, her walls throbbing around me. Being face to face with her, our eyes locked, a different wave of warmth spread through my body. Mixed with affection and protectiveness. And something else. Something deeper, more physical. Hooked into me like claws.

'You're falling in love with her,' Erik commented through our bond.

The words slammed into me. I almost stopped, but pressed on. Stunned, I became aware that his words rang true. She and I had only known one another for a short time, but spending a day or two caged and being tormented and starved, I hadn't just developed affection for her, I'd fallen head over heels for her.

Instead of letting the realisation pull me from the moment, I kissed her again, hard. I filled her, stretched her, and drove my body to move fast. I was claiming her, and she responded, her own pace keeping up with mine. Another orgasm raced toward me. I held her gaze as we came together, letting myself feel the tenderness and affection for her. Then I bit her shoulder again, her fangs sinking into my throat.

Chapter 44

Aria and Josef were caught in a trance of blood sharing. His mind had become full of wonder. The way they looked at each other, the way they kissed, a closeness had formed. The warmth I felt in Josef was familiar. It was what I'd felt from him when I'd first told him I loved him. His shock at my words only confirmed it.

They lifted their heads, their eyes locked. I'd wanted my own turn with Aria, to allow her to claim me; but this was a moment they needed. I moved away from the bed. She tore her gaze from Josef. Her eyes were bright red.

"Join us," she offered, and reached for my hand, inviting me to her.

Josef's smile was welcoming. "Please," he added.

They moved out of the way. "Lay down," she said. "We can't have you feeling left out. Let us take care of you, Erik."

I could not deny their request. I lay on the bed on my back. The blanket against my skin was coarse, so I pulled it from the bed. The cotton sheets felt rough, lacking the cool silk that covered my own bed.

Josef nodded, possibly an answer to a silent question through his bond with Aria. The two of them moved to plant kisses over my chest and stomach. Aria straddled me. Josef's hands slid over her, his eyes showing the new affection for her. When he brushed my thighs, the connection was gentle, reverent. She leaned in, breath against my mouth, lips finding mine with a tenderness that filled me with aching need. Our warm bodies moulded together, and I tightened my arms around her.

"Erik, I want to claim you," she whispered.

I bared my throat. "Then do it."

"You're mine," she declared.

Her fangs entered my throat at the same time as Josef bit into my thigh. I bit her throat as well. With me already bonded to Josef, the three of us connected as one, our minds open to one another. Josef's love for the both of us blazed, his protective nature strong. Aria's wonder at our connection was sharp, and I sensed her joy. I let the pleasure of their bites carry me.

Josef fondled my balls. I threaded my hand in his hair.

Aria lowered her pussy onto my cock. As her muscles gripped my cock, she lifted herself up, driving down again. We released each other's throats at the same time, and she continued to move. Up and down, my cock sliding into her. She straightened, eyes on my face as her fingers twirled over my chest. Some of my blood dripped down from her lips. I pulled her towards me, licking my own blood away. The action turned into a deep kiss.

Josef pulled back, watching us intently.

Growls rose from Aria, and she bit me again, deeper. Her need echoed through our connection, so I obliged. She held her arm out to Josef. His fangs tore into her wrist and she whimpered.

Aria's pace quickened, pushing us to orgasm together. She lifted herself off my cock and flopped down on my chest. I rolled over, and Josef embraced her from behind. We lay in a tangle, breathing hard.

"We should probably wash up and return to the Hunters' house," Aria said after a few minutes.

"Damnit. I want this to be over and done with so we can return to our nest and not be rushed anywhere," Josef complained.

I tapped his leg, indicating for him to move. "All in good time," I promised. "Let's kill these Bestowed Hunters first, then. And that damned Hunter who became a vampire because of Josef."

Josef glared. I snapped my teeth at him, bringing out his smirk.

We showered together, fighting hard to resist temptation. Yet I still couldn't resist touching both of them, running my hands over their bodies, kissing them both. I wanted to forget about everything else, to hold these two in my arms and share this moment with them.

Discarding our bloodstained clothes from feeding, we searched the house. Josef found a blue shirt and jeans. He pulled it on, leaving the shirt open. I lifted the pendant that still hung around his neck, recalling the day I'd given it to him.

"I wouldn't object if you gave this to Aria," I offered.. "This can be a token from us both."

He glanced down at it. "Maybe," he said.

I pressed my hand against his cheek. "It's alright, Josef. Having a connection with another doesn't change what's between you and me. You've seen King Carlos loves equally. That's who he is. We're no different."

'You're right, I love her,' he whispered through our bond. *'All I wanted to do in that cell was protect her. I didn't care that I was in pain and hungry.'*

I'd felt it myself through our connection. He'd fallen fast and hard. With the new bond I now had with Aria, I could feel that his affection was reciprocated. They'd bonded during their traumatic experience.

I kissed his forehead. *'You know this pendant has deep meaning to me. I know it has deep meaning to you. Would it not be the perfect gift for her? We've both claimed her; that could be a symbol of her belonging to us.'*

He gave me a half smile.

"My men, what is taking you so long?" Aria asked from another room in the house.

"Our lady awaits," I said.

We found her in a black and red top, with a black skirt. Her eyes ran over the length of my body. "You're still naked," she said. "We should go soon. You're not planning on fighting Pierre and the Hunters naked, are you?"

I chuckled. "I didn't find any clothes that fit," I explained. "Maybe I should show up naked." I deepened my voice. "Behold! You face a god among men. Tremble before my glory!"

I grabbed my own crotch.

Aria raised an eyebrow. "Your glory?"

I indicated my body. "All this! Let them admire my visage!"

Josef scoffed. I retrieved my blood-soaked tee-shirt and pulled on my jeans.

"Come on then," I said. "Let's go to war."

Dark joy crossed over Josef's face. "With pleasure," he replied.

They followed me from the house. I examined the streets around us. It wasn't that late, but humans had made themselves scarce. Mere hours had passed since the Bloodking had revealed our existence to the world.

"Remind you of anything?" I asked Josef, pointing around us.

He scanned our surroundings. "The scent of fear clings to the air," he acknowledged. "It does remind me of when I was human. We knew about the monsters that came from the shadows, and we thought hiding from them kept us safe. Humans know about us now. They're responding the same way we did. With fear and irrationality. Their four walls of any shelter will stop no vampire who wants in." He shot me a grin. "Is this how it felt for you?"

I recalled a time long past. "We never hid ourselves from humans like we do now. They knew of our existence long before you were born. They told themselves they were safe in the light. In their homes, convinced that we could not pass the threshold if they prayed to their entities. When we burst through their doors, they told us we were not invited in the eyes of their gods."

"Is that how the myth began of us needing to be invited in?" Aria asked.

I nodded. "Humans have a habit of changing stories to fit whatever makes them comfortable. If they believed we couldn't enter uninvited, they felt safe." I met Josef's eyes. "It was a temptation, listening to humans whisper to each other. Being called forth by their fear." I laughed. "Ingrid started to play with them early, where she would hide her vampirism, beg them for help, say that someone was chasing her. They'd let her in without question. She'd then show them her true nature and let me in. Oh, the games we played with them."

Memories of Ingrid mixed with pain. She'd died when the Hunters took down Gabriela, and I hadn't had a chance to say goodbye. Both of us Northerners, we'd shared a fondness for our discussions of the Norway we'd left behind. We'd spent hours watching inaccurate television shows of our time, both hating it, yet missing our home.

It didn't take us long to get back to the Hunters' safehouse. Carlos opened the door as we approached.

"You're late," he said. "Diego is briefing the Garcia Perez brothers." He glanced over his shoulder. "They're not opposed to allowing themselves to be Bestowed."

"I'm assuming you'll grant them that privilege?" I asked as Josef and Aria walked past us into the house.

"Andreas, Quinn, Matteo, and Celeste will," he said. "By the way, I wanted to talk to you about something."

I followed him outside, and we walked away from the house.

"What did you want to talk about?" I asked.

"We've known each other a long time," he started. "I could not have become King without you, Erik. Your support and guidance in those early years were valuable. I should not have used my voice on you earlier."

"No, you shouldn't have," I agreed. "You swore to all of us you wouldn't rule your clan like Gabriela had. But let's not dwell on what's happened. We have Hunters to kill, and a rogue vampire."

His eyes met mine. "You knew the Elders before I did. Do you think they lied about anything?"

This was not what I'd expected at all. "About what?"

"About us being bonded with more than two vampires," he said. "We were told it was dangerous. It's been a couple of weeks since I shared my blood with Quinn, to save her. I'm bonded to three people. Other than a feeling of being crowded, the only thing I feel is stronger. I have Elder blood in me, and the three bonds add to my power. What about Josef? He was bonded to three for a short time too."

"Josef didn't say anything about that." I stroked my beard, mulling over his words. "Knowing Luis the way I do, he would have wanted to ensure he, and the others, remained the strongest among us. It's possible they could have constructed a lie to keep other vampires from gaining such power."

"No one tested it?" he asked.

I shrugged. "No one had need to. We were content living our lives the way we did. We had everything we wanted."

"I want to put my theory to the test," he said, and held his wrist out to me. "Feed from me, Erik."

"You want me to be bonded to you?" I asked. "To make you stronger?"

"It will make you stronger, too," he said. "I'm assuming you've bonded with Aria by now."

"Hmm, it might be a good thing while going into battle with these Hunters," I agreed. "Don't fall into the trap of getting power hungry or abusing your status as our King."

He grinned. "I'll always have you to pull me back, old friend."

Now there was no hiding the truth from him. The moment I bit him, he'd know. My venom would reveal what I was. "You should know," I said quietly. "I'm a first generation. Amara was my maker."

Carlos's eyes darted across my face, disbelief drawing his brows together. "I'm the King of a First Gen?" he asked in awe. "Why didn't you tell me?"

I shrugged. "I didn't want you to treat me differently. You know how some vampires bow and scrape when they meet first generations."

Carlos stared for a moment, then laughed. "Have you forgotten I was turned by a first generation? You thought it would change how I see you?" A silence stretched between us. "I should have known," he said finally. "Your nesting with Luis and Amara. How close you were with her. Your strength. You never had a need to fear talking to me about it, though. I've had twenty years of being your King; this makes me feel a little…"

"Don't," I interrupted him. "I knelt to you, Carlos. We chose you as our King. First generation or not, that changes nothing." I sighed. "Not even Gabriela knew. She was elsewhere when I was turned. Amara warned me that vampires get a little…awestruck, with First generations. So I told her I didn't want to be treated like that. She and Luis compelled anyone to forget who'd turned me and not ask questions. I wasn't the only vampire they did that for. Centuries passed, and people stopped talking about who their makers were."

I grabbed his wrist. "Enjoy my bite," I told him with a grin, and bit hard before offering him my own.

I grunted as his venom hit my system, and pushed down the urge to bite into his throat instead. Our minds connected, and I felt his sharp awareness and worry for his clan. The determination to protect us all mixed with cold calculation as to how to win. I'd never been bonded with more than two vampires before. Carlos was right; it *did* bring power.

"What a rush," he murmured, releasing my wrist. "If I'd ever known your bite, I would have known you were first generation. There's nothing as intoxicating as first generation venom. Except for Elder venom and blood, of course. But you'd know that better than I."

I'd known the effects of Elder blood. Luis had only ever bitten me, never sharing his blood with me. But Amara's blood and venom were enough to create a frenzy. A pang pulsed through my heart. She'd been dead longer than I'd known her, but I still yearned for my maker.

"I felt her death as I watched her die," I confessed. "The most painful thing I've lived through."

"You never told me you were there," he said.

I laughed bitterly. I'd only ever spoken to Josef and Ingrid about this. "The three of us were in the middle of fucking and feeding when the Hunters attacked. Luis left; I followed. I found Josef, taunted him a little, but Amara's fear pulled me to her. I walked in in time to see that Hunter decapitate her. With all my strength and speed, I never had a chance to save her."

I'd watched Luis grieve his beloved in silence.

Carlos embraced me. "I had no idea, Erik. You keep a lot to yourself. We supported Luis in a time that you were hurting, too. I'm sorry." He pulled back.

"If we're blood bonding, I'd like in on this," Josef said from behind us.

Carlos smiled, and the two of them exchanged blood.

Before we could return to the house, Carlos dropped to his knees.

"My King?" I crouched before him. "Are you alright?"

His eyes glazed over, as if he didn't see me.

"What's wrong with him?" Josef asked, searching Carlos. "Was he shot?"

"I think the Bloodking might be talking to him," I said.

"A warning," Carlos confirmed. "I'm not to do that again. Tell no one of our discovery here."

"It gives you an ace up the sleeve that no one will see coming," I pointed out.

"The clan should know," Josef added.

Carlos nodded. "I will not hide this from the others, but we don't discuss it outside of the clan. That includes our Hunter friends in there." His eyes lifted to mine as I helped him up. "You were right to challenge me, Erik. Now, let's present ourselves as one front and take down these damn Bestowed Hunters and their traitorous vampire King."

Chapter 45

The Hunter brothers were talking in low voices to Diego when I walked into what Erik referred to as our 'War Room'. Recognition sparked in their eyes as they stopped talking, staring at me.

"It's Josef Alfaro," one of them muttered. "He looks exactly the same, but with shorter hair."

I said nothing, growing tired of my celebrity status amongst Hunters. I moved to the far side of the room. I'd cursed sitting for that portrait a thousand times—insisting we needed to record the war for history's sake. That generations would follow us, should we fall. What had started as journals had become an entire online library when the internet took over. Only my own journal had survived that transition, a keepsake I'd claimed at the first opportunity after I'd turned. I'd even continued writing for a while; about my life as a vampire, the battles we'd won and the different hunts. Now every Hunter knew my face.

The brothers whispered amongst themselves, but I tuned them out.

"We learn about you from a young age," Camila joined me. "You were a man who lost everything and found the strength to fight for humanity. A man whose courage and resolve others drew strength from. You and many of the First Hunters were a beacon to many generations that followed." She smiled up at me. "That first day I saw you, I knew you looked familiar, but couldn't place your face, even though I'd learned about you. Hunters hate who you are now, but admire that man you were."

"I'm not sure telling him he inspires Hunters will have its desired effect," Celeste said.

I laughed. "But I do appreciate your attempt," I said. "Thank you, my Queen."

Camila beamed up at me. I smiled back at her.

Carlos drew everyone's focus back to him. "This is an unlikely alliance. Our people have been on opposite sides for a long time, and war has been declared once more. But today, the enemy of my enemy is my friend. So here we are, vampires and Hunters, working together to take down a former Hunter and his Bestowed descendants." He spoke in a clear voice. "This is what we know about Pierre. Josef's history is what inspired him. He has already taken down vampire clans, and the clan of San Marino is next in his sights; potentially us, too. The Hunters he has shared his blood with are here for the sole purpose of killing us. They believe it gives them an advantage."

Every vampire in the room laughed.

"Pierre has underestimated us," our King continued. "We are no longer bound by The Accords. While he understands the strengths and hunger of a vampire, he has not known life before the war. He has not seen what vampires will do when not held back by such restrictive laws." Carlos smiled, showing fang, but it was one of menace. "He tried to take two members of my clan, and Matteo's daughter. He wanted us here, so we will show him the nightmare he summoned." He pointed to the Hunters. "We have nine trained Hunters." His eyes flickered to Camila, and a sliver of fear shifted through my new bond with him. "Our newer arrivals have suggested we Bestow them to give them an advantage against our enemy. Celeste, Andreas, Quinn, and Matteo will be bonded with four of these brothers. The fifth one will remain un-Bestowed. Unlike our enemy, these Hunters will be bonded. They do not wish to become feral if any do become vampires. But we will prevent that from happening." He stepped aside, allowing Diego to step up.

"If you kill Bestowed Hunters, make sure they cannot come back," Diego said. "Hunters, in my absence, listen to King Carlos."

Erik and Matteo's eyes found mine. A noticeable shift for the seasoned Hunter. Usually, to call a vampire by their title was only ever done with a mocking tone. There had been respect in the way Diego had spoken.

"We've discovered that our enemy can only be compelled by Pierre. So Carlos will compel us to only take orders from him. When this is over, he will free us from that influence," Diego added.

We watched in silence as the Hunters lined up, and Carlos planted a command in all of their subconscious with his compulsion. "You will resist all compulsion that isn't mine."

Camila went last. He gazed down at her, his hardened expression softening. Through the blood bond I now had with him, tenderness and warmth flowed.

"You are my Queen," he said. "No other vampire can give you commands except for your King,"

"No other vampire can give me commands," she said, falling under his compulsion.

He tilted her chin up, and lowered a kiss to her lips. She moaned into his mouth, their kiss becoming somewhat heated.

"Damn, do we all get special treatment like that?" one of the Garcia Perez brothers joked. He glanced at Celeste. "I want that one."

Celeste drifted over, planted a kiss on his lips, then walked away. His eyes remained on her.

"Be careful," another Hunter warned. "She belongs to the Vampire King too."

Diego cleared his throat, and Camila pulled away. The smile she gave Carlos was one of love before tearing her gaze from him.

"Thank you for trusting him," she said to her brother.

"It's *you* I'm trusting," he replied, then looked around at us. "Who wants to put this to the test?"

I stepped forward. "I will."

Diego approached me with hesitation.

"Don't look so worried," I said with a smirk. "The enemy of my enemy is my friend. You can go back to fearing and hating me tomorrow."

He stood in front of me, and I appreciated the fact that normally, no Hunter would willingly let a vampire compel them. Yet there he was, allowing Carlos to do so, and again with me.

"I don't fear you," he said, lifting his crossbow. "Not when I have this."

Erik growled. "Watch who you threaten, Hunter."

"Diego, they shot him; maybe put the crossbow away," Camila said.

Diego handed his weapon to his friend. "Sorry," he said, forcing a wry smile. "Habit." He squared his shoulders. "Okay, I'm ready."

I pushed my will onto him. "Get on your knees, Hunter."

Diego didn't move, and a smile broke out over his face. "Again," he said.

"Suck my cock," I commanded.

Diego scoffed. "You wish."

I raised my eyebrows. "No desire whatsoever to get on your knees?"

"I can *feel* your command," he admitted. "But I can *resist* it." He looked over at Carlos. "It works."

Four of the Garcia Perez brothers approached Andreas, Matteo, Quinn, and Celeste, exchanging blood.

"You only had a small amount," Matteo told them. "It should leave your system in a couple of days. Three at the most. We can't compel you, but we can use our bond to keep you from giving in to the hunger."

"Everyone ready?" Carlos asked.

He moved through the room. First he stopped in front of Celeste, kissing the top of her head, then caressed Quinn's cheek, and put his hand on Matteo's shoulder. Carlos stopped in front of me.

"If you were wanting to be sucked off, you could have asked," he said. "I would have happily obliged, or Erik, or even Aria. You didn't have to ask a Hunter to do it."

I burst out laughing. "I was trying to be funny, my King."

He grinned at me, but his smile faded. "Everything you do is for our clan; that has not gone unnoticed, Josef. You and Erik both put our clan above everything. I thank you both for that. But I'm happy you and he have found Aria. Perhaps you can finally take your own joy, without the burden of the clan weighing you down."

"Our life is *La Voz,*" Erik said from behind Carlos.

"But live for yourselves, too," Carlos said. "I want to see you both happy. You hid your own bond and love of each other for twenty years to put the clan first. Once we get through today, I don't want to see either of you for at least two weeks. Maybe a month. Not just the nesting, but find your place in the world again." He pulled Camila to him, wrapping one arm around her. "Leave Venice if you need to. Maybe we all need to leave Venice at one point or another. Humans take breaks; perhaps we need to as well." He met Erik's eyes. "Don't you own a couple of hotels?"

"I do, my king. One in Verona, Norway and in Scotland," Erik confirmed.

"Then take Josef, maybe even Aria and have all the time you need to enjoy life's pleasures outside of the clan." Carlos glanced around the room. "Let's go."

Diego walked next to Carlos, Camila behind them. Together, we followed them out. Hunter and vampire alike.

Chapter 46

Outside, the Garcia Perez brothers released three small drones into the air, watching on his tablet. I watched them, the quiet buzz breaking the silence. Erik looked over the shoulder of one Hunter.

"Even the drones have night vision?" Erik asked and lifted his eyes to the nearest drone.

His image on the screen was bright green, brighter than that of his surroundings.

Beside me, Andreas chuckled. "Our weapons expert," he said to me. "Although I can't blame him for taking an interest in those drones. I've never seen them so small before."

"Our tech expert," my father added, grinning at Andreas.

"There's thermal imaging too." The Hunter showed Erik. "Your heat signatures show as normal. If you hadn't recently fed, you'd be easier to pick out of a crowd. All Hunters have this tech, so you should be careful when you go home."

Erik pointed to the tablet. "What's that button for?"

"That is a button you'd better hope I don't push," the Hunter said. "It emits a high-pitch sound that only vampires can hear. Probably us, too, with your blood. It'll drop you to your knees. Useful when we need to make a hasty exit."

"Oh, we're well familiar with that sound," Carlos said. "It doesn't only drop us to our knees; it makes our ears bleed."

Camila winced, and Carlos dropped a kiss to the top of her head.

"This one turns on a concentrated light that is almost as bright as sunlight," the Hunter continued.

One of the brothers handed a tablet to Erik. "Would you like to try it?"

I watched as Erik took the tablet and a drone circled us. His face lit up.

"Okay, maybe we should refocus on the task?" Diego suggested.

Camila elbowed him. "Let the vampire play."

"You want the oldest, whose weapon choice was an axe, to "play" with something that can explode?" Quinn asked.

"It can't explode," Camila scoffed.

Watching how the clan interacted with Camila, I let some of my own mistrust of her go. They'd accepted her. As Camila grinned at Quinn, attempting to imitate the Australian accent, I saw they were treating her as one of their own. Even her brother was trying, for her sake, to speak to her clan as if they weren't enemies.

"You'll get used to the ways of our clan," Andreas said with a warm smile.

I smiled back.

The walk to where we'd been caged was twenty minutes. Carlos had burned that house down as we left, but the one next door now housed Hunters. I leapt onto the opposite rooftop with Andreas.

"I only hear eight heartbeats inside." Carlos eyed Diego. "So much for the numbers."

"Then they're nearby," Diego said. "Probably waiting for you and your clan before they close in."

"He knows you're working with us," Carlos reminded Diego. "So they'll be waiting for you, too."

The low, mechanical hum of the drones set me on edge as they circled above.

"Five houses over, unless someone's having a party, there are twenty people, not moving," one of the Hunters said in a low voice.

"Another twenty in the house at the end of the street," Erik added. "If they're Bestowed, they already know we're here."

Carlos said nothing in response as we waited. He turned towards Diego, making a hand gesture like he was starting a lighter. Diego pulled small items from the bag he carried over his shoulder. Carlos pointed at Erik and Josef, who grabbed the items. Diego showed a throwing motion.

'We're flushing them out,' Josef told me as they disappeared. *'Be ready.'*

'You do that, and we'll be surrounded on three sides,' I warned. *'Not to mention any humans who get curious when houses burst into flames.*

Erik's laughter echoed in my mind. *'I don't care about the humans. Let them come. They'd be a distraction for the Bestowed Hunters.'*

A moment later, bright orange glowed against the cover of night followed by a roar of flames. Josef and Erik returned without a sound, taking to the shadows with my father. Angry voices came from the houses now on fire. The Hunters weren't fools; they knew where the fire had come from.

"It feels a little unnatural using something that can kill us against humans," Josef remarked.

The Hunters moved out onto the street.

"I don't like this. They're being boxed in," I worried aloud to Andreas.

"Trust in them," Andreas said. "Three of our clan fought in the war. They'll have some plan."

The Bestowed rushed towards where Carlos waited with Celeste, Quinn, and the Hunters. They paused, as if confused by the lack of vampires. Carlos stood back to back with Diego.

"Here we go," Diego muttered.

"Don't sound so stressed," Carlos returned. "This will be fun."

Diego scoffed. "Fun?"

A Bestowed Hunter charged towards Quinn, raising his crossbow. My father closed the distance, breaking the Hunter's wrist. But not before a bolt was released, striking Quinn in the shoulder. She pulled it out and shoved it into the Hunter's eye. The wet squelch was followed by the Hunter's screams as he fell to the ground, clutching his eye.

The eight inside the house showed up.

"Our turn," Erik said. He and Josef joined the fight.

Someone punched Diego, and he punched back. The five brothers circled around three of Pierre's Hunters, eliminating them quickly. The thumps of fists against bodies and gush of blood filled the air.

"I feel like we're missing out," Andreas commented.

Camila and Celeste paired up, taking on their own Hunters, while Quinn and Matteo faced what looked like the leader.

"Do we go down and join them?" I asked.

"No," Carlos instructed as he tore the heart out of a Bestowed Hunter, advancing on the next. "Watch our backs. I need a warning if Pierre shows up. Or your clan."

Humans came from their houses, saw the fight, and fled back inside, their fear heavy in the air.

"All clear on the humans," I said. "They're too scared to intervene."

I had to agree with Andreas. We were missing out. I scanned the street, but no more Bestowed Hunters advanced. Andreas fell to his knees, pulling me with him, and pointed.

Pierre stood at the end of the street, watching the fight, anger apparent on his face, nostrils flaring.

'Pierre has arrived,' I told Erik and Josef through our blood bond. *'He doesn't look happy.'*

Pierre's eyes darted around until he found us and smiled. "Already on your knees," he stated. Even above the noise of the fight below I could hear him clearly. "Tell your King to kneel and I'll let him live."

I rolled my eyes, and Andreas chuckled. "You clearly don't know the strength of our King," he shot back, rising to his feet. "Or The Feral."

Andreas disappeared, only to reappear in front of Pierre. "How about you face me?" he growled. "Without the cage between us, without your army's arrows, you'll fall this time."

"Oh, shit. Andreas has engaged Pierre alone." My voice rang out.

I didn't wait for any commands or replies. I leapt from the roof of the house and raced towards Pierre, a growl erupting from my chest. "I'll tear your heart out," I threatened.

"Aria, stop," my father's voice reached me, pulling my anger back a little.

"That's right, listen to your father," Pierre said.

"Shut up," I said.

One by one, Carlos's clan joined us. A quick glance over my shoulder showed Diego and the brothers still fighting the rest of Pierre's Bestowed Hunters.

Carlos pushed me aside. "So, you're Pierre. Didn't you *kneel* to me?"

Celeste gasped, stepping forward. "I thought I recognised your scent back in Venice, but I couldn't place it," she murmured. "Patrice?"

Chapter 47

"Patrice?" Carlos snapped his head towards Celeste. "*That's* Patrice?"

"Who's Patrice?" Aria asked.

Celeste spoke to Aria in a shaking voice. "We took him in. He said he was the last survivor of his clan after Hunters destroyed their den." Her breath caught, eyes flickering towards Pierre. "He was with us for a year. I—We trusted him. Then one morning, the Hunters attacked. Set our den on fire." Her voice dropped to a whisper, a tear leaving a trail down her cheek. "I thought I was the only one who made it out."

"Hello, Celeste," Pierre said with a smirk, tone cruel, mocking.

Carlos growled, a warning. "Don't speak to her!" He pulled Celeste to him, caressing her cheek. "You didn't know," he murmured.

"I thought you were dead," Celeste said to Pierre with a shaky breath. "I didn't realise you were the Hunter who destroyed your own clan. Then mine. Was there even a clan? I…" She turned her face away, and another tear slid down her cheek.

"If it means anything, I loved you, too," Pierre said, voice gentle before his eyes hardened. "But I had a job to do."

"I told you not to talk to her!" Carlos warned.

Celeste took a step back, shaking her head. "It was a friend of mine you captured. You violated her in taking her blood. Is she still alive?"

"She is," Pierre said. "Under heavy guard. She's the reason I haven't forgotten my mission. Hunters force her to use her voice on me, to kill vampires. They've tortured her all these centuries, so there's not much of her mind left. I suppose I would have lost myself centuries ago, the way Josef did."

The idea of a vampire being tortured brought me a burning rage. Especially in the knowledge we'd failed in freeing her. A friend of Celeste's. Carlos's anger vibrated through the connection we now had. I stepped forward, placing myself between Pierre and Celeste. Josef followed. Then Matteo and Quinn. We all formed a line. Andreas was the last to join us.

"I mourned you!" Celeste cried. "I mourned everyone! You murdered them?!"

"It's okay, *ma chérie,*" Carlos whispered to her.

"How does it feel, knowing she loved me first?" Pierre asked. "We fed together. I fucked her before you even knew her. She was so beautiful, I couldn't resist." His eyes shifted towards Aria. "She didn't resist like you though."

Carlos growled again, and pushed his way between me and Matteo. "How does it feel knowing I'll pull your heart from your chest and give it to her?" he said.

"You can try," Pierre said.

Carlos advanced on Pierre. "I'll do more than try. You took members of my clan, and my Second's daughter." He pointed to us. "Besides, I think you're outnumbered."

"We're not in your territory this time," Pierre said. "Now, *I'm* King, and you're in *my* domain." His smile returned. "So, *kneel,* King Carlos. Recognise me as your equal."

I laughed. Andreas, Josef, and Matteo also. Carlos's laughter boomed from him.

"My equal?" he asked. He turned to face us with amusement glinting. "He thinks being king makes him my equal!"

Carlos's eyes turned red, fangs lengthening, and he turned around again to face Pierre. "You will *never* be my equal. Your former King knelt to me. Your clan is my clan."

"I was not King when I knelt to you," Pierre said. "I am a King now, and I do not kneel to you, or your small clan." He lifted his gaze to Aria. "It's not too late to be a King's Queen."

She made a sound of disgust.

"She's mine," I said to Pierre.

"And mine," Josef added.

We surrounded him. Diego chose that moment to approach. "Pierre Moreau, you Bestowed Hunters. You risked making ferals. It is my right to kill you where you stand."

"I am a Hunter, you fool!" Pierre told him. "I did the work of the Hunters. I killed vampires."

Carlos moved enough to allow Diego to stand beside him.

"I heard you climbed into bed with the vampire you were sent to kill," Pierre said to Camila. "I'm the reason you were in Venice in the first place, so you can thank me for meeting your sweetheart." He laughed, glancing at Carlos. "Look at me, bringing you together with your beloveds. Not one, but two."

"What do you mean?" Diego demanded.

Pierre barely acknowledged Diego. "That body in the canal? Something I left in the hopes to draw Hunters. That didn't go as planned. They were supposed to descend on Venice, and take your clan out."

It unsettled me that he'd come into our territory without anyone noticing. We'd been lucky that only Camila had answered that call.

Pierre finally focused on Diego. "I also heard that your father died. Killed by the same vampires you stand with." He glanced at the Garcia Perez brothers. "Yet your own men are Bestowed. You are quite the hypocrite, aren't you?"

"I did what I had to to take you down." Diego pointed to Pierre's dead Hunters behind us. "Now you're alone, it's my privilege to watch King Carlos kill you. You're a traitor."

I realised those he came with weren't beside him, and glanced around; not finding them.

Pierre laughed this time, and pointed to Josef. "You can thank him. His actions inspired me. I've killed hundreds of vampires in three centuries."

"Enough talk!" Carlos boomed and attacked.

He struck Pierre hard, the blow landing with a loud crack. The force sent Pierre stumbling back, blood spraying from his mouth. Carlos didn't hesitate and followed through with another punch. This one with enough force to break bones. Satisfaction surged through our bond, as the sound of each impact filled the silence.

Pierre tried to fight back, swinging wildly, but his punches hit nothing but air. Carlos moved with a predatory grace—lethal, deliberate. Every strike revealed his power as he unleashed his full strength—a blur of movement. Growls and the heavy impact of bones cracking filled the night. Bones broke. They healed in seconds, but each strike left Pierre rattled, weakening before our eyes.

Carlos dominated the fight. Both as a King and as someone bonded to five vampires, one of which was the Bloodking. None of us moved, knowing we were not needed. A three-hundred-year-old didn't stand a chance against someone who had fought in a war and led a rebellion. Pierre had been fooling himself to think he could take on Carlos.

Finally, Pierre crumpled—exhausted, humiliated, and defeated. On his knees, he stared up at Carlos as our King pressed a foot to his chest, pushing him to the ground.

"You say you took inspiration from Josef," Carlos said. "But he put up more of a fight than you when he was human." He smiled at us. "Who wants the honour of killing this pathetic excuse of a vampire?"

"I do," Aria said. "He killed Luca and Angelina."

"I want his heart," Celeste added.

Fear rose from the fallen vampire as he struggled under Carlos's foot.

Vampires sped towards us from all angles. He must have called to them using his King's voice. They surrounded us. Silent, watching. Waiting for Pierre's command. *Famiglia di Sammarinese* had arrived.

Chapter 48

My clan stood in silence.

"They invaded our territory. Aria let them in, and they killed Luca," Pierre said. "Kill them, now."

Ricardo met my eyes. "Is this true?" he asked. "You were his Second. What reason did you have to kill Luca?"

"She wanted to be Queen," Pierre gasped under the increasing pressure of Carlos's foot. "Get this idiot off me."

Vampires ran at Carlos, knocking him to the ground. Ten vampires surrounded them. Carlos remained still, unwilling to hurt my clan.

"He lies," I said, appealing to the clan. "*He* killed Luca, and he caged me, along with Andreas and Josef. You've known me for *centuries*. I would *never* kill another vampire without reason."

"She has lied to you all. For centuries," Pierre said. "She is Aria Barone, The Feral's own daughter. Luca sent her to Venice, and she plotted with them to take over our entire clan. Kill them. And the Hunters who stand with them."

"Ricardo," I pleaded as his red eyes lifted to me. "You were there when Marco brought me to the clan. You've known me longer than Pierre. He's a Hunter, and he killed clans in France before he joined us. He only came to San Marino to kill us."

"Listen to your King!" Pierre grunted. "You knelt to me. Obey me now."

My clan advanced.

'He's using his voice on them,' Erik's voice in my head was quiet. *'They have no choice but to do as he commands.'*

'Why did his voice not work on me?' I asked Erik. *'I haven't officially joined La Voz. This is still my clan.'*

'Because you didn't kneel to him,' he replied as Ricardo rushed him.

We were outnumbered by a clan that had no choice but to obey Pierre's order.

"Don't hurt them!" I pleaded with *La Voz*, and the Hunters who stood with them.

"No killing," Carlos confirmed as he pushed vampires away from him. He climbed to his feet, only for vampires to close in, menacing snarls rising from them.

"They're trying to kill us!" Diego argued.

"They have no fight against their King's command," my father replied.

"So we kill Pierre, then. Got it." Diego said. "Don't kill the vampires, but take down their King!"

I fought against Carmen, the two of us growling as we lunged at each other.

"Don't let the siren sing," Pierre commanded.

I didn't have time to find Quinn as I faced Carmen "Stop," I pleaded.

"I can't," Carmen whispered. "You know this, Aria. Our King has *commanded* us."

She lunged at me again, faster this time. I met her halfway, blocking, my own blows making contact. Her blows reverberated through my bones. I fought to keep her from my throat, from reaching for my heart. Erik's growls sounded from behind me; primal, cutting through the chaos. He faced off against Ricardo and three other vampires.

Out of the corner of my eye, I saw Pierre climb to his feet, one hand wiping the blood from his mouth. A satisfied smile curved his lips.

I closed my hands around Carmen's throat. "I don't want to hurt you," I said.

Andreas stepped from the shadows, holding Carmen back. She snarled, struggling against him. He retreated back to the shadows, taking her with him.

"I didn't realise you could do that," I muttered.

Pierre had done what he'd set out to do. Pit *La Voz* and *Famiglia di Sammarinese against each other.* He didn't have to do anything to kill *La Voz,* as my clan would kill them. I'd learned about this clan, and drawn close to Josef, and appreciated Erik's protective presence. Andreas, Quinn and even Camila, I couldn't let them die. I gazed across at my father, and for the briefest of moments, he smiled back before punching Ricardo hard enough to knock him out cold.

"Perhaps you should let The Feral out," I whispered.

His smile faded. "Your clan will die if I do that."

"I was Luca's Second!" I shouted at those around me. "By rights, *I* replace him, *not* Pierre. It is *me* you should kneel to!"

"Nice try," Pierre said. Right next to me.

A sound I'd never heard drilled through my head. It came from above me. A second sound joined it, and I fell to my knees, pressing my hands to my ears. Every vampire around me had also dropped, including the Bestowed Garcia Perez brothers.

"You're hurt," Camila said to her brother, reaching a hand to his swollen face.

"I'm fine," he grunted.

He lifted his crossbow and fired three rounds into Pierre's chest. Satisfaction surged through me when the usurper's body crumbled to the ground. Blood trickled from my ears as the sound continued. Camila ran towards the tablet Erik had dropped. She picked it up, and the sound stopped.

My ears rang as I removed my hands.

"Good thinking, Erik," King Carlos said, climbing to his feet. "Maybe next time, a warning?"

"Sorry, my King," Erik said.

The rest of us rose from the ground. *La Voz* faced *Famiglia di Sammarinese.*

I stepped between the two clans. "Pierre killed Luca," I said. "He had me caged with Josef and Andreas. He tried to starve us into a frenzy."

"Aria, you're working with Hunters," Ricardo said. "He warned us you were." He stalked towards me. "Whatever the cause, they're our enemies. They've spent centuries killing our kind."

Erik and Josef stepped in front of me. Andreas reappeared, releasing Carmen. "That's far enough," Erik commanded. "She was caged; it wasn't Aria who called the Hunters in. It was our King. Let me remind you, he's *your* King. too. Luca knelt to him. That still stands."

"Pierre was a Hunter," I said. "He betrayed us all." I pointed to Celeste. "She can tell you of his betrayal, three hundred years ago."

My clan murmured amongst themselves. There was mistrust there as they glared towards Diego. I noticed then that my father, Andreas, Quinn, and Celeste were holding back the four brothers whom they'd Bestowed. Their brother who wasn't Bestowed lay on the ground near Pierre's dead Hunters, his heart stilled, throat sliced open. Wails of grief mixed with growls of their hunger. Diego knelt over the bodies of the friends who'd come with them.

"They both died," Camila said. "Diego, I'm sorry."

"I rescued them from Rome, only for them to die anyway," he said, voice thick with emotion. "We must take them back to Spain."

"You know I can't go back with you," Camila said.

I let their conversation fade as I focused on Ricardo. He hadn't moved. No one had.

"If you try to kill me, I think you'll find yourself surrounded by Erik and Josef," I said. "They've claimed me."

"Was Pierre right? Are you The Feral's daughter?" Carmen asked.

I nodded. "I am. Marco turned me, promising to help me find him."

"Why did you keep it from us?" Carmen asked. "I've known you for centuries, Aria. We've fed together. You couldn't trust us with that?"

"I did not want to be used as a way to get to him," I said.

Carlos crouched over Pierre's body, and punched into his chest, removing his heart.

"Did you have to do that?" Diego asked. "I'm sure he's dead."

"Now we know he is," Carls said, standing. He gave the heart to Celeste.

"You killed our King," Ricardo said.

"He was no king," Carlos said. "Aria speaks the truth. I came here to free my clan, and Aria, from Pierre." He pointed at the burned house. "We burned it down, but that is where they were held captive. Fifteen bodies of Hunters lay inside; even Bestowed didn't stand a chance against my clan."

"I was bonded to Luca when he died," Josef added. "No vampire wants to cause the death of one they're connected to."

Ricardo considered Carlos's and Josef's words, staring at me for a long time.

He then addressed my clan. "I know of King Carlos, and with all his reputation, he is not known to lie. I know that of Aria, too. Luca fell at the hands of a usurper," he said. He glanced down at me. "Aria was Luca's Second. She succeeds as Queen."

Ricardo knelt at my feet. The rest of them followed.

Carlos's features showed a smug triumph. My father smiled at me with pride.

"Well, this was unexpected," Andreas said.

Erik and Josef grinned at me. "Not really," Erik added.

"I think as Queen, she outranks you as Alpha now," Josef said to Erik.

Carlos moved until he stood beside me. "Well, Queen Aria, do you accept their pledge? You need to drink from them all."

I recalled Giuseppe drinking from me when Marco had presented me to the clan. Luca had not done so when he returned from Venice. "Our clan has had no King since Giuseppe died," I realised. "Luca didn't do that."

"Then cement your rule over *Famiglia di Sammarinese*," Carlos instructed me. "They kneel to you, Aria. They choose you as their Queen."

"I never wanted this. I never sought to be a Queen," I said.

Carlos turned, making eye contact with each of his clan. "I didn't choose to be a King. They chose to follow me, just as your clan chose you. They would not kneel to you if they didn't have faith in you." He leaned forward to whisper in my ear. "I would have inserted you as Queen, anyway. So accept it."

I moved between each vampire on their knees, taking a small taste of their blood. I'd never felt such power before. Each of my clan incanted, "My Queen."

I returned to where Carlos still stood.

My father had joined him. "My daughter, a Queen," he lauded.

"Address your clan," Carlos instructed. The rest of his clan stood behind him. Camila placed herself at his side. Diego and the Garcia Perez brothers watched.

"Stand," I ordered my clan.

They obeyed.

"War has been declared," I said. "Our existence has been revealed to humanity. I kneel before King Carlos, as Luca did. But not out of the ignorance he did. I want to form a close connection with his clan. For us to offer assistance to one another if needed." I took a knee before King Carlos. "King Carlos, Queen Camila, my clan is yours. We offer you welcome to San Marino. If ever a time arises that you need sanctuary, you have it with us."

He leaned over, biting into my throat. He only drank briefly before pulling away. "On your feet, Queen Aria."

I rose and faced him.

"I agree, we need to assist one another," he affirmed. "While I am the King of *La Voz* and *Famiglia di Sammarinese*, I ask that you rule your clan as you see fit in my absence." He pointed to the bodies. "Although, perhaps we clean up the mess we made. This is still your home, and I see no need to frighten the humans who live here. Don't give them a reason to need to evacuate, or to draw Hunters here. Compel the humans who saw the fight."

Josef chuckled. "There may be one more mess," he said. "We got a little carried away."

Diego glared. "I do not need to hear that."

"I don't think our den is safe," Ricardo said. "You can guarantee that the Hunters know the location. Pierre had to have told them."

"Then we need to find a new den," I agreed.

"What about the safehouse?" Camila asked her brother.

He hesitated. "Sure," he said."Its location was never in the records, as it was a private establishment our family owns. We'd have to build on it to fit the whole clan; maybe a second level."

"Why should we trust you?" Ricardo demanded. "You're a Hunter. You stand with four other Hunters. Bestowed, but Hunters. We're at war. How do we know you won't return in the middle of the day and burn us alive?"

Diego pointed to Camila. "My sister is the Queen of *La Voz*. I will cause no harm to her, or her clan," he promised. "I will communicate any threats you face to King Carlos and Queen Aria." He faced Carlos. "I am not my father. I was raised a Hunter, but I wish you no ill will. I know you'll keep my sister safe, and that's all I care about right now. I will remain in San Marino to help relocate the clan here."

"So will we," one of the Garcia Perez brothers said. "We must bury our brother. We have no reason to return to Spain, as the Hunter community already wants nothing to do with us. We will remain here, to protect the clan here."

I stared at the brothers in shock. "Why would you help vampires?"

"Because we don't follow the hate of our ancestors. We believe our people can live in harmony." He smiled at me. "We worked well with King Carlos and his clan, as did Diego. Proof that our people do not have to hate each other. War or no war, we want to live in harmony with you.."

He had a point. "Then I welcome you to my city," I said. "I will secure a home for you."

Chapter 49

After helping *Famiglia di Sammarinese* move into Diego's safe house, we returned to Venice with Aria. She named Carmen as her Second, and Ricardo as her General, leaving them in charge. The moment we returned to Venice, we were met by Matteo and Aria's descendants.

"Diego advised me that you were returning," Lenora said. "It's not every day a Hunter tells me ahead of time that vampires are returning." She smiled at Aria. "It is good to see you again, Aria."

Both of them hugged. "And you, Lenora," Aria agreed. "Although, you aren't as young as you once were." Laughter rose between them. "The offer is still there, if ever you wish to be immortal."

"I may consider it one day." Lenora's smile faded. "You need to hide. This city has been invaded by Hunters who are looking for King Carlos." She sighed. "While the existence of vampires is now widely known, our deal still stands. No killing. And you do not touch Venetians. In return, they have agreed to shelter you. They thank you for the protection you've provided over the past twenty years, and I hope you'll continue to do so."

"You've spoken about this?" Erik asked. "Humans agreed to protect us?"

"You provide safety from other clans who may not be so willing to agree to our terms," Pietro explained.

The last few days had revealed many surprises. First, Hunters working with vampires. Now, an entire city who knew of us; willing to keep our secret.

"You have my word," Carlos agreed. "I will take my clan home. But we'll need food."

"That can be arranged," Lenora said.

Carlos grinned. "Erik and Josef will be escorting Queen Aria to her villa. They need some time to themselves. Arrange food for them, too. They're nesting."

"*Queen* Aria?" Lenora asked.

"Queen of *Famiglia di Sammarinese*," Aria said.

"Oh, I cannot wait to hear this story," Lenora smiled at Aria with affection. "But go. I'll send people to your villa and the den. There are a lot of Hunters here. So be careful."

We left Carlos and the others, using every ounce of speed we could. Arriving at the den, we scanned our surroundings to ensure no Hunters were watching.

Inside, I stripped off before the door had even closed.

"Let me take care of you both," Erik said as he removed his clothes. "Get on the bed now."

He sat against the headboard, legs apart. "You first, Josef."

Before I climbed on to the bed, I pulled the pendant over my head, turning to Aria. "I want you to wear this," I said. "It was important to Erik because it belonged to his brother. It's important to me because Erik gave it to me. I'm giving it to you because it's important to both of us. As you are."

She reached out for it. "It's a beautiful gift," she said, eyes glimmering. "Thank you, both of you."

I placed it over her head, kissing her. Then I approached the bed. Erik gave me a smile, patting the bed between his legs.

"Sit," he instructed. I placed myself on the bed where he indicated. "Now lean back."

I let myself melt against him.

"You've both had a rough couple of days," Erik said. His lips touched the back of my neck, sending a shiver through me. "Aria, come, sit in front of Josef."

"You know I'm a Queen now," Aria said with a small smile.

"We're not in your territory right now," Erik replied. "I'm still your alpha. Now do as I commanded, or I'll go over there and make you."

Desire lit up in her eyes, and for a moment it looked like she was going to resist so he would follow through with his threat. Finally, she approached the bed and placed herself between my legs.

"Good girl," Erik said, and Aria's whole body trembled.

"Do you like being called a 'good girl'?" I whispered in her ear. "Queen Aria, I want to worship you. I've never fucked a Queen before."

"I want you both to relax," Erik said, wrapping his arms around the both of us. "Lean back, close your eyes, and sleep."

"Are we not nesting?" Aria asked.

"We have plenty of time for that. You two need time to recover from what you've endured. Sleep."

I closed my eyes, leaning into his embrace.

A knock at the door woke me up. I growled, listening to the heartbeats: one vampire and two humans. Erik tightened his arms around me.

"Shh, it's not a threat," he said. "You're safe, Josef."

"How long were we asleep?" Aria asked.

"Twelve hours," Erik said. "I'll get the door. It's a gift from our King."

He slid out from behind me and walked, still naked, to the door, before opening it.

"A little risky, don't you think?" Erik asked. "I thought Lenora would be the one to send humans."

"I offered," Andreas said and smirked. "No one saw me."

The humans entered the house.

"Andreas," Aria said. "Won't you stay? Feed with us." She left the bed, approaching the door.

I followed her.

"You heard her," Erik said. "You're welcome to stay. I'm sure you're as hungry as we are. Have you slept since we returned?"

The door closed. I entered the living quarters and admired the humans standing with vacant expressions on their faces. Two women who were pale; one with dark hair, the other blonde.

"Mmm, they smell delicious," I said. "I'd love them more if they weren't in a trance."

Erik clicked his fingers in front of their faces and they blinked, taking in their surroundings.

"You're naked," one said with alarm. "Where are we?"

Aria walked around the women, examining them. She leaned in, taking in their scent. "You're in a vampires' nest," she said. "Your arrival is quite welcome." She stopped in front of one. "I'll take you."

Their fear rose, pulling me forward.

"Are you going to kill us?" one asked.

I laughed. "Not while you're in Venice, little human. A night of feeding vampires, and if you're lucky, an orgasm or two."

Erik claimed the second woman. "Josef, won't you enjoy a drink with me?"

I didn't wait, and we both bit into the throat at the same time. Her fear was doused by the effects of our venom as she gave in to our bite.

"Andreas, I'd be delighted if you'd share this one with me," Aria offered.

I fed, lifting myself from the woman's throat at the same time Erik did. He caressed her cheek. "Shhh, it's okay. sleep," he said. She dropped to the ground, falling under his compulsion.

Aria was already licking Andreas's chin. His eyes were closed. Erik grinned at me and wrapped his arms around her. He dropped a kiss onto her throat. I could only assume he asked her something through their bond as she smiled.

"Mmmm, I would like that," she whispered out loud. "Are you okay with that? And Josef?"

Erik's eyes met mine, before he moved around her towards Andreas. I followed his lead. Erik lifted Andreas's chin and lowered a kiss to his lips. Aria stepped forward, completing the circle, each of us surrounding him. Andreas groaned into the kiss, sliding his arms around Erik. When they broke the kiss, Andreas panted. I spun him to face me, dropping a kiss to his lips. Andreas didn't try to resist.

"I'd say we're okay with that," Erik reassured Aria. "Andreas, I want you to join us."

"Join you?" Andreas asked, appearing uncertain.

I met his eyes. "You're going to pretend you didn't come here in the hopes to see Aria?"

Erik grabbed Andreas's jaw. "I am inviting you to join our nest. What do you say?"

His eyes darted from Aria, to me, to Erik. A slow smile spread across his face. "I would like that, very much," he admitted.

Aria started to tug at his tee-shirt. "I admired the way you protected me in the cage," she said. He let her pull his clothes from him. "You and Josef took arrows for me." She kissed his chest. "The way you smashed Pierre's head on the bars." She reached towards me, pulling me towards her. "You both took care of me. I want to take care of you." Her smile lit up her entire face. "But I want to be worshipped like a Queen first, of course."

"Of course," I said, unable to keep my hands off her. "Then get on the bed, so we can."

She moved, and I followed her to the bed. Erik stood over Andreas.

"Kneel." Erik said. "In this nest, I am the alpha."

Andreas dropped to his knees, gazing up at Erik.

Chapter 50

I lost track of the days. Humans were delivered to the door, and we fed together, letting them enjoy our venom. We fucked, fed, and slept. Then we started over. I was in utter bliss.

I awoke to find Andreas and Aria gazing at each other. He tucked stray strands of her hair behind her ear.

"The first moment I lay eyes on you, I couldn't look away," he whispered. "Erik and Josef had already claimed you, I felt a great sense of loss. I'd never believed in love at first sight, but I felt like I'd fallen in love and lost you all at once." He leaned forward and kissed her. "My sweet angel."

"My shadow," she whispered back. "My protector."

"*Our* shadow," I corrected, and climbed over a still sleeping Josef. He better wake up soon, I had a surprise for him. I kissed Aria before turning to Andreas, the new connection between us pulsing. "You are our shadow. You always have been, haven't you?"

Andreas smiled. "You're the ones who pulled me out of captivity all those years ago," he said. "I think I loved you that day. I'd never seen such a welcome sight. My rescuers looked like a mirage."

I kissed him again, the scent of Aria clung to him, mingling with his own. He melted against me, his cock hardening. I smiled down at him. "You could have voiced your affections." I caressed his cheek. "If we had known, we would have welcomed you to join us. Aria did not have to be the one to bring you to our bed."

"Let's not worry about that. He's here now," Josef added, lifting his head.

"Is anyone hungry?" Aria asked.

Josef stretched out. "How long have we been here?" he asked. "Do you think the Hunters looking for King Carlos are gone yet?"

"Ten days," Andreas said.

"Who cares about the Hunters?" Aria asked. "They won't find us. I want to stay in here forever. Maybe ask King Carlos for a delivery again." She nuzzled her head under my chin. "Although, I still feel a little blood drunk from the last delivery."

"You probably are," I said with a chuckle. She was right though, we'd been a little less restrained with the last meal, a sign of intoxication, enjoying the feed a little too roughly. The humans still slept in the corner, drawing my attention. It would be time to release them soon, minus the memory of what had occurred here.

Over ten days, I'd tied Aria in shibari, lashed Andreas, marked all three of them, given the men head, eaten her out, and been in a constant state of euphoria as we fucked. Occasionally we'd allowed humans to join us in our bed, feasting and fucking. I could not have imagined how vigorous Andreas was. He liked to be dominated, all three of them accepting my commands. All three of them submitted to me, and then Josef, Andreas and myself worshipped the Queen and her body.

Since the time my maker had given me her blood, I had embraced the existence she'd granted me. I'd gained a hunger for blood. I couldn't get enough sex. But Amara had delighted over my hunger for life itself. I'd loved her and suffered with her death. But now, I stood before three naked vampires who accepted me as their alpha within my new nest, yearning on their faces. What had started out as desire for Aria and Andreas, was becoming as deep a love as I held for Josef; one I had once experienced with Amara.

Aria, a new Queen. Beautiful and strong, with a gentle love that she showed towards Andreas and Josef; while displaying a demand for recognition of her strength with me as she accustomed to her new status. I couldn't help but admire her.

Andreas, a man I'd known long enough to know when he wanted something, despite him never asking for anything. He'd wanted Aria as much as I had the first time he laid eyes on her, and I couldn't blame him one bit. The man of shadows.

Josef—the man whose wife I'd killed, awakening a rage in him as he sought my death. But now he looked at me with warmth, waiting for me to join them on the bed.

"What are you waiting for?" I asked. "We have a Queen who wants every part of her body worshipped."

"I want to know what else you have in your bag that we haven't yet used," Aria said.

"Agreed," Josef added.

"I do have the collar," I said.

Josef's red eyes shone, need blazing through our bond. He licked his lips.

I tilted his chin up. "Are you a good boy, Josef? Do you want the collar?"

He whimpered. "You waited ten days to tell me this?"

I grinned. "I saved the best for last."

I reached for the bag I'd brought with us, unzipping it slowly. As I pulled the collar out, a wide smile broke out on Aria's face.

"It's safe to say that collar is not for me," she asserted.

"It's Josef's," I said. "But I can have one made up for Andreas too. And one for you."

The collar was wide, leather for around the neck, with my name in Norse runes, declaring that the wearer of the collar was *mine*. I buckled it around Josef's neck.

"Is it too tight? I asked Josef.

"No," he said, his eyes holding mine.

Aria grabbed the smaller collar attached by a leash, placing it over Josef's cock, then lowered her mouth over his head, licking it.

"I like this look on you," she whispered, and reached for Andreas. "Don't you agree, Andreas?"

Andreas ran his eyes over Josef's body. "It does suit him," Andreas said with a grin.

Leaning forward, she nibbled on his ear, fingers wrapping around his cock.

I gave the leash a gentle tug, and Josef whimpered again. Aria licked Josef's throat and snapped at his jaw, then turned to kiss Andreas. A growl of contentment rose from him and he pinned Aria under him on the bed right next to Josef. Andreas bit her throat and she moaned.

'You're mine," he whispered. "My Sweet Angel."

I watched, enthralled. When he released her throat, she bit his. Josef turned his head towards them. Aria kissed Josef, fingers gliding across his abs and chest.

She lifted herself off Andreas, snapping at my jaw. "The Queen and the Alpha. I want to tease them." She smiled at him. "Would you like to be teased, Andreas? Josef?"

"Teased, bitten, anything you want to do, I will lay back and take it with a smile," Andreas replied.

"I will do what my alpha asks of me," Josef said.

"With that collar on, he has to obey me," I explained. "Or whoever holds the leash."

I pulled out a Venetian mask, handing it to Aria. "Put this on." Her mask was black and gold, matching mine, but the mask and gold paint were more delicate. I slipped mine over my face. Aria slipped hers on.

"Paint us," I commanded Andreas and Josef, giving them gold paint.

They dipped their fingers into the gold glittery liquid, smearing it over my arms and body in a solid layer. With their hands sliding over my skin, I forced myself to sit still, letting the sensations warm me.

Finished with me, they turned their attention to Aria. Unable to resist, I dipped my fingers into the paint, and the three of us covered her body and arms.

"You really do look like a Queen," I admired.

"Worship me," she whispered. "Like the Queen I am."

We cleaned our hands on the tee-shirt I discarded, the paint drying quickly on my skin.

Aria turned her face towards me.

"Can I have the leash?" she asked, her voice muffled. I handed Josef's leash to her.

A gentle tug had Josef scrambling towards her. She took her time stroking Josef's cock. She moved between Josef and Andreas's cocks, and they started to pant. She turned her face up to me, eyes red through the mask.

"Will you watch, or take part?" she asked.

"Oh, I very much want to take part," I assured her.

She lifted her mask, the smile she gave awoke heat that coursed through me. Her lips closed over my cock. Her tongue swirled, and she pulled back. She pulled Josef and Andreas towards us, taking the time to kiss all three of us. We formed a circle around her, caressing her golden body. She tugged on the leash again. Josef fell on her, lips locking with hers. My lips traced the lines of his crossbow tattoo that covered his entire back, while trailing my fingers over Aria's gold covered body.

"Andreas, will you tend to Josef, while I take care of Erik?" she asked.

Andreas didn't hesitate, the two embracing, paying attention to one another. Aria lowered herself over me. I slid into her wet pussy easily. She reached for my mask. "You truly do look like a god," she whispered. "Carved out of perfection." Her hands dropped to my chest, gliding over my painted skin. "I want us to have thralls, who will kneel before us, begging for our bite."

"We shall," I promised. "I will deny you nothing. We'll have as many as you like. I own a hotel in Verona, we can keep them there so it won't break the agreement we have with your descendants."

"I want you to bite me," she ordered.

I removed my mask and bit her throat. Picking up on the scent of blood, both Josef and Andreas made their way to her, biting. The three of us fed from her, and deep shivers tore through her body. A low moan burst from her.

I leaned her back, both of us maintaining a rhythm. I lowered my head, taking her nipple into my mouth, the paint tasting slightly of lemon. Josef and Andreas took to kissing our bodies. Aria let go of the leash, clinging to me. Her nails dug into my back, drawing blood.

"Erik," her voice came out low.

I growled in her ear, taking pleasure in the way she tensed right before she came, her walls squeezing my cock, pushing me over the edge.

I ran my eyes over all of them, recalling what Amara had once said to me.

"You're all mine!" I murmured. "Bare your throats. Let me have what is mine."

Epilogue

Elise (Reporter)

A chill raised the hairs on the back of my neck. Someone was watching me. I spun around. A shadowed figure leaned against the door frame with arms folded over his chest, balcony and city lights at his back, his face in darkness. He hadn't been there a second ago.

"Elise?" he asked, in an accent.

"That's me," I agreed, taking a chair and pulling out my notebook and pen. I crossed one leg over the other. "The balcony was empty before. How did you get up there?"

He entered the hotel room with movements I could only guess were to put me at ease. "I wanted to make an entrance." The smile in his voice was unmistakable.

"Thank you for agreeing to sit down with me," I said, watching him. "This is an intimate setting though. One could almost think you planned for more than just an interview."

He stepped into the light, and his eyes raked up my legs and body. His hair was dark, his complexion Mediterranean, eyes blue. He met my gaze, a small smile on his face. "Are you afraid of being alone with a vampire?" he asked. "Or is that what you want? This room has seen thousands of lovers. Possibly vampires too. I do like the romantic atmosphere of the room."

We were in a large hotel room with a king-sized bed made with black silk sheets, a table, a small fridge, and two chairs. This room was known to be used for honeymooners, and the Italian elegance was noticeable. Heavy velvet curtains framed the windows with lush carpet and frescoes and marble walls decorated the rest of the room. I caught the vampire watching me again.

"I didn't think that I'd be interviewed by someone so beautiful," he said, voice deep but gentle, calming. I had to admit, the guy had charm.

Certain he was flirting because he could, a blush still warmed my cheeks and neck. I indicated the empty chair for him to take.

He moved across the room fast, hands on the armrests. and leaned over me. "Does anyone know where you are?" he asked.

"No." The word forced its way out of my mouth. I knew what he was doing. There had been many news reports about vampires' ability to compel people. Knowledge of it gave me no power to resist it, though. I looked at his mouth, curious. No fangs.

"Good. And no one shall. You will not tell anyone. If anyone asks, you don't know where you went. Just that you met me in a hotel."

"I don't know where I went," again the words I spoke were pulled from me. But it was more than that, it was a command that sunk into my mind, one that I would obey. I sighed. "Are you done compelling me?"

This close to him, though, staring into his blue eyes, the shock of dark hair, I realised how attractive he was. He pulled away from me and dragged the empty chair closer to me.

"Do I get a name for this story?" I asked. "You emailed from an anonymous email address, and you didn't tell me who you were."

He laughed as he sat again, our knees touching. "Josef Alfaro," he said.

I wrote down his name. "You said in your email that you were once a vampire Hunter. One of the first?"

"I was *the* first. In the late twelve hundreds," he replied. "I'm the one who recruited the first of the Hunters. I declared war."

That explained his email address. "The twelve hundreds? You've been alive since the thirteenth century?"

He chuckled, a relaxed laugh. I let myself laugh, too, releasing tension a little. I was alone in a hotel room with a vampire, in the middle of a war. But he hadn't given me reason to fear him. Yet. He seemed more interested in flirting with me, rather than killing me.

"Why did you reach out?" I asked. "The world fears vampires, and you took an opportunity to sit down with a journalist. Why?"

I'd heard from dozens of vampires, but for some reason Josef's email stating: *'I'll see you on Friday in the Romeo suite in Verona. You'll want to hear my story,'* had appealed to me. He'd been so confident that I couldn't help but reply, and had caught the next available flight from London.

"The humans are panicking, but you wanted to tell the story of a vampire. What can I say? You got my attention," he said.

Humans. Not people.

I nodded. "Okay, then, tell me how it started. What set you on the path to becoming the First Hunter?"

"Right down to business. I like it." His eyes took on a far-away look. "Before I became a Hunter, I was happy. My son had recently married, and I finally had my wife to myself. However, word had reached us of vampires. Shadows in the night who terrorised entire villages, snatching people, sucking the life from them. People became afraid." He paused. "We'd already fled Spain to escape them." I didn't see any emotion in him. Just a faint smile as he spoke of his wife and son. "One night, I awoke to the sound of my wife's moans. A vampire had broken in, and he was feeding from her. I tried to help her, by attacking the vampire. He rewarded my efforts by ripping her throat out. He told me he'd just wanted to feed in peace, and would have left, had I not angered him. Then, he was gone. The next morning I found that my son and his wife were among the others who'd been killed in the night. I met with villagers, declaring I was tired of living in fear and we needed to fight back. Many agreed with me. I didn't care about other vampires, I just wanted to take down my wife's murderer. I wanted to know who'd killed my son."

I gave him a sympathetic look. To lose his wife and son on the same night.

"So, you started to hunt them?" I said, my pen scratching over paper as I took notes.

"It wasn't as simple as that," he said, laughing. "We had no idea how to kill them. So we took months to track them and capture one. Only then did we discover that it would take large numbers of us to stand a chance.

Three human lives were lost, trying to take one vampire. They were too strong for us, and we needed an army. But we *did* learn how to kill them, and we went looking for people willing to join us. We found many villages hit by vampires. Many humans had lost loved ones at their hands. And so, we started the war."

He paused again, and I looked up from my notebook.

"I know you're curious," he said. "You looked at my mouth earlier; just ask."

"How about you finish your story," I suggested.

He grinned at me. "Not until you ask."

I sighed, forcing myself to look bored. "Alright, fine. Let me see them."

Fangs emerged in his mouth, long and sharp. His eyes turned red. He smiled, the tips of his fangs pressing against his bottom lip. A change shifted over his face. He even *looked* inhuman. An unearthly visage that hadn't been there a moment ago.

Something in him pulled me in. For a monster, he was beautiful, and I was caught in his primal net. He leaned forward, gently grabbing my wrist with a cold hand. "Perhaps I can have some of that payment you promised me."

My heart skipped a beat. I had offered him my blood in payment for this interview. But sitting here, with his thumb massaging my wrist, I felt uncertain.

"Just a taste, then we can get on with our meeting. You'll enjoy it," he promised.

While his cool grip was gentle, I could feel his strength in the way he'd grabbed my wrist so easily. I decided that fighting him would be a bad idea.

"Very well," I said, voice shaking.

"Shhh, don't be afraid. I promise this won't hurt, Elise." His voice was soothing, soft. He lowered his head, sliding his tongue over my wrist, eyes on my face.

There was only a brief sting of pain when his fangs pierced my wrist. I gasped at the pleasure that suddenly wrapped itself around me. I was flying, heat spreading through me. Then his fangs were gone, and he licked at the blood on my wrist.

"Mmmm, delicious," he whispered. "Just the right amount of desire."

My head was spinning, and I pulled my wrist back, surprised to find the punctures he'd made slowly closing. I stared at Josef.

"What you're feeling are the effects of my venom," he said. "This is why many humans enjoy our bite. Now, where were we?"

I stared down at my notes. "Uhh, you started a war," I reminded him.

He licked his lips and smiled at me again. Only this time it didn't feel warm, but the smile a predator would give its dinner. I suppressed a shudder. "Yes, of course. We had our army, and the vampires worked out that we were hunting them. We tracked them to a village, set fire to it, and waited." He got up and walked across the room, bringing back bottled water, taking a sip. I found it a strange thing for a vampire to do. Did they need water? "What we started that night, it would lead to many deaths on both sides. But I caught sight of the vampire who'd killed my wife. He stood, almost glowing in the firelight, smiling at me."

"So, you found your wife's killer," I recapped. "What happened next?"

"I became a man obsessed. All I could focus on was killing him. On revenge. Each time I tried, he laughed at me. Other Hunters started to notice that I was solely focused on one vampire, but they said nothing. We'd all lost someone and had reasons for being where we were. But I saw him one night, and I took twenty Hunters, and followed them.".

I had a feeling I already knew what came next.

"It was Carlos's idea to turn a Hunter. He'd built a vicious reputation himself, being the one to turn many ferals. I found out he'd killed my son. But my wife's killer, Erik, chose me to turn. I tried to fight. Fangs were in my throat, then I was being force-fed blood. I resisted every step of the way, but it was pointless. As I fought against the rising slumber, Erik stood over me, watching me try to fight to stay awake. To live."

I stared at him, my mind still a little foggy from the effects of his bite, making a mental note to ask him about ferals later. "What happened when you woke up?"

He shrugged. "I woke up hungry, with no memory, only instinct. They pointed me in the direction of my own men. I killed every last Hunter that I'd led, tearing their throats open to get at their blood."

"That doesn't bother you?" I asked.

"Why would it? I was doing what is only natural." He turned his head towards the door as if listening, and a small smile pulled at his lips. "I was surprised to find the vampires all willing to welcome me. Especially Erik."

"Did you still want to kill them?" I asked.

"Oh, that desire faded fast!" He shook his head. "They taught me to hunt, and became my new family. My maker, Ana, was a woman with quite an appetite. Carlos was brutal, and always went straight for the kill, living for their fear." He reached a hand across, caressing my throat, his cold touch sending a chill through me. "But Erik taught me to seduce the meal, to make them want it, just as much as I did. To make them desire my bite, yearn for it." His eyes bored into mine, and I couldn't look away. "My favourite that he taught me was bringing my meal to the point of satisfaction before I finished them off. That moment when they realised that they were going to die, but that their fight was useless. When the desire in their blood mixed with fear. Oh, it was delicious!"

"You enjoyed killing?" I asked. "Tell me what it means to be a vampire. I understand you survive off blood. Are you all murderers, as they say?"

He laughed, the sound low. The hairs on my arms stood on end. "I enjoy drinking to the point of intoxication," he admitted, voice smooth. "I enjoy giving chase, the thrill of the hunt. That pull of fear. You can't imagine what that scent does to us. We survive off blood, yes. Make no mistake, we are a predatory species. We are at the top of the food chain." He tilted his head, watching me. "The kill is something else entirely. That final struggle, the heartbeat quickening as they fight to hold on to life. The begging, oh the begging." His voice dropped to a whisper. "That is an acquired taste. Granted, we don't always kill. Feeding stations, feeding galleries, clubs, they are a delight, where people come to us wanting to be fed upon."

His words both mesmerised and terrified me. Every instinct screamed at me to run, but I was frozen in place. "The Accords," I whispered. "They stopped you from killing."

"They were put in place to restrain us," he agreed. "But they don't exist anymore. It's a new age."

"This won't exactly paint you in a positive light," I said. "People don't want to know that vampires enjoy killing. They won't want to live alongside you, share their society with you."

His chuckle was full of darkness. "You're food. Why would the thoughts of food bother us? Do you care what cows think when you enjoy a good steak or burger?"

I shuddered. "We don't seduce cows," I interjected. "Why do you make such an effort to seduce people, if you feel that way about us?"

"Oh, it's no effort," he mused. "Humans are drawn to us. Only a few sense the danger, but even that can draw some in. We just take joy in the effect we have. If that means fucking, then we take that pleasure, too. Only if the human wants it, of course. We're not *that* kind of monster." He leaned forward, kissing my throat. Another shiver tore through me. "You've already had a taste of my venom, it's in there, worming its way through you." His breath brushed over my neck. I couldn't move. Another kiss. "I can smell you, Elise. You want it, don't you? Perhaps we can take a break." He licked my throat, a deep rumble rising from him. "Mmmm, let me give you a taste of the pleasure you seek. I could smell your lust the moment you walked into the hotel. You didn't come here to interview me. You came for the thrill of feeding a vampire, for my bite. Maybe more. You've heard how intoxicating our bite can be, how seductive we are, and you wanted to see for yourself. We fascinate humans as much as we scare you."

He was right. I was alone in a hotel room with a hot vampire who'd reassured me I'd get my story.

"I really did come here for your story," I insisted.

Josef laughed and leaned back, hands on the armrests. "Of course you did. If you want to continue, we can. Or, you can get onto the bed. Let me show you why humans are so needy for us."

Heat surged through me. He wasn't compelling me, but I wanted to do what he was suggesting. No one had to know. I could finish asking questions later. Josef smiled as he watched me.

"Admit it. You came here to be seduced by a vampire. And I like to think I'm well versed in seduction. I won't force you, but I also know I don't have to. You're already wet." As he leaned forward again, hand dropping to my leg, inching up my skirt, but stopping short of where I wanted his touch.

Oh, fuck. Without another word I put down my notebook and climbed onto the bed.

"Take off your clothes," he said, lifting his tee-shirt over his head.

The words *La Voz* were tattooed across his chest, and Nordic runes and the name Aria over the other side, combined with dark shadows. I decided I didn't want to know who Aria was.

I hesitated. Josef noticed. "Are you nervous? You don't have to be. Will you let me undress you?"

He was already on the bed, crawling towards me. But instead of undressing me, he whispered in my ear. "I have a friend, he's outside the room. He'd like to come in and watch, if you'd allow him." His hand slid under my shirt then, and I gasped at his cold touch. "He'll only touch you if you say he can." He pointed. "He'll sit there, on the other side of the room. If you feel more comfortable in the dark, I can turn the lights out."

I wanted to turn the lights out, but was dealing with vampires. There was no point. His body lowered, thigh grinding against my pussy. My mind was fuddled. "Okay," I said, not completely sure what I was agreeing to.

"Come in," Josef said, eyes on my face.

The door opened as Josef started to kiss my throat. The man who entered was taller than Josef, his shoulders and chest wide. Long blond hair, pulled back, and a neat beard. He held a key card with the hotel's logo on it.

"How did you get that?" I asked. "Did you compel the staff?"

He smiled. "I don't need to compel them when I own the hotel." He waved around the room and his gaze shifted to Josef. "This is my favourite of all rooms in this hotel. We'll fill every suite with thralls. A home away from home. Our King did tell us to take a break. I will lay a hundred thralls at your feet my Beloved. Have you found us one already?"

My heart pounded. Thralls. I had interviewed people who claimed to be thralls, speaking of their lives serving vampires, enjoying luxuries many people would never experience, well paid for their services. Plus, a life of being fed on, orgies and never to live outside of a vampire's hold. With the small taste Josef had taken from me, I understood why thralls accepted such a life.

"This is Elise," Josef said to his friend. "Elise, I'd like you to meet Erik."

Erik. the vampire who'd killed Josef's wife.

Erik took his shirt off, revealing a body covered in tattoos, including La Voz on his chest, and a Venetian mask, an arrow and shadows wrapped around his bicep. Josef's fingers pressed against my chin, closing my mouth. Erik sat in the chair on the other side of the room, eyes on the two of us. I couldn't look away, the guy was massive.

"Are you going to stare at Erik, or are you going to pay attention to me?" Josef asked. He unbuttoned my shirt, exposing my skin to him. "If you want me to bite, bare your throat to me."

I hesitated for a moment, then lifted my head, baring my throat to him.

I opened my eyes, finding myself between two sleeping vampires with their arms draped over me. Memories washed over me. Josef had been so gentle, placing kisses over my body. Being watched had been intimidating, but Josef had made it easy to forget that a man sat in the corner, touching himself as he and I fucked. He'd bitten my throat, and the euphoria had forced away all my doubts and fears.

Then Erik had inched closer, asking to touch me. Once I'd said yes, he'd trailed soft kisses up my arm, hands moving over my stomach. They'd been as interested in each other as they were in me, suggesting they had a deeper connection than just friendship. I'd never shared a bed with two men at once before, and their intensity had worn me out.

I squirmed out from under their arms and shifted to the end of the bed. They didn't wake, much to my relief. Their stamina had surprised me, and I could hardly keep my eyes off their perfect, naked bodies. I lifted fingers to both sides of my neck, finding their twin punctures already healing. *Interesting*. I recalled the heat and pleasure unfurling within as they'd both bitten me.

I pulled my laptop from my bag and began to type, making notes on what Josef had told me. This was a lot to absorb. His story, but also how he viewed people, and held no remorse for being a killer. There had been public anger at the Hunters for not being honest with the world about the existence of vampires, but I appreciated that their Accords somewhat restrained more deaths. Were we doomed, now that these Accords no longer bound the vampires?

I started to write the article, outlining what I'd learned about vampires, before shifting the story to Josef and his relationship with the murderer of his wife. Warm breath caressed the back of my neck, and I froze. I hadn't heard anyone move.

"I wouldn't use that word," Erik whispered. "We're not really 'lovers'. What we are, it's deeper. Humans can't really comprehend the connections in the vampire world. The bond a maker and their fledgling have. A clan to their King or Queen. Nest mates with their alpha."

"If not lovers, then what?" I asked.

He chuckled. "Would you like to explain it, Josef?"

Josef kissed my back, hand reaching around to cup my breasts, caressing them. His warmth surprised me, as he'd been cold earlier. I leaned into him as his lips trailed over the back of my neck to my shoulder.

"He's my alpha," Josef said, and nibbled my ear. "My Beloved."

"Alpha?" I asked.

"We belong to a nest. There's four of us. Nests always have an alpha. The more dominant member of the nest. Usually the eldest. The one everyone submits to." Erik moved around me, hands caressing my thighs, pushing them apart.

I wouldn't be getting much work done tonight, so I placed my laptop on the table at the end of the bed. "Do you have an endless supply of energy or something?" I asked jokingly as I moved back.

They both laughed. "You could say that," Josef said. "I don't think we're a match for Queen Aria though. She is insatiable. Except for that one time she blacked out."

Well that explained who Aria was. "Wouldn't she be annoyed that you're here, with me?" I asked.

"Humans are so naive," Erik said to Josef. "They have no understanding of us."

Josef wrapped his arms around me, a possessive embrace.

"What do you mean?" I asked.

"We are a nest," Josef explained. "But we're creatures of desire and lust. When it comes to feeding, we take pleasure. Aria won't care. Neither will Andreas."

Erik chuckled. "They might be upset that we didn't invite them." His mouth lowered to my clit. "Maybe we should have."

"So, Erik's your wife's killer," I recalled, squirming between them, trying to stay focused on my job. I'd already failed at that.

"Shhh, the interview is over," Josef whispered. "Now's the time to enjoy yourself, Elise. Let go. Bare your throat."

I did as he asked, and his fangs pierced my throat again. Erik bit into my inner thigh. Their bites were intoxicating, the heat spreading through me. I let out a moan, sure that I could come from their bites alone. Erik moved kisses from one thigh to the other; then his tongue swirled over my clit. I twitched as pleasure spread through me again. Erik bit again, the effects of his bite feeling like they were affecting me more than they had before. Josef dropped his hand, fingers circling my clit with expertise. His touch had me wanting more. Waves of pleasure consumed me, and sent me spiralling. I gave into them, letting myself soar at the pleasure pulsing through my body, writhing under his fingers.

I tensed, my orgasm hitting hard, letting out a loud wail. My toes curled, and I melted into Josef. Panting, and trying to catch my breath, I couldn't believe how quickly I'd come. But my light-headedness was becoming overwhelming, my heart erratic. The vampires were still latched on, still feeding from me. Panic closed around my throat, and I struggled to break free

"Stop." My speech slurred, and I tried to fight against their grip. But my struggles had no effect on them. "Please, you're taking too much."

They're going to kill me. Terror clawed at my chest, a crushing fear I'd never experienced before. Josef's arm tightened around me, holding me against him, holding me immobile. I couldn't breathe.

Erik's red eyes met mine from between my thighs, and I saw no humanity, no trace of mercy. Only the cold stare of an apex predator as his fingers dug into my hips. He lifted himself, towering over me—my blood trickling from the side of his mouth.

"Bare your throat," Erik commanded.

"No," I mumbled. I wouldn't do as he asked this time. "You're taking too much. Please, let me go."

Erik only smiled. "Oh, I do love the begging."

"He said bare your throat." Josef yanked my head back, exposing my throat to Erik.

The blond vampire's body pressed against mine, sandwiching me between his and Josef's chests. He bit into my throat. I whimpered at the new wave of pleasure from the effects of his bite, relieved at least that it wasn't hurting. Ice and adrenaline surged through me, my movements desperate. I was trapped.

"Please," I pleaded again, thrashing against an iron grip. The room dimmed, as the sound of my heartbeat thundered against my ribs. A tear slid down my cheek. Everything started to spin and blur.

The low rumble from Josef vibrated deep into my bones. Erik reached a hand for him, his growl I felt in my chest. My laptop was only inches away, but beyond my reach. I had a timed email that would go to my boss, but not until the following morning. All my notes, my location, and who I was writing about. I would be dead by then. I could feel each pull of their mouths as they gorged themselves on me. They had no intention of stopping, and my body felt heavy, my struggle weak. A strange sensation of tearing filled me with horror. Yet the warmth of their venom continued to spread throughout. I had no strength left to fight, and my body slumped.

Finally, they released me, Erik climbing towards Josef with smooth, graceful movements. The two of them shifted towards the head of the bed. Unable to hold myself up, I fell back.

"Oh, the fear in her blood was delicious," Erik's voice sounded far away. "We should have invited Andreas and Aria."

"I told you we'd have fun with this one," Josef replied. "Not all humans are afraid of us; some are curious. Especially when word got out about the effects of our bite, and the clubs. I suppose we can thank thralls for that."

"Perhaps she thought she'd be a thrall." Erik chuckled. "Damn, I do believe I'm blood drunk. Oh, the way the flavour of her blood changed, that spice of fear flavouring the sweet desire at the end. An absolute delight. The begging was a nice touch too."

He spoke as if he'd just finished dining at a restaurant, discussing the taste of wine.

I somehow managed to move my head back, to find Erik on top of Josef, licking his chin. Then, the two of them kissed; Josef hooking a leg around Erik's. I tried to speak, only a whisper coming out. Erik glanced back at me with a smile. The sight of my blood on his mouth sickened me—it dripped from his jaw, colouring his beard. There shouldn't be that much blood. I barely had the strength to touch my neck, finding deep gashes, blood still seeping from the wounds. I winced. They'd mauled me while their venom kept the pain at bay.

"She's still alive," Erik said.

"Not for much longer," Josef added, lifting his head to look at me, chin and mouth also slick with my blood. Again, not a sign of humanity, only a dark glee as he watched me. "Her heart's beating its last beats. I do love that sound." His mouth widened into a smile, and he met my eyes. "Thank you, Elise, you were delicious."

Erik turned his attention back to Josef, licking at my blood, the two of them kissing again.

Erik glanced back at me a second time. He left Josef, lifting me as if I weighed nothing, moving me across the width of the bed guiding my head so I could only see Josef where he lay. He returned to Josef, closing a hand around his throat. I couldn't move and could feel my life ebb, forced to see Erik and Josef as I slipped closer to my own death.

"My Beloved, let's give her a show. Submit to me. We'll be the last thing she sees."

Erik, Josef, Aria, and Andreas will return in Bloodking.
Prepare yourself for more blood, spice and all over vampireness.

Acknowledgements

Jess and Michelle, my alpha team. Daphne, Nicole, and the other Jess, my beta team. I appreciate you. Always! Having you all on my alpha or beta team has helped me so much with this process.

Alicia, my best assistant evah! Our conversations started about Venice, and became a solid friendship. I appreciate all you have done to help me prepare for the launch of this book.

Tanya Nellestein, a fellow author who had done research for her own book, and corrected me on my Old Norse translations for some of the words of affection spoken, in particular between Erik and Josef.

Ellen, as always, your input is invaluable. You sat next to me at an ECCC panel as if you targeted me out of a crowd, we chatted and now years later, you're my editor. Our collaborations just work so well!

My gratitude goes out to the sensitivity reader who reviewed the polyamorous and MM/MMF elements of this story with kindness and care, helping me portray representation correctly, without tokenism, romanticisation, or perpetuating damaging misconceptions and harmful rhetoric. Working with you was invaluable. Thank you.

About the Author

Serra is an author of dark historical fantasy and paranormal romance books with stories that draw you in from page one. Within these worlds that she created, you will find unbreakable family bonds, darker aspects to humanity, shadow realms as well as passion, lust, strong FMC's and men who would risk anything for the women they love.

Serra's journey to becoming an author started from a young age, when her first creative writing attempt—a poem titled 'The Mighty Oak Tree,"—was published in her primary school newsletter. An avid reader with a vivid imagination, her Mum always encouraged her to keep writing. She proceeded to write poetry and short stories before discovering a deeper passion for novel writing and screenplays.

In 2021, she adapted a screenplay she'd been working on, into her debut novel 'The Shadow Within,' which was published in November 2023.

Serra is a Melbourne-based author from New Zealand. As a reader and a writer, she's drawn into the dark fantasy and paranormal romance genres. Like many authors, she balances her writing alongside a day job in which she works in the communications part of a marketing and digital team; by night, she's a weaver of words, creator of worlds bringing forth stories that hold readers captive.

If you wish to subscribe, please visit:

www.serrarosewrites.com

Be the first to receive updates and sneak peeks at character art, quotes, chapters, next projects and early access to pre-orders.

Also by Serra Rose

The Horsemen Chronicles:

The Shadow Within
Death's Shadow

Upcoming Titles in The Horsemen Chronicles:

The Whispers of War
The Echoes of War
The Scourge of Famine
The Plague of Humanity

The Bloodsong Series:

Bloodsong
Consumed

Upcoming Titles in The Bloodsong Series:

Bloodking

The Bloodsong Series Spin-offs:

Heart of the Wolf
Eternity
Lovestruck
Lovesong

Bloodsong

Quinn thought launching this new step in her singing career would be the only thing on her mind. But fate, it seems, has other plans. Because the sexy and mysterious stranger who comes to watch her sing immediately grabs her eye—and stirs all her wildest fantasies.

Except Matteo has deep secrets, and when Quinn catches him mid-feed, a whole new world of vampires is opened up to her. And she's his new obsession.

In all his centuries, Matteo has never seen a masterpiece like Quinn. The second he hears her voice, he knows she's meant to be his. His to claim. His forever. Just his.

Torn between normalcy and this dark new reality, she's unsure how long she can resist her desire and the danger it brings—now that his hunger has drawn deadly attention.

He wants to taste her, she wants the thrill of his embrace. In the end, their love could consume them…or be the one thing that sets them free.

Consumed

The King is on the Hunt…

Carlos has lived for nearly a thousand years. His human life ended, and he never looked back. As a vampire, he could take what he wanted, feed and kill without remorse. The Vampire War ceased centuries ago, but the animosity lives on. Now, Venice is his domain, and his clan are his responsibility. Anyone who dares to challenge him will face his wrath.

Camila's entire life purpose has been to eradicate vampires. It's all she's ever known. Her mother is killed in a hunt, and she's sent to Venice to investigate a possible vampire related-death. What was supposed to be a solo vampire is actually one of the most bloodthirsty killers in history, and King to his loyal clan. Hunters find strength in numbers, but she must face him alone.

Carlos and Camila's attempts to kill each other pull them into the most brutal battle either one of them has fought yet. Will the King be brought to his knees, or will Huntress and vampire be consumed by the fire within?

www.ingramcontent.com/pod-product-compliance
Lightning Source LLC
Chambersburg PA
CBHW030352310726
48979CB00001B/273

* 9 7 8 1 7 6 3 8 4 4 8 9 6 *